A DOG'S PROMISE

W. BRUCE CAMERON

A TOM DOHERTY ASSOCIATES BOOK

NEW YORK

This is a work of fiction. All of the characters, organizations, and events portrayed in this novel are either products of the author's imagination or are used fictitiously.

A DOG'S PROMISE

Copyright © 2019 by W. Bruce Cameron

All rights reserved.

A Forge Book
Published by Tom Doherty Associates
120 Broadway
New York, NY 10271

www.tor-forge.com

Forge® is a registered trademark of Macmillan Publishing Group, LLC.

The Library of Congress has cataloged the hardcover edition as follows:

Cameron, W. Bruce, author.
    A dog's promise / W. Bruce Cameron.—First edition.
        p. cm.
    "A Tom Doherty Associates book."
    ISBN 978-1-250-16351-6 (hardcover)
    ISBN 978-1-250-26675-0 (signed edition)
    ISBN 978-1-250-16350-9 (ebook)
    1. Mutts (Dogs)—Fiction. 2. Dogs—Fiction. 3. Families—Fiction.
    4. Human-animal relationships—Fiction. I. Title.
    PS3603.A4535 D638 2019
    813'.6—dc23

                                                    2019457048

ISBN 978-1-250-16349-3 (trade paperback)

Our books may be purchased in bulk for promotional, educational, or business use. Please contact your local bookseller or the Macmillan Corporate and Premium Sales Department at 1-800-221-7945, extension 5442, or by email at MacmillanSpecialMarkets@macmillan.com.

First Edition: October 2019
First Trade Paperback Edition: June 2020

Printed in the United States of America

0 9 8 7 6 5 4 3 2 1

For Gavin Polone, friend, animal advocate, calorie denier,
laptop critic, and one of the main reasons why my work
has reached so many people on the planet.

My name is Bailey. I have had many names and many lives, but Bailey is what I am called now. It is a good name. I am a good dog.

I have lived in many places and of all of those, the farm was the most wonderful—until I arrived here. This place has no name, but there are golden shores to run along, and sticks and balls with flawless mouth-fit, and toys that squeak, and everyone who has ever loved me is here—and they all love me still. There are also, of course, many, many dogs, because it wouldn't be a perfect place without them.

I am loved by so many people because I have lived many lives with many different names. I've been Toby and Molly and Ellie and Max, I've been Buddy and I've been Bailey. With each name came a life with a different purpose. My purpose now is a simple one—to be with my people, and to love them. Perhaps that was my ultimate purpose from the start.

There is no pain here, only the joy that comes from being surrounded by love.

Time was unmarked, passing in serenity, until my boy Ethan and my girl CJ came to talk to me. CJ is Ethan's child. I sat up alertly when they appeared, because of all the people I had ever cared about, these two had the most important role in my lives, and they were carrying themselves the way people behave when they want a dog to do something.

"Hello, Bailey, you good dog," Ethan greeted me. CJ ran a smoothing hand over my fur.

For a moment or two we just shared our love with each other.

"I know you understand that you have lived before, Bailey. I know you had a very special purpose, that you saved me," Ethan said.

"And you saved me, too, Bailey, my Molly girl, my Max," CJ added.

When CJ said those names, I remembered how I had accompanied her on her life's journey. I wagged at the memories. She put her arms around me. "There's nothing like a dog's love," she murmured to Ethan.

"It's unconditional," Ethan agreed, patting my forehead.

I closed my eyes with pleasure at being cuddled by the two of them.

"We have to ask you to do something now, Bailey. Something so very important, only you can do it," Ethan told me.

"But if you fail, it will be okay. We will love you, and you can come back here and be with us," CJ said.

"He won't fail. Not our Bailey," Ethan replied, grinning. He held my head in his hands, hands that once smelled like the farm but now just smelled like Ethan. I gazed at him with a rapt focus, because when my boy speaks to me, I can feel his love pouring out like warmth. "I need you to go back, Bailey. Back to fulfill a promise. I wouldn't ask you if it weren't necessary."

His tone was serious, but he wasn't mad at me. Humans can be happy, sad, loving, angry, and many other things, and usually I can tell by their voices how they feel. Dogs are pretty much just happy, which might be why we don't need to talk.

"This time will be different, Bailey," CJ advised. I looked to her and she, too, was loving and kind. I sensed, though, an anxiety in her, a worry, and leaned into her so that she could hug me more tightly and feel better.

"You won't remember anything." Ethan was speaking softly now. "None of your lives. Not me, not the farm, not this place."

"Well," CJ objected, her voice as quiet as Ethan's. "Maybe not *remember*, exactly, but you have been through so much, you will be a wise dog now, Bailey. An old soul."

"Here's the tough part, Buddy. You won't even remember *me*. CJ and I will fade from your mind."

Ethan was sad. I gave his hand a lick. Sadness in people is the reason there are dogs.

CJ petted me. "Not forever, though."

Ethan nodded. "That's right, Bailey. Not forever. The next time you see me, I won't look like this, but you'll recognize me, and when you do, you will remember everything. All of your lives. It will all come back. And maybe then you'll also understand that you are an angel dog who helped fulfill a very important promise."

CJ stirred and Ethan looked up at her. "He won't fail," Ethan insisted. "Not my Bailey."

ONE

A t first I knew only my mother's nourishing milk, and the sheltering warmth of her teats as I fed. It wasn't until I had become much more aware of my surroundings that I realized I had brothers and sisters with whom to compete for Mother's attentions, that as they wiggled and squirmed against me they were trying to shove me to the side. But Mother loved me, I could feel it when she nuzzled me, when she cleaned me with her tongue. And I loved my mother dog.

Our den was formed of metal floors and walls, but Mother had arranged a soft roll of cloth into a warm bed up against the back side. Once my siblings and I could see and move well enough to explore, we discovered that the surface beneath our pads was not only hard and slick but cold. Life was much better on the blanket. The roof over our heads was a brittle tarp that flapped in the wind with a crisp rattling chatter.

None of this was as interesting to us as the alluring, empty rectangular hole at the front of the den, through which light and outdoor smells poured in an intoxicating blend. The floor of the den jutted out past the roof at that point. Mother often went to this window to the unknown, her nails clicking on the metal shelf that thrust out into the world, and then she . . . vanished.

Mother would leap out into the light and be gone. We puppies would huddle together for warmth in the chill of her absence, squeaking comfort to each other, and then collapse into sleep. I could feel that my brothers and sisters were as distraught and anxious as I was that she might never return, but she always came back to us, appearing in the middle of the rectangular hole as swiftly as she had departed.

When our vision and coordination improved, we pooled our collective courage and followed her scent out onto the ledge, but it was terrifying. The world, dizzying in its compelling possibilities, was open to us there below the shelf, but to access it meant a free fall of impossible distance. Our den was literally off the ground. How did Mother jump down and then back up?

I had a brother I thought of as Heavy Boy. My siblings and I spent most of our time trying to shove him out of our way. When he would climb up over me to sleep on the pile it felt like he was trying to flatten my head, but extracting myself from the compression was not easy, especially with my brothers and sisters pushing back. He sported the same white muzzle and chest, with the same mottled white, gray-and-black body as the rest of us, but his bones and flesh were just somehow heavier. When Mother needed a respite from feeding us and stood up, Heavy Boy always complained the longest, and he was always seeking to nurse, even when the other puppies were satiated and wanting to play. I couldn't help but be irritated with him— Mother was so thin that her bones were visible through her skin, and her breath carried a rancid, sick odor, while Heavy Boy was plump and round and yet still always demanded more from her.

It was Heavy Boy who strayed too close to the lip of the ledge, his nose sniffing at something in the air, maybe eager for our mother to return so he could continue to try to drain the life out of her. One moment he was precariously stretched out at the very edge, and the next he was gone, falling, an audible thump reaching our ears.

I wasn't sure this was a bad thing.

Heavy Boy began a panicked squalling. His terror infused all of us in the den, so that we, too, began squeaking and crying, anxiously nosing each other for reassurance.

I knew right then that I would never go out on the ledge. That way meant danger.

Then Heavy Boy went completely quiet.

The silence in the den was instantaneous. We all sensed that if something had gotten to Heavy Boy, it might very well be coming for us next. We huddled together in soundless dread.

With a loud scratching sound, Mother appeared on the ledge, Heavy Boy hanging, chagrined, from her teeth. She deposited him in the center of our pile and of course immediately he was squeaking in demand for a teat, heedless of the fact that he had frightened all of us. I am sure I was not the only puppy who felt our mother would not have offended us if she just left Heavy Boy out there to face the consequences of his venture.

That night I lay on top of one of my sisters, considering what I had learned. The ledge at the front of the den was a dangerous place, not worth the risk of trespass regardless of the succulent odors offered by the world beyond. By staying near the bed; I reasoned, I would be completely safe.

I was entirely wrong, as it turned out a few days later.

Mother was napping with her back to us. This upset my litter-mates, especially Heavy Boy, because the fragrance of her teats called to us and he wanted to feed. None of us were strong or coordinated enough to climb over her, though, and she was wedged in the back corner of the den, denying us access around head and tail.

She raised her head at a sound we heard every so often: a humming machine noise. Before, the sound always rose and fell swiftly, but this time it came close and whatever was making it was obviously motionless for a time. We heard a slam, and that's when Mother stood up, her head tenting the flexible ceiling, her ears back in alarm.

Something was coming—heavy thuds were getting closer. Mother pressed herself to the back of the den and we followed suit. None of us went for her teats, now, not even Heavy Boy.

A stark shadow blocked the light from the rectangular hole, and with a loud boom the ledge to the world was slapped up, making the den a sealed enclosure, no way out. Mother was panting, white rims under her eyes, and we all knew something was about to happen, something *awful*. She tried to force her way over the side of the den, but the ceiling was down too tight; all she could do was stick the tip of her nose out into the air.

The floor of the den rocked, and there was another slamming sound, and then with a grinding roar the surface beneath our feet began to tremble. The den lurched, flinging us all to one side. We slid on the slick metal surface. I looked to Mother and she had her claws extended and was struggling to stay on her feet. She could not help us. My siblings were crying pitiably and trying to make their way to her, but I hung back, concentrating on not be-ing thrown. I did not understand the forces pulling at my body; I just knew that if Mother was afraid, I should be *terrified*.

The bouncing, banging, and shaking went on for so long, I began to believe this would now be my life, that my mother would forever be dismal with fear, that I would be flung back and forth without cease—and then suddenly we all were tossed in a crush at the back wall of the den, where we piled up and then fell when the noise and the sickening stresses on our bodies magically ceased. Even the vibrations stopped.

Mother was still afraid. I watched her as she alerted at a metallic slam, and saw her whip her head around as she took measure of a crunching sound tracking to the place where the ledge had always thrust out into the world.

I felt real fear when I saw her lips draw back from her teeth. My calm, gentle mother was now fierce and feral, her fur up, her eyes cold.

With a clank the ledge fell back down into place and astoundingly there was a man standing there. The instinctive recognition came to me in a flash—it was as if I could feel his hands on me, or remember how it felt, even though I had never set eyes on such a creature before. I caught sight of bushy hair below his nose, a rounded belly, and eyes widening in surprise.

Mother lunged and savagely snapped her teeth, her bark full of angry warning.

"Yaaah!" The man fell away in shock, vanishing from view. Mother kept barking.

My littermates were frozen in helpless fear. Mother was retreating to where we were collected, drool flecking her mouth, fur up, ears back. A maternal rage radiated from her—I felt it; my siblings felt it; and, given his reaction, the man undoubtedly felt it as well.

And then, with an abruptness that made us all flinch, the ledge banged up, shutting off the sun, so that the only illumination was the dim glow filtering through the covering over the top of the den.

The silence seemed as loud as Mother's snarls had been. In the gloom, I saw my littermates begin to unclench, though they set upon my mother with a need made frantic by what had happened, and she acquiesced, lying down to nurse with a sigh.

What had just occurred? Mother had been afraid but had channeled that fear into something fierce. The man had been afraid but hadn't turned it into anything but a startled shout. And I had felt an odd composure, as if I understood something my mother did not.

It wasn't true, though. I didn't understand anything.

After a time, Mother crossed to where the ledge had been flipped up, sniffing along the top edge. She pressed her head up against the tarp, raising it slightly, and a shaft of light shot into the den. She emitted a slight sound, a moan, chilling me.

We heard the crunching noises I associated with the man, and then voices.

"Ya wanna take a look?"

"Not if she's vicious like you say. How many pups, you think?"

"Maybe six? I was just figurin' out what I was lookin' at when she came at me. Thought she was gonna take my arm off."

These were, I decided, men speaking to each other about something. I could smell them, and there were no more than two.

"Well, why would you leave the tailgate down in the first place?"

"I dunno."

"We need this pickup. You gotta go get that equipment."

"Yeah, but what about the pups?"

"So what you do is take them down to the river. You got a gun?"

"What? No, I don't got a *gun*, for Pete's sake."

"I got a pistol in my truck."

"I don't wanna shoot a bunch of puppies, Larry."

"The pistol's for the mother. With her out of the picture, nature will take care of the pups."

"Larry . . ."

"You going to do what I say?"

"Yessir."

"All right then."

Within moments we were back to sliding around, again subjected to noises and sickening forces we did not comprehend. Yet among the mysteries of the day, this particular event seemed less threatening with its repetition, somehow. Was it too farfetched to believe that soon the noise would end, our bodies would settle, the ledge would reappear, Mother would snarl and bark, a man would yell, the ledge would bang upward? This time I was therefore more interested in the smells wafting in through the gap between the flapping roof and the metal walls of the den: a blast of exotic, wonderful odors that brought with them the beckoning of a promising world.

When we were flung into a pile and the vibrations ceased, Mother tensed, and we probably all knew that a man was walking outside the den, but then nothing happened for some time except that our mother paced, panting. I noticed that Heavy Boy was following her around, focused on what was, for him, the issue of the moment, but I knew Mother had no intention of nursing us right then.

Then came voices. This, too, was something we'd experienced before, so I yawned.

"Okay, I'm not sure how this is going to work." That was a voice I hadn't heard. I pictured another man.

"Maybe instead of droppin' the tailgate, I just roll back the tarp?" This was the voice belonging to the man who had yelled.

"I think we're just going to have one shot at the mother. Once she sees what we're up to she'll bail over the sides."

"Okay."

"I forgot to ask, you said you have the gun on you?" New Voice asked.

"Yeah," Familiar Voice replied.

"Would you mind?"

"Oh, hell no, here it is. I ain't never shot a pistol in my life."

I looked over at Mother. She seemed less stressed. Maybe all dogs calmed down once something seemed to be occurring over and over.

There was an unrecognizable clicking sound. "So, you ready?"

"Yeah."

With a loud crackle, hands appeared on both sides of the den, and daylight began flooding into our enclosure. The roof was being peeled back by the men, who were peering down at us. Mother was growling ominously. There were two humans—the one with the hairy face from before, and a taller man with a smooth face and more hair on his head.

The smooth-faced man smiled, his teeth white. "Okay, girl. Be still, now. This will go a lot better if you hold still."

"She 'bout ripped my arm outta the socket before," the hairy-faced man said.

{ 19 }

Smooth Face looked up sharply. "She actually bit you?"

"Uh, no."

"That's good to hear."

"She ain't friendly, though."

"She's got a litter. They get protective."

Mother was growling more loudly. Her teeth were on display now.

"Hey there. Just hold still," Smooth Face soothed.

"Look out!"

Her nails scrabbling, Mother turned to the exposed side of the den and in a flash leapt over, vanishing. Instantly, my siblings reacted, swarming in the same direction.

"Well, I guess I could have predicted that," Smooth Face chuckled. "See how skinny she was? She hasn't had a home for some time. She's not going to trust a person no matter how gently I talk."

"Big, though."

"Mostly malamute, as far as I can tell. These pups have something else in them, though. Dane?"

"Hey, thanks for taking the bullet outta the gun, I didn't know howta do that," Hairy Face said.

"I removed the clip, too. I can't believe he handed it to you with a round in the chamber. That's dangerous."

"Yeah, well, he's my boss, so I guess I won't be complainin'. You, uh, won't tell anyone I didn't follow his instructions? Wouldn't wanta have this get back ta him."

"Tell him you did what he said. It explains why there aren't any bullets left."

My siblings reacted in various ways as the men lowered their hands into the den. Some cowered, but others, like Heavy Boy, were wagging and submissive.

"Can I see the puppies?" I looked up at this, a third voice, pitched high.

"Sure, Ava, here." Smooth Face lifted a small human off the ground. It was, I realized, a little girl. She clapped her hands. "Puppies!" she squealed in her high, delighted voice.

Smooth Face put the girl down. "Time to get them in the crate."

He deftly scooped me up. I was placed in a basket with my littermates, who all had their forepaws on the sides, noses raised, trying to see.

The little girl's smiling face appeared over the edge of the basket, gazing down at us. I stared up at her, curious about all the different smells wafting from her—sweet and spicy and flowery.

"Okay, Ava, let's get these little guys inside where it's warm."

The basket shifted and the world was once again unstable, made worse by the absence of our mother. Several of my siblings squealed in alarm, while I concentrated on trying to stay out of the way as Heavy Boy came tumbling by.

Suddenly the air was warmer. The new den stopped moving. The little girl reached in and I found I welcomed her touch as she lifted me up to her face. Her light eyes stared at me from very close, and I felt an impulse to lick her skin, though I did not know why.

"We have a problem, Ava," Smooth Face said. "We can bottle feed them, but without a mother I am not sure they'll survive."

"I'll do it!" the little girl piped in immediately.

"Well, I know that. But we'll be late getting home tonight, and that's not going to make your mother happy."

The little girl was still gazing at me, and I stared rapturously back. "I want to keep this one."

The man laughed. "We probably can't, Ava. Let's get going with the bottles."

Every experience was utterly new. When the little girl sat holding me on my back, pinning me between her legs, I squirmed in discomfort, but then she lowered a small object toward my mouth and when I smelled the tiny drop of rich milk oozing from it I took it in my mouth like a teat and sucked hard and was rewarded with a meal rich and sweet.

In the den with Mother, night fell as a gradual process, but in this new place it came in a single instant, with such swift abruptness I felt several of my siblings twitch in alarm. Anxious without our mother, we were restless and took a long time before we dozed off. I slept on top of Heavy Boy, and it was much better than the other way around.

The next morning the little girl and the man returned and once again we were given nourishment while lying on our backs. I knew my littermates had fed because they all carried the smell of the dense milk on their lips.

"We have to get the mother to come back, Ava," Smooth Face said. "We won't be able to bottle feed these little guys as much as they need, otherwise."

"I'll stay home from school Monday," the little girl replied.

"You can't do that."

"Daddy . . ."

"Ava, remember how I explained that sometimes we pick up an animal and we can't save them because they are sick, or because they have been badly mistreated? It's like these puppies are sick. I have other animals to take care of and I don't have anyone to help me right now."

"*Please.*"

"Maybe the mother will come back. Okay, Ava? Hopefully she'll miss her babies."

The little girl, I decided, was named Ava. She reached for me a short time later, and her hands made me feel safe and warm. She carried me out into the cool air, cuddling me to her chest.

I smelled Mother before I saw her. Suddenly Ava drew in a sharp breath.

"Are you the mommy?" she asked in a small voice.

Mother had edged out of some thick trees and was creeping hesitantly toward us across the grass. She lowered her head when the girl spoke, her distrust obvious with every uncertain step.

Ava set me down, leaving me by myself in the grass. I saw my mother watch warily as the little girl retreated until she was standing at the door to the building.

"Daddy! The mother came!" Ava called shrilly. "It's okay, girl," she urged in softer tones. "Come see your baby."

I wondered what we were doing.

{ T H R E E }

Ava patted her thighs with her palms flat. "Please come,
Mommy Dog! *Please*. If you don't come save your babies,
they will die."

Though I didn't understand, I heard the anguish layered
through her words. This tense situation, I decided, called for a
puppy. I turned my back on my mother, making a conscious
choice. I loved my mother dog, but I knew in my heart I belonged
with humans.

"Mommy Dog, come get your little boy!" Ava called. She
scooped me up and eased through the door to the building, moving backward down a hallway. Mother crept right to the threshold, but stopped suspiciously, not budging.

Ava set me on the floor. "Want your baby?" she asked.

I did not know what to do. Both my mother and Ava were
brittle with anxiety. I could feel it crackling off them, it was in

my mother's sour breath and came as a scent off the little girl's skin. I whimpered, wagging, confused. I began inching toward Mother and that seemed to decide it. Mother took a few steps inside, her eyes on me. I flashed to a memory of her leaping into the den, Heavy Boy's nape in her teeth, and knew what was coming. Mother darted for me.

Then the door banged shut behind her. The noise seemed to terrify Mother. Her ears back, she darted back and forth in the narrow hallway, utterly panicked, then dashed through a side doorway. I saw Smooth Face Man looking in the window, and for some reason I wagged at him.

When he dropped from the window I followed Mother's scent into a small room. There was a bench at the far end of the space and Mother cowered under it, panting, her face tight with fear.

I sensed the little girl and the man behind me in the door-way.

"Don't go any closer, Ava," said the man. "I'll be right back."

I was going to run to Mother, but the little girl gathered me up. She nuzzled me and I wiggled in delight.

Mother didn't move, was hunkered down, hiding. Then the man reappeared, trailing a strong odor of my siblings, and put our cage on the floor, popping open the door. Heavy Boy, followed by the rest of my littermates, poured out, trampling over one another. When they spotted Mother they stampeded her in an uncoordinated rush. She eased out from under the bench, ears up, staring at Ava. Then the wave of puppies was upon her, shrieking and squealing, and Mother flopped down by the bench, allowing her puppies to nurse.

The girl put me on the floor and I ran over to join my family.

"That was so smart, Ava! You did it exactly right," the man praised.

The man was, I learned, called Dad by Ava, and Sam by all

the other people in the building. This was far too complex of a concept for me, and I eventually just thought of him as Sam Dad.

Ava wasn't in the building all the time, or even every day. I nonetheless regarded her as my girl, belonging to me and nobody else. There were other dogs sharing our big room, dogs to see and smell and hear in their cages nearby. One of them was a mother dog like ours; the scent of her milk wafted through the air, and I heard the peeps and squeals of another litter, out of sight in a cage at the other end of the big room. I also detected a different sort of animal, coming to me as a strong and alien scent from another part of the building, and wondered what it could be.

Life in the metal den with the rattling roof seemed long ago and far away. Mother's milk was suddenly richer and more plentiful, and her breath was no longer fetid.

"She's gaining weight even with the nursing; that's good," Sam Dad told Ava. "When she's weaned them, we'll spay her and find her a new forever home." Mother always shied away from Sam Dad but after a time went willingly to Ava, who called Mother "Kiki."

Ava addressed me as Bailey, and eventually I understood that was who I was, I was Bailey. Heavy Boy was Buddha. All of my siblings had names, and I spent the days playing with them in our cage and out in a grassy yard with high wooden walls.

None of my littermates understood that Ava and I shared a special relationship, and they would crowd her when she opened our cage door. I finally decided to rush to the opening the moment the little girl entered the big room, to be ready if she was there to let us out.

It worked! She picked me up, while all the others remained teeming at her feet and probably feeling jealous. "Well, Bailey, you're so eager, do you know what's happening?"

She carried me because I was the special one. My siblings trailed after us down the hallway. She pushed open the door and set me down and I jumped on Heavy Boy Buddha. "I'll be right back!" Ava sang.

We were old enough now that we no longer tripped over our paws when we ran. Heavy Boy Buddha leaped on a hard rubber ball, so we all leaped on him. It was satisfying to realize I wasn't the only puppy who resented being crushed by our brother.

The door opened again and Ava astounded me by setting down three new puppies! We all rushed to one another, sniffing and wagging and climbing up to chew on each other's ears.

One puppy, a girl, had a black, pushed-in muzzle and a brown body with a splash of white on her chest—her two brothers had white marks on their faces. Her fur was short and when we were nose-to-nose, it seemed as if all the other puppies in the yard faded away, not present even when one of them careened into us. When the black-faced girl dog ran the perimeter of the yard, I ran right with her.

The mingling of the two puppy families became routine, and Ava called the girl dog Lacey. Lacey was close to my age, with a muscular but compact frame and bright black eyes. We sought each other out and played together in the yard with exclusive devotion. In ways I could not understand, I felt I belonged more to Lacey than to Ava. When I slept, Lacey and I wrestled in my dreams; when I was awake, I raised my nose in an obsessive hunt to isolate her scent from those of all the other animals. My chief frustration with my otherwise marvelous life was that no one thought to put Lacey and me in the same cage.

When Mother began evading our pleading approaches to her teats, Sam Dad set out small bowls of mushy food, which Heavy Boy Buddha seemed to think he could only eat if he was standing in it. This new circumstance, this food, was such a wonderful development I would dream about it as often as I dreamed of Lacey.

I was overjoyed when Lacey and I were finally put in a cage together, inside what Sam Dad called "the van." It was a high-sided metal room with dog cages stacked on top of each other, though the interior of the van was redolent with that same mysterious, absent animal. I didn't care: Ava had observed how much Lacey and I loved each other and had rightly concluded we needed to be together always. Lacey rolled on her back and I mouthed her throat and jaw. Lacey's stomach was mostly white and the fur there was as dense and short as on her back, as opposed to my siblings, who had bushy gray hair and a face mostly white with tracings of gray between the eyes and around the snout. I supposed, when I thought about it, I probably appeared the same. Lacey's ears were so soft and warm, I loved to nibble them gently, my jaw quivering with affection.

"Will there be cats at the adoption event, Daddy?" Ava asked.

"Nope. Just dogs. Cats are in two months—May is the start of what we call kitten season."

In the van we were subjected to the same torsion and pull that I remembered from the day we met Sam Dad and Ava. It went on so long that Lacey and I fell asleep, my paw cradled between her jaws.

We awoke when, with a lurch, the jostling stopped. The side of the van opened up and admitted a flood of dog smells!

We were all whimpering, eager to run free and sniff everything this new place had to offer, but that was not to happen. Instead, Sam Dad moved each cage, one at a time, out the door. When it was our turn, Lacey and I flattened to the floor, made dizzy by the way Sam Dad carried us. We were placed on some sandy ground, still in the cage. Across from us I saw Heavy Boy

Buddha and two of my brothers, and realized that all the dogs from the van were now here, their crates arrayed in a rough circle. The canine odors were even more rampant and available now. Lacey and I sniffed, and then she climbed on top of me and it turned into a long wrestle. I was aware of humans young and old darting around the kennels, but Lacey absorbed most of my attention.

Then Lacey shook me off and I saw what she was staring at: a girl not much older than Ava, with completely different features— Ava's eyes and hair were light, her skin pale, but this girl had black hair and dark eyes and a darker cast to her skin. She smelled very much like Ava, though—sweet and fruity.

"Oh, you are the prettiest baby. You are so beautiful," the girl whispered. I felt the adoration coming off her as she poked her fingers through the wires and Lacey licked them. I pushed my way to those fingers for my share of the affection, but the girl was only focused on Lacey.

Sam Dad crouched down. "That's Lacey. She's obviously mostly boxer."

"She's the one I want," this new girl declared.

"Ask your parents to come over, and I will let her out for you to play with," Sam Dad offered. The little girl skipped off. Lacey and I exchanged baffled expressions.

Very soon a man around Sam Dad's age approached, followed by a boy older and bigger than Ava. I was wagging because I had never seen a boy before: it was like a male version of a girl!

"Are these two from the same litter? The female looks smaller," New Man observed. The boy stood with his hands in his pockets, hanging back. I had never before met anyone who didn't want to play with puppies.

"No. We're thinking the male's father might be a large breed of some kind, maybe great Dane. Pup's probably ten weeks old and already pretty big," Sam Dad replied. "The mother is mostly malamute. The girl there is from a different litter; she's a boxer mix. Her name is Lacey."

"It's a big dog we're needing."

"Well, unless by big you mean tall, like an Irish wolfhound, you're not going to get much bigger than a malamute with some Dane in him. Not stockier, anyway. Look at his paws," Sam Dad noted with a chuckle.

"Your rescue is in Grand Rapids? A bit of a haul."

"Yes, we drove up with some of our bigger dogs. Up here people like large dogs; in the city they like them small. When I head back I'm filling the rescue-mobile with Chihuahuas and Yorkies and other small breeds from shelters around here."

I fell on my back so that Lacey would attack my neck. An older woman joined the new man and smiled into the cage, but I was too busy being mauled by Lacey to pay her much mind.

"Like I said," New Man continued, "it's the bigger dogs we're interested in. It's for my other son, Burke. He was born with a spine problem. The doctors want to wait until he's older to operate, so he's in a wheelchair. We need to get a dog to help him around, pull his chair, all of that."

"Oh." Sam Dad shook his head. "There are organizations that train companion animals. It's hard work. You should contact one of them."

"My son says the trained dogs should go to people who have no hope of walking again. He refuses to consider taking a companion dog out of the system." New Man shrugged. "Burke can be sort of . . . stubborn about things."

The boy with his hands in his pockets snorted and rolled his eyes.

"That's enough, Grant," New Man said. The boy kicked at the dirt.

"You want to have your son come meet the male? His name is Bailey."

New Man, the older lady, and the boy all looked up sharply. Lacey and I caught the sudden motions and froze, wondering what was happening.

"Did I say something wrong?" Sam Dad asked.

"It's just that my family has a history with dogs named Bailey," New Man explained. "You, uh, mind if we changed his name to something else?"

"It would be your dog. That's fine. You want to bring your other son over? Burke?"

No one said anything for a moment. The older woman touched a light hand to New Man's shoulder, saying, "He's . . . he struggles with people seeing him in the chair right now. He didn't used to mind, but this last year has been difficult. He'll be thirteen in June."

"Ah, the end of the preteen years," Sam Dad observed dryly. "I've heard about them. I've got a few more years before I have to worry—Ava's only ten."

"I think I can make the command decision, here," New Man declared. "I assume there's a fee?"

"Fees and forms," Sam Dad replied cheerfully.

The new people went away, talking together. Suddenly the little girl with the dark hair came running back, followed by two adult humans.

"This is her, Daddy!" she cried out. She knelt, opened the cage, and scooped out Lacey. When I made to follow, she clanged the cage door shut right in my face.

I watched in concern as she turned away. Where was she taking Lacey?

FOUR

The little girl with the black hair took Lacey over to meet the two adults—the girl's parents, a part of my mind decided. Mostly I was just trying to catch a glimpse of Lacey in the little girl's arms. For some reason, this felt different, more threatening, than when Ava carried one of us. Lacey was just as desperate: when she was lowered to the ground, she ignored the dark-haired girl and ran straight over to my cage and stuck her nose through the bars to touch mine.

"Lacey!" the little girl called, leading her parents over and snatching my Lacey back up.

New Man and his family were returning, and I saw him stiffen at the sight of the little girl's family. The boy regarded New Man curiously.

"Hello," said the man with the dark hair. New Man reacted

oddly, ignoring Dark Hair Man and kneeling to pull me out of my cage, hopefully so I could be with Lacey.

"Hello," the older lady replied to Dark Hair Man. "Are you adopting a new puppy, too?"

"I'm getting Lacey," the black-haired girl sang.

I decided there were two separate families—Black Hair Girl and her mother and father; and New Man, a boy, and an older woman who didn't seem to be the boy's mother. Though the two families were both human, they smelled slightly different from one another.

New Man picked me up and turned away from the conversation with Dark Hair Man. "Are you coming, Mom?" he asked after he took a few steps. An odd tension flowed through New Man's hands as they held me.

"Nice speaking to you," the older lady (who New Man called "Mom") said to the Black Hair Family before she hurried after us. She was frowning at New Man. He waited as she caught up to us. "What in the world was that?" Mom asked in low tones. "I've never seen you so rude."

Held against New Man's chest, I couldn't see Lacey and could barely smell her. I squirmed, and he patted me reassuringly. "Don't you know?" New Man replied. "He's one of the robo-farmers trying to put us out of business."

The boy ran ahead to the side of a car. Inside the vehicle I could see another, younger boy, smiling at me.

"Wait!"

Little Ava was dashing up and New Man turned.

"I want to say goodbye to Bailey!"

I was lowered so that I was nose-to-nose with Ava. "I love you, Bailey. You are such a good puppy. We can't keep every dog we rescue, because that would be foster failure, so we have to say goodbye, but I will always remember you. I hope I see you again sometime!" I wagged at my name, Bailey, and at the kiss Ava put on my nose.

Then I was in the car. Why? What were we doing? What happened to Lacey? The younger boy gathered me to him. He was essentially a smaller copy of the first boy—same dark hair and light eyes, same smell of bread and butter. I was so anxious I whimpered.

"Don't worry, little guy, everything is okay," the younger boy whispered. I was intimidated, but he rubbed his face on mine so fondly I was charmed into licking his cheeks.

Everyone was sliding into the car with me.

"Can I drive?" the older boy asked.

"Or maybe we should just try to survive the trip," the younger boy replied.

"You can drive when the whole family's not in the car, Grant," New Man said.

"I don't know why it's called a learner's permit when you won't *permit* me to learn," he complained.

The car started moving. "What was the deal with the Asian dude?" the older boy asked.

New Man shook his head. "That's not the way to ask the question. His being Asian has nothing to do with it."

"What happened?" The boy holding me wanted to know.

"Dad acted weird," Older Boy explained.

"He was rude," Mom interjected.

New Man sighed. "We have nothing against Chinese Americans. What we do have a problem with is where he works. They're buying up the farms and replacing the workers with drone harvesters. They're running down prices so that we can barely make a living. Meanwhile, workers who used to bring home a decent wage can't feed their families."

"Okay, I get it, sorry," Older Boy mumbled, looking away.

"Your father isn't angry at you, Grant. It's the situation," Mom said pointedly. "Isn't that right, Chase?"

New Man grunted. The younger boy had me on my back and was tickling me and letting me bite his fingers. "I'm going to name him Cooper!" he announced.

"Dumb name," Older Boy observed.

"That's enough, Grant," New Man said.

Older Boy's name was Grant. That's one of the things I learned over the next several days. His name was Grant, and the younger boy was Burke. The woman was mostly Grandma, so I stopped thinking of her as Mom. New Man, though, was more of a challenge because he couldn't seem to get names straight. He called Grandma "Mom," and she called him "Chase," and then, most confusingly, the boys called him "Dad," which was what Ava called Sam Dad. It was too much for a dog, so I began thinking of New Man as "Chase Dad." Were all men "Dad"?

And everyone addressed me as "Cooper." I had been Bailey when I was with Lacey, and now I was Cooper and was without her. I was happy to be surrounded by people who loved me, but a part of me was always waiting for Lacey to show up. Thinking of her made me feel oddly hungry, hungry even after I'd filled my belly with dinner. I was burdened with a persistent, empty ache.

When Burke wasn't lying in bed, he was sitting in a chair that moved swiftly from place to place with thrusts of his hands on two wheels. Sometimes one of the other family members would stand behind Burke and push. Burke wanted me in his lap, and I discovered he really couldn't touch me otherwise, though he would bend over and try, his fingers wagging in the air. He taught me to climb up on a low, soft stool and from there to leap into his lap. "Up, Cooper!" he called, slapping his thighs and laughing when I complied. Once I was there Burke would cuddle me and I could chew on his face, the same sort of affection flowing through my jaws as when I held Lacey's leg in my mouth.

"If Cooper is Burke's dog, how come I have to do the house training?" Grant asked one day.

"Why do you think?" Dad replied.

Several times a day Grant would take me outside, sometimes in a rush if I were about to squat in the house. He would feed me treats. "I'm the fun boy in the family. You'll see. Burke says you're a working dog, but when you're older I'll take you on hikes and throw the ball for you. You'll see," Grant whispered to me as he gave me a treat. I loved Grant.

Grant wasn't always home, and neither was Chase Dad, but Grandma and Burke were. "School," Grant would say, and then he'd be running out the door. I learned to expect that I'd be hearing "time to get to work" from Chase Dad, or something similar with the same tones in his voice, and then it would be just Grandma and Burke. "Let's start with your French lesson," Grandma might say, to Burke's loud groans. I would roll on my back or jump on a toy or run around the room to make sure they knew there were plenty of alternatives to what they usually did, which was to sit quietly and gaze at an odorless, flickering object, and make small clicking noises by tapping their fingers, and generally ignore the fact that they had a dog in the house. They didn't even get up to follow me when I pushed through the dog door and trotted down the ramp to sniff around and mark my territory outside.

I wondered where Lacey was. I did not understand how I could be so certain we would be together always and then see her pulled away from me by a little black-haired girl.

Gradually I came to understand that while I lived with everyone in the family, I had a special responsibility to Burke. It was

Burke who fed me, setting my food bowl on a shelf he could reach from his chair and I could access by climbing up on a wooden box. I slept on Burke's bed in a small downstairs room—Grandma had a bigger room downstairs, and Grant and Chase Dad had beds in rooms upstairs.

It was Burke who taught me to respond to commands. "Come. Sit. Stay. Lie down."

Stay was the hardest.

Everyone in the family loved me and played with me, of course, but I had a sure sense that Burke *needed* me. He cared enough to teach me things. And being needed felt more important than anything, engendering a bond between us as strong as the attachment I felt to Lacey. Sometimes I would gaze at him in sheer wonder that I had my own boy. I loved everyone in the family, but within a very short time it was Burke who centered my world, Burke who was my purpose.

Where we lived was called the "farm." There was a barn and a fenced-in area where an old goat named Judy chewed distractedly on grass but never threw up. I sometimes approached the fence, and Judy the old goat and I would stare at each other. I marked the fence, but the goat didn't show me the courtesy of sniffing the area. I wasn't sure what an old goat was good for. Grandma spent a lot of time speaking to her, but goats can't talk any better than dogs. Judy was not invited into the house, so I decided I was the favorite. I was allowed to run around on the farm, but my sense of obligation to my boy kept me from going much past a large pond with worthless ducks swimming around in it. I just needed to know where he was at all times.

Come, Sit, Stay, Lie Down. I had work and it made me happy.

I also had a box of toys. Whenever I felt the mood growing stagnant, I would plunge my face into the open box and pull out a ball or some other object—most of them were rubber because the cloth ones I shredded and ate. The only item I didn't care for in my toy box was something Grant gave me: "It's a nylon bone for him to chew; it's good for his teeth," Grant advised Burke. He would thrust this odorless, tasteless, hard "nylon bone" at me. "Get the bone! Want the bone?" Grant would shake it and I would pretend interest because I felt sorry for him.

After a time, I didn't need the wooden box in order to reach the food bowl. "You're a big dog now, Cooper," Burke declared. I decided "big dog" was the same as "good dog."

Or, maybe not, because around the same time my boy started saying "big dog" he began speaking with the obvious intent that I was to do something in response—something harder than Sit or even Stay. "Let's do some training, Cooper," Burke announced every day, and I would know it was time for me to pay attention to what was always a bewildering set of spoken commands.

There was a loop of rope on the door of what I learned was a "refrigerator." Burke shook it. "Open" he said. He kept shaking it until I just had to have it in my mouth. Growling playfully, I backed up, the door swinging on its hinges and wonderful food odors ghosting out on cold currents. Burke gave me a treat! Open meant "tug the rope and get a treat."

Leave It was very confusing because it *started* with a treat, this one under a heavy glove on the couch. I recognized that glove from when Grant and Burke would throw a ball to each other in the yard—a game I loved because when one of the boys missed I would leap on it and then it was *my* ball.

Burke held a chicken treat under the glove and just sat there, even though we both knew where the chicken was! Finally deciding I needed to take the initiative, I went to move the glove away. "Leave It!" he snapped at me. I was utterly baffled. What did that mean? I stared at the glove, drooling, and went for it again. "Leave It! No! Leave It!"

No? What did he think a chicken treat was for? "Leave It!" he commanded again, this time handing me a *different* treat, a liver-flavored one. I preferred chicken, but with this madness going on I decided liver was the best I was going to be able to do.

After several repetitions of "Leave It!" I decided to wait him out, and he gave me more liver. It made absolutely no sense, but as long as it ended in a treat it was fine with me. I learned to cheat by turning away from the glove as soon as he said "Leave It." Treat! Then the morsel was under the glove on the floor and Burke was no longer holding it. I calculated I could move the glove and gobble the chicken easily enough, but when he said "Leave It" I almost couldn't help myself, turning away from the glove automatically.

Treat!

Eventually I decided that whenever my boy said "Leave It" I should ignore whatever had my attention and focus on his hand, which was a much more reliable source of treats.

Those delicious morsels were not the best part, though—it was the affection pouring from Burke as he said, "Good dog, Cooper." I would do anything for him. Burke loved me and I loved Burke.

Pull was easy—I marched steadily forward with a rope on my harness that looped back to the chair. But Pull had variations that took me many days and many treats to learn.

"Watch this," Burke said to Grant. "Okay, Cooper, Pull Right!" That meant tug in one direction. "Pull Left!" That meant tug the other way. This was hard work for a dog, but Burke's praise plus Burke's chicken made it all worthwhile.

"What's that for?" Grant asked.

"Like if I am having trouble in the snow. Cooper can pull me."

"You're not going to try to go out in the snow. That's stupid," Grant replied.

"Not deep snow, but you know, even if it's shoveled, sometimes it's tough to get traction."

"What else have you taught him?"

"Okay, this is the best one." Grunting, Burke lifted himself out of his chair, sliding onto the couch and then, his arms out, rolling onto the floor. I watched tensely as he crawled with his arms into the middle of the room. "Okay! Cooper? Steady!"

I went immediately to my boy's side. He reached up and seized my harness with both hands. "Assist!"

He gripped me with one hand and helped push himself with the other as I slowly dragged him across the floor to his chair. "Steady," Burke commanded again. I held completely still, taking his weight as he scrambled into his seat. "See? Cooper can get me back into the wheelchair."

"Cool! Do it again!" Grant said.

Though I had just managed to get him into the chair, Burke fell out of it a second time. I did not understand what had changed for him, lately, because it seemed like he could barely manage to stay in the thing now that we had learned Assist.

This time, when Burke called me to him, Grant stepped over to the chair and dragged it into the kitchen, which was all the way across the room.

"Why'd you do that?" Burke demanded.

Grant laughed.

"Come on, Grant. Bring it back."

"Let's see if Cooper can figure it out. Like Dad always says, an easy challenge is no challenge at all."

"So you're saying this is somehow good for me."

"Or maybe good for the dog."

Burke was quiet for a moment. "Okay, Cooper. Assist."

I did not know what to do. How could I do Assist when the chair wasn't there?

Burke pulled on my harness until I was facing the kitchen. "Assist, Cooper."

I took a tentative step forward. "Yes!" Burke praised. "Good dog!"

Did he want me to drag him into the kitchen? This was a different Assist than we'd been doing, feeling more like Pull Left. But I remembered how "Leave It" went from "don't try to eat what's under the glove" to "ignore what's on the floor even if it smells delicious." Perhaps "training" meant everything in my life would keep changing.

I started moving steadily toward the kitchen. "Yes! See? He figured it out!"

Grant waited in the kitchen with his arms folded. Burke was panting a little by the time we got there. "Good dog, Cooper!"

Treat!

Grant picked up Burke's chair. "How about this?" He carried the chair into the living room and up the stairs. "Can he get you up here?" Grant called down with a taunting laugh.

Burke just lay on the floor. He seemed sad. I nudged him with my nose, not understanding.

"Okay, Cooper," he whispered finally. Something like anger was pushing the sad out of him. "Let's do it."

Burke seized my harness and steered me around so that I was facing the living room. I thought I knew what was coming: when he said "Assist," I headed toward the couch, figuring that's where he wanted to go. Then he surprised me, twisting me again. "Assist!"

The stairs? I dragged him that far and stopped, bewildered. Grant was grinning from up at the top. Burke put one hand on the first step and his other hand gripped my harness.

"Assist!"

I took a faltering step upward. Burke shoved himself with his free hand, grunting. "Assist!" he commanded when I stopped. This seemed wrong; Burke's weight was dragging me back. Why didn't Grant come down to help? "Let's go, Cooper."

I took another stair, then another. We developed a rhythm,

moving more fluidly. Burke was breathing deeply. "Yes!" he whispered. "We're doing it, Cooper!"

Grant had stopped grinning and had his arms folded again.

I smelled Dad but was focused on making it to the top. I did not know what would happen when we got there but hoped it would involve chicken.

"What's going on here?" Dad asked behind us.

Both Burke and Grant went silent and tense the moment their father spoke. I didn't wag so the boys would know that even though I didn't understand, I was taking whatever was happening very seriously.

"You want to tell him, Grant?" Burke asked pleasantly.

Grant swallowed.

"I asked a question," Chase Dad said. "What are you two doing?"

Burke was smiling at his brother. "I'm showing Grant how Cooper is helping me up the stairs."

I heard my name, so I figured it was okay to wag now.

"Oh." Chase Dad rubbed his face. "Okay, can he help you *down*?"

"Probably. We haven't practiced that one yet," Burke replied.

"Let me know if you need me to come get you," Chase Dad advised. "Wet start to the summer, need the rain." He turned toward the kitchen.

Grant blew out a breath.

Burke shook his head. "You couldn't have looked more guilty if you had a smoking pistol in your hands. Why, do you think Dad would be angry if he knew you were torturing your brother?"

"Torturing," Grant scoffed. "Anybody can crawl up the stairs using just their arms, plus you had a *dog*."

"Try it."

"You don't think I can do it?"

"Nope," Burke declared.

"Okay. Watch this."

Grant folded Burke's chair and clumped down the steps, snapping it back open and placing it at the bottom. Then he got on his hands and knees. I tensed—did he need Assist?

"No, you're using your knees," Burke objected.

"Am not."

"Drag your legs."

"I know!"

"Okay, that's just one step and you used your legs."

"This is stupid."

"So you admit you can't do it."

"You know what?" Grant stood, jumped down past the bottom step, and savagely kicked the chair. It fell over with a crash.

"Hey!" Chase Dad yelled from the kitchen. He strode out, his shoes making angry-sounding impacts on the floor. "What do you think you're doing?"

Grant stared stonily at the floor.

"Grant? What do you have to say for yourself?"

"I *hate* this stupid wheelchair!" he shouted.

Dad stared at him.

"Really?" Burke countered quietly from his perch next to me. "Because I love the thing."

"We don't abuse equipment around here, Grant. Understood?"

Grant wiped his eyes. I could smell his salty tears. Without another word he bolted for the front door.

Chase Dad's mouth opened. "Grant!"

Burke cleared his throat. "Dad?"

Chase Dad had taken two steps to follow Grant, but now he paused, looking up at us.

"Would you carry me down, please?"

Chase Dad glanced back in the direction Grant had run.

"Let it go, Dad," Burke whispered softly.

Chase Dad lifted Burke and put him in the rolling chair, even though I was right there and could have done Assist.

After several days we were outside playing a game of Get It. Burke scattered a few items—a shoe, a ball, a stick, a sock—and then told me to "Get It!" I had never heard the word before and, though I felt I probably was being asked to do something in the name of "training," I didn't really feel much like trying to figure things out that day. Instead, I pounced on the stick and gave it a good shaking.

"Leave It," Burke commanded.

I stared at him in disbelief. Leave It a *stick*?

"Leave It," he repeated.

So I dropped the stick. He pointed at the ball. "Get It!" I picked up the stick. "Leave It!"

I decided to lift my leg on a flower and hope Burke would Leave It this new game of Get It.

"Get the ball! Get It!"

The day was warm, the grasses so intoxicatingly fragrant I wanted to roll on my back and then probably nap, but Burke apparently did not want to celebrate with a fun stick. I went over to him and licked his fingers to let him know I still loved him despite his crazy behavior.

Chase Dad came walking up. "How is this going?"

Chase Dad smelled like mud—apparently *he* knew how to have fun on a day like this!

Burke sighed, a sad sound, and I went to him and did Sit attentively to cheer him up. "Not well. I think maybe I need to start by throwing things and pointing at them so he learns to follow my finger."

"Nothing worth doing comes easy, Burke. You're doing great

with that animal. You're a natural. But even a natural needs practice."

"Like you and your guitar?" Burke probed shrewdly.

Chase Dad laughed. "People did say I was a natural. After twenty-five years of practice, I'm still only about as good as when I picked up the darn thing the first time."

"But you never practice."

"No, you're wrong. I do when you and Grant are not here. I go out to the barn so as not to deafen your grandma."

"How come you never play so we can hear you, Dad? Why can't we ever come listen when you're with your band?"

"The bar is only for adults over twenty-one, son."

We all looked up as, down on the road, a long line of cars came trundling up, each almost on top of the other—huge, gleaming machines.

I had learned some things. Cars had more seats inside for people. Trucks often had fewer seats but more room for other things, like the loads of plants Chase Dad often drove with. Vans carried stacks of cages and were loaded with animal scents. Then there was the slow truck—a loud, rattling vehicle with a single seat perched high above the wheels. But these things on the road were very strange, enormous and nearly silent, following each other in tight, single-file formation.

I barked to let them know that whatever they were I had my eye on them and I was a dog.

"That's right, Coop." Chase Dad stooped and petted my head. "Those are the enemy."

"Grandma calls them the future," Burke replied.

"Yeah, well," Chase Dad stood and swatted at his pants. "Hopefully not *our* future. Drone harvester-combines. Robo-farmers. You used to see twenty, thirty workers out on a day like this for every asparagus field; now there's not a single person, just these things. Same with potatoes, same with everything."

"Not us, though."

"Right. I've got Grant out there right now, picking asparagus for the farmers' market this Saturday."

Burke's hand stroked me in a way I had learned to mean he was sad.

"Wish I could help, Dad."

"Oh, you will someday, Burke."

I saw those same machines cruise by every day Burke and I were out in the yard working on Get It. I learned to follow Burke's pointed finger gesture and do Get It on the glove; the ball; and sometimes, thankfully, the stick. Then other things in the house, like pillows, a shirt, a dropped fork. "Get It" just meant I should keep picking up things and doing Leave It until I finally selected something that earned me a treat.

Not my favorite game.

No one ever played Get It with Judy the old goat—or anything else, as far as I could see. Everyone petted Judy, even though she was not a dog and probably didn't even enjoy such treatment, but it was only Grandma who would go into the pen and sit and talk to Judy. Judy didn't wag or seem to respond, though she did cling to Grandma's side.

"Oh Judy, you are such a sweetie; I remember when you first came to us as a baby," Grandma said. "Miguel couldn't wait to show me; he knew I would love you. He was a good man, Judy." I wagged at the affection I could feel, which seemed shadowed with melancholy.

When Grandma wasn't sitting in the chair in the goat's pen, Judy would often climb up on it. I wondered if Grandma knew that.

Burke liked to spend time at a table in his room, silently taking little pieces of plastic and dripping a pungent liquid on them. The stuff was so strong it made me sneeze.

"What are you working on?" Burke and I looked up. Grant was leaning in the doorway.

"It's a solar energy plant. I'm going to use it to power the whole town."

Grant shoved himself out of the doorway. "Show me."

Burke looked his brother up and down. "Okay," he agreed slowly. "These are the houses I built. And this is the hotel, the city hall . . ."

"What have they been doing for power all this time if they didn't have solar?"

"It's not a story, Grant. I'm not building a town in chronological order. I just like laying it out so it will all make sense when it's finished."

"If that's how you want to do it, sure. Seems like it would be more fun to have a farm, and then housing for the workers, and then businesses on Main Street. Like, with kerosene, then coal, and horses and then cars. Your way is boring. At least my way there would be an adventure, a purpose. What's the point of any of it if it never evolves?"

"So if you wanted to put in a trolley system, would you start with a town hall meeting? Do an environmental impact study?"

"You're playing with dolls. It's stupid," Grant sneered.

When Grant and Burke spoke to each other, I often sensed an irritated anger rising off both of them. I felt it now.

"So you need something, Grant?"

Grant took in a breath, regarding his brother carefully, then nodded and blew it out. "So I want to go with my friends and play basketball this weekend and as usual Dad tells me I have to work. So I said I was going to go help the Millards pick strawberries—

you know how big Dad is on having us help thy neighbor and all that."

"What does any of this have to do with me?"

"Just, you know, when Dad comes back, tell him Mr. Millard came to get me. He'll believe *you*."

"I don't get why I should do that. Lie to Dad."

"Don't I do all the work around here? Do you have a single chore? No, you just sit here and build a crappy pretend city with Barbies."

"Don't you think I would help Dad if I could?" Burke hit the arm of his chair in real fury. I flinched and then nosed his arm.

"Okay, just . . . Sorry. I'm just a little pissed because I only want to play basketball and I know Dad would say no. Can I count on you?"

"So Dad goes, 'Who picked up Grant?' and I say, 'It sure wasn't a bunch of guys for basketball.'"

"God, Burke."

Later, while Grant was outside stacking firewood with Dad, I helped Burke climb the stairs and then did Assist as he steered my harness into the room where Grant slept. My boy was laughing but also oddly tense, and he froze at the sound of Grandma opening a cupboard. He guided me to the closet and pulled out some shoes and put a few drops of the really smelly fluid in each one of them, the air filling with an eye-watering tang. What was he doing?

We were downstairs when Grandma came out of the kitchen and told Burke, "I just put some cookies in the oven." I was very interested in "cookies."

I heard pounding steps on the front porch. "I'm late!" Grant called as he burst in.

Grandma held up a hand. "Take off those muddy boots, please."

"Sorry, Grandma." Grant reversed course and sat and yanked off his boots. I went over to sniff at them, delighted at what he had tracked in.

"I just put in some cookies. Why are you in such a hurry?"

There was that word again!

"I, uh, told the Millards I would help pick strawberries this afternoon and they're going to meet me at the end of the driveway in like five minutes." Grant shot past me and up the stairs.

Grandma stared after him and then turned to Burke. "Do the Millards have a daughter?"

"I don't know. Why?"

"I've just never known Grant to be so excited about picking strawberries."

"Burke!" Grant's yell seemed to shake the house. "What did you do to my shoes?" He came thundering back down the steps. "There's like rocks glued into them or something!"

Burke was laughing.

"Burke, what did you do?" Grandma asked.

People are like that. Cookies had been mentioned, but now they had stopped talking about them completely.

Grant stalked over to Burke and shook a shoe. "I need these shoes!"

I lifted my head because I heard a car coming up the road. After a moment, Grant heard it, too. "They're coming! I gotta go!"

Grandma was shaking her head, but she was also smiling. "You should wear your work boots anyway, Grant."

"My *work boots*?" He stared at her in disbelief.

"It's been raining. The strawberry fields will be muddy."

"*Really* muddy," Burke chimed in. "Boots are by far the best choice. You'd just get your basketball shoes all mucked up, out there helping the Millards with your love-thy-neighbor efforts."

Grant narrowed his eyes at his brother. We all looked out the front windows when we heard the honk of a vehicle. I could tell it was down where the driveway met the road.

"That's them." Grant thrust his shoes at Burke. "Fix it!" he hissed in tones I am not sure Grandma could hear. He went to his work boots, struggled them on, and then clomped down the ramp and down the driveway toward the road.

"Can whatever you did be undone?" Grandma asked.

"What do you mean, Grandma?" Burke asked innocently.

"No cookies until you've fixed the shoes."

Burke laughed and had me Get It on Grant's shoes, though I would rather have done Get It on the cookies, whose sweet odors were tantalizing me with every sniff.

Later Burke ate several cookies and gave me a few crumbs and then we were down the ramp and out into the yard. He had me do Pull a little, drawing him down the driveway. I saw a man in the road, kneeling by a truck. Burke saw him, too, and put his hands to either side of his mouth. "Flat tire, Mr. Kenner?" he called.

The man looked up and nodded, wiping his mouth with his sleeve. I saw that there were some metal tools lying in the road. One of them was like a thin metal rod, dangling loosely from the man's hand.

"Anything I can do to help?" Burke yelled.

The man stared at Burke and I felt my boy stiffen, his hand going tight on my back. The man finally shook his head.

"He doesn't think I can do anything, Cooper," Burke muttered. "Because I'm the crippled boy."

I barked: those same gigantic cars were headed down the road toward us, and it was my job to call attention to the fact. I watched as the man with the tools put his hands on his hips and spat. He stepped right out into the path of the cars! Burke inhaled, and I felt the tension in his hand as it gripped my fur.

With a clatter, the line of cars stopped. One of them made a loud honking noise.

The man with the tools seemed enraged. The cars flashed lights and made the same sound. The man took a step forward. "What you gonna do, run me down?" he demanded in a raised voice. I could sense his fury.

"What is he doing?" Burke breathed.

The car in front started to jink back and forth a little. The angry man raised his metal rod high over his head and swung it.

The hard smack of it made me jump. A shiver of motion traveled down the length of the cars as he hit the front one again, and then again.

Suddenly the line of cars made a hard turn, off the road, up the shoulder, and then up our driveway, straight toward where we were sitting. They were going to hit Burke! I had to protect him. I ran forward, teeth bared, barking.

"Cooper!" Burke yelled.

Burke's shout rang in my ears and I knew he wanted me to return to him, but the line of cars was still approaching and I was determined they would not harm him. When they abruptly halted, I did too, my fur up, lips back, my bark as threatening as I could make it.

"Cooper!" Burke yelled again.

The forward car jerked to one side, the side that matched up with Pull Right, trying to get past me there. I darted in that direction too, snapping at the tires, blocking progress. *You will not hurt Burke!* The lead car went the other way and I shifted Pull Left, lunging again. The machines were huge and I was afraid of them, but my fear just made me more determined to protect my boy. They were halted, making an ominous humming sound. The front wheels on the first one swiveled in the dirt, one way, then the other way. I attacked, biting the hard rubber, growling. When I backed away, dirt flew from the lead machine's wheels and it cut hard Pull Right and trundled past me into the yard. The other cars didn't move and I barked at them to let them know not to try anything, then turned my head at the sound of a crash. The front car was smashing right into the woodpile! The entire stack toppled, wood spilling everywhere, and then the other cars decided to follow, moving in tight formation to link up with the lead car, banging into each other and stalling. The front car was rocking back and forth, emitting a loud, distressed beeping.

"Burke! Get back!" Chase Dad shouted. I looked and saw him striding down from the house, his face scowling, his arms clutching a long, wood-wrapped metal pipe. Grandma stepped out onto the front porch, her hand to her mouth.

Chase Dad was furious, I could feel it boiling off him as he strode past Burke without speaking to me. He was doing his angry walk. Intimidated, I stopped barking. He approached the car that was stuck in the woodpile, pressing the pipe to his shoulder and pointing it high above the front wheel. *Bang!* I flinched, and an acrid tang cut the air, obliterating other scents. Another bang, then another, and then the air filled with a different smoke, oily and thick, pouring out of the front car.

All the cars ceased making noise.

Burke glanced down at me. "It's okay, Cooper." I went to him and nosed his hand.

The tension left Chase Dad. He pointed the metal pipe at the ground, turning to peer at Burke. "You okay?"

"Yeah. I can't believe you shot the drone, Dad! That was so cool."

"Well." Chase Dad sighed. "We'll see how cool it is."

"Cooper protected me, Dad. He wasn't going to let them come any farther."

Chase Dad knelt and ran a hand down my neck. "Good dog, Cooper." I licked Chase Dad's face.

Grandma was approaching, shaking her head. "Was that really necessary, Chase?"

"You saw what was happening," Chase Dad replied defensively. "The things were on a rampage."

I glanced toward the road. The man who had hit the car was marching up the driveway with a big smile on his face. He carried his own pipe. "Chase!"

"Hey there, Ed."

The man walked up to the machines and hit one with a clang, turning to give us a fierce grin. "This'll show the bastards! Let's make a stand right here!"

"Well, I wasn't trying to show them anything. My son was in danger," Chase Dad replied mildly.

"Their navigation systems may have malfunctioned when you smashed them with a tire iron, Mr. Kenner," Burke observed.

Grandma stared at the man. "You did that, Ed?"

He shrugged. "Maybe a little."

Chase Dad and Burke laughed, so I wagged.

"You men are behaving like children," she chided. "Trident Mechanical Harvesting is a multinational corporation. If they decide to come after us, what are we going to do?"

The man hung his head. "I was just fixin' my flat," he mumbled.

Chase Dad laughed again. I sat and scratched behind my ear. The sharp scent had mostly left the air, but Chase Dad's pipe still reeked with it.

Grandma was shaking her head. "I don't know why you think this is funny. Look what happened." Grandma's hands smelled a little like meat. I examined them carefully.

"Uh, Dad?" Burke said. "Look."

A car was coming quickly down the road, a cloud of dust trailing behind it.

"Here we go," the man murmured. He looked at Chase Dad. "You need me to make a call? I can get five guys out here, back us up."

Chase Dad frowned. "No, I think this has gone far enough. Your tire fixed?"

"Yeah."

"I got this, then. You go on."

The man turned down the driveway. I wagged, but he didn't even glance my way.

Chase Dad, watching the approaching car, bit his lip. "Mom, why don't you go on inside?"

Grandma put her meaty hands on her hips. "What are you planning to do, Chase?"

SEVEN

I sensed Chase Dad's unease and so did my boy; I could tell by the way he stiffened in his chair, his hands tightening on the wheels.

"Chase?" Grandma said. "I asked you what you're planning to do to the men in that vehicle."

Chase Dad cleared his throat. "There might be words exchanged, Mom."

"Please don't do anything foolish. This has gone far enough already."

"It'll be okay. I'd feel better if you took Burke inside, though."

Grandma frowned. "Well . . ."

Burke vigorously shook his head. "No! I should stay with you, Dad."

I felt a tension swirl between them. I had figured out that

people mostly communicate by talking, but other times they don't talk and communicate more with their bodies, like dogs.

"All right," Chase Dad finally agreed. "You can stay, Burke. But Mom . . ."

"Don't even start with me. If my grandson is here, I'm here. You've turned this into a family affair, so we'll face whoever is in that car as a family."

The car turned up our driveway. When it stopped, men exited out of all the doors. They were wearing hats on their heads. "What the hell?" one of them shouted. He had a small amount of hair around his mouth. They walked in a manner similar to the way the cars moved: in a line, one behind the other, headed toward the woodpile.

I sat, watching them carefully. I did not like how mad the Hairy Mouth man seemed—his angry walk was more pronounced than anything I'd seen from Chase Dad. I instinctively knew these men were not friends and that I was not to wag unless maybe they started tossing treats. "Good afternoon," Chase Dad greeted dryly.

The men were picking over the car in the woodpile. Hairy Mouth turned to Chase Dad. "You *shot* it?"

"I thought it was going to run over my son and his dog."

"This drone is worth more than a million dollars, you moron!"

Chase Dad gestured with his pipe. "You come on a man's property without being asked, he's got a loaded shotgun, you insult him to his face, and *I'm* the moron?"

All of the men stopped looking at the car and were staring at Chase Dad's metal pipe, instead.

"Chase," Grandma urged in the barest whisper.

I could feel the heat rising off Hairy Mouth's face. He turned to the men behind him. "Jason, why don't you get them headed back."

A man climbed up on top of one of the cars and began stabbing at it with his finger. Every time he jabbed, the car beeped.

Chase Dad shook his head. "You and your robots are destroying a whole way of life, here, and you don't even know it. Men and women who had real jobs, who could afford their own homes, have nothing."

Hairy Mouth scowled. "What are you hanging on to, here? Things change. Adapt."

"Adapt," Chase Dad repeated softly. He looked away, his mouth a bitter line.

With a lurch, the line of cars backed up and then swiveled and went down to the road and departed in tight formation. Only the one in the woodpile remained.

"I've called a wrecker drone," another man told Hairy Mouth.

Hairy Mouth pointed a finger at Chase Dad. "This is far from over, you know."

I snapped my head up at the man's rage.

"You have more you need to say?" Chase Dad's voice was quiet, but I heard anger sizzling on his every word.

"Your land is in our way. And now you've given us a way to take it from you," Hairy Mouth said.

I heard a faint twisting sound as Chase Dad tightened his grip on his pipe. I began panting with anxiety, not at all able to understand any of this.

Hairy Mouth was sneering. "Why don't you put your shotgun down, we'll see what you've got, old man."

"All right." Chase Dad bent over and lay his pipe in the grass.

Grandma made a small distressed noise and I couldn't help myself—at that tiny sound I growled from deep in my throat, ready to launch myself at Hairy Mouth, at all the men, who were frozen, staring.

Hairy mouth backed up, his palms out. "You're siccing your *dog* on me?"

"Burke," Chase Dad said.

Burke slapped the arm of his chair. "Cooper! Come!"

I immediately went to his side and sat, but my eyes never left the strangers.

"We're here getting our property and you're putting a vicious dog on us," Hairy Mouth said.

"I did no such thing," Chase Dad seethed.

"Soon as we leave I'm calling Animal Control," Hairy Mouth declared.

"Cooper didn't do *anything*," Burke cried.

The man laughed, but it was an ugly sound and I did not wag. "Not how I see it."

A big truck was coming down the road. It turned slowly up our driveway. Chase Dad wiped his face with his sleeve. "I've had enough of this. You're on my property and you're no longer welcome. Take your damn harvester and go."

With a derisive snort, Hairy Mouth turned away and walked over to his friends.

I started in surprise: a dog had broken from the tree line and was romping down the hill toward us, wagging. I instantly turned away from the people and scampered joyously to meet it. A dog!

When I was close enough for her scent to wash over me I realized it wasn't just a dog, it was Lacey! I stopped and exultantly lifted my leg on a small tree.

Lacey barreled into me and I was so happy I was crying. We frolicked and tumbled and jumped on each other.

Burke's shout "Cooper!" cut through my elation. I turned and dashed back to be with him and Lacey was right there, pressed up against me as if doing Steady as we ran.

Burke laughed when we nearly crashed into his chair. "Who are you?" He reached out and snagged Lacey's collar. She sat obediently and I took advantage of the moment to grab the back of her neck in my mouth.

"Get down, Cooper!"

I did not see how Get Down applied to this situation.

"Who is this dog?" Chase Dad asked.

Burke was still pulling on Lacey's collar. "Dogs! Cut it out! I'm trying to read her tag. Okay, Lacey. Lacey? Is that your name? Good dog, Lacey."

Burke released her collar and Lacey flopped on her back and I dove on her, aware as I did so that the remaining vehicles at the woodpile were leaving down the driveway.

Chase Dad grunted. "Looks like the show's over, Burke. I have to get back to work. When your brother shows up, send him out to the orchard for me."

"Dad . . . what happens if they call Animal Control on Cooper?"

I glanced up at my name and Lacey froze also.

"I don't know, son."

"Will you get in trouble for shooting the drone? Can they really take our land?"

"It is what it is, Burke. They want to make trouble, they'll make it."

Chase Dad picked up his acrid pipe and trudged away. Burke sighed unhappily, and even though I was chewing on Lacey I took a moment to go to him to let him know his dog was here.

Grandma watched me play with Lacey. "Lacey," she mused. "Who does she belong to?"

"Her tag says the Zhangs," Burke replied. "You know, the Chinese family?"

Grandma looked surprised. "*Really*. Wonder what she's doing here; they live all the way across the valley. I guess I'll call them to come get her."

I was proud to show Lacey I knew Pull as I helped Burke back up the driveway, but she seemed unimpressed. She sniffed appreciatively at Grandma's meat-scented hands, though, impressed with *them*. Before long we had tumbled off the porch and were wrestling in the grass. Burke sat and watched us, smiling.

A car stopped at the bottom of the driveway and Grant got out. He stood and gaped in bafflement at the fallen woodpile, then walked up to where Lacey and I were playing. Lacey, I decided, would probably be Grant's dog, but the two of us would sleep together on Burke's bed.

"Looks like I missed some excitement," Grant observed. "What happened?"

"Dad said you're supposed to go to the orchard."

Grant frowned. "So I can't even get something to eat first?"

"I didn't say that, Grant; he just said to give you the message."

Grant blew out a puff of air. "So what happened?"

"A drone came up the driveway and Dad shot it with a shotgun."

"*What?*" Grant's mouth dropped open. "Seriously?"

"No lie. And they say they're going to call Animal Control on Cooper and sue us and take our land."

"Huh. This dog theirs? The robo-farmers?"

"No, that's Lacey, she just wandered up in the middle of it all. You heard me about Cooper?"

"Yeah."

"And our farm?"

"Yeah. Guess we'll see what happens."

"Jesus, you're as bad as Dad." Burke was quiet for a moment and I looked up at him, giving Lacey a chance to pounce on me. "How was basketball?"

Grant made a disgusted noise and sat down on a chair, wrestling off his boots. Lacey broke off play to go sniff them, so I followed suit, even though I had smelled them already. "I had to borrow someone else's shoes and they were too big. I played like a clown. What's in *my* shoes, broken glass?"

"Just drops of airplane glue. I already scrubbed them out of there."

"When I said I needed to borrow shoes, everyone in the car went quiet. You know why? Because they think we're so poor, we can't afford shoes."

"Well, we *are* poor."

"God. It was humiliating. I hated every second. I hate my *life*."

"You going to go help Dad?"

Grant looked at Burke for a long moment. Lacey and I stopped playing, sensing something. "No, I am going to go get something to eat, first."

Burke stayed out on the porch while Lacey and I rolled in the yard. She was heavier now, but I was even bigger, still able to flip her on her back. She lay panting, her tongue lolling, while I chewed gently on her neck and her feet. My affection for her poured through me and out from my mouth, my jaws shivering as I nibbled on her. I was glad Lacey had found me because we belonged together as surely as I belonged with Burke.

Eventually, exhausted, I lay sprawled on Lacey, barely conscious. I was so tired I didn't register a new car in our driveway, though Lacey and I both leaped to our feet when we heard a girl's voice call, "Lacey!"

A girl and a man stood up out of the car and Lacey ran straight to them, so I did, too. I had seen this girl before: she seemed to be about Burke's age and had black hair and dark eyes.

"Lacey, what are you doing all the way over here?" she sang in a high, affectionate voice. Lacey jumped to lick her face, so I shoved my head under the girl's hand to get petted. Behind us Grandma appeared at the screen door. The man said something to the little girl and she nodded and ran up to the porch. Burke swiveled his chair as she moved past him to the door.

"Thank you for calling us and saving Lacey," she said to Grandma, but the girl was staring at Burke, and he was staring at her. Grandma opened the door and came out.

"Of course, honey. What's your name?"

"Wenling Zhang, ma'am."

"You can call me Grandma Rachel. And this is Burke."

Burke raised a hand.

"Grant!" I heard Chase Dad yell from across the field. He was marching toward the house in a way that fell a little short of his angry walk—more of a not completely happy walk.

"What grade are you in?" Burke asked suddenly.

"Uh, I'll be in eighth," the girl said.

"Me too!"

"Oh. Do you go to Lincoln Middle School? I don't think I've seen you before."

"No. I'm homeschooled. You might have seen my brother, Grant, though. He was at Lincoln, but now he's going to be a freshman."

"Oh. No, I don't know him. But seventh grade is like being a new inmate in prison, so I tried to avoid the older kids."

Burke laughed, nodding.

Chase Dad strode up the ramp and onto the porch. He seemed a little confused to see the girl. "Where's your brother?" he asked Burke.

"I gave him some pie," Grandma replied.

"I need Grant's help. He can have pie after dinner." Chase Dad looked out and saw the man standing by the truck. "What is *he* doing here?"

Chase Dad headed back down the ramp. *Now* he was doing his angry walk.

"Chase," Grandma cautioned.

"Hey!" Chase Dad yelled.

EIGHT

I felt everyone's tension rise, sharp as a slap, as Chase Dad proceeded down the driveway, the girl running after him. Lacey was on the girl's heels and I stuck close to Burke's chair as he followed. I wondered if they would need me to growl again.

Burke was slower, so by the time we reached the man by the truck, Chase Dad was pointing his finger at him. "You're too late, your people already towed the damn thing off. They left things in a mess, though. Your drone could have run over my boy and his dog, and it crashed into my woodpile, and all anyone was concerned about was the machine."

The man stood stiffly and stared at Chase Dad while he was being lectured. "He only speaks Chinese," the girl said. She turned, speaking at length to her father, who then looked at Chase Dad and said something.

"He says he is very sorry. He did not know any of this," the girl advised.

Chase Dad frowned. "Didn't know? What do you mean?"

"He means nobody told him about a drone being on your property. Or hitting your woodpile."

Chase Dad looked at her. "He's not here because of the drones?"

"No. We came to get my dog who ran away. This is Lacey." Lacey looked up at her name. "My name is Wenling, and my father is Zhuyong Zhang, but everyone at work calls him ZZ."

I saw the man with black hair nod at this. He held his hand out and, after a moment, Chase Dad shook it awkwardly. He didn't seem as angry anymore. "I misunderstood the situation," he told the girl.

"You want to see my model city?" Burke asked her.

Chase Dad looked back and forth between the girl and Burke and scratched his head. The girl spoke to the black-haired man, "Bàba, wǒ kěyǐ hé zhège nánhái yīqǐ qù kàn tāde wánjù chéng ma?" The man nodded and spoke back. "He says okay, for five minutes," the girl told us.

"Fine, then," Chase Dad muttered. "Nice to meet you, uh, ZZ." He turned and led the way back to the house. Lacey and I ran in circles around Burke and the girl as we followed.

"Do you need me to push you?" she asked.

"No, I can do it."

"Your dog is really big!"

"He's part malamute, part stegosaurus."

The girl smiled. "Can I ask why you need a wheelchair?"

"I'm a paraplegic. I was born with a rare condition."

"Oh."

"There's an operation I can have, but I have to wait until I stop growing, and then there's no guarantee it will work. Are you from China?"

"My mom is American. She and Dad met in China and fell in love, but I was born here. We lived in China until I was five, and now we're here permanently."

I was listening to hear any words that I knew, but now decided not to bother. It's easier to be a dog if one accepts there are many things that are incomprehensible and just concentrate on being happy. Then Lacey discovered a stick and I focused on what was really important, which was getting the stick from her so that she would chase me.

We all were soon in Burke's room. I was starting to conclude, though, that the girl with the black hair was Lacey's person, which meant my Lacey might be leaving me again, though if the girl wanted to sleep in Burke's bedroom with us that was fine with me.

While the two of them talked, Lacey and I pulled on a rope toy. Then we ran out to see Grandma, who had cookies for Burke and his new friend but none for the dogs, even though Lacey followed my example and did Sit. How someone could stand with cookies in hand and not give them to dogs who were being so astoundingly good, I would never understand.

In the living room I pounced on a squeaky toy, chewing it into loud squealing. Lacey was astonished. I tossed the thing up in the air, deliberately allowing Lacey to catch it because she had clearly never encountered one before. I delighted at the frantic squeaks as Lacey pranced.

Chase Dad stepped to the front windows. "What's he doing? Aww, damn." He set down his cup. When he walked out the door, the girl and Burke and Lacey followed, so, with a final look to give Grandma one last chance with the cookies, I did the same.

Lacey still carried the squeaky toy. The man by the truck was at the woodpile, stacking logs. Chase Dad held out a hand. "You don't . . . ZZ. Hey, I didn't mean you should do that."

The man spoke. "Wǒ kuài wánchéngle."

"He says he is almost finished," the girl reported.

Chase Dad started gathering up logs, too. Logs are sticks that are too thick to have fun with, though Lacey apparently didn't know this because she spat out the squeaky toy, picked up a log, and tried to run with it, her whole head tilted to one side as it dragged through the dirt.

I was saddened when, a short time later, Lacey, the girl, and the black-haired man climbed into their car. Why couldn't they stay? Lacey barked at me out the window as they left. Burke stroked my head, but I felt the same way I had felt when Lacey was taken from me the first time: sad and almost hungry, somehow, with an empty feeling inside.

I decided to go see the old goat, who wasn't a dog but was otherwise good company. I slid under the rails of her fence and saw her sleeping by her wooden house.

But Judy wasn't sleeping. She didn't stir as I approached, and I saw some flies around her face. I sniffed cautiously. The goat was here but what made her a goat was gone, not just her smell, but her vibrancy. I had never encountered death before, but I somehow understood what it was. I stood and wondered what Burke would want me to do.

I looked back to the house. Grandma had some plants she liked to stroke and pet as if they were dogs, and she was on her knees doing this now. No one else was in sight. I yipped, putting a notice of loss and alarm in my voice. Grandma stood, holding a hand to shield her eyes. I yipped again.

She came to me and spotted the old goat, and I felt the sadness rising in her. I nosed her, letting her know she had a dog's love. She wiped away her tears and smiled down at me. "You know

I adored that silly old girl, don't you, Cooper? You're a good dog. Thank you for telling me."

When Chase Dad returned from the fields, he buried the goat in the yard near her house. Grant pushed dirt and Grandma's face was wet with tears. Burke sat with his hand on my neck, but we all turned when a truck crunched up the driveway.

"Animal Control," Grant murmured.

A jolt of alarm coursed through Burke, his hand spasming on my neck. "*Dad,*" he gasped.

"Burke," Chase Dad said. "Have Cooper take you down there in your chair. Don't help—have him do all the work. Mom, I'll join you and Grant in the house in a minute."

"Cooper, Pull!"

I happily surged forward, glad to have something important to do. He had me guide him down to where a woman was standing by the newly arrived truck. Her arms were folded. Her hair was very short, and her clothes were a dark color. "This the vicious animal?" the woman asked.

I could smell chicken treats in her pockets!

"That's Cooper."

I wagged because of my name and the treats.

"Afternoon, officer," Chase Dad greeted. "Help you with something?"

She stared at him. "Chase?"

I glanced at Chase Dad, because he seemed oddly stiff. "Ahh . . . ," he replied.

"Rosie. Hernandez? We met . . . you were playing the guitar?"

"Oh, sure. Rosie. Hi." Chase Dad reached out his hand and they moved their arms up and down.

"I'm Burke," Burke advised. I noticed he was staring at the woman very intently and wondered if he, too, smelled the treats.

There was a long silent moment, and then the woman blinked.

"Well. Okay, we got a complaint you threatened someone with a dog. Is this the dog?"

I wagged. With her saying "dog," could the treats be far behind?

"Some men came on my property after a TMH drone knocked down my woodpile. They were acting aggressive and Cooper growled. What I *threatened* them with was a shotgun, if you want to know the truth."

Another silence. With a groan, I flopped down on the ground, my legs up in a clear invitation to give me a tummy rub.

The woman laughed. "All right. I think I've got the picture. TMH thinks they own the town, but I work for the sheriff. I'll file this as BS, and that should be the end of it."

The relief in Burke's sigh led me to sit back up.

"Thanks very much," Chase Dad said.

"Chase . . . could I talk to you for a moment?" She glanced down at Burke and me and I wagged hopefully.

"Sure. Burke, why don't you head on up to the house."

I did Pull. When we rolled into the house, Grant and Grandma were standing at the front windows. "What's going on?" Grant asked.

"That's like an old girlfriend or something," Burke replied.

Everyone tightened their posture, all staring out the window. I assumed that Burke had told them about the chicken treats and they were watching to see if she would toss a few of them on the ground for me to find later.

When Chase Dad walked through the door, he took in everyone standing there. "Whatever conversation you think we're going to have, we're not," Chase Dad said, his palm up to show us he didn't have any chicken.

"Who was that, Chase?" Grandma asked.

Without a word, Chase Dad passed through the living room and went up the stairs. "She was hot," Burke said.

"I'm standing right here, boys," Grandma replied.

They left the living room and no one gave me a treat of any kind.

Judy's smell lingered all summer, as Grant and Chase Dad went off to play with plants while Burke mostly sat in his room and applied his smelly drips to toys I wasn't allowed to touch.

Sometimes Grandma would set food on an outdoor table and Chase Dad and Grant would emerge from the fields to eat. We were sitting there enjoying a wonderful game of Toss the Treat to the Best Dog (I am very good at snatching pieces of food out of the air) when several different cars hummed down the road and turned up our driveway. These were smaller than the machines that collided with the woodpile, and people emerged from each one.

Chase Dad stood. "What in the world?"

There were men and women but no dogs or children, so I stayed focused on Grant, who was tearing off little pieces of meat and pitching them at me. Chase Dad went down to talk to the people, then he turned and waved. "Burke! Come here a minute."

"Come, Cooper," Burke said as he wheeled off toward the line of cars.

People are always doing this: I was being a good dog, as evidenced by the treats from Grant, but now I was being asked to do something else where there seemed to be no rewards of any kind. I hesitated, unsure, while Grant tossed me another morsel.

"Cooper! Come!"

That tone of voice meant I was potentially being a bad dog. With a last mournful look at Grant, I ran down to catch up with Burke, who was sitting in the back of one of the cars while someone loaded his chair in the trunk. Car ride! I leaped in next to my boy, wagging. Chase Dad sat up front.

"Where are we going?" Burke asked.

"Surprise," said the man driving.

"Quite a parade you've got here, Dwight," Chase Dad said.

"Yep," the man driving replied.

The procession headed down the road. My window was open a crack, so I put my nose up there and inhaled deeply, smelling animals—horses and cows, mostly, and then something pungent and wonderful. I wagged frantically.

Burke laughed. "You like the goat ranch, Cooper?"

Yes, I would love to play with the goat ranch!

"Oh. We're going to the middle school," Burke observed after a little while. He stirred uneasily.

"Yep," the man driving replied

The cars all stopped and everyone got out. Car ride over! I sniffed, marking territory carefully, while Chase Dad helped Burke into his chair.

"Well? Try it out," urged the man who had been driving.

Everyone gathered as Burke wheeled himself up a ramp like the one off our front porch, and I padded after him. "We got tired of waiting for the district to move the ramp, so we just did it ourselves," one person told him.

"Now Burke can go in the side door instead of having to wheel in the delivery door and through the kitchen," another one added.

We made it to the top of the ramp and Burke turned his chair and regarded the people, who were all smiling up at him. They held out their hands and brought them together so that it sounded like a hard rain. I watched my boy curiously—his tension showed in the tight way he gripped the wheels of his chair.

"What do you think, Burke?" Chase Dad asked. He was smiling, too.

"It's very nice," Burke replied stiffly. I wagged because I didn't know what we were doing.

"This is a wonderful thing. We're grateful to all of you," Chase Dad said.

We rolled back down the ramp and into the car again. Car ride, yes! Then we returned to the farm. What a great day.

We stood in the yard and watched the people leave in their vehicles. "They moved the ramp so that Burke can get in the side door now. The way they had it before, he'd have to go through the kitchen. Really nice of them," Chase Dad told Grant.

"Side door," Grant repeated.

"Yes, by the library," Chase Dad said.

"Nobody goes in that door."

"Well, Grant, it is where the ramp is."

"All the kids sit on the steps in front of the school before class," Grant explained. "Nobody ever uses the side door except the teachers, maybe."

"I don't see how this is helpful, Grant," Chase Dad said.

"It doesn't matter," Burke interjected tightly. "I'm not going to school anyway. I'm going to stay and be homeschooled by Grandma."

Chase Dad folded his arms. "I think maybe my mother could use a break."

"I'm not going." Burke wheeled himself up the ramp into the house and I followed him to his room. He climbed into his bed but not to sleep; he just stared at the ceiling, so I jumped up and put my head on his chest. With every exhalation, I felt his troubled sadness, and wondered if I should get the squeaky toy to turn things around.

After a time, Grant walked in the room. "I mean, not everybody sits on the steps," he said.

"I don't care. I don't want to go to a school until after I've had my operation."

Grant sniffed, looking around. "Dad and Grandma went to town."

Burke didn't say anything.

"You sick or something?"

Burke shook his head. "Just don't feel like doing anything."

"Want me to teach you how to drive? We can take the old truck."

Burke sat up. "What?"

"Sure. I'll sit next to you and work the pedals, gas and brake and whatnot. You steer."

"You can't. Your permit says there has to be an adult."

"Suit yourself."

"No, wait. Seriously?"

"We'll go out on a county road where there's nobody."

"Dad will kill us."

"You planning to tell him?"

Another car ride! We sat together in the truck, which smelled of decaying food and old mud. After a time Burke slid over and drove with Grant sitting very close, almost on top of him. I stuck my head out the window. This was turning out to be one of the most wonderful days ever!

"This is great. When I take my driver's test, you can go with me and sit in my lap," Burke drawled.

"It's not my fault you can't work the pedals."

"So it's my fault?" Burke demanded. I felt his anger and did Sit, being extra good.

"Jesus! I was just trying to be nice!" Grant shouted back. "But you want to turn everything into a poor me about your chair! It's like if anything is ever normal for a second, you have to remind us all you can't walk."

"I'm done driving."

"Fine!"

I felt Grant seething with an unstable rage as he drove. I yawned nervously. We crested the top of a long, steep hill. The truck stopped. "Hey, I have an idea." Grant sprang out of the truck and grabbed Burke's chair.

"Grant? What are we doing?"

"Just get in your chair."

"This is stupid." After Burke grabbed my collar and slid into his chair I jumped out onto the pavement, shaking myself. "What's going on?" he asked.

"Do you know they call this Dead Man's Hill?" Grant asked. "It's like the steepest road in the county." His voice grated with an odd stress—he didn't sound like Grant at all.

"I never heard that." Burke stiffened as Grant began to push him. "What are you doing?"

"What's the fastest you've ever gone in the chair?"

"The *fastest*?"

We were headed downhill and Grant was trotting, then running. I galloped along, not sure what we were doing but enjoying it.

"Grant!" Burke shouted, his voice sharp with fear.

Grant gave a thrust with his arms and the chair took off ahead of me. I ran to keep up. The chair began drifting to the Pull Right side. When it went off the pavement and into the gravel it made a crunching sound and then the chair tipped over and went flying. Burke tumbled headfirst down the embankment, rolling and crashing down through the bushes. I felt a flash of terror at the way his legs flopped and splayed through the air. I scrambled after him, whimpering.

When he came to a stop he was facedown, lying very still.

"Burke!" Grant shouted. "Burke!"

I was racing to Burke's immobile body, but Grant's agonized

cry pulled me up short: I had never heard such panic in a person's voice before. Burke and Grant *both* needed me. What should I do?

Grant ran stumbling down the hill, his mouth open, his face in such distress it looked almost injured. I did not understand any of this, but Grant's terror was absolute, and my own alarm rippled down my spine.

"Burke! Burke!"

NINE

I peered down at Burke at the bottom of the slope. His face was in the dirt, his arms and legs were splayed. I half fell down the hill, leaping through the rocks and grass. I reached Burke and shoved my nose at his face. He was warm and alive; he was not like Judy the old goat.

Grant fell to his knees, grabbed Burke, and flipped him over.

Burke's eyes were shut, his face slack. He had pulled in a breath and was holding it.

"Burke! God, oh God!"

Burke's eyes popped open and he grinned. "Gotcha."

"Oh. You . . ." Grant looked away, clenching his fists. His fear was gone—now he was angry.

"Okay, Cooper. Assist!" Burke commanded. I dutifully went to his side, wagging, glad things were back to normal. He grabbed my harness with one hand and began pushing against the dirt with the other, heading back up the hill.

Grant put a hand on Burke's arm. "Let me help."

"Let go of me. You want to help, like how you *helped* me down the hill? What's next, you want to 'help' me in the head with a rock? You're feeling so helpful, you can get my chair out of the ravine."

The ascent to the side of the road was far more difficult than any set of stairs. Burke lay panting at the top while Grant struggled to carry the chair up the steep slope. Grant did not call for me to Assist—it occurred to me that Grant never gave me a command except Sit. He finally made it to the top and snapped the chair open.

"Cooper, Steady."

I stood rigidly while Burke hoisted himself up on me and into his chair. Grant ran his hand down the side of it. "Kind of got scratched up, here."

"Maybe something you should have thought about before you shoved me over a cliff. You'd be like, 'Hey, Dad, sorry I bent up Burke's chair, and also he's dead.'"

"Whatever."

"You want to take a turn?" Burke rocked his chair back and forth a little.

Grant blew out a puff of air. "Pass."

"What was your plan for how you were going to get my corpse out of the ravine?"

Grant shook his head, his lips twisted in a disgusted expression. "I'm not like you, Burke. I don't *plan* everything. Life's about surprises."

"Oh, like, 'Surprise! I murdered my little brother.'"

"Let's just go."

"No, seriously. I want to know. You could have killed me, Grant. Is that what you wanted to do?"

"I'm not having this conversation."

"I know you hate me!" Burke shouted. I shrank away from his loud voice. "And I know you blame me for everything. And you're right, okay?"

Grant was staring at Burke.

"I know it was my fault!" Burke choked, his voice raw. "But I couldn't help it! I couldn't help any of it!" He buried his face in his hands. For a long moment he cried and cried, while Grant sat stiffly and stared at him. I had never felt such pain and grief coming from my boy and I did not know what to do. I put my paw on his leg and cried out my own distress, begging this horrible sadness to go away. I laid my head in his lap and felt tears land on my fur.

"Hey." Grant touched a hand to Burke's shoulder. "I know. I know you couldn't help it. I know."

Neither of them spoke for some time, and then Burke and I slid into the truck.

Car ride! I did my best to show the proper enthusiasm, hoping it would cheer everyone up, but whatever horrible mood had seized the both of them sat in the truck with us like a third person. When we arrived back at the farm, I was so excited to be back home where things made sense that I ran to the pond and chased the ducks off the dock. They were idiot birds: they fluttered away but then came swimming back, as if I couldn't just jump in the water and catch them if I wanted.

When I slid inside the dog door, I circled my forlornly empty dinner bowl and then padded into the living room where Grandma and Burke were sitting without treats.

"It isn't that I am not willing to keep doing home school, though I will admit some of the math lessons are getting to be a struggle," Grandma was saying. "It's just that school is more than learning what is in books. Especially middle school—that's when you discover how to get along with other kids against the backdrop of growing into the adult you're going to be. Understand? I can't offer you the social aspects of school."

"They'll make fun of me, Grandma! I'll be the kid in the wheelchair."

"I believe that you'll handle that just fine. You're very resilient, Burke. Much like your father, in that way. But resiliency and stubbornness are close cousins, and stubborn just means unwilling to consider other points of view I want you to try it for a few weeks, for me. Please."

Burke sighed and looked away as Chase Dad and Grant tromped up the outside ramp and into the house. I went to them in greeting. They had nothing to eat in their pockets. "Chicken pot pie tonight," Grandma announced. I heard chicken and looked at her hopefully, though my name had not been spoken.

"Now that's good news," Chase Dad said. He stopped, then went to Burke's side. "What did you do to your chair, Burke?"

Grant drew in a breath.

"Oh. Uh, I was seeing how fast I could roll down the driveway and I kind of crashed."

Grandma's mouth opened. Chase Dad scowled. "You did what? Burke, do you know how expensive this chair is? You can't treat it like it's garbage."

"Sorry, Dad."

"Well, you're grounded."

Burke raised his hands and then let them fall in his lap. "Aren't I sort of already grounded?"

"Don't pull that on me. No connectivity. No streaming. You get bored, you can read a book; there's a whole shelf of them in the den."

Chase Dad and Burke were both angry. I sat anxiously, hoping that having a good dog would diffuse the situation.

"I'm trying to teach you boys not to take everything for granted. We're barely hanging on, here. Understand? We can't just throw money away for no good reason."

Grant inhaled. "I, uh, told him to do it. To see how fast he could go."

Chase Dad pursed his lips and shook his head. "I'm very disappointed in you boys. You're grounded, too, Grant."

Grant and Burke were both looking at the floor, though there was nothing there to play with or eat. Later, though, Grant passed me some warm pieces of chicken under the table.

I knew something was different the morning Burke had me do Steady so he could swing into the shower and sit and soak in the water pouring down, and then he put on new-smelling clothes. "School," everyone kept saying. Apparently we were doing School, whatever that was. Then we rode in the car. Grant drove and Burke sat up front and I sat in the back with Grandma. It was a warm morning and Grandma smelled like the bacon she had fed the boys for breakfast. I barked at a dog out the window. Then we drove past the goat ranch and I barked at it, too.

"Just tell them you're my brother. All the teachers loved me," Grant said.

"I tell them you're my brother, they'll send me straight to the principal's office."

I saw a squirrel!

"Cooper! Stop barking, you idiot," Burke laughed. I wondered if he was trying to tell me he also had seen the squirrel.

Grant stopped the car. I watched with interest as he walked around to Burke's door with Burke's chair, helping Burke to sit in it in a human version of Steady. We were parked in front of a large building with a huge set of stone stairs. I urgently wanted to jump

out and run up those stairs because there were children Burke's
age sitting on every step, but I was locked in the car with
Grandma and she didn't seem to want to go anywhere. I put my
feet up on the glass and stared as Grant began pushing Burke
away. I whined loudly, the other children forgotten. I needed to
be with Burke!

"It's okay, Cooper." Grandma stroked me with her bacon-
scented hand.

Grant slid back in *without Burke*. "You want to come up
front?"

"We'll switch when I drop you off. Cooper! Be still."

Grant turned and put a hand on my back. "Cooper! Settle
down."

I cringed. Everything I was doing seemed to be wrong and
my boy was gone and Grant and Grandma sounded mad. Where
was Burke?

She petted my head and I licked her hand, almost able to taste
bacon. "That was pretty hard for Burke, you know," she said after
a moment. "He really hates for people to see him in the wheelchair."

"I don't get it. He's always *been* in the wheelchair. He's gone
to birthday parties, football games, and it was never a problem.
Don't know why it is such a big deal now."

I stared out the back window in disbelief. Now we were driving away. Without Burke!

"I think it's just hard for your brother right now."

Grant shrugged. "Sure, but I mean, everyone knows he's going
to have an operation, and then he'll be able to walk."

Grandma sighed. "If the surgery is successful."

They were quiet for a while. The smell of my boy was fading
the farther away we drove. I yawned anxiously, not understanding.

We eventually stopped in front of another large building. Boys and girls Grant's age were streaming into it. Grant closed his eyes. "Grandma," he said quietly.

"What's wrong, honey?"

"I need to tell you something. I did something bad. Really bad."

"What is it, Grant?"

"The reason his chair is dented on one side is because of me. I was pushing him. I pushed him down a hill, I mean."

Grandma started and stared at him. "Why would you do that?"

I nosed her hand, concerned at the alarm in her voice.

"I don't know. I don't know! I just . . . Sometimes I hate him so much it's like I can't think of anything else. And I think I wanted him to *hurt*." Grant was talking in a rush. "As soon as I let go of the chair I was sorry." He turned in his seat, wiping his eyes. "Every day of my life is the same, you know? School, then chores, then homework, then do it again. Unless it's summer, and then Dad wakes me up at dawn."

Grandma was regarding Grant closely. "But how is any of that Burke's fault?"

"I can't explain it."

"You're holding something back, I can tell."

Grant turned and looked out the front window. I followed his gaze but did not see Burke and could not smell him. He was not here.

Grandma shook her head. "When you boys were little you frightened me, the way you two would clobber each other. Now you're old enough to do real damage, Grant."

"I know."

"You can't turn Burke into your whipping boy for your frustrations."

"Am I a bad person, Grandma?"

Grandma laughed dryly. "I think we old people sometimes

forget that childhood isn't all fun and games. You're coping with
a lot of things right now. But hurting other people because inside you're hurting yourself is no solution to anything. I don't
think you are a bad person at heart, Grant. But if you feel that
impulse again you can't act on it. It doesn't matter how righteous
you are if you let yourself do awful things."

Grant slid out and so did Grandma, but she kept me from
following her. I watched them through the window. "I love you,
Grandma," Grant said, hugging her. I wagged because of the hug.

Grant ran off. Grandma drove and I jumped over to the seat
next to her and spotted for squirrels and other prey. We visited
several nice people but no treats were given. After we went home
for a nap it was time for another car ride. Normally two car rides
in a single day would be a wonderful thing, but I was worried
about Burke. Was he ever coming home? We picked up Grant and
then I was sitting in the back with Grandma again. I wondered if
we were going to get Burke next, and we did! He was out in front
of the big building. There were still children on the stone steps,
though not as many. The way Grandma held me suggested I wasn't
supposed to leave the car, but I wrestled free of her and ran to
Burke, leaping into his lap and licking his face.

"Okay! Okay, Cooper!" he sputtered.

As Grant drove us away, Grandma leaned forward and touched
Burke's shoulder. "How was your first day?"

He twisted to look at her. "It was *horrible*."

Burke seemed upset. I stared at him intently, wanting to lick him or do Assist or anything to make his bad feelings go away.

"Oh dear," Grandma said. "Were they cruel?"

Burke shook his head. "No, it was worse. Everyone was so *nice*. They all wanted to sit with me at lunch, and everyone kept complimenting my wheelchair, like it's a Ferrari or something. I was invited to like ten kids' houses after school, and they made a big point of telling me that of course I am welcome when there's a party. *More than welcome*. What the heck does that even mean? 'More than welcome.' You're either welcome or you're not."

Grant laughed.

"I think they were just trying to be friendly, dear," Grandma said.

"And Grant was right. Everyone sits on the steps out front. The cool kids are at the top, but even the complete dorks are out there, like on the bottom steps. And then there's me, on the cement in front of the steps, like I'm my own category of dork. I'm not even human."

"We don't do that kind of stuff in high school. It's so middle school," Grant noted.

"Yeah because I'm *in middle school*," Burke retorted.

The next morning we took the same sort of car ride, Grandma sitting with me in the back. "You sure you have permission to take Cooper to school?" Grant asked Burke.

"I didn't ask. You don't ask, they can't say no."

Grant snorted. "The wisdom of an eighth grader."

"I worry about this, Burke," Grandma said. "Did you tell your father you're taking Cooper to school with you?"

There was a long silence. "I may have forgotten to mention it," Burke finally replied.

Grant laughed.

This time I did get out of the car at the big building, but I barely had time to lift my leg before Burke asked me to do Steady. I was at his side as Grant drove away. Then we wheeled over to the stairs. When we arrived at the bottom step, Burke told me Steady again, so I stood patiently as he slid out of the chair, clutching my harness. "Assist," he commanded.

The children fell completely silent. I carefully picked my way upward, Burke at my side, everyone scooting over a little.

"Nice doggy," a girl whispered.

"Hey Burke," a boy greeted. I smelled a lot of wonderful meats and cheeses on some of them, but focused on climbing. Soon we were at the top step.

"Think someone could get my wheelchair?" Burke asked. Several boys sprang up and ran down and grabbed Burke's chair and hauled it up. Then everyone was talking and girls were petting me. A boy scratched me at the base of my tail and I moaned in pleasure.

"What's his name?"

"Cooper."

"Good dog, Cooper!"

"Hi, Cooper!"

Burke buried his face in my fur. "Thank you, Cooper," he whispered. "You make me feel like I'm *normal*."

When a loud bell rang, everyone jumped up at once. I did Steady so Burke could climb into his chair. Children were milling everywhere in the hallway, many of them reaching out to touch me. "Nice dog!" I smelled other dogs on their hands.

"His name's Cooper."

"Good dog, Cooper!"

We found our way to a room full of tables and children. Burke had me do Sit and Stay next to his chair. A man about Grandma's age came over to talk to us and to admire what a good dog I was being. "So, does Principal Hawkins know about this?" the man asked as he petted my head.

"Uh, no, but she said whatever she could do to help . . ."

The man shrugged and smiled. "Fine by me. What kind of dog is he?"

"We think maybe Malamute and something else, great Dane, maybe."

"No wonder he's so big."

It was strange to be at a table for so long without any food making an appearance. I could smell some ham in a boy's pack, but when I'm on Stay I'm not allowed to investigate such things.

Burke was happy, though, I knew that, could tell by the way he was breathing, and smiling down at me, the way his hand stroked my ears. Whatever I was doing here, if it made him happy, I was willing to do it all day long.

Eventually I circled and lay down with a yawn, but I jumped up when that bell rang and all the children leaped to their feet. We made our way through the throngs in the hallway to another room. Was this going to be our day? If this was School, it seemed pointless.

In the new room there were no tables, just rows of chairs. Burke wheeled to the back of the room and told me to Sit and Stay. He looked up when a woman opened the door. She smelled like flowers. She was about Chase Dad's age and her long, light hair was curly. "Burke," the woman said.

"Yes, Mrs. Hawkins?"

She held up a finger and wriggled it toward her. "Come with me to my office, please."

I sensed a lot of tension from the children as I followed Burke out the door.

The woman's legs made a rubbing sound as she walked next to us. We passed through a big room with people sitting at desks and then entered a smaller room in the back. She closed the door. There were chairs but no tables and no children, and I could smell no food.

School was going from bad to worse.

The woman sat down. When she tapped her fingers on her knee I could smell an animal, not a dog, but not a goat either—it was the unseen animal I had detected at Ava's building. I hoped the mystery creature would make an appearance and I'd finally get to meet it.

"Why are you provoking an incident, Burke?"

I looked at him when she said his name. He was frowning. "I'm not."

"You brought a *dog* into my school."

The way she said "dog" sounded like the word "bad" was in front of it. I nosed Burke's hand.

"He's my service dog. He helps me with my chair."

"I was told you could propel yourself without help."

"Well yeah, *propel*, but . . ."

"This school has been outfitted to accommodate your chair. I even gave permission for the ramp to be moved so you wouldn't have to wheel through the kitchen in the morning. Your dog is disruptive—it's all anyone is talking about. And he's huge. I would hate to think what would happen if he bit one of the students."

"Oh, Cooper would never bite anyone."

I glanced up at my name. I could feel Burke getting angry.

"So you say. I can't take the risk."

Burke folded his arms. "There is no risk."

"That is not for you to determine."

"You don't have the right to keep my dog out."

She scowled. "I have every right, young man. Do not talk back to me."

There was a long silence. I yawned, feeling tense.

The woman's shoulders relaxed a little, her posture softening. "Look, I understand you have been homeschooled the past several years. And I promise, I will do everything in my power to see that you get caught up with the other students. But that requires that you follow the rules. This isn't what you're accustomed to; this is an institution."

"I don't need to be 'caught up.' I take the same tests as every other student. I always get an A. But I need my dog with me."

"The answer is no."

Burke took in a deep, trembling breath. "Cooper stays with me."

I wagged just a little at my name.

The woman stood up. "Then I will call your parents and tell them to come pick you up."

Burke shook his head, his lips twisting in an odd, cold smile.

"Well, not my parents. My dad," he corrected flatly. "My mom left because I was born crippled and she couldn't deal with it."

There was another long silence. The woman opened her mouth, then closed it. "You can wait in the front of the office."

She opened the door and Burke and I went through it. Now we were in the bigger room. I wagged at the people sitting at desks and they smiled at me. Burke wheeled over to a place by some windows where we could see children flood the hallway when a bell rang. He watched them silently. Several of them stuck their heads in the open door and said things like "Hi, Cooper!" and "Hi, Burke!" I wagged at all of them.

A girl came in and I knew her instantly. Lacey's person! "Hi, Burke. Remember me?"

"Wenling?"

Her name was Wenling.

"Yes!" She smiled, while I sniffed her frantically. Her skin and clothes were redolent with my Lacey. She sat in a chair. "Why are you here in the office?"

"I'm getting kicked out."

She clapped a hand to her mouth. "Of school? Seriously?"

"I guess there's a no dog rule, whether he eats my homework or not."

She ran her hand down my side and I licked it in gratitude. "That can't be cool, isn't there like a law or something? I'm pretty sure a service dog is allowed everywhere."

"Everywhere but middle school, I guess."

A large boy poked his head in the doorway. "Hey, Burke!"

"Uh, hi, uh . . ."

"Grant."

"Right. Grant Karr."

I looked around in bewilderment. Grant?

The boy tapped his hand on the doorframe. "So I was thinking you should maybe come down to the gym after school. First day of football practice?" The boy made a throwing motion and I looked quickly but didn't see anything land.

"Football?" Burke repeated.

"Yeah."

"What position would I play?"

The boy stood still. "I just meant, you know, hang with the team. Not . . ." The boy looked at me, then at Burke. "We were thinking maybe more like equipment manager or something?"

"Or cheerleader?" Wenling suggested.

Burke laughed. "Actually, I'm busy, but thanks, Grant."

I looked at Burke when he repeated Grant's name. The other boy knocked his knuckles on the door. "Okay then! Maybe we'll hang later." He turned and left. Burke sighed.

"I know," Wenling said. "When I first came here, everyone wanted to be friends with the Chinese girl. And you know what they serve me when I'm invited to their house for dinner? Still? Chinese food. Every. Single. Time."

Burke laughed. I wagged at the happy sound. "Do you even like Chinese food?"

"I like my *mom's* Chinese food." The girl stood up. "I have to get to class. Did you get in trouble for shooting the drone?"

"I guess not. Animal Control came out and was more interested in my dad than in Cooper."

"First the drone, then you bring a vicious animal to school. You're like a family of outlaws."

"My brother, Grant, is picking me up after school so we can rob the bank."

"Be sure to take Cooper! See you later, outlaw."

She left, and then Grandma walked in! I was very excited to see her. She told me I was a good dog, then sat in the chair Wenling had been occupying. "What happened, Burke?"

"Mrs. Hawkins pulled me out of class. She says I can't have Cooper because I am capable of independent propulsion. Also I'm stupid because I'm homeschooled."

Grandma's face tightened. "Your reading and math are both at college levels."

"I don't think she wants to hear about that."

The woman with the foreign animal smells opened her door and she and Grandma touched hands, then they went into the smaller room and shut the door. I wagged because I didn't know what else to do.

Burke moved his chair back and forth, and he picked up some papers off a small table and looked at them and set them down and picked them up and set them down, and he petted me. "Hey, Cooper. Good dog," he murmured

Sometimes people will tell you you're a good dog but forget to back it up with any treats. In the end, though, hearing "good dog" always makes me happy.

Grandma left the office and she and Burke didn't speak until we were in the car. I sat in the backseat. When the doors were closed, Grandma touched the wheel, then dropped her hands.

"Grandma?"

She turned to look at Burke. "Oh Burke. Principal Hawkins told me what you said, about Patty. About your mother."

Burke lowered his head and stared at his lap.

"Please look at me, honey."

Burke sighed and raised his eyes.

"Your mother didn't leave because of you. She just . . . It's complicated. She's a different sort of person than the rest of us. She missed the city. She talked about wanting to walk to shops and restaurants—this wasn't the life she wanted."

Burke made a soft, sad sound. "You weren't there, Grandma. You didn't see her when she said we could pick her or Dad. When

I started to talk, she knew I was going to pick her, and she, like, *dreaded* it."

"You mustn't tell yourself that, Burke."

He looked away and I nosed his hand to remind him we were happy just moments ago.

Grandma pursed her lips. "And then Patty moved overseas and got married, and her husband, from what I understand, is a real controlling bastard."

Burke drew back in surprise. I glanced out the car window. Squirrel?

Grandma laughed softly. "I know, my language, but that's how I feel. The last time I spoke to Patty she told me he wouldn't *let her* have any contact with you." She shook her head, staring out the window herself.

"Are you okay, Grandma?"

"Am I okay? *Me?* Oh Burke, you've got the warmest heart in the world."

Later we sat in the car and ate out of deliciously fragrant papers. Burke fed me cheese, which I could still taste even after we returned to the farm.

When Grant showed up I wondered if he knew how many people had been talking about him all day. He crawled on his knees, waving that stupid nylon bone in front of my nose until I just had to take it from him. I snuck around behind a chair and spat it out.

Chase Dad's boots smelled of dirt and insects. I carefully inspected them while he talked to Grandma and Grant and Burke in the kitchen. Then I realized, they were in the *kitchen*. I hustled in to see if any food was about to make an appearance.

"Well, that's it, then," Chase Dad was saying. "You have to go to school, Burke. Mrs. Hawkins has a point—the school's wheelchair accessible." Grandma was at the stove and I was smelling something meaty in the air, so I went over to do Sit and be a good dog next to her.

"But she's wrong, Dad. I looked it up. If I say I need a service animal, she's not allowed to say otherwise," Burke replied.

"For you to get kicked out in two days, that's got to be a new record," Grant laughed.

"Grant," Grandma chided.

"Show me what you found out," Chase Dad requested. There was a long silence as Chase Dad leaned over Burke's shoulder and stared at something on the table. I kept my focus on Grandma. I didn't know what she was making, but I smelled butter and I'll eat anything with butter on it.

"Okay, but Burke, it's one thing to read a law, it's another to get someone to obey it. I'm sure she's got some rules on her side," Chase Dad finally said. "I remember Mrs. Hawkins from when she coached basketball. She's tough as they come."

"You always say we should stand up for what's right, Dad. This is what's right. When Cooper's with me, I'm not the guy in the wheelchair, I'm the guy with the big dog. I can climb up the stairs and sit with my friends. It makes all the difference."

Chase Dad shook his head. "You're being dramatic, son."

My boy wordlessly turned away from the table and I followed him as he rolled into his bedroom. Later I was lying on Burke's bed while he sat in a chair. I lifted my head when the door eased open. Chase Dad was standing there, his expression serious. "Burke, I'm going to drive you to school tomorrow. I'll go in and talk to Mrs. Hawkins about Cooper myself. Okay? Maybe I can get her to listen to reason."

"Thanks, Dad."

Chase Dad petted my head and left. I sighed, remembering the cheese.

ELEVEN

We were back to doing School, it looked like, only this time Chase Dad drove, taking us in the truck. He did it wrong; dropping Grant off at his building before Burke at School. But at least Chase Dad knew the right place: I wagged excitedly when I saw all the children on the steps.

Chase Dad turned to us. "Wait here." He left us and walked to the building. As he mounted the stairs, the boys and girls scooted out of his way.

After a moment, Burke opened his door. "Come on, Cooper." I did Steady. We rolled over to the stairs and I did Assist until, about midway up, my boy sat next to Wenling.

"Cooper!" she greeted, holding out her Lacey-scented hands. I buried my nose in them, inhaling with forceful snorts. I wondered why Wenling would come to this place and not bring Lacey. Everyone would be so much happier if Lacey were here!

Several people called out Burke's name, and he was waving and responding, so I let Wenling pet me and I put my head in her lap. I knew I was getting my scent on her, and that when she got back home, Lacey would smell her and think of me.

"My dad sent himself to the principal's office," Burke told Wenling.

"Oh, for the drone?"

"I figure at least two hours' detention."

Wenling laughed softly.

"He's going to try to talk Mrs. Hawkface into letting me bring Cooper to class," Burke explained. "I'm going to write a theme paper on what happens when two immovable objects collide."

"Everyone says they have to allow it. Legally, I mean," Wenling noted.

"Everyone meaning the entire eighth grade? Well, we haven't talked to a lawyer, but I did some research, and yeah, they can only ban him if he maybe bit somebody."

Wenling stroked my head. "You would never hurt anybody, would you, Cooper?"

"Of course he wouldn't."

"Do you smell Lacey on me? Is that why you're sniffing me, Cooper?"

I looked up at her. Lacey? Was Lacey coming?

A stirring above me drew my attention. The children were sliding over and Chase Dad was descending the steps. He was doing his angry walk. He saw Burke and stopped. "Burke." He took a deep breath and let it out. "We're leaving. Come on."

Chase Dad stooped as if to pick Burke up and Burke held out both hands, his arms stiff. "No! Let Cooper, Dad."

"Suit yourself." Chase Dad angry-walked to the truck.

Burke turned to Wenling. "I think probably it didn't go all that well with Mrs. Hawkins."

"I'll visit you in prison."

Burke chuckled. "Bye, Wenling."

"Bye, Burke."

I did Assist down the steps and Steady for the chair. When Burke lifted himself into the truck, Chase Dad put the chair in back.

I blinked at how loudly Chase Dad shut the door. "I told you to wait in the truck."

"I wanted to say hi to my friends."

Chase Dad shook his head. "Your . . . I don't want you having anything to do with that girl."

"Who, Wenling? What do you mean?"

"I mean her family is trying to put our family out of business. Her father is an engineer for the robo-farmers." Chase Dad drove for a time and my boy was silent. "I mean it, Burke."

"What did Principal Hawkins say?"

Chase Dad's hands made a twisting noise on the steering wheel. "She says Cooper was disruptive, that the teachers couldn't teach with him in class, and that children were afraid because he's so big."

Burke's laugh was quick and harsh. "What? That is such bull. Nobody did anything but try to pet him before class. Cooper knows how to stay."

"Well, that's what she says. So you're going to have to leave the dog at home."

Burke stared out the side window. His hand on my neck felt tense. "I get it then."

His voice was bitter and his face was dour and scowling. I watched him anxiously. What was wrong?

Chase Dad glanced at him. "Get what? What are you talking about?"

"Because you have a fight with Wenling's dad, you want me

to get involved, even though Wenling and I have nothing to do with it. But when I have a fight with a school, you not only won't help me, you want me to just give up."

We drove in silence past the goat ranch, which smelled as wonderful as always. "Look, son, this is a battle we can't win. The institutions have all the money and all the power. If we try to fight, they'll crush us."

"Then why not sell out to the robo-farm corporation?" Burke wiped his eyes and I licked his face, concerned for the sad and angry emotions radiating off his hot skin. "Why fight for *anything*?" Burke turned in his seat. "This means everything to me, Dad. Don't you get it?"

"I do get that it seems important, but believe me, when you're older . . ."

"This is happening *now*!" He yelled loudly. I flinched from the harsh tone in Burke's shout and from the torrent of hot emotions pouring from him. "Why don't you care how I feel?"

"Settle down, son."

Nobody said anything else all the way home. Normally car rides make me happy, but this one was sad and tense and I was glad to get out and run and terrify the ducks.

On my way up from the pond, I saw something black slinking out of the barn, and my nose told me it was the mystery animal! It was small and smooth and when it glimpsed me it dashed around the corner and seemed to vanish—I tracked it to a big hole in the side of the barn. I shoved my nose in that hole and inhaled deeply, disappointed the creature hadn't wanted to play with me. And I wondered, if they lived out in barns, why did so many people carry that odor on their clothing?

After that, things were normal. Grant left most mornings, Chase Dad played outside with plants or drove around in the slow truck, and I sometimes watched him, especially when all Burke was doing was talking to Grandma or sitting and staring at a light on a table, barely moving. "I'm impressed you're doing Calculus II," she remarked to him one day. "But it's over my head. I'm afraid I can't help you anymore."

"That's okay, Grandma, the online lessons are fine. I love it, but I get that some people find math boring."

"Oh, not at all, honey. Watching your brain develop has been one of my life's thrills. You make me so proud."

Grandma leaned down and Burke put his arms around her and I climbed up to shove my head in between them to make the moment even more special.

We went outside and I trotted straight to the barn. The mystery creature's fragrance was everywhere, but there was no sign of the creature.

Burke wheeled down to the dock to ruffle dry-sounding papers in his lap, and the leaves were pouring from the trees in a steady rain that made a similar rustling noise. I sprawled contentedly at his feet and was mostly asleep when a special scent jolted me to my feet.

"Cooper?" Burke called as I scrabbled off the dock, my nails digging into the wood. Lacey! She was running to me and it was as if we had never been separated for a moment. Of course Lacey found me! We belonged together and we both knew it. I couldn't go find her because I needed to take care of my boy, but Wenling could walk on her own without Lacey.

What a wonderful day! While Burke sat and watched, Lacey and I chased ducks and leapt in the water and sniffed along the shore. I smelled Wenling on her and knew this meant that Lacey would have to leave again, but at that moment I had her all to myself.

Whenever Burked called "Cooper! Lacey!" we made our way back to him, but soon were absorbed in each other again. Nothing is better than when your person and your favorite dog are both there. My sense of the lateness of the afternoon told me that Grant would be home very soon and then it would be all of us having fun together.

The ducks were gathered in a grumpy knot in the marshy area across from the dock, but when Lacey and I dashed through the muck the birds squawked and flapped out to the center of the pond, scolding us.

I was first to see the snake. I froze for a moment and it did, too: it was curled back on itself, its tongue flicking out, eyes cold as they watched me. I barked at it and it raised its head higher. I didn't know why but I instantly wanted to attack it, bite it, even kill it—a compulsion went through me like a shiver. The fur was up on the back of my neck and my bark carried a furious tone. In response, the snake shook its tail end, not in a wag but more like a tremble, making a scratchy sound.

"Cooper? What is it?" On the dock, Burke wheeled his chair to peer at me.

Lacey charged up to see what I had found. The same ferocious rage crackled along her spine, forcing her tail rigid. She started barking and snarling, too. She circled around behind it, and the snake wove its head back and forth, trying to keep each of us in view.

"Dogs? What do you see?"

I darted forward and the snake snapped out, nearly reaching my face, and I scrambled back. It was *fast*. It instantly turned toward Lacey and I went after it again and it struck at me and Lacey jumped on its back and picked it up like a stick. Instantly the snake curled, biting Lacey's face.

"No! Lacey, no! Drop it! Leave It! No!" Burke screamed at her.

Lacey shook her head, her eye twitching just above where the fangs were sunk in her jowl. The snake struck again and Burke was still screaming and finally Lacey dropped the snake, which immediately fled into the reeds.

"Lacey! Come! Cooper!"

There was no mistaking the fear in his voice—something very serious had just happened. We ran to Burke. Lacey had her ears lowered and I knew she felt she had been a bad dog, because I felt the same way. Burke, however, did not seem angry as he extended his arms. "Lacey. Oh no, come here, girl."

Lacey went to Burke and sat. He seized her jaw in his hands and twisted it, peering at the side of her face. Lacey's tail tapped the dock. I pushed forward, because Burke was radiating a horrible fear and I knew he needed me, though it was Lacey he hugged, pulling her up into his chair, squeezing tears out of his eyes. I did Sit, not understanding. "Oh God. Lacey, I'm so sorry. It really got you bad." He looked up at the house. *"Dad!"* Burke's frantic wail came as a voice I'd never heard before, raw and scared. "Dad! Hurry! Dad!"

The wind pushed Burke's shout back at us. He turned to me. "Cooper! Come!"

I obeyed and felt the snick as he attached my short leash to my harness. "Pull, Cooper!"

With Lacey in his lap and his hands not helping move his wheels, Burke was much harder to drag, but I dug in my claws and strained up the hill, making slow progress.

"Dad! Dad!" Burke cried. "Dad! Help!"

I expected Chase Dad but instead, after a moment, it was Grant who burst out the front door and came running downhill toward us.

"Hurry!" Burke yelled.

Grant's boots thudded on the hard-packed dirt. "What is it?"

"Lacey got bitten by a massasauga!"

"A what?"

"A northern rattlesnake!"

"What? You sure?"

"Grant, I saw it. It's poisonous. Its venom is more toxic than a regular rattlesnake and it got her again and again! You've got to drive her to the vet *now*."

"Did it get Cooper, too?"

"No. Thank God."

"Should we suck out the venom?"

"No, that might kill *us*. Just go!"

Grant clapped his hands together. "Come on, Lacey!"

Lacey seemed to hesitate, gauging the leap from Burke's chair to the ground. Burke unsnapped my leash and I went to Grant, thinking he wanted both dogs. Lacey finally sprang out, her forelegs folding under her when she hit the ground. She got up, shaking herself. Grant turned and began running up the hill.

But Lacey didn't run after him. Instead, she took a very slow step, as if afraid the ground would bite her.

"Grant!"

Grant turned around. Lacey was walking sideways. Her back legs quivered, and she fell. I put my nose to her and she licked my snout.

Something was very, very wrong with her.

"You have to carry her!"

Grant picked up Lacey and ran toward the house, staggering under the load. The way Lacey's head lolled terrified me. I anxiously tried to follow, but Burke needed me to do Pull and the two of us ventured up much more slowly. By the time we reached the farmhouse, Grant and his truck were gone and the scent of Lacey was on the wind, slowly fading away in the direction of the road.

In the house, Burke talked to Grandma and they hugged each other. Soon Chase Dad came rumbling up on the slow truck. "Any word?" he asked as he walked in.

"Grant doesn't have his phone with him," Grandma responded. "He left it sitting here when he heard Burke. I was napping in my room."

"I suppose under the circumstances that it's okay that Grant's driving, but if he gets stopped they'll yank his permit."

"You said he's a good driver."

"For a fifteen-year-old, sure."

Burke petted me and I did Sit. "Dad. I called Wenling. It's her dog. They're on their way over, her and her dad. The Zhangs. The robo-farmer."

Burke and his father looked at each other for a moment. "Fair enough," Chase Dad finally said. He went to Burke and put a hand on his shoulder. "You're sure it was a massasauga. A rattle-snake."

"Yessir. I studied them in my biology unit last year. Our state's only poisonous snake. They are supposed to be almost extinct."

"I've never seen one. Burke, I'm sorry you had to go through this."

Burke looked away, waves of sorrow flowing off him. I whimpered. I did not understand. What had just happened? Where was Lacey?

"You couldn't have prevented it, Burke," Grandma told him.

Burke's mouth formed in a bitter line. "If I had been able to get off the dock. If I had been there in the reeds with the dogs, I would have seen the snake. I could have called them off."

I dug in my box of rubber balls and pulled out the squeaky toy. The smell of my Lacey was painted all over the surface. I carried it with me to my dog bed.

Later, we all reacted when we heard the unmistakable chug of Grant's truck. We waited on the porch and gazed out at him as he stood up. He shook his head and Grandma put a hand to her mouth. "Oh no," she said softly.

When he trudged up the ramp to join us, I smelled Lacey, but the sadness was pouring out of him and it washed over everyone, and I somehow understood: Lacey wasn't coming back. She was like Judy the old goat—what made her Lacey, made her my dog, had departed. The snake had somehow hurt her that badly.

I whimpered and my boy reached out and stroked me.

Grandma stooped to hold my head in her hands and stare into my eyes. "You understand, don't you, Cooper? You understand what happened to Lacey. You're a young dog but you've got an old, old soul."

I licked her face.

"Thank God Cooper didn't get bitten," Chase Dad said.

Another truck came up the driveway. It was Wenling and the man who always drove her. He had a long metal rod in his hand. Chase Dad turned to Grandma. "He's got a rifle. Get the boys into the house."

There was fear and anger in Chase Dad's march down to the car. I remained by his side, as if doing Assist. The girl, Wenling, was crying, wiping salty tears from her face. Her father held the rod pointed toward the ground.

Chase Dad put his hands on his hips. "What the hell do you think you're doing?"

"He came to shoot the snake that killed Lacey," Wenling explained. I trotted up to her and she stooped to put her arms around me, the scent of Lacey wafting off her skin. I could feel her grief in the desperate way she clutched me. I was not Lacey, but I could be a dog for her to hug.

"You don't bring a gun onto another man's property without asking permission," Chase Dad said coldly.

Wenling spoke to her father, who replied and then lowered his head. "He says he's sorry. He meant no disrespect. He asks permission."

"Permission . . . Ask him to put his gun in the truck, please."

Wenling's father opened his door and set the metal rod inside. "He can't speak much English, but he has learned to understand more," Wenling advised.

I felt some of the tension leave Chase Dad. "Look, uh, ZZ. I understand how you feel. God knows I'd probably feel the same way. But that snake is an endangered species. We can't actually kill it. It's against the law. You could go to jail."

The man looked at his daughter and she spoke to him and he replied to her. "Zhè shì yītiáo dúshé. Rúguǒ tā yáole lìng yīzhǐ gǒu huòzhě yīgè xiǎohāi, zénme bàn ne?"

"My father asks, what if it bites a child, or another dog?"

I heard a noise and glanced up: Burke and Grant had left the house and were advancing cautiously toward us, Grant pushing the chair.

Chase Dad shook his head. "They're not aggressive. They only strike out of fear. I've never even seen one, and I've lived here my whole life."

Wenling spoke to her father and then reached down to touch me some more. "How did it happen?" she asked in a soft voice, wiping her eyes.

"I wasn't there. It was Burke," Chase Dad answered, gesturing to his two sons.

Burke came forward. "Hi, Wenling. I'm so sorry." Grant stood a little bit back from us. "The dogs found a snake and before I could react, Lacey picked it up and it bit her right in the face." His face winced. "She didn't seem to suffer."

Wenling nodded. "Thank you for what you did for Lacey," she replied in choked tones.

"Oh, it wasn't me. It was my brother, Grant. He took her to the vet."

Grant stepped forward. "Hi, I'm Grant. I'm so sorry I didn't get her there in time."

"Hi, Grant," Wenling said softly. "I'm Wenling. Thank you for trying to save Lacey. This is my father, ZZ."

"I am just . . . I mean I'm so sorry," Grant told her.

Everyone stood for a moment. Her father spoke and Wenling nodded. "He says we will call the vet and have the bill sent to us."

Everyone seemed to be too sad to talk anymore, so Wenling and her father departed, taking with them the smell of my Lacey.

I knew I would never breathe in Lacey's scent again.

That night Burke woke me up, running his hands through my fur. "Why are you crying, Cooper? Are you having a bad dream?"

Restless, I padded out into the living room. Grandma was sitting in a chair, the window open. I lifted my nose to Lacey's fading scent. In that moment, it seemed possible she might bound into the house through the dog door, jump up on Burke's bed to sleep with us. "Do you hear, Cooper?" Grandma whispered. "Listen." She ran a hand down my back. "Let's go watch."

I was surprised when she led me outside. I lifted my leg on some bushes as we made our way to the barn. A slash of light fell onto the ground from the partially open door. I smelled both the mystery creature and Chase Dad in the barn through that crack, and could hear his voice and feel an odd vibration on the air. Grandma pulled the door all the way open and I trotted in to greet Chase Dad, sniffing curiously at the box with metal strings he held in his lap.

"Please keep playing," Grandma urged.

Chase Dad smiled. "You caught me."

"What was that? It was pretty."

"Just . . ." Chase Dad shrugged. I carefully sniffed along the walls, picking up that unknown creature's scent but not seeing it. "I don't think I'm handling either of my boys very well right now. Especially Burke. I don't understand why he can't just go to school without Cooper."

I had closed my eyes, but now I opened them.

"Do you remember eighth grade?"

"Tell you the truth, I sort of blocked it out."

"You don't remember carrying your guitar with you?"

"What? Well sure, when I had band."

They didn't seem to be talking about me after all. I sighed sleepily.

"No, Chase. Every class, nearly every day. You claimed it was too big for your locker. The principal told me it's how you felt you fit in. He didn't mind. Some boys, he told me, wear the same Detroit Lions jersey every day, and that was a lot worse." Grandma pinched her nose.

Chase Dad chuckled. "I do remember the smell of pituitaries in the morning. I get what you're saying, Mom, but this is different. We hire a lawyer—I just don't think I have that kind of money."

Grandma left. I decided to sit at Chase Dad's feet while he made his sounds, but I shook and wagged when Grandma returned. She held out a piece of paper to Chase Dad, who accepted it. "What's this?" he asked.

"My contribution to the legal defense fund."

Chase Dad regarded her. "This is a lot of money, Mom."

"I've been saving for something important. I think this qualifies. Just . . . don't tell Burke about it. We're fighting this as a family."

The next morning, after Grant had left and the delicious smells of breakfast no longer perfumed the air, Chase Dad came to see us in Burke's bedroom. "You planning to sleep all day? It's ten thirty," he said from Burke's doorway.

Burke groaned. "Cooper was twitching and crying all night."

"I need to tell you something, son. Your grandmother and I had a talk last night after you went to bed. You're right. There *is* sense in standing up for what you believe in."

Burke looked up at him in surprise.

Chase Dad nodded grimly. "I called my lawyer first thing this morning. He agrees with you—he says if the dog is disruptive or dangerous, maybe it can be banned, but Mrs. Hawkins has to prove it. In court. We're taking them to court."

Burke's mouth dropped open. Chase Dad held up a hand. "I don't have the money if the district wants to turn it into a big battle, but Paul—our attorney, Paul Pender—thinks they'll fold after an informal hearing. The optics look bad, he says."

Snow came, the days turned cold, and the water on the pond froze slick. Burke liked to throw a ball for me and laugh when I overran it and couldn't stop, my nails digging into the ice. When I was down at the pond, though, I could not help but remember romping there with Lacey. Burke was my person, but Lacey had been my mate.

We were headed up to the house after one such afternoon, me doing Pull through the packed snow, Burke grunting a little as he worked the wheels on his chair. I had heard a car earlier and it was still in the driveway, one I had never smelled before, as we rolled up the ramp and into the house.

"Burke, you remember Mr. Pender," Chase Dad said.

Burke raised a hand. "Hello, sir."

"Hi! Is this Cooper?" I trotted over to sniff the offered hand of a man who seemed to be around Chase Dad's age. His fingers harbored a sweet odor very unlike any of the men who lived with me. "Call me Paul," the man said. He patted my head. "I'm glad you're here. I was just telling your father that the judge granted our motion. Cooper will be allowed to be in court with us at the hearing." The man smiled.

"That's good news," Burke observed cautiously.

"What does that mean?" Grandma asked.

"It means," the man explained, "that we're going to war."

I saw that man again because he gave us a car ride, not to do School, but to a building with steps but no children. Burke was up front and I sat in the back with Chase Dad and Grandma. We were parked right in front of the stone steps, and then we just sat there not doing anything. People are funny that way: all anyone had to do was open a door and we could get out and run and play and maybe find a stick or a squirrel, but they like to sit doing nothing, not even eating or giving good dog treats.

How strange to think of being able to eat anytime you want, but not doing it.

"So the Animal Control officer isn't on their witness list," the driver with the sweet hands said.

"Is that good?" Chase Dad asked.

"I'm going to say yes. The fact she was called out on a complaint works in their favor. But from what you said, her testimony probably would not help their case. I don't know if they made a conscious decision, or if they're just lazy. I like it when they're lazy." He leaned forward. "Okay, that's the judge's car. Go, Burke; we'll follow with the chair."

"Come on, Cooper!"

Once we were out of the car I thought maybe I would get to run around a little, but Burke wanted me to do Assist to the bottom of the stairs. He further baffled me when he asked me to Stay. He was waiting for something, I decided, and imagined a bell ringing and children pouring out the doors at the top of the steps. I discreetly lifted my leg where another male had previously marked.

When a woman turned the corner on the sidewalk, Burke ordered me to Assist, and we mounted the stairs together. I noticed the woman had stopped to watch, so I worked hard to show her what a good dog I could be. You never know who is going to have a treat in her pocket.

Chase Dad followed up the steps with Grandma and the chair. The man who gave us a ride pulled away from the curb and drove down the street. I did Steady and Burke hoisted himself up and we entered a building that echoed with the loud clack of Grandma's shoes. I followed everyone into a small room that reminded me a little of doing School because it had seats and a table up front.

Our driver walked in a short time later. He slid into a chair. "Here we go," he said. He seemed excited, as if he were about to bring out a squeaky toy.

Some more people filtered in, but they didn't sit with us even though we were the only group with a dog. They sat at another table. I recognized one of the women from doing School. She had the odor of the mystery animals clinging to her so strongly it was almost all I could smell in the room—but a different scent from different, distinct creatures than what I could smell in our barn. She did not come over to talk.

Everyone stood up so I thought we were leaving, but all that happened was that the lady from the front steps came in and sat at a raised desk, and then everyone sat down again. I yawned, but at that point had no idea just how boring things were going to be. The people were seated at tables, but there was no food.

I sprawled out for a nap, but awoke when the animal-scented

woman from school said the word "dog." I noticed she had left her table and was sitting adjacent to the raised desk.

"My number-one concern is for the safety of the students. *All* the students. From what I understand, Cooper hasn't even been formally trained as a support animal," the woman said.

Our driver nodded, leaning forward at our table. "So am I understanding you to say that if Cooper were to be professionally evaluated and deemed a fully capable and trained service animal, Burke would be allowed to have his dog with him, Mrs. Hawkins?"

Everyone was saying my name! I wagged, wondering what we were doing.

The woman from doing School frowned. "No," she replied slowly. "I was merely pointing out that I have to watch out for my students. The dog was disruptive I have the absolute authority to take whatever measures I deem appropriate to maintain a safe and productive learning environment."

"Well, Mrs. Hawkins," our driver observed softly, "that's why we're here, to determine if you do have absolute authority. When you say the dog was disruptive, could you give us some examples?"

The School woman was silent for a moment. "It was all anyone was talking about."

"Anyone being . . ."

"My staff."

"You mean the office staff?"

"Yes."

"What about the teachers, what did they say?"

"I was a teacher myself for years. I know how hard it is to get kids to focus. A dog would make it impossible."

"Unresponsive, your honor."

The woman behind the high desk stirred. "Mrs. Hawkins,

Mr. Pender is asking you what, if anything, the teachers said to you about the dog."

Everyone was saying "dog" a lot. I was sorry I didn't have any toys with me.

"No one said anything to me. They didn't have to. I didn't let it get that far. I pulled Burke out of class as soon as I heard about it."

"From his first class?" our driver asked.

"No, second hour."

"First hour for Burke was taught by Mr. Kindler, I believe, is that right?"

"Yes. American History."

"The dog was there for Mr. Kindler's class?"

A man who had been sitting with the School woman cleared his throat. "I object to that, your honor. How would she know?"

"Withdrawn. Mrs. Hawkins, I have a signed and sworn statement from Mr. Kindler about the hour in question. He confirms the dog was there the whole time. Your honor?"

"Go ahead," said the lady at the high table.

Our driver got up, handed a piece of paper to the man at the other table, and then approached the School lady and gave her a paper, too. Of all the things humans play with, papers are my least favorite. They smell dry and stick to my tongue. The School lady put on a pair of glasses that were swinging from strings on her neck.

"Please, Mrs. Hawkins. If you don't mind, read the third paragraph."

She frowned.

"Mrs. Hawkins?" our driver asked.

"At no point did the service dog disturb me, the class, or the other students. He lay quietly by Burke's side. When the bell rang, Cooper sat up but otherwise did not move until Burke gave him some command. Frankly, I wish my students were as polite as Cooper."

Grandma and Burke and Chase Dad laughed, so our driver did, too. The mere mention of my name seemed to put everyone in a better mood.

The do School lady removed her glasses, the motion sending wafts of the strange animal smell into the air. "I have been principal of Lincoln Middle School for eight years. By all measures, our performance has improved under my administration. It requires making difficult decisions. I am sorry for Burke's other-abled challenges, but the school meets all requirements for his access. For the dog to . . . to *drag* him up the steps, his paralysis in full view of nearly the entire student body, goes beyond disruptive. It was disturbing."

The woman at the high desk was shaking her head. "I don't agree. I saw Cooper assisting Burke this morning. I thought it was beautiful."

Grandma grabbed Burke's hand.

After some more conversation, the do School lady sat back down next to the man at the other table—maybe he was *her* driver. Then everyone talked and I slept a little, and then I sensed everyone getting tense, so I woke up and looked at Burke. He scratched the itchy area under my chin.

"Very well, thank you," the lady at the tall desk said. "Due to the pressing nature of this matter—this young man deserves an education—I will render my decision here tomorrow at nine a.m."

Everyone stood up, so I wagged.

THIRTEEN

Was this the new do School? We were back in that same place with the same people the next morning. Everyone seemed tense but me, and I was trying to think how to lighten the mood—lie on my back for a tummy rub, perhaps?—when all the humans in the room jumped up, the lady came in and sat at the tall desk, and then everyone sat down.

It was very peculiar.

The woman at the tall desk leaned forward. "I don't need any more time to render my decision—the facts speak for themselves. This has already dragged on needlessly. What is important is to get this young man back to his school."

Grandma drew in a breath. Chase Dad's hand was on Burke's shoulder and I saw his grip tighten.

"Mr. Pender is absolutely correct: barring evidence that Cooper poses a significant, ongoing impediment to the teachers' abil-

ity to teach, and the students' ability to learn, the administration
is not justified in removing either the dog or his owner from
school. The language in Title II is clear."

I flopped down with a groan, heading into another nap.

"And yes," she continued, "if the dog is aggressive, the school
has every right to protect the other children. So while I do agree
that he is a very big dog, I do not see that he poses any immedi-
ate threat. I mean, look at him, he's the personification of pas-
sive. Burke, you and Cooper are to be admitted to school starting
tomorrow."

I scrambled to my feet because everyone started hugging each
other. And, of course, they also hugged me. Our table was very
happy. I looked over at the other table as they were leaving and
they did not appear at all happy, but I didn't go over to try to
change their moods. Sometimes people can't be cheered up, no
matter how much attention they get from a dog.

Driving home, I sat in the back with Grandma, Burke, and
Grant, wagging and watching for squirrels. The next morning
Grandma drove and Burke and I got out to do School with the
stone steps. I did Assist, and we stopped midway up.

"Hi, Wenling," Burke said.

Wenling did not smell like Lacey anymore—nor like any dog,
which I found puzzling. How could a girl not have a dog?

This time Burke enjoyed doing School so much we kept returning. The snow melted and the air filled with the fertile scent
of new grasses and leaves. I was by my boy's side when he needed
me and otherwise I napped. I often did not see the unhappy do
School lady, but I sure could smell her, with her alien-animal
odors wafting throughout the building.

"Having a dry start to the summer," Chase Dad said at dinner. "Better get some moisture soon."

When summer brought bugs and tall grasses, we abruptly

stopped seeing my friends on the steps, but I was able to spend more time with Burke. I did Pull and Assist, but I also curled up next to my boy at night, just being his dog.

We never did do School again, but that fall we did go to Grant's building, which had no children on the steps. Grant and Wenling were there, too, and I could smell him and Wenling even when I couldn't see them. I recognized many of my friends, and made many new ones. I did not miss do School or the unhappy lady with the alien barn animal odors—this new place was just as fun!

The snow came and was heavy and thick and Burke needed me to do Pull many, many times. I loved being a good Pull dog. Sometimes Grant would push while I did Pull, as good a boy as I was a dog.

When the snow melted and the air warmed and thickened with the scent of grasses and flowers, I knew it meant we would soon be staying home and that I would miss everyone from Grant's building. But this was the pattern of my life as I understood it.

I liked to sit on the porch and enjoy the fragrances of the farm as the sunlight faded. Sometimes the goat ranch was on the air, sometimes horses, often cows—of all of them I'd only actually played with a goat and was happy to leave the other ones alone. I could smell my human family, the elusive barn animal, the ducks. . . .

Dog. I sat up, drinking in the scent of a canine on the night currents, strengthening as it came closer. My nose told me it was a female, out on the road, headed in my direction. Excited, I jumped down off the porch and trotted off to greet her.

A thin, young female burst from the gloom, her tail wagging as she galloped up the driveway. We ran to each other, veering at the last moment, approaching nose-to-tail. Her long blond coat was full of bits of plant material and she didn't have a collar. I lifted my leg, making a mark, which she politely took a moment to inspect. Then she was bowing and jumping so enthusiastically I wasn't able to sniff her as investigatively as I wanted. Her breath was rancid in a strangely familiar way. I was intrigued by the dried blood around one ear and the way I could feel her bones when I jumped on her—this was a very skinny dog! And the way she played, the way she ran at my side, chewing gently at my jowls, reminded me of my Lacey. Everything about her reminded me of Lacey!

I stopped running. The female loped up and threw herself on her back, allowing me to finally give thorough scrutiny. She licked me as I sniffed her ears, which were covered in unruly hair.

As much as I knew Sit and Stay, I knew who this dog was. She was a different dog, but she was the same dog. This was *Lacey*.

Lacey! We ran side by side, tearing around the yard, retracing paths we'd worn in the grass long ago. I jumped up onto the porch and came down with the squeaky toy, chewing it and then dropping it at her feet so she would see that I recognized her.

I did not know that a dog could be taken away in a sudden, fearful car ride, that she would be gone and people would be sad, but then she would find her way back to the farm as a new, different dog. But it made perfect sense to me now. Of course Lacey came back to me! We belonged together.

Whatever journey brought her here had also changed her, because when Grant opened the door and came out, Lacey turned and ran off into the night. I raced after her but when Grant whistled I faltered, watching her disappear in the shadows. She was afraid of Grant, now, which I found incomprehensible. Other than try to get me to play with the nylon bone, Grant had never done anything wrong, in my experience.

That night I lay on Burke's bed with my nose pointed at the

open window. Lacey had not gone terribly far; I could track her scent out there in the woods.

The next evening Grandma gave me a bone with succulent meat and fat clinging to it. I slipped through the dog door, my mouth salivating. I prepared for my feast by placing the bone between my feet, lying prone, but before I could even chew, an image came to me: skinny Lacey, a sickly, sour tang on her breath—so similar to my mother dog's exhalations in the metal den. But then we all went to live with Sam Dad and Ava, and Mother's frame grew stocky and she no longer emitted the odor of a desperately starving animal.

Lacey needed food. I padded over to a corner of the porch and left the fabulous treat lying there, and later that night smelled Lacey and heard her stealthy feet. She crunched that bone in the yard, too hungry to take it any farther away.

I concluded Lacey must be living with her person, of course, but when Wenling came to visit there was no smell of any dogs on her legs and sleeves. Who was Lacey's person now?

What did cling to Wenling's sleeves was the odor of my boy, Burke. The two of them were often pressed so close together, murmuring to each other, it was as if they had forgotten they had a dog sitting next to them. I usually wound up having to shove my nose in the small gap between them to correct their focus.

"What time are you and Grant coming to pick me up for the party?" Wenling asked.

"You know, since it's a formal, I think maybe I'll get a ride from someone other than He Who Turns On Two Wheels," Burke replied. "Maybe my dad."

That night Chase Dad and Burke departed in the car but did not take me. Lacey had wandered off. I sat on the floor, hoping for attention, but Grandma didn't respond even when I rolled on my back with my legs in the air in a clear invitation to rub my tummy. Chase Dad soon returned, but without Burke. I examined him carefully for clues as to what might have happened to my boy.

"Looks like a wet start to the summer," Chase Dad remarked. "Supposed to rain all week."

"How did she look?" Grandma asked him.

"Who?"

"Oh Chase. Wenling, who do you think?"

"Mmmm . . . well, she had on a dress and her hair was curled."

"My, you are so observant. Do you give the same lack of appreciation to what Natalie wears?"

Chase Dad was silent for a moment. I was watching him carefully for signs he might be getting ready to summon up some bacon, but he seemed distracted by Grandma. "How did you hear about Natalie?"

"How big do you think this town is?"

"I gave specific instructions to every person in the county not to talk about this."

"My son has another girlfriend and you don't think my phone doesn't start ringing?"

"*Another* girlfriend. Interesting choice of words, Mom. So the old girl network lights up every time I go on a date?"

"I've met her, you know. She's nice. She brought her nieces to the book fair and made a point of saying hello to me."

"It isn't serious, Mom."

"Maybe it *should* be serious."

"I've got enough on my plate."

"Spoken like a true bachelor. So is that where you were Saturday night? Or did your set last until five a.m.?"

"Mom. This is embarrassing."

"My son," she observed lightly, "seems stiff as a board, then he goes to town to play guitar and I hear he's up there dancing and laughing. Rumor has it you're a completely different person on that stage. Why doesn't that wild man ever show up here?"

Chase Dad grunted. "I have to set an example for the boys. Farming is a hard way to make a living."

I decided to give up on the both of them. Sighing, I put my head down. For a moment there I had been so committed to the idea of bacon I could almost smell it.

"I think part of that example should be offering them a view of their father as being a man with more than one note to play."

"They need stability. They need to know they can count on me not to change."

Grandma's tone softened. "They know they can rely on you, Chase. They know you'd never abandon them."

"Really not enjoying this conversation."

"Suit yourself."

I was curled up on Burke's bed when I heard a vehicle in the driveway. I eased out through the dog door and trotted up to where Wenling's father was setting Burke's chair on the ground. Wenling hugged Burke and kissed his face by his ear. I went to his side to see if he needed me to do Pull, but he just sat and waved at the car and then he spun his chair in circles.

I had no idea what he was doing.

When we rolled up the ramp and into the house, Grandma was the only person in the living room. "Did you have a good time at the dance, dear?"

"It was pretty much the best night of my life!"

"Oh Burke. That's sweet. I'm happy for you."

I could sense Grant standing just around the corner, but whatever was going on didn't interest him enough for him to join us.

Grandma and Burke talked a bit more and then Grandma said, "I'm going to bed," and Burke accompanied me into his room. I pressed my nose to the window to search for Lacey, but she wasn't close.

I heard a noise and Grant was at the door, leaning against the wall. "How was the 'freshman spring fling'?" he asked in a flat tone.

"I didn't get very far flung," Burke replied. "But it was a fun party."

"You make out with Wenling?"

"What's your problem?" I could feel Burke getting angry.

"You'll be fifteen in June. I kissed my first girl when I was a lot younger."

"Yeah? Were you in a wheelchair?"

"God. That's your answer for everything."

"Or maybe it is just that when you're in a wheelchair you don't get much opportunity to *date*."

"I just can't wait for you to have your operation. Then *you* can do all the chores."

"*You* can't wait?"

Grant turned and left. His angry walk looked just like Chase Dad's.

When Lacey returned she had a healed cut on her shoulder. What drew my attention, though, was something else, a scent so enticing and obligating I could not control myself. I was seized by a compulsion I had never experienced and did not understand, and in my play I wanted only to climb up on her back, gripping her with my forepaws. In that moment it was more important to be with my mate than my people, and if Burke had called, I would not have been able to respond.

Later Lacey sprawled out in the dirt and I lay with my head resting on her side, rising and falling with her breathing. She still did not smell like Wenling.

As I approached the porch, Lacey shied away, remaining in the shadows, and when I slipped through the dog door I knew she had turned and left. Where were her people? Why didn't Wenling and her father come to get Lacey and *feed her*? And where did Lacey go when she left me for so many days at a time, if not to her person?

When the air turned hot the family schedule abruptly changed. As I anticipated, we stopped going to see my friends, and Grant and Chase Dad would leave together every morning to go out and play with dirt in the fields. Burke would talk into his phone, saying "Wenling" a lot.

On a day when the rain was pounding the roof and slapping the car windshield so emphatically the sound was overwhelming, Grandma drove Burke and me a long distance, stopping occasionally to dash into a building and then returning with a box or a bag but no treats. Every time we halted Burke slid down a window, which was how I tracked the weather as the rain lessened and then stopped completely. I sat with my boy and breathed in the mud and leaves and water.

"So Grandma," Burke said slowly after Grandma returned yet again to the car, "tell me again why you needed me to come with you?"

"I had to run errands."

"Right," Burke agreed, "but I can tell something is going on."

Grandma blinked, smiling. "Why, I have no idea what you're talking about."

"It just feels like there's some reason you wanted me away from the house for a few hours," he noted. "Does the fact that I turn fifteen on Wednesday have anything to do with it?"

"I'm glad it's stopped raining."

Burke laughed, so I wagged. The car moved and the windows slid shut, but I could still drink in the glorious moist air of the wet outdoors. I sniffed hard as we passed the goat ranch; we were headed home.

When we pulled into the driveway and jumped out, I was excited to see that everything from in the barn had been moved outside and stacked against the side of the building! I delightedly marked the items, something I felt I should not do when they were in the barn itself. Many of them smelled like the slinky barn animal, so I was careful to make sure I wet those.

There were also two cars nearby, and I diligently lifted my leg on these as well.

Grandma went into the house and Grant walked out of the barn, smiling. "Happy birthday, brother."

"Thanks. You're a few days early, but I do appreciate that you emptied the barn for me. Truly the best gift, ever."

"Come on inside for a sec," Grant replied, gesturing.

My boy did not have me do Pull as we wheeled over to the barn and up the short ramp. I was startled to see what awaited us inside: several boys all standing and grinning in the big empty room. Burke hesitated on the threshold, then slowly wheeled himself in. "You put a basketball net up in the barn," he observed. "Is that my birthday present? If so, you've truly managed to surprise me with this one. I was expecting a running track."

Some of the boys chuckled, and they came up to grab Burke's hand or slap his palms and then reach out to pat my head.

Grant produced a large ball that rang loudly when he bounced it on the floor. I tensed because I knew that I could never get my jaws on the thing, though I would, of course, try. "We thought it might be fun to play a little round ball," he said. He put the ball in Burke's lap. "Game on."

"Huh," Burke replied.

FOURTEEN

The boys exchanged glances, grinning, and then followed one another out the back door and returned pushing chairs just like Burke's! I was bewildered, especially when they sat down and began wheeling around in jerky circles. Even Grant had a chair!

"Let's see what you got, birthday boy," someone called out.

Things quickly became even more confusing: the boys began rapidly rolling back and forth, throwing the ball and yelling. My boy told me to do Stay, but it was simply too difficult and I pranced out to get involved with that ball. Burke eventually clipped my leash to a pole. I watched tensely as the boys scrambled about, periodically heaving the ball up in the air.

Though I did not understand what they were doing, the expression on Burke's face and his laughter told me he was happy.

I noticed that he was moving much more quickly than everyone else, weaving in and out among the other chairs.

"How does he *do* that?" one of the boys panted at Grant.

Burke was out in front of everyone, rolling fast, and he threw the ball up in the air and it fell back down and several boys cheered, somehow having fun without a dog.

"Practice," Grant told the panting boy with a laugh.

I tried to stay involved by barking and wagging but eventually resigned myself to just sitting there and keeping my eyes on my boy.

Later that afternoon the boys all left in their cars, so it was just Grant and Burke and me.

My boy reached down to scratch my ears and I groaned. "Where did you get all the chairs?" he asked.

Grant grinned. "A couple of them are rented, and we got some from garage sales, pawnshops, places like that."

"So you have been planning this for some time?"

Grant nodded. "Yeah. How was it?"

I turned my head to stare at Burke because a wave of emotion came off him as sudden and sweeping as the morning's rainstorm. "Grant," Burke said. Then he stopped, looking away for a moment, and then started again. "Grant, I have never been part of any team before, not ever. And to not just play, but to be the, the . . ."

"You smoked us all. You were the best," Grant said simply.

"Thank you, brother."

Grant and Burke grinned at each other. The pull between the two of them in that moment was so strong I had to jump up, putting my paws on Grant's chest, wanting to be part of it.

I usually sat under Grant's chair at dinner because he dropped more food than Burke. I was lying there when Chase Dad said,

"I ordered new doors for the storm cellar. The ones we have now are so rotten you could put a foot through them. Tornado hits, not much good to have a shelter with doors falling apart. After we get done tomorrow, Grant, why don't you see about getting the old doors off. The things weigh a ton."

Grant kicked his legs a little. "Sure. I'll work all day and then work a little more."

"Watch your tone," Chase Dad replied.

"I can do it," I heard my boy say.

Grant made a snorting noise.

"Grant," Grandma pleaded quietly.

"I'm serious. I'll figure something out," Burke insisted.

There was a silence. "All right, Burke, you do that," Chase Dad agreed.

The next morning Burke seemed very interested in a pair of wooden doors lying on the ground. "This is going to work, Cooper," he told me.

I watched with absolutely no curiosity as he started tying ropes, running the line to a tree, where an object clanked as he lifted it. "See? With the hinges removed, I can pull the doors off using the block and tackle."

I yawned, then curled up for a nap. I was intrigued, though, when the slatted wooden doors were removed, revealing steps that went down into a space under the building.

"Go ahead, Cooper! Check it out!"

The steps were stone and no children were sitting on them. Whereas the barn was lofty and airy, the small room down there, the under barn, was dark and damp. I found nothing of interest in the cramped space: some soft blankets I could smell even though they were wrapped in plastic, some containers, a metal box reeking of burned wood. No sign of the barn animal. I trotted back up to where Burke was playing with the ropes. "Let's not tell anyone how I did this," he said to me.

I went back to my nap.

"How did you get the doors off?" Chase Dad asked Burke at dinner.

"It was easy," Burke replied.

"Who helped you?" Grant challenged.

"Nobody."

"Liar."

"Moron."

"Boys," Chase Dad said in a firm voice.

I listened mournfully to the sound of eating. There was beef up there on the table and none down here on the floor.

"Burke, why don't you invite Wenling to dinner some night," Grandma said.

The sounds of eating stopped. Grant's legs kicked.

"Uh," Burke said.

"Mom? Where did that come from?" Chase Dad asked.

There was a long, long silence.

"Why don't you boys give your grandmother and me a moment to talk," Chase Dad suggested.

Grant and Burke left, but I lingered under the table because of beef.

"I'm serious. What was that?" Chase Dad asked in low tones.

"I know what you're going to say and I don't want to hear it. It's Burke's first girlfriend. What you have against her father is your own business, but it doesn't have anything to do with your son."

"It's not just that they're robo-farmers. I don't like the idea of her being a 'girlfriend.' How do we know what's really behind it? What if she's just dating him out of pity, or worse, if she just wants to be seen as the girl who is so, so *generous*, she is willing to go out with a disabled boy?"

"Oh Chase."

"Oh what? I'm his father. I am just looking out for his best interests."

Grandma stood. I got up and shook myself, sniffing, watching her hopefully. "I think that when Patty left it made you so mistrustful of women you can't just celebrate that your son is in love. Of course she's going to break his heart, or he'll break hers—they're in high school, for heaven's sake. But what you're trying to do is avoid all emotional risks for yourself and for your sons, which means you're not really participating."

"God, is this about Natalie?"

"It's about *life*. Don't you think I miss your father every single moment of every day? But would I pass up the opportunity to be with him, to marry him and raise a family with him, if I knew that I would come home from the store one day and find him lying dead in the kitchen? No, because life is to be *lived*, Chase. Encasing your heart in stone doesn't make it stronger, it makes it cold."

I could not remember Grandma ever doing an angry walk before. Chase Dad sat at the table for a long time after she shut the door to her room.

Grant and Burke decided to visit the dock the next morning, but not to harass ducks. Grant took off his shirt and jumped into the water and Burke watched from his chair.

Grant floated on his back. "You should come in."

"You know I can't swim," Burke replied.

"You don't think I'd save you?"

"Why would I think that?"

"Come on. Why'd you put on your swimsuit if you aren't going to swim?"

"Changed my mind."

"Chicken."

"Seriously? That's the best you got?"

"You know you want to."

I looked up at a noise, and at the same time caught the scent of Wenling. She was on a bicycle, standing on the pedals as she ascended the driveway. She didn't look over at us and neither of the boys saw her. I wagged, anticipating her hands on my fur.

"Cooper! Steady!"

I alertly darted to my boy's side. He gripped my harness, sliding down onto the edge of the dock.

"Go for it," Grant encouraged.

With a sigh, Burke pushed himself off and landed in the water. I bounded forward and stared down into the green water, seeing and smelling him as he sank.

And sank.

And then he was completely erased from my sight. A tense silence fell in the still air. A duck chided another. Somewhere far off, a cow complained. Alarmed, I panted, willing my boy to reappear.

"Come on," Grant muttered.

I gave an anxious whine. I glanced at Grant, then up at the house, where I could see Wenling talking to Grandma. Grandma pointed in our direction, and Wenling turned, putting a hand up to shade her eyes.

I paced, my claws gripping the ends of the dock. Something bad was happening to my boy! *Burke!*

With a splash, Grant dipped under the surface. I barked. Now *he* was disappearing! I had to do something!

I launched myself over the side in utter panic, diving down into the depths of that pond, and as I descended something extraordinary happened: I remembered doing this before. I remembered swimming through gentle, warm waters. A voice came to me: *Good dog, Bailey.*

Yet as powerfully as the recollection captured my mind, I couldn't at all place where I had been. Or *when*.

And then the boys bumped into me on their way up and the moment passed. I followed them to the surface. Grant was sputtering, holding Burke with both hands.

Burke spat water in Grant's face. "Gotcha." Laughing, he pushed himself off his brother's chest, while I swam in circles around them, so relieved I couldn't stop the little yips that escaped my mouth.

Grant wiped his eyes. "What?"

"Of course I can swim, you idiot."

"Hi," Wenling called from the dock. Both boys turned and gaped at her.

"How did you get here?" Grant asked.

"I'm happy to see you, too, Grant. I rode my bike. Did you know there are a lot of bumps in the road? My butt knows."

"Hey, want to come swimming?" Burke asked her, treading water.

"Oh. I, uh, didn't bring a suit."

"Huh." Burke sucked in a breath and slipped under the surface.

A moment later, Grant gasped and spun himself around. Burke surged up out of the water, throwing Grant's bathing suit on the dock by Wenling's feet. "Here! You can borrow Grant's!"

After a bit, Burke climbed out of the pond and I did Steady to help him back to his chair. Grant stayed in the water much longer, not emerging even when Burke, carrying Grant's bathing suit, wheeled with Wenling back to the house. Finally Grant hauled himself onto the dock and ran really fast to the stairs down under the barn, emerging wrapped in a blanket.

I just do not understand people sometimes.

Later the three of them ate ice cream off sticks at the wooden outdoor table. I was enraptured. The boys were eating with crunchy bites but Wenling was licking hers in a way that made me almost dizzy. "So I had my first flying lesson," she said.

The boys stared. "Flying lesson?" Grant repeated.

"You said you were working at the airfield, but you never said anything about flying lessons," Burke added.

"You're like fourteen still," Grant objected.

"So wait, a *girl* is getting her pilot's license, and it's bothering the *boys*?" Wenling taunted.

A drop fell off her stick and landed on the seat next to her. I stared at it.

"Of course not," Burke replied uncomfortably.

"I can't fly solo until I'm sixteen, but I can take lessons now." Wenling grinned. "My father won't let me drive until I'm eighteen, but it never occurred to him that I might *fly*. My mom knows, but she won't tell."

That drop of ice cream was just sitting there!

"Do you have a parachute?" Burke wanted to know.

"Stop it. I'm going to get my pilot's license before I even have a driver's license. So." She turned to Burke. "You want to come out and fly with me sometime?"

"You mean leave the earth?"

Wenling laughed.

"I'll go," Grant offered.

"Would there be flames?" Burke asked.

"No, no *flames*. The instructor sits at the controls next to me."

"Oh, then there probably isn't room for me. I was *so* looking forward to it." Burke sighed.

"I'll go," Grant repeated.

"There's room for both of you. Cooper, too," she said.

I heard my name and lunged, slurping up the ice cream splat in one lick.

Many days passed by with no sign of Lacey. In my dreams, though, Lacey and I ran together, and sometimes she was the dark-faced, short-haired brown dog I first met and sometimes she was the yellow dog with the scraggly fur I knew now.

Then one night she filled my senses so powerfully I woke up, and I still smelled her. I padded out the dog door and into the darkness. Her scent led me to the stone steps to the under barn. She was down there; her scent strong and constant.

And something was down there with her.

FIFTEEN

I cautiously descended the cement stairs to the room under the barn. Lacey had pulled out a folded blanket and was curled up on it. She wagged her tail as I approached, but otherwise did not get up to greet me. She was panting in distress and I was frightened because something was going on and I did not understand. The area at the bottom of the stairs was very dark. I strained to see what she was doing.

The air was rich with the presence of what I had assumed was another animal but now realized was coming from Lacey. I decided to examine her more closely and was shocked when she halted me with a growl, a warning from deep in her throat. She did not want me any nearer. *What was happening?*

I stood awkwardly on the steps peering at shadows, feeble light from the house providing the only illumination in the under barn. I heard Lacey licking and then, astoundingly, I heard a tiny peep, an animal sound. Lacey had just given birth to a puppy, and the dense odors told me another one was coming.

Lacey had made a den down here. I needed to protect her. I was her mate.

Yet when Burke whistled for me, I had to obey. I left reluctantly and lay on the floor in his room with my nose pointed toward the open window because his door was shut. I panted anxiously all night. When he finally let me out the next morning I dashed to the steps and could see my Lacey and several tiny puppies lying down there. She wagged when she saw me.

My affection for her in that moment was overwhelming. I realized then that I not only needed to protect my new dog family—I needed to *provide* for them. I trotted back up to the house. My human family was sitting at the table. I went to my food bowl, but the first meal of the day wasn't there yet.

Chase Dad cleared his throat. "Almost time to start bringing in the zucchini, Grant. Let's go out and check on them this morning."

"You sure, Dad?" Grant replied. "Wouldn't it be better if I stayed and helped Burke with his model city?"

There was a silence. I went to peer at my food bowl. Still nothing.

"Grant, you're just going to have to get glad in the same clothes you got mad in," Chase Dad said, "because I'm going to need you out there every minute, and even then I think some of it's going to wind up rotting. Used to be we'd have a hundred migrant workers coming up to help with the harvests, but not anymore."

I returned to my bowl, picked it up, took it to Burke's chair, and dropped it at his feet, where it clattered. Burke laughed. "You hungry, Cooper?"

I stared at him expectantly until he wheeled to fill my bowl. My dinner came from an open bag on the floor. I could stick my head in the bag, but I understood this was bad dog behavior and did my best to ignore its wonderful odors. As soon as the bowl was full, I ate greedily and quickly.

When Grant and Chase Dad left I slipped out the dog door and anxiously followed them, hoping they wouldn't go to the under barn. They were my people and harboring a secret from them made me feel like a bad dog, but I couldn't help it— something told me that part of protecting the den was keeping it hidden. The two of them went off in the direction of the fields, so I padded down the cement steps.

The scent of dinner still clung to my lips, and Lacey stood up to a chorus of squeaks from the tiny puppies pressed to her side. She nosed me and I held still, letting her inspect me. When she licked my lips, I felt a strange compelling sensation come over me, starting with my throat and working its way down to my stomach, and then everything I had just eaten came back up in a swift and neat regurgitation. Lacey began to feed.

"Cooper! Come!"

I tore myself away, racing out of the under barn and into the morning sunshine. Burke had wheeled himself out into the yard. "Where were you, Cooper?"

Lacey's scent was strong in the air and I was anxious to return to her, but my boy clearly expected me to remain with him. I finally sank down into the grass with a sigh. When I slept, I didn't dream Lacey and I were running. I dreamed we were playing with puppies.

Later Burke rolled to his room. When I abandoned him I felt like a bad dog. I creeped back to the little room behind the kitchen and seized the bag of dinner in my mouth. Then I froze: I could tell Grandma was lying down on her bed but wasn't asleep. Slinking quietly, I dragged the food bag with me through the living room. A noise came from Burke's room, was he coming out? I felt as if people were running at me shouting, "Bad dog! Bad dog!" I squeezed through the dog door, the bag catching on the frame. I walked backward, pulling, finally breaking free. Then I halted, listening guiltily. Was someone coming? My heart was making the same sort of noise as when Grant ran down the stairs.

The bag bumped on my legs as I ran across the yard and down the steps to the under barn. Lacey did not get up, but I knew she could smell what was in the bag. I did not know if the puppies could, and they didn't seem to be very interested in me at all.

I was interested in *them*, though. They made tiny peeping noises, their eyes tightly closed, each face scrunched. I stared, learning every one by sight and smell. These were my puppies.

I was back at the house when Chase Dad and Grant arrived for their dinner. I was very hungry and sat hopefully under the table.

"The new storm shelter doors come yet?" Chase Dad asked.

"No, sir," Burke replied.

"Not much of a storm shelter if it's open to the elements."

"You planning to put the new ones back on yourself, Burke?" Grant asked slyly.

"Maybe. I'll bet you I could."

Chase Dad cleared his throat. "I think it will go better if we all help. The new ones are steel and probably weigh a ton. We'll never have to replace them again."

Grant stealthily lowered his hand and gave me a tiny piece of bread. A good, attentive dog doing Sit, and that's all I got, bread.

The next several days I took up a post at the top of the stairs to the under barn. Lacey only emerged at night—she would head down to the pond to drink. I would stay and guard our puppies until she returned. Lacey smelled of delicious milk and of the tiny puppies in the den.

I was shut in Burke's room at bedtime—my nose up and

attentive—when a feral animal smell arrived on the breeze. A growl formed deep in my throat.

My boy stirred. "Go to sleep, Cooper."

Whatever it was, I knew it was out there *stalking Lacey*. I jumped off the bed and ran to the door and scratched it frantically.

"Cooper!"

I barked, my lips pulled back from my teeth. Burke sat up and blinked at me. "What's going on?"

The thought of something happening to my puppies drove me into a frenzy. I wasn't just scratching the door now, I was pounding it.

"Hey!" Burke shouted.

He swung into his chair and rolled to the door and opened it, and I shoved past him and raced across the living room and burst through the dog door. I instantly spotted the creature I'd smelled—a low, fierce-looking animal with pointed ears. It was the size of a small dog and had canine-like features. Lights popped on above the porch, flaring out into the yard.

The predator saw me and froze, and I did not hesitate, I ran right at it.

"Cooper!"

It was fast, too fast for me to catch. I bounded after it but soon lost track when it fled into the woods.

My boy was calling and I reluctantly returned to him. Chase Dad was standing with him.

"You saw the fox?" Chase Dad asked.

"Yeah. Cooper chased him off."

Chase Dad petted me. "Good dog, Cooper."

My boy called me to go to bed, but I went down the ramp and sat in the yard, watching warily for the predator to return. Burke came out and regarded me from the porch.

"What are you doing, Cooper?"

I heard my name and felt like a bad dog, but I would not leave my post. After a moment, Burke sighed. "All right," he said.

After that, I spent the nights outside in the grass. I did not smell the stalking creature again, but I was not taking the chance that it would return and go down into the under barn. Burke eventually gave up calling for me to sleep with him.

"He just wants a piece of that fox," Grant observed.

"We better hope it doesn't come back," Chase Dad replied.

"Oh, I think Cooper could handle it," Burke said.

"Right, but not without some vet bills on the other side of the fight."

One evening Grant and my boy left in Grant's truck without taking me. "It's okay, Cooper," Grandma said. "They are just going to pick up Burke's girlfriend." I did not know what she was saying to me, so I went out to lie at the top of the stairs to the under barn. When the boys returned and parked, Wenling was with them!

I sat under Wenling's chair at dinner, both to be friendly and to give her suggestive nudges with my nose. I was delighted when she figured out I was a good dog who deserved little pieces of meat, which I gently lifted from her hands.

I knew dinner was over when Burke pushed himself back from the table. "Hey, you want to maybe go for a walk?"

Walk! I trotted ahead of Burke and Wenling as they slowly strolled along the path. I glanced up ahead at the open hole to the under barn. Lacey's scent told me she was down there taking care of our puppies.

"So you said maybe you'd have your operation this year?" Wenling asked.

"I guess not." Burke sighed. "I'm still growing, which normally should be good news, but not this time. It's not like I'm trying out for basketball. I just want to get it done, you know? If it's not going to work, okay, but at least I'll *know*."

Wenling put her hand on Burke's shoulder and his chair stopped. "It will work, Burke. I know it."

"Thanks."

They hugged, then pushed their faces together. I sighed—they seemed to be doing that a lot, lately. Finally, after a long wait, they began moving again.

"Hey, what's that?"

"It's the storm cellar. You know, for tornadoes, zombies, like that."

They turned in the direction of the under barn. I followed, anxious. I both wanted them to find the puppies and *not* to find the puppies.

"Tornadoes? We don't get tornadoes in *Michigan*," Wenling challenged.

"Oh yeah we do! What about Flint-Beecher? It was like the deadliest tornado in U.S. history until there was this one in Joplin, Missouri."

"So is that what you do all day, watch the weather channel?"

Burke laughed. "I did a report about Michigan tornadoes in seventh grade. We're not Kansas, but we're competitive."

"Okay, good, as long as we're in the tornado Olympics."

My boy laughed again. Wenling, I realized, made him happy.

"So what's down there?" she asked.

"Like, water, canned goods, a woodstove. I mean it really is so that if you had to spend a couple days there you could, like if there was a nuclear attack."

"Or zombie invasion. Can I go down there?"

Burke wheeled right up to the top of the steps. I panted anxiously, afraid for what might happen next. I was acutely aware of the empty dog food bag, of each of my puppies, of Lacey. She was tense, too, I could sense her staring up at us.

"Sure. There's a light at the bottom, just pull the string."

"There are no rats or anything, are there? Or *snakes*?"

"No, of course not."

"Promise?"

"Just go."

Wenling descended the steps, moving slowly, her hand brushing the wall. I followed helplessly. I thought when her scent flooded the small room that Lacey would growl, but instead, the moment a bright light filled the space, Lacey began wagging her tail, her little puppies squealing.

"Oh my God!" Wenling gasped.

SIXTEEN

Burke started at Wenling's exclamation. I heard his chair squeak as he leaned forward. "What is it? What's wrong?"

"There's a mother dog with little puppies down here!"

"You're kidding!"

I knew what would happen: Wenling would approach and Lacey would growl. But Wenling put her hand out and Lacey licked it—of *course* Lacey licked it! Wenling was her person! "You're a sweet mommy dog."

"Cooper! Come!"

I did Assist. This time Lacey did growl as we approached the bottom step. Wenling held up a hand. "Don't come any closer, she's getting upset. She might've been abused by a man at some point."

Burke tugged and I stopped on the steps. "Okay. Wow. This is really cool."

Wenling turned and looked at him. "Sure. Except this is a stray dog. Look at her, she's had a rough life. No collar. And now she's down here in a storm cellar because she didn't have anywhere to go."

"Sorry."

Lacey was no longer growling, but she was staring stonily at Burke, who had braced against me to sit. I nuzzled him to show her he posed no danger, but her whole posture remained rigid.

"You know what, Wenling?"

"What?"

"These puppies look a lot like *Cooper*."

"Like Cooper," Wenling repeated.

"Yeah."

"But that's not possible, right? You had Cooper neutered."

They kept saying my name, but I could not tell if I was a good dog or a bad dog. I wagged my tail hopefully.

"Burke? You had him *neutered*."

"No, in fact, we didn't. We couldn't afford it at the time. We're not robo-farmers."

Wenling shook her head. "I'm going to ignore that. So we need to call animal rescue and have them come out. And we need to give her food and water in the meantime."

Wenling returned to the house and brought out a bowl of food and a dish of water and Lacey wagged and ate hungrily while the puppies crawled around on their blanket, calling for their mother. I cautiously approached and this time Lacey let me sniff them—I think being back with Wenling made her feel safer. I nuzzled them, drinking in their scents, eventually sprawling out so that I could be with them on the floor of the under barn. Did they understand that I was their father? They squirmed and squealed and I wagged, certain they must. Lacey watched, and the love I felt for her flowed to these little dogs, my puppies.

"You're a good dog. Good mommy for your puppies," Wenling praised. I wondered if she knew this was Lacey. Humans can do amazing things, but they don't always understand what is going on with dogs.

Over the next several days, everyone spent time at the top of the stairs, watching the puppies. When Wenling was there, Lacey would let Grant come down the steps without growling at him, and when Wenling handed him a puppy, Lacey didn't object.

Grant held the little pup to his face and kissed its nose. "This one has Cooper's face! Have you thought of any names for them yet?"

"I thought the rescue organization should do that."

Grant nodded. "Don't name the chickens."

"Exactly. If I gave them their own identities it might be a lot harder to say goodbye, even though it is best that they all go to forever homes. I did name the mother, though. Lulu. Right, Lulu?" Wenling reached out and stroked Lacey's head.

"Are you going to keep one?"

"No. My father says not."

"Hey, could I play with one?" Burke called down. Wenling took him a male puppy, placing it in his lap.

"What about when you adopted your first dog? The one the snake got? He let you have her," Grant said when she returned.

"Lacey," Wenling affirmed. Both Lacey and I whipped our heads up and stared at her. Wenling did know! Of course, why would I think she wouldn't? Lacey and Wenling belonged to-gether. "Right, well, I think getting me a puppy was because when I was that age I could do no wrong in his eyes. Now our relationship is . . . complicated. He feels like saying 'no' to a dog is reestablishing control or something. My mom fights with him about it a lot." She stepped forward and lowered her voice. "Dad's not happy I'm going out with Burke. He thinks I should date someone more . . ." She waved her hand in front of her face.

"Chinese?"

Wenling glanced up at Burke, keeping her voice a murmur. "Exactly."

Grant laughed. "Here? Has he looked around at the local populace?"

"I'm terrified that a Chinese family will move to town and they'll have a son and my dad will try to make me marry him, even if the guy is a psychopath."

"What are you guys talking about? I can't hear you," Burke complained.

Wenling called up to him, "I just figured out you're not Chinese."

"What?" Burke responded in a voice that sounded aggravated. I looked up at him, concerned, but he wasn't acting upset. "Come on, Grant, why did you have to tell her?"

Everyone laughed. Wenling traded puppies with Grant. "I know there are too many dogs on the planet already, but I can't help but love them, especially the ones who look like Cooper," she said. I wagged.

"You have such a big heart." Grant made his voice quiet. "I don't think Burke knows how lucky he is to have you."

Wenling blinked at him. "What do you mean?"

Lacey and I both reacted to the sudden rise in tension in the two humans. Grant stepped closer. "I have been trying to figure out how to tell you and I just have to say it. I can't hold it back anymore."

"Hold back *what*?"

"You really don't know? You can't see it every time I look at you? I'm in love with you, Wenling."

Wenling took a deep, shuddering breath. Lacey sat up, nuzzling her hand.

"It just happened, okay?" Grant continued urgently. "I know it's wrong. I know I shouldn't feel this way. But I have, I have for a long time, and sometimes when you're looking at me I think you feel the same way, and it's been so hard. . . ."

"Hey, if we're going to hang here, I'll have Cooper help me down," Burke offered.

Wenling was staring at Grant. "No, I have to go," she called up. She put her puppies down and Lacey lowered her head to them.

"Wenling," he whispered plaintively.

When he reached for her she turned away and bounded up the stairs.

"Wenling?" Burke said.

"I have to go!" she replied. I climbed the stairs to be with Burke. I did not understand any of this.

Many days later Burke knelt and kissed me and said, "I'm going to the doctor. You'll be okay, Cooper." I wagged because he said "Cooper." Then he and Grandma drove away and I watched them go, his scent drifting away from me. I did not understand why he was leaving, but I didn't try to chase after him because I needed to stay near Lacey and our puppies. When I trotted over to check on them, Wenling was in the under barn! She had recently taken to bringing meat treats for Lacey and me, a development I regarded most favorably. We played with the puppies for a while, but we climbed back out when a big van pulled into the driveway.

A man and a girl a little younger than Burke were getting out and I was astounded: it was the very first girl I ever met, Ava, and her father, Sam Dad! Her light hair was shorter and she was taller, but everything else about her was the same. I ecstatically ran to them, jumping up, whimpering. Were they going to live on the farm with Grant and Burke and Lacey and the puppies? I couldn't think of anything that would make me happier!

"Hello, you!" Ava greeted, kneeling so I could kiss her. I plowed into her and she fell on her back, laughing.

"That's Cooper," Wenling advised, coming up behind me.

Ava turned her head from side to side, sputtering, so that I could lick her entire face. "Cooper!"

I was so excited I ran circles around them. They all laughed. "I'm Sam Marks and this is my daughter, Ava," Sam Dad said.

"I'm Wenling Zhang. The puppies are in the storm shelter. I'll take you over—the mother doesn't warm up to strangers very easily."

Ava reached down to pet me. "Is Cooper the father?"

"Oh yes. There's no doubt about that, once you see them."

We were walking toward the under barn. I was excited for Lacey to see that Ava and Sam Dad were here!

"Thanks for coming all this way," Wenling said.

Sam Dad shrugged. "It's no bother. We're up here twice a week with the rescue-mobile anyway. These rural areas have more of a problem than Grand Rapids. In fact, we're opening a branch office up here soon." He cleared his throat. "So, we will spay the mother, of course."

"Her name is Lulu."

"Good. We'll spay Lulu, and, even though he's not a stray, we could also pay to fix Cooper if you'd like. Our mission isn't just to rescue animals, it's to try to make rescue unnecessary. In fact, we never adopt out animals anymore without commitments from the new families to spay and neuter. We learned our lesson on that one."

Wenling regarded him thoughtfully. "Cooper's not my dog, he's my friend's dog. But I can speak to him. I'm sure he'll agree."

They were saying my name a lot. I wondered if I should go get the squeaky toy.

As I assumed, Lacey remembered Ava, too! It was obvious from the way Lacey brightened, wagging, when Ava knelt, offering a palm to Lacey. "These are the cutest puppies ever! Hello, Lulu. Good dog."

Sam Dad was smiling as he watched the puppies tackle Ava. "Mom's got terrier for sure, also maybe . . . shepherd?"

Wenling shrugged. "Lulu just came out of nowhere. It's going to be hard to say goodbye to her and these pups, but I know you'll find them wonderful homes."

Sam Dad nodded. "That's the paradox of rescue. We bring together such happy families, but we'd rather it wasn't necessary. How did you hear about Hope's Rescue?"

Wenling grinned. "The Trevinos adopted Cooper from you. I got a dog from you, too. Lacey."

Lacey had been loving Ava but now, hearing her name, she went to Wenling and nosed her hand.

Ava smiled. "I'm sorry I didn't remember."

"You were pretty young, Ava," Sam Dad observed.

Ava shrugged. "I'm twelve."

"I turn fifteen in September," Wenling replied.

"So is Lacey here?"

Wenling knelt to pet Lacey and shook her head mournfully. "Lacey was bitten by a northern rattlesnake and died."

Ava put a hand to her mouth. "Oh no!"

Sam Dad looked startled. "Here? A massasauga? I thought they were basically extinct."

Wenling smiled sadly. "It was a freak thing."

They were all silent for a moment. Lacey waded into her pile of pups and collapsed.

"We'll find a good home for the mother, too, of course," Sam Dad finally said.

My hopes that Sam Dad and Ava had come to stay were soon dashed: with a puppy under each arm, they returned to their van—the same one I had once ridden in, with stacks of dog cages inside. Lacey pursued them anxiously, her nose in the air. She followed her brood right into a cage in the back of the van, but when I tried to join them Wenling restrained me with a hand. "Stay, Cooper."

Stay? I did not understand this at all. I watched helplessly as the rest of the puppies were placed in the van. From where I sat I could just see Lacey inside her cage, and she was staring at me in dismay. I felt like a bad dog, because I couldn't help her. Then Ava and Sam Dad drove away, the scent of Lacey trailing after them. Wenling patted my head. "It's okay, Cooper."

I went back to the cement stairs and descended them to the under barn. Though the whole area was redolent with Lacey and my puppies, they were gone. I put my nose to their blanket. It was still warm. I breathed in deeply, separating out each individual scent, remembering my puppies climbing on me and nipping at my jowls. I knew people could take away my dog family if they wanted, but why did they have to?

I didn't leave the under barn when I heard Burke and Grandma return. I stayed curled up on my puppy blanket until Burke called me for dinner.

Not long after that I went to the vet and had a long, dreamless nap. When I came home I was very itchy between my legs but could do nothing about it because of a heavy, stiff collar that restricted my movements. By the time I got the collar off, the itch had gone away. I felt different, now—not bad, just different, and the stubble of hair between my legs was rough on my tongue.

I was sad when Chase Dad and Grant lowered heavy metal doors over the steps to the under barn.

Would I ever see Lacey and my pups again?

Grant and Burke started saying the word "school" again, but we never went back to do School, we just returned to Grant's building. There was not much for me to do but nap, except when a bell would sound and all the people would go crazy, running out into the hall and dashing around and shouting and slamming doors, and then we'd be in a new room and everyone would be quiet again. There was nothing in any of this activity that a dog could comprehend, but I had fun just the same.

I was always at Burke's side but would often smell Wenling and Grant and see them in the halls. My boy had many friends and they were all very nice to me. "You can pet him, but please don't give him any treats," Burke often said. Yet despite saying the word "treats" over and over, no one ever gave me any.

I noticed how stiffly Wenling and Grant spoke to each other, if they spoke at all. There was an odd, unsettled feeling passing between them, and I never encountered them alone with each other.

One afternoon, when the sun was warm in the sky, a car full of girls around Burke's age came over and they sat on the porch and talked and laughed and gave me treats—a perfect day! The girls reeked with sweetness and flowers and musk. One of them had a scent on her clothes that I instantly recognized as belonging to the mystery creatures that lived in barns and ran from me in such an unfriendly fashion.

Grant and Chase Dad emerged from the direction of the fields and I ran to greet them, wagging. Their hands were rich with traces of soil.

"Hi, Grant!" several girls called, waving. "Hello, Mr. Trevino."

Both of them came up and everyone talked for a little while. "Leaves are just starting to turn," Chase Dad finally said, passing into the house. Grant remained behind.

"And where's Wenling today?" Grant asked his brother.

Everyone went quiet and looked at Burke. He frowned, and I could feel that he was uncomfortable. I went to nose his hand in a reminder that the best way to cheer up is to toss a dog a chicken treat.

"We heard you guys broke up," a girl said.

Grant cocked his head. "Oh?"

"Well," Burke said.

"So sorry, Burke," another girl said.

Burke looked down in his lap for a moment. "It's not really . . . we had a fight. It's not like we've broken up."

"Oh, okay," a girl said.

Grinning, Grant went into the house. Shortly after that, the girls departed, which meant all treats stopped. I followed Burke as he wheeled into the kitchen. "Thanks, for that, Grant," he said flatly. "It wasn't really the moment I wanted to talk about Wenling, you know?"

Grant held up his hands. "Sorry, you don't keep me posted on your celebrity love life."

"You know what I mean."

"What I know is that you've peaked, brother."

"Peaked?"

"As in, you're only a sophomore and you're already with the best-looking girlfriend you're ever going to have in your life. After this it's all downhill for you."

"You do know you're adopted, right?"

Not long after that, Burke and I were down at the pond for duck patrol. Wenling came over on her bicycle and Burke said

"I'm sorry" over and over and sounded sad, so I brought him a stick. Eventually Wenling hugged him and they pressed their lips on each other in a long kiss. I chewed the stick into bits.

Grandma sometimes drove us to Wenling's house and left us there, but she always came back later. One such night I sat in the backseat with my nose up, smelling cheese in the air, though no one was eating and no one gave me any. It seemed to be coming from Grandma's hair. The car stopped and I did Assist and Steady. "See you in a while!" Burke called

I did Assist on the front steps and Burke knocked on the door. A loud shout, a man's voice, came from within the house, and a moment later a woman's angry yell answered it. I gazed at my boy anxiously.

Wenling opened the door. She was crying.

"My God, Wenling, what's going on?" Burke asked her.

SEVENTEEN

Wenling wiped at her eyes. "Come in," she invited. I gave her hand a lick, tasting salt. "My parents are fighting over me."

"What? Why?" I did Assist and Steady so Burke could climb into his chair.

"My dad says he would never allow me to apply to the Air Force Academy. He says it is out of the question, that he doesn't want me going away to college, he wants me to live at home and go to school," she said. She held thin paper to her face.

"At home? Around here there's just community college," Burke objected.

The yelling continued, and I pressed up against Wenling's legs, wishing we could leave this angry place.

"I know, but he thinks I should be here to 'take care' of them. Now she's saying, she's saying we'll leave him. Oh Burke!" Wenling's voice was anguished. I raised my paw, touching her leg. "She says she'll move with me, get a job, and put me through school."

"I'm really sorry. Do you want us to go, Wenling?"

"God, no." Wenling knelt and threw her arms around me and I leaned into her, grateful to be able to be the dog she needed.

There was a loud bang that I recognized as the sound the door makes when it swings shut with force, and then the yelling stopped. Burke and Wenling sat in the backyard, and I sat with them, being a good dog, until eventually Wenling's sadness left.

Winter was approaching and both the air and the grasses were moist on a day Grant took us for a car ride.

Alone in the backseat, I pressed my nose to the partially opened window, delightedly breathing in the wet leaves that were lying pressed to the ground. I wagged when we passed the goat ranch, and inhaled deeply when we drove over a river. I would gladly have jumped into that water, but instead we traveled to a flat, hard place with small buildings and strange cars tied to the ground.

Wenling was there! I did Steady as Grant held the chair for Burke but then was allowed to dash to her and greet her properly, licking her face when she bent down to me. She stood up, grinning.

"Are you sure you want to do this? Wouldn't it be more fun to eat some cake or something?" Burke asked as she reached to hug him.

She laughed. "I'm sure."

She faced Grant and there was a moment of stiff awkwardness, and then he stepped forward with his arms extended. "Okay, hi, Wenling," he said quietly. They held each other for a moment, then broke apart and both glanced down at Burke, for some reason.

Wenling smiled. "So, you guys ready for this?"

Burke peered at the sky. "It's a good day to die," he noted dryly.

"Oh," replied Wenling, "you'll be perfectly safe unless we decide to throw you out of the airplane because of your comments."

"Or even if you don't say anything, I'd be up for that," Grant offered.

We wheeled over to a car and met a nice woman named Elizabeth. She briefly gripped hands with Grant and Burke and then held out her palms for me to sniff. The boys' scents were intermingled with hers.

The inside of the car was small, and Burke left his chair parked outside on the ground. Elizabeth and Wenling sat up front and I sat in back on the floor between the boys' seats. When the car started it was very loud. I wagged because I was unsure what was happening.

"You've done this before, right?" Burke asked. I sensed his nervousness and nosed his hand.

Wenling and Elizabeth smiled at each other. "Never!" Wenling shouted above the noise.

With a lurch, the car roared and I felt us starting to move. An odd, heavy sensation ran through my stomach, reminding me of a time long ago when I was with my mother in the metal den and she had her nails extended to keep from sliding. Burke drew in a sharp breath. "How about if we keep it maybe ten feet off the ground?" he asked loudly.

Grant was grinning. "I didn't realize you would be doing it all!" he yelled. "I thought Elizabeth would fly and you would just observe."

"I can't solo yet but as long as I am with my flight instructor I am allowed to fly the plane," Wenling advised above the rumble.

"I see Grandpa telling me to move into the light!" Burke called.

It was a boring car ride. Nobody opened a window, and the oily smells were not very interesting. When the noise lessened somewhat, I felt Burke's anxiety loosen its grip and his hand relaxed on my fur.

"Look," he said. "You can see how the rivers are formed by little streams and how the lakes all have small creeks flowing into them. The whole hydraulic system is laid out as if someone designed it."

"Yeah," Grant agreed, "and you can see how the robo-farms are taking over the entire county."

I slept, vibrating, but jerked awake when the car hit something and then stopped. We climbed out and Burke lay on the ground and kissed it.

"Very funny," Wenling said.

"Wenling, that was amazing. You are amazing," Grant told her.

She lowered her eyes. "Thanks."

"I mean it."

Burke asked me to do Assist. The car ride back home was much better because the window was down and I saw a horse running and smelled goats.

Very often in the evenings I would stay home with Grandma and Chase Dad and Grant would drive away with Burke sitting next to him. When they returned, both boys always smelled like Wenling, but the fragrance was much stronger on Burke.

I always paced and passed in and out of the dog door while Burke was gone, until Chase Dad spoke to me sternly. I didn't know what he was saying, but it seemed clear he didn't understand that Burke needed to come home. So I was thrilled when, one night, I went along for the ride! We picked up Wenling and drove to a building and talked to a man who had been standing in a doorway waiting for us. He wore a hat and smelled like burning leaves.

"Any one of you twenty-one years old?" the man asked.

Grant and Burke and Wenling glanced at one another.

"Thought not," the man said.

"I'm seventeen," Grant volunteered.

"Cooper is twenty-one!" Burke said brightly. I wagged.

The man in the door had a stick in his mouth that he now took out and held between two fingers. It was such a tiny stick that if he threw it I decided I wouldn't even bother to go try to pick it up. "Sorry, kids, we got a policy."

"Our dad is Chase Trevino," Burke said. "We just want to hear him play."

The man eyed us silently for a moment. "We got a manager's office upstairs with an open window, but I don't know how you'd get up there," he drawled. He gestured with his little stick toward Burke's chair.

"I can get up there if Cooper helps," Burke assured him. I wagged.

I did Assist up some very narrow and steep steps, Grant carrying the chair behind us, and then we were in a small room. It was noisy because people were talking in big voices and then it became even noisier, the building filled with such strong vibrations that the walls hummed. Wenling and Grant started jumping around and Burke was nodding his head. I yawned, wondering if this was my new life: I would go with Burke and Wenling and Grant to small places and then it would be very loud. Would Elizabeth arrive next?

"He's really great!" Grant exclaimed with a grin.

Though I could sense that everyone was excited, as far as I was concerned this was about as interesting as watching ducks swim around in the pond. I eventually sprawled myself out in front of Burke's chair and fell asleep.

Assist down those stairs was difficult, but I moved very slowly and then did Steady so Burke could slide into his chair. I started wagging because I smelled Chase Dad, and a moment later he was standing in front of us.

"I'm a little surprised to see you boys here. Hello, Wenling." He reached down to pet me and I licked his hand, tasting salt and cheese.

"We wanted to hear you play, Dad," Burke explained.

"You are really good," Wenling said. "The whole band is."

Chase Dad cocked his head. "Sneaking around is never the way to go about being an honest adult," he finally said. "You could have asked me."

"We knew you would say no," Burke objected.

"It was my idea, Dad," Grant offered.

He nodded. "If I had said no, you'd be in trouble, so you didn't ask. You parse your arguments the way you build your models, Burke. Be careful where that takes you." He looked at Grant and Wenling. "I hope we didn't ruin music for you."

There had been a tension between the humans that I only noticed now, as it left. They all chuckled. "I need to get back up there for another set. Head on home and I'll catch up," Chase Dad said.

We left but Chase Dad remained. Out on the sidewalk, Burke encountered some people whose smells I recognized from being in Grant's building. Wenling and Grant went and sat in the car while Burke talked and laughed with his friends. I wagged, but other than a few halfhearted pats on my head nobody paid any attention to me and none of them had treats in their pockets. Bored, I went to the car door and Grant opened it for me without otherwise paying attention. He was twisted and facing Wenling in the seat next to him.

"How could you even suggest such a thing?" Grant was asking. He seemed upset. I wagged uncertainly.

"She's nice," Wenling responded.

"No, I mean how could *you* say it, when I told you how I feel about you? For you to try to fix me up with one of your friends is like spitting in my face."

Grant turned and faced the front and didn't react when Wenling reached out and lightly touched his arm. He seemed tense and angry and moved briskly to put Burke's chair in the trunk when I was allowed to do Steady.

Burke ran his hand down my back and I wagged.

Grant started the car. "You are always leaving me alone with your girlfriend," he observed tightly. "Maybe someday we will forget and drive off without you."

No one said anything and I could sense that Wenling was tense all the way to her house, where she slipped out, opened the back door to give me a hug, and also hugged Burke.

"You know what I wish?" Burke said as we drove off. "I wish that just once Dad wouldn't make a lesson about everything. If he was pissed, okay, but instead I get a moral lecture."

"This whole thing, like if we see him playing in his band, we'll think he's going to move away, like Mom? Is that it?" Grant asked Burke.

"It's like he's ashamed. Like if we see him having fun, it means he's a bad father. Or bad farmer. Or something," Burke replied.

"It's psycho," Grant said hotly.

"So says the man who keeps trying to kill his brother," Burke observed.

Grant made a disgusted noise.

The next morning was one of those days when we didn't go to Grant's building. Wenling came over and she and Burke went down to the dock. "Was your dad mad?" Wenling asked.

"He's a hard person to figure out sometimes. Most of the time.

He has this code of conduct—it's all bound up with being our father, and running the farm, and my mom leaving."

They were silent for a while. "So was it weird? Going out as just friends, last night," she asked softly.

"Did *you* think it was weird?"

They were silent some more. A duck flew in from overhead and landed with a splash right in front of me. I eased to the end of the dock and glared at it.

"No, actually I thought it was fun," Wenling said. "I mean it doesn't feel much different being broken up than when we were dating."

"You and me and Grant and Cooper, like any other night," Burke agreed.

They smiled at each other, but I could tell that Wenling was sad.

On the way up from the pond, I saw the slinky barn animal! I dashed toward it, and it ran into the barn where I knew I could catch it. Except when I burst in the open door, I couldn't find the thing. My nose told me it was up above me somewhere, up where Chase Dad and Grant sometimes climbed up. Why didn't it want to play with me?

When we arrived back at the house, Chase Dad and Grandma were in the living room, sitting next to each other with tense postures. I wagged, not sure why they were afraid. Burke and Wenling stopped in the middle of the room. Burke was staring. "What's going on?"

Grant came down the stairs and halted. "Hi, Wenling."

"Hi, Grant."

He looked at everyone. "What happened?"

Chase Dad held up a hand. "It's not bad. No, just the opposite. Dr. Moore called. He's happy with what he's seen in your latest X-rays, Burke."

Wenling gasped. I noticed Grandma was crying and went to her.

"So . . . ," Burke said slowly.

"It's set for Christmas break. You're going to have your operation, son."

EIGHTEEN

Grant was the first to react. "So you're fifteen and you're as tall as you're ever going to be," he snorted.

Chase Dad frowned. "Really, Grant? That's all you've got to say?"

Grant's grin dropped. He gave Wenling a look, and then glanced away.

"It is true?" Burke asked softly.

"Is what true? What Grant said? No. You could still grow a touch. I guess they just feel you've mostly reached adult size. You're taller than I am, Burke."

Burke licked his lips. "No, I mean, that I am going to have my surgery. Is it really true?"

We had many nights after that when Burke did not sleep much. I sensed he was anxious and afraid and did my best to do Steady in bed, lying there next to him and offering him all the support I could give.

"What if it doesn't work, Cooper?" he whispered to me in the dark.

I licked his hand.

I was perplexed when Chase Dad and Grant moved the couch out of the living room and in its place put in an upright structure that had rails like the ones Grandma held when she went up the stairs, except these didn't slant up or down. I was very suspicious of the thing. It reminded me of the ladder lying on the floor of the barn, except there were no rungs and it was almost as high as Grant's shoulders. In the corner they pulled and twisted on a machine with cables and lead plates until, panting, they stood back and looked at it. Grant sat on a low chair in front of the machine and pushed pedals and the metal plates glided up and down, clanging. I sniffed it and found it utterly unremarkable except for the fact that my bed was now across the room and the couch was out in the barn. Whatever they were doing, they were certainly causing the dog of the house a great inconvenience, though I later discovered I could lie on the couch in its new location and no one told me to do Off.

Not long after the machine displaced my dog bed, everyone left in the morning and I stayed behind and felt abandoned. I restlessly crawled in and out of the dog door, leaving footprints and marks in the snow. I paced and sniffed my dog bowl, and eventually I wound up lying on the couch in the barn. I missed Lacey.

When the family returned I ran out to greet them, wagging and jumping up, hoping they wouldn't find out about the couch. Then I realized Burke wasn't with them.

I slept upstairs on Grant's bed the next several nights but kept going into Burke's room to see if he had returned. I remembered Lacey and the puppies being taken away from me by Ava and Sam

Dad. Was this what had happened with Burke? Would I never see him again?

"Hey, Cooper. Hey," Grant whispered to me in the darkness. "I know you're worried. He'll be home soon, I promise." Grant's hands on my fur was comforting, but I needed my boy back. "God, I hope it worked," he muttered. He wasn't sleeping well, either. Maybe we *both* needed Burke!

Grandma and Chase Dad spent a lot of time speaking quietly, with Grant out of the room.

"I didn't understand there would be so much pain," Grandma lamented. I sensed her sadness and fear, and went to her chair and lay at her feet.

"His leg muscles have never communicated with his brain before, and they've got a lot of things to say. It's overwhelming his nervous system," Chase Dad observed. "They said it is normal, to be expected. They don't want to give him too much in the way of painkillers because they don't want to interfere with his nerves establishing a connection."

"He's so brave," Grandma said. "You can see in his face how much it hurts him."

Grandma left every day but was always home in time for dinner. I could smell Burke on her sleeves, and it occurred to me that perhaps she was able to find him, so the next time she walked to her car I tried to get in with her, but she ordered me out. I knew, though, that his scent meant he was not like Lacey after the snake, not like Judy the old goat in the yard. He was out there somewhere. I paced the house, panting, imagining he might be at the base of some stairs, needing Assist.

"They gave Burke a sponge bath today, thank God," Grandma told Chase Dad at dinner, while they were having fish. I like chicken better. Also beef. But I will eat fish if offered and was sitting under Grandma's chair.

Grant had left with some friends. Now I was anxious *he* wouldn't come back. I realized that over time I had developed a real longing to have all the people I cared about—Ava, Sam Dad, and Wenling included—together here, where I could keep an eye on them.

Chase Dad was laughing. "He's full on teenage boy, that's for sure. I don't know why they can't smell themselves."

Grandma was laughing, too. I wagged at all the mirth, but sometimes even though people are really happy they don't give fish to a dog.

Then there was a long pause before Chase Dad spoke again. "Any improvement? Progress?"

"Not yet. Chase, I'm worried it didn't work," Grandma replied.

"You're worried?" Chase Dad asked. *"I'm scared to death."*

A moment later Grandma fled to her bedroom and I followed. I put a paw on her leg, but she did not stop crying for some time.

Not too many days after that I was napping on the floor but jerked awake when I heard a car door.

"Cooper!"

Burke. I bolted through the dog door and ran to him, sobbing. He was sitting in his chair and I jumped right into his lap. "Cooper!" He was laughing and sputtering as I licked his face. My boy was home! "Down! Stop!"

I could barely do Pull to help his chair in the snow, I was so excited. Wenling came over and everyone sat in the living room to talk, and then Chase Dad and Grant went out to the barn. Grandma made a foul-smelling drink. "Do you want green tea too, Burke?" she asked.

"Sure."

"So what do the doctors say?" Wenling asked Burke as Grandma handed him a cup of the liquid. I have eaten a lot of things in my life, but I could barely stand to be in the same room with that steaming cup, which was billowing vile odors into the air.

"I guess it's going to take a lot longer. I mean, I knew I wouldn't jump out of bed and start playing basketball, but I thought I'd be able to at least move my feet. I have sensation, though. Like, my legs sort of itch, a burning itch. It's a lot better than it was just a few days ago—I had the worst cramps you can imagine."

"I'm so sorry."

"Oh no. *I can feel my legs*, Wenling. Not the way I can feel my arms, but there's *something*. The neurosurgeon told me everything went fine. I start PT tomorrow."

"When are you coming back to school?"

"When I can walk in that front door."

Wenling frowned. "Okay, but, you're already a week behind. What happens if you miss too much of second semester? You won't be able to graduate with our class."

"So I'll repeat a sophomore semester in the fall. I don't actually care about when I graduate. Being older has always worked out for Grant," Burke replied. He took a sip from his cup. "Oh my God, you drink this stuff?"

Every day after that a man named Hank came to see me and to play with Burke. I liked him. He had clean-smelling hands and his hair wasn't on top of his head, it was under his chin. He carried the scent of several different dogs with him. Hank would hold Burke's feet and tell him to *push*. I didn't know what that meant and apparently neither did Burke, because he didn't do anything. "There you go! There you go!" Hank would say. "See that? I felt that."

"Nothing happened, Hank," Burke replied dismally.

"What are you talking about? You practically punted me across the room. We're going to have to build some goal posts in here."

We also started spending time on the strange wooden contraption. Burke would stand, holding the wooden railings, and Hank would stand behind him and Burke would twitch his feet a little. What was he doing?

Hank clapped his hands. "Look at you dance! You're a dancing fool."

"Stop lying to me, Hank!" Burke snapped.

Sometimes Grandma would watch. "I don't understand why I'm not making any progress. Why can't I walk?" Burke complained to her one day after Hank left.

"They said it would take time, honey," Grandma said.

"No! It's been more than two months. They told me I would be able to take steps after sixty days, but I can't even move my feet!" The anguish in Burke's voice made me whimper.

"Cooper knows you're upset. You are such a wonderful dog, Cooper," Grandma told me.

Whatever had happened, Burke was not the same person. "Sit, Cooper! Stay!" he told me harshly when Hank was not there and he was struggling to climb up onto the living room ladder. I had been trying to do Assist, why wouldn't he let me help him? One time he lay facedown and slammed his fist on the floor. Grandma came to the doorway but didn't say anything. I went to her, wagging, seeking comfort. She stroked my ears.

I felt so little happiness in the house, even as the days grew warmer and noisy birds fluttered in the trees. We had a dinner and everyone said "happy birthday" to Grant, something I had come to associate with an intoxicating sweetness in the air, flowing from the table and into my nose. Though I'd never had an opportunity to sample whatever it was, I certainly was on hand to take advantage of any offers. That day I sat and stared with all the intensity I could muster, but no one correctly interpreted my expression.

"Pretty wet start to the summer," Chase Dad said into a quiet moment.

"Oh my God, Dad, I knew you were going to say that!" Grant howled. "You say it every time I have a birthday!"

Everyone was laughing until Burke spoke. "I told myself a long time ago that the day Grant turned eighteen I would race him out to the apple orchard and beat him. I can't even stand up."

"Burke," Grandma whispered. I knew my boy needed me and went and put my head in his lap.

"We need to face it," he continued, not stroking me though I was right there. "Something went wrong. I'm never getting out of this chair."

NINETEEN

The gusts of sadness off my human family were so pronounced, I felt a whine building inside of me.

"No, man, that can't be right," Grant pleaded.

"Happy birthday," Burke replied. He wheeled into his room
and climbed into his bed, where he had been spending so much
time, lately. I put my head on his chest. From the table I could
still breathe in the thick sweetness, but right now Burke needed
his dog.

That summer Wenling didn't come to visit me as often as I
would have liked. When she did, Grant was always out in the
fields. I was never able to find any trace of Lacey or any other
dog clinging to her.

On a morning when Hank didn't come but Wenling did, Burke
was sitting in the chair in front of the device with the metal cables. "How is it going?" she asked.

"It's *not* going. I haven't budged anything. School starts in two weeks and I'll still be in my chair," he responded grimly. "I can't even wiggle my toes." Burke slapped his thigh and I jerked, startled.

"Will you go back to school anyway?" Wenling asked.

"I don't know. Why bother?"

Wenling sighed. "Well, I have news. You know I turn sixteen September fifteenth?"

"Yeah?"

"That will be the day I take my solo flight test. Can you believe it?"

"That's great," Burke muttered. I looked back and forth between them, feeling dark currents of emotions from both of them.

"Burke, is there anything I can do?"

"Like what?"

"I don't know, Burke, that's why I'm asking you."

"I'm fine."

"I have to go."

Burke shrugged his shoulders. "Bye."

Wenling left the house. I could tell my boy was very angry and wasn't sure if I was a good dog, so I followed Wenling outside and over to where her bicycle lay in the grass. It had brought so many foreign odors with it that I felt compelled to lift my leg on a shrub nearby. Grant came out of the barn.

"Hey, Wenling! How have you been?"

"Hi."

"You okay?"

She ran a hand through her black hair. "Just . . . yes, I've been fine."

"You leaving?"

"Thought I would."

"Because my dad asked me if I knew anyone who would like

to earn some money helping to harvest the next crop of zucchini. This hot weather, they get too big in like two days. So I asked around, but of course no one wanted to do it. 'Cause, you know, it's *work*."

Wenling laughed. "So I'm not exactly your first choice."

"I didn't say that."

She laughed again. "No, you did say that. But okay. Why not."

Grant brightened. "Really?"

I followed her and Grant out to the fields. Chase Dad wasn't there. Grant handed her a bucket. "Okay, so, you know how to do this? You look under the leaves, 'cause the little suckers are hiding. Anything longer than five inches, you cut at the stem. Here's a knife."

"Where's your dad?"

"He's working the apple orchard today. So the zucchini crop is all mine. Lucky me. The zucchini king."

Wenling laughed. "I was already impressed you were a big senior, but *king*? I'll have to remember to curtsy."

They played with leaves and stalks, bent over, their heads almost touching. They filled buckets with plants and emptied the buckets into boxes and then did it again. They were talking and laughing. I did not understand how what they were doing could make anyone happy enough to laugh. I picked up the scent of a rabbit and tracked it a little bit, but it probably saw me coming and ran away.

"Cooper! Don't go too far," Wenling called. I trotted back to them.

"Oh, he never strays. He's a good dog."

I wagged at "good dog."

"Let's take a break," Grant suggested. They went to a picnic table and sat next to each other. The table was very old and tilted to one side. Grant handed Wenling a bottle. "Just water, sorry."

"I had expected champagne."

He laughed. "So, my brother still pretty crabby?"

"He's not the same Burke."

"Yeah."

I squeezed in under the table to be in position for when some food made an appearance.

"Hey," Grant exclaimed. "Do you remember the first time we met?"

Wenling frowned. "No, not really."

"Sure you do. The pet adoption. I was there when we got Cooper."

I looked at him at the sound of my name.

Wenling smiled. "I was mostly about adopting a dog, that day. Sorry."

"I probably didn't make that big of an impression. The dorky older brother."

"Oh no, don't say that. I never think of you as *older*. Just dorky."

Grant laughed softly. "There you go. That's the thing about you and Burke. You both have such quick wits. My wit is mostly half."

Wenling slapped a hand over her mouth. "Oh my God! Grant tells a joke!"

"Stop it. I tell jokes, I'm just conscious how lame they must sound to you. Because you're so good at it. You're good at everything."

"*That's* not true."

Though they were still seated at the table, the lack of food smells convinced me I had been misled. I flopped down on my side with a sigh. They were quiet for a bit.

"You know what I miss?" Grant finally said. "Driving you and Burke to the movies, or out for a burger."

"Me too, Grant."

"Do you think you two will ever get back together?" Grant's leg was bouncing. I eyed it curiously.

"Oh no, not like as in a couple."

"So then maybe *we* could go to a movie. Just us."

"Would that make me zucchini queen?"

Grant laughed. "No, I'm just saying how great it would be to sit next to you in the movie theater again, listen to you laugh."

Wenling inhaled audibly. "I would like that, too, Grant."

I could feel something happening, something filling the air with an emotion somewhere between fear and excitement. I crawled back out from under the table to see what was going on. Grant and Wenling had turned to face each other. "I know you don't feel the same way, but nothing has changed for me, Wenling. And I don't think it ever will. Because when I look at you . . ."

"Shhh, Grant." Wenling's hand went around his neck and she pulled his face to hers and they pressed their lips in an endless kiss. I yawned and scratched my ear with a back leg and lay back down in the dirt with a sigh, raising my head when Wenling leapt up. "Oh God, this is going to be so hard."

Grant also stood. "I know. I don't care. I love you."

"I should go, Grant."

"Wenling, please."

"I love you, too," she whispered. They kissed again. "Okay, really, I need to, I need to think."

We walked out of the fields and Wenling jumped on her bike and rode away. Then we turned and headed to the house. Burke was lying spread out on the floor.

"Hi, Burke!" Grant greeted cheerfully.

Burke turned his head. "I know what I have to do. I told Hank that if I'm going to learn to walk I need to do it the way a baby does. I have to start off *crawling.*"

"Huh. Well, do you want to show me your models or something?"

"No."

"Can I help? Get you something from the kitchen? You want to go see a movie tonight?"

"Stop feeling sorry for me, Grant. Leave me alone."

"Okay, but if you need anything, let me know, okay?"

"What's wrong with you?"

Grant sighed and went outside. I had a feeling he was going back to play with his plants and buckets, and I certainly had endured enough of that for one day. I watched Burke straining on the floor and went to Assist. "No, Cooper."

No? I watched in frustration. He needed his dog!

"No! Lie down!"

I obeyed but did not understand why, with a good dog right here, he was sprawled on the rug, grunting and gasping, tears in his eyes.

From that point on, Wenling arrived early every day and rode the slow truck out to the fields to help Grant and Chase Dad. When Chase Dad wasn't there, Grant and Wenling spent a lot of time hugging and kissing. "Are you sure you don't want me to tell him?" Grant asked.

"No, it has to be me."

"Are you okay?"

"Not really." She laughed, a single, harsh sound. Grant put his arms back around her and they kissed some more. "Grant, I love you so much."

"I love you, too, Wenling."

"I'm going to go tell him now before I lose my nerve."

"I have to help my dad in the orchard. Come talk to me after, okay?"

They kissed again. I found it pretty boring, but they kept doing it. I followed Wenling as she went to the house. Hank had left for the day and Burke was lying on the carpet, rocking back and forth. He turned his head as we came in. "This is going to work! You know how babies creep? Look, I'm doing it!"

Wenling stood watching him as he grunted. I went to see if he needed me. I licked his ear. He stopped moving and frowned at Wenling. "What's wrong?"

TWENTY

B urke called me to Assist and Steady so he could get into his chair. It felt so nice to be doing good dog work! He wheeled over to Wenling. He didn't say anything, just stared at her.

She cleared her throat. "You are my best friend, Burke. In the whole world. You know that, right?"

He took in a long, deep breath, and then let it out. "Who is it?"

"What do you mean?"

"Stop. You know what I mean. The guy."

Wenling looked away. "The guy. You were the one who said we were seeing other people."

Burke coughed out a harsh laugh, and I glanced at him, concerned. "Well, since my operation I haven't exactly had much of a social life."

"That's your choice, Burke."

"I told everyone I was going to walk again. I don't want to go

on a date in a wheelchair. I don't want to do anything in a wheelchair!"

I cringed from his shout. I slunk to my bed and curled up in
it, making myself as small as possible.

"I'm so sorry, Burke."

He brooded for a moment. "So do you love him? You must be
in love with him, the look on your face right now."

"No, that's not it. I mean yes, we're in love, but you have to
understand. Neither one of us wanted this. Neither one of us
planned it."

Burke's hands tightened on his chair. "Wait a minute. It's
Grant? My *brother*?"

"I'm so sorry, Burke."

I eased up out of my bed, shrinking away from Burke and his
anger, feeling like a bad dog.

Burke clenched his teeth. "Time for you to go."

"No, can't we talk, Burke? Please?"

Burke wheeled out of the room. I followed but he shut his
door with a slam, so I turned around. Wenling was running to her
bicycle, and I didn't follow her. She rode down the driveway and
away.

Grandma came home, but Burke was still in his room. It was
much later in the day when I heard his bedroom door open. He
glided into the living room and I followed, but he didn't speak to
me. Grandma was lying down in her room. I saw Grant and Chase
Dad walking toward us. Chase Dad turned to the barn and Grant
stomped up the ramp and through the front door. He stopped,
his shoulders slumping, when he saw Burke sitting there. "Burke.
God, I don't know what to say."

Burke began wheeling across the floor, moving faster and
faster, and when he reached Grant, Grant said "Hey!" and Burke
launched himself out of the chair and onto Grant's chest and both

boys crashed to the floor. Burke lay on top of Grant and raised his fist and hit Grant in the face. Grant twisted, trying to get away, but Burke held on to his shoulder with one hand and punched him again with the other, and then again. Then Grant slugged Burke and I couldn't help it, I started barking. The rage was boiling off both of them. I smelled blood and didn't understand and kept barking even when I heard Grandma come out of her room.

"*Boys! Stop it!*" she screamed, anguished. "Chase! Hurry!" She clenched her fists over her chest. Grant finally managed to roll on top of Burke, but then Burke hit him in the lips and I heard Grant's teeth click together.

"Hey!" Chase Dad burst in the door and ran to Grant and yanked him off. Blood was coming from Grant's split lip. Both boys were panting.

"Cooper. Assist!" Burke commanded.

But I was afraid. I lowered my head.

"Stop!" Chase Dad pushed Grant so hard, Grant stumbled and fell against the wall. "What are you doing?"

"You always take his side!" Grant shouted. "Always!"

Chase Dad looked bewildered. "No, I just . . ."

Grant made an inarticulate sound. He put his hand up to catch the blood from his face. Grandma handed him a towel.

"Tell him, Grant," Burke said in a hard voice.

"Tell me what?" Chase Dad wanted to know. "Grant?"

There was a long silence. Grant looked away. I felt the anger leaving the room, but no one seemed happy.

This time, when Burke told me to Assist, I helped him into his chair.

"I've seen you two fight before," Grandma observed, "but not in a long time, and never like this. Whatever has come between you, this is not how to settle it. You are brothers."

"Not anymore," Burke snapped.

"Do *not* speak to your grandmother like that," Chase Dad thundered. "Explain yourself, Burke. Now."

"Wenling isn't my girlfriend anymore."

It seemed as if everyone in the room took in a breath. I trembled anxiously. Something very bad was occurring and I did not know what.

"Didn't that happen a long time ago?" Grandma asked softly.

"No. She dumped me for another guy." Burke pointed a finger. "*Him.*"

Grandma gasped. Chase Dad whirled on Grant. "Is this true?"

Grant, still holding the towel to his mouth, closed his eyes. "Not exactly. Yes, we're together, Wenling and me, but she and Burke broke up."

"But Burke is your own brother," Chase Dad responded sternly. "How could you do something like that?"

Grant opened his eyes and pulled the towel away from his bloody lips. "I don't know how it happened," he whispered helplessly.

"Well, I'll tell you what you're going to do," Chase Dad began, his voice tight.

"Chase," Grandma warned.

He looked at her and she shook her head. After a moment, Chase Dad nodded, his body sagging.

"I hate you, Grant," Burke declared quietly. "I've always hated you and I always will hate you."

"Enough, Burke," Chase Dad pleaded wearily.

"You understand me, Grant?"

"Like I care."

"All right," Chase Dad said, "I've had it with both of you. Go to your rooms. I'll tell you when to come out."

Grant laughed harshly. "Go to my room? I'm eighteen years old!"

"Are you either paying rent or obeying my rules? Your choice," Chase Dad snapped.

Burke did not call me or look at me. I started to follow him, unsure, but he shut the door on me again. I slunk back to the living room and approached Grandma. She knelt and held my head. "Oh Cooper, that was upsetting, wasn't it? I am so sorry. But you're a good dog." She looked at Chase Dad, who had collapsed on the couch. "Sometimes I think Cooper has a secret. If only he could tell us."

"No idea what you're talking about."

"I think I'd like a drink; would you mind making it?"

Chase Dad went into the kitchen and soon the room was filled with pungent odors. He and Grandma raised glasses to their lips with a tinkling sound.

"Grant should ice that lip, Chase. Can you take it up to him? My hips are not up to those stairs today."

"In a minute."

"You're still angry at him."

Chase Dad scowled. "Of course I'm angry."

"Chase. They're boys. She's a young girl. Don't you remember being that age?"

"It's her I'm most angry with. I told Burke to stay away from the Zhangs, that they're a bunch of robo-farmers, so what does he do? And then she leads him on and breaks his heart. And takes up with his brother. Who does that sort of thing?"

Grandma took a sip of her drink. "Fidelity is very, very important to you," she observed carefully.

"God, Mom, give it a rest. I know what you're going to say, but I'd feel the same way even if Patty and I were still married."

"And you think that Burke has a life claim on Wenling? Like she's some sort of, of, cow?" I stared at Grandma because I had never heard her voice so harsh.

Chase blinked at her. "I didn't say anything like that."

"As I see it, you've raised two fine sons, two young men who know Wenling better than anyone else. Of *course* she loves both of them. This isn't something she is trying to *do* to either of them. And Burke's got a lot of rage in him right now, or haven't you noticed? Don't you think his reaction might have a lot more to do with something else than a girl he stopped dating half a year ago?" She stood. "I'll get that ice."

Everything after that appeared normal, but it wasn't—far from it. We all still ate and still went to bed, but it was as if I lived with a completely different family, and it took me a long time to figure out why. Grant and Burke were never alone together, and at dinner they barely spoke, not to Chase Dad and Grandma and certainly not to each other.

Also, Burke started dragging himself by his arms everywhere, which upset me. He told me to Sit and Stay, but I couldn't remain still when I saw him trying to make his way across the floor. I went to him to do Assist, but he pushed me away. Why? I was right there, a good dog who could help him to his chair. I didn't understand what he was doing. I tried everything to put things back the way they were. I brought him toys, I whined, I even barked.

"No!" Burke told me sternly.

No? I was just trying to do my job, to be my boy's dog, and he wasn't letting me. Didn't he love me anymore?

"Do you need anything at the store?" Grandma asked him.

"Actually, could you take Cooper with you? He's jumping on me and crying. I think he's bored."

"Sure. Come on, Cooper."

Grandma took me for a car ride! It felt so good to be out of that unhappy house, with my boy painfully creeping along the carpet. I stuck my nose out the window and barked when we passed the wonderful goat farm; when I thrust my face directly into the wind, the air rushing up my nostrils made me sneeze. Grandma laughed.

Then, among all the exotic smells being forced up my nose, I picked up an intoxicating scent: *Lacey*. It grew stronger and stronger and then we passed a farm and it faded. Lacey was there, right back there!

We drove farther, and then Grandma stopped the car and rolled down all the windows. "All right, I know you are good dog, Cooper. You stay," she told me.

I sat, doing Stay. There were nothing but parked cars all around me. Grandma's scent slowly dissipated as she walked into a big building, but it wasn't her I was fixated upon. I now knew where to find Lacey.

Stay. But Grandma had not even slowed as we passed the farmhouse where Lacey's presence was most powerfully felt. Grandma clearly didn't know what I knew!

I whined. Sometimes a dog will be told to do something but will know it isn't right. At that moment, I knew Stay was the wrong thing to do. I stared in the direction Grandma had gone, indecisive.

Stay.

Lacey.

The side of the car was cool on my feet when I climbed out. I landed lightly, shook, and went to go find Lacey, my mate.

Before long I had her on the wind, and I trotted confidently in her direction. I started running when I reached the driveway of a place with a house and a barn and some other big buildings. The whole area smelled like horses.

Lacey gave a yip when she saw me. She was in a small, open-topped pen. We could press our noses through the fence. We bowed and wagged, and I was so happy I spun in a circle. I had found Lacey!

Lacey's doghouse was in the back of her kennel. I tracked her as she went to it and sprang nimbly on its roof. I didn't know what she was doing until she put her paws on the top of the fence and then, glancing over her shoulder at the house, she leapt, her back legs scrambling. There was a ringing sound as the fence rattled, and then she landed and I joyfully climbed on her.

We rolled and played. I was as happy as I had ever been and had no thoughts of anything else but being with her. Then she shook, nosed me, and set off toward some woods. I followed her, trying to play, but she merely started running—she had a destination in mind, I could tell. I figured we were headed to the farm; where else would we be going?

I was wrong. After some time, Lacey led me up to a house in a row of houses, and I knew where we were. She trotted up to the front door, scratched, and sat and barked. I meandered into the yard to lift my leg on some bushes.

The door opened, smells wafting out. The girl in the doorway was, of course, Wenling. "Lulu? What in the world are you doing here?" She looked out in the yard, her expression bewildered when she caught sight of me. "*Cooper?*"

She led us through a wooden gate, closing it behind her. We were in the flat backyard of mostly grass. She set out bowls of water and we drank thirstily. Then we played and played, tearing around the yard, wrestling, tugging on the opposite ends of a stick. This must be where Lacey lived, because Wenling was here!

When Wenling's father came out, we ran to him joyously. "Down," he said.

"I called. Lulu's owner is on her way, but I want to take Cooper back to his house myself. Can you drive me over to the Trevinos', Dad?"

Lacey and I resumed our play. Not long after that, the back

gate opened and a woman came in. She smelled like spices and cheese. "Lulu," she scolded, "how did you get out?"

Lacey ran to her. I lifted my leg on a fence post, unsure.

"They just showed up here," Wenling told New Woman. "It's funny, I know them both. Cooper belongs to my, to a friend, and he and I were the ones who found Lulu after she had her litter. They were Cooper's puppies. And I was the person who called Hope's Rescue to come get them."

"That's where I adopted Lulu," New Woman replied. "So she followed Cooper here, then."

"I suppose," Wenling replied dubiously. "It's weird, though. Why would they come to my house instead of Cooper's?"

I heard a snap as New Woman put a leash on Lacey. I figured we were going for one of those walks where we would be restrained from running, probably because of squirrels. I trotted up to Wenling expectantly, but she just petted me.

I was alarmed when New Woman led Lacey to the fence. "Come on, Lulu." Lacey stared at me, resisting the leash. I ran to her and as the New Woman dragged her through the opening, I tried to nose my way to follow, but the woman blocked me with a leg and then the gate banged shut. I whined and scratched anxiously at the wood slats—I needed to be with Lacey!

For some time I paced and circled in the backyard, smelling Lacey, listening for her return. Then Wenling took me for a car ride, with her father driving and me sitting in the backseat. When we passed the goat ranch I realized we were headed back to the farm.

I felt Wenling's tension as we pulled up the driveway. The car stopped and she put a hand to her mouth. "Oh my God," she breathed.

Burke was watching us from the doorway.

He was standing.

TWENTY-ONE

When Wenling opened the door I broke from the car and galloped joyously up to Burke. He was so tall! I could hear Wenling running right behind me. "Burke!" she cried. "You're standing!"

A few moments later I heard "Burke!" That was Grandma, coming out of the barn door. I started to dash to her, but then heard a long shout and turned—Chase Dad was running out of the fields.

"Burke!" he was yelling, his voice strained as he pounded across the flat earth toward us. "Burke!"

"Burke!" Wenling shouted again. I was excited everyone was calling my boy's name.

She and I got there first. His wheelchair was pressed to the back of his knees and he was holding on to the doorframe with both hands. He was wobbling, and when Wenling charged up the ramp he asked, "Are you here to see Grant?" Then he fell back in his chair. He sighed. "I can stand if I hold myself upright. No walking yet. Haven't mastered standing on one foot and lifting the other. You make it look so easy."

Wenling was crying. "To see you standing there was like a miracle."

"Well, a miracle that took about a million hours of effort."

"Not to mention my genius," Hank said from behind him.

"Oh Burke," Grandma said as she came up the ramp. She put her arms around my boy and started sobbing. Moments later Chase Dad followed, panting, his face wet, joining the hug. Everyone was crying but no one was sad

"Hey, enough," Burke protested. I wagged because I could tell he was happy.

"This is the best day of my life," Chase Dad declared, his voice thick and raw.

Only one thing could make everyone even happier. I dashed into the living room and jumped on the squeaky toy.

"I knew when I was able to crawl that I was going to stand up soon," Burke told them.

"You have to crawl before you walk. Hey, did I just make that up?" Hank asked.

Everyone laughed, so I tossed the squeaky toy high in the air, pouncing on it.

After a time Hank left, Dad returned to the fields, and Grandma went to her bedroom. Wenling followed Burke out onto the porch. "Come here, Cooper," Burke called. I pushed through the dog door and put both feet on the chair and reached up to lick his face. "Okay, good dog enough, Cooper. Enough! Where did you go, huh? Grandma drove all over looking for you."

Wenling sat. "It was the most amazing thing. Remember Lulu

the mommy dog? Cooper was running *with her*, and they came to my house!"

"How did they find each other?"

"I know!"

"Huh. Probably he was out running around and smelled her. Maybe Cooper doesn't know he's been neutered." Burke was quiet for a long moment. "Well, thank you, for bringing back my dog."

"Burke."

He didn't reply. Wenling took a deep breath. "I miss my friend. It seems weird not to talk to you."

"Because you decided that's all we were. Just friends."

Wenling shook her head. She was sad, but Burke seemed angry. "No, never *just* friends. You were my first boyfriend, Burke, and you'll always be my *best* friend. But it's been six months since we broke up—broke up because you wanted us to see other people!"

"Other people not meaning Grant, Wenling. I think if you had brothers and sisters you'd understand what a betrayal it is."

Wenling looked down into her lap. I went to her and touched my nose to her leg. "That's . . . fair," she admitted softly.

"So when the three of us would go to the movies, or grab a burger, because your dad won't let you drive, were you and Grant together then?"

"No. No, Burke."

Burke was silent, staring at her. Wenling glanced away. "To be honest, I think I was having feelings, but I promise you neither one of us acted on them. You have to know that I would rather it be anyone but Grant. I know it hurt you. But, 'whatever our souls are made of, his and mine are the same.' That's from *Wuthering Heights*."

"I kind of don't care where it's from, Wenling."

"Oh."

I sensed Grandma coming up behind us and I wagged a greeting, happy to see her again. She pushed open the door. "I just can't stop thinking about seeing you standing up, Burke. It was the most wonderful thing."

He shrugged. "As long as I'm holding on to something." My boy wheeled his chair around. "I guess I'm not ready for small talk. I'm going to work on some stuff in my room."

I followed, but he shut the door behind him so I returned to the porch. Grandma was speaking to Wenling. "I know this seems like the biggest thing in the world," she was saying, "that he'll never recover, never forgive you, but you're both young. Believe me, as the years go on, this won't seem so important."

"Grant says they hate each other now. Or at least Burke hates Grant."

"Those boys have been fighting since they were little. I think they just can't figure out a way to love each other yet. They'll get there. You didn't cause this, it's just the latest in a long line of grievances they keep racking up with each other, silent indictments that explode into the open from time to time."

"That's what my mom says about him." Wenling pointed to the car in the driveway. "That he doesn't know how to express love."

"Oh! Why is your father out in the car?"

"He's—he knows Mr. Trevino hates him."

"Well, that's ridiculous. Go tell him to come in. I'll make tea."

"Okay. Uh, Grandma Rachel?"

"Yes?"

"Nobody in my family really likes green tea. We like Earl Grey or any black tea."

"Oh!" Grandma Rachel laughed. "Well, I feel silly; I should have asked." She went into the house and I followed, because she was headed to the kitchen. She began opening cupboards and getting things out, which I took as a very good sign. She opened the refrigerator and all the wonderful smells came wafting out: cheese, bacon, chicken. I licked my lips in anticipation. Someday I would love to climb into that refrigerator.

Wenling and Grandma and Wenling's father arrayed themselves in the living room. Small pieces of bread, some nuts, and some cheese were on a plate on a low table. I stared at this arrangement intently.

Grandma Rachel clinked a cup with a spoon. "Thank you very much for coming over."

The father spoke and Wenling turned to Grandma. "He says, 'Thank you for having us. The tea is excellent.'"

Grandma smiled.

"He understands English much better than he can speak it," Wenling said.

"My English is not too good," her father added.

I kept my focus on the plate on the table. I didn't even look up when, a moment later, Grant and Chase Dad entered the house. They both halted when they saw us sitting there.

"Chase, our neighbor returned Cooper and now we're having tea. Come join us," Grandma said firmly.

Chase Dad sat stiffly in a chair, as if his angry walk was translating itself into his seated posture. Grant bounced down on the couch next to Wenling and I saw him grab her hand and hold it. They smiled at each other.

There was a long silence. Grant reached for a fistful of treats and I licked my lips because I knew him to be the most generous member of the family.

"We could use some more rain," Chase Dad finally observed.

Nobody said anything to this. Chase Dad poured some fragrant liquid into a cup, took a sip, and made a sour face. He put the cup down. "So. ZZ. What is it like to be a robo-farmer?"

Wenling's father turned and looked blankly at his daughter.

She spoke and he frowned, shaking his head and replying: "Gàosù tā wǒmen zhīqián de shēnghuó."

Wenling nodded. "Dad used to be a farmer like you," she explained. "He had tomatoes and apples. Then he met my mother when she was on a trip. She was American, but that was okay. He, like, totally fell for her."

Wenling's father spoke some more. Everyone seemed so stiff that I abandoned sentry duty on the cheese and pounced on a squeaky toy. It didn't squeak anymore, but I thought it might liven things up.

"So anyway," Wenling continued, "Mom moved to China to marry Dad and they lived on his farm. That's my earliest memory. He says she was happy, but I know she wasn't, not really. She wanted to live in America." Wenling listened to her father and then shook her head. "He knows I'm not repeating word for word. Anyway, he had no sons to help him on the farm. I was no good because I'm a girl."

Wenling's father said, "Wǒ cóngxiǎo jiù gēnzhe wǒ bàba zài nóngchǎng gōngzuò. Zhè shì dà bùfèn de jiātíng duì er zi de qīwàng."

She nodded. "So he agrees with that part, that he needed sons, but Mom didn't have any more children, and when I was nine her brother died and left her the shoe store here in town, and Dad was able to get a good price for the farm so he sold it because all he had was this worthless daughter and no sons, and they moved here. He says selling shoes is no way to make a living, that women keep changing their minds on what they want, and the store was losing money and finally he had to close it down. Dad took a job with Trident Mechanical Harvesting because that's all he could find. Mom works in a clothing store part-time. He wanted to work on a farm, but he says Americans don't use men, they use machines."

"Those drones are destroying our community, our economy, the country," Chase Dad declared severely.

Wenling's father nodded. "Yes."

Chase Dad's lip was fixed in a hard, straight line. "But you work for them. If you didn't fix their damn machines, they wouldn't be in the fields putting me out of business."

"Chase," Grandma warned.

I yawned, worried at Chase Dad's stern tones.

"Oh! No, he doesn't fix the drones," Wenling corrected. "He works in janitorial. He cleans the bathrooms, replaces lightbulbs, like that."

Chase Dad stared for a long moment. He pursed his lips. "Really? Sorry. I guess I assumed he was an engineer."

"Why, because he's Asian?" Wenling asked.

Grant laughed.

Chase Dad nodded slowly, shrugging his shoulders. "Yeah," he agreed uncomfortably. "You got me. I'm sorry."

Grandma giggled. Wenling spoke to her father and then they, too, were laughing, and Chase Dad joined them. This is the sort of thing no dog can understand: a moment ago there was anger and tension and now there was laughter and Grant was eating more cheese. I wagged.

Wenling's father spoke again. She listened, nodding. "Dad says he *could* fix the machines, if they let him. And they're making stupid mistakes with how they plant their crops. They cut down a stand of trees so they could put in more and now the wind shreds everything. But he doesn't speak English or have a college degree, so they think he is an idiot who doesn't know anything about farming."

"My English is not too good," Wenling's father stated.

"I didn't go to college, either," Chase Dad admitted.

"I'm going to major in business," Grant declared. Wenling smiled at him.

Chase Dad said, "I've diversified a lot more lately. I sell to vendors who take my crops to the farmers' market and to organic restaurants. Now I've got asparagus in the spring; cucumbers, zucchini, tomatoes, and peppers in the summer, apples and pears into the fall. I finish it out with carrots."

Wenling's father had leaned forward to listen. Now he nodded. "Good."

"But I hear the robo-farmers are getting into organics and are going to have a booth at the farmers' market. That'll just drive down prices further. And I've got crops I can't bring in because I don't have any help except for my son, Grant. He's a damn good worker, a lot better at farming than I was at his age. But even with his help, I'm not making it."

Grant was staring at his father in astonishment.

Wenling's father spoke animatedly to his daughter and she listened, her eyes widening in surprise. "Yes, okay," she said. "My dad says he knows how fast squash grows and when the right time to prune apple trees is and how to cut asparagus below the soil line without damaging nearby growth. He says if you would let him work for you, he doesn't care what you pay, he hates his job. He has never said a word about this to me or my mom before, I promise."

Chase Dad blinked. "I would pay what I always pay. It's more than a decent wage—it's just that the work is so hard and there's no one to do it. You really want to work for me?"

Wenling's father closed his eyes for a moment. When he opened them, he smiled. "Yes." He stood and held out his hand and Chase Dad grabbed it and then let go. Wenling's father ducked his head a little.

Everyone was smiling, as if they had given me a piece of cheese or something, but it was still just sitting there on the table.

After that, things changed, but not for the better. I learned that Wenling's father was ZZ. He and Wenling came over every day, but not to play with me. They would go out and fiddle with plants with Chase Dad and Grant. Burke did not go with them; he stayed in the house and crawled on the floor and would stand up briefly and then sit down, over and over. I was so frustrated: I was right here, why didn't he want my help? I could almost hear his voice. *Assist, Cooper. Steady. Good dog.* I even dreamed about it, and would jerk awake and stare at him in the night. My boy no longer needed me. I began wondering if I should leave the farm and go find Lacey.

"Bad dog!" Burke yelled at me when I chewed up a boot in his closet. "I don't understand," he complained to Grandma, "he's behaving so strangely, like he's an entirely different dog."

"Come here, Cooper," Grandma urged. She had no treats in her hand. I looked at her. It just didn't seem worth the effort to obey her under such circumstances. "Do you think he's sick?" she asked worriedly.

I put my head down and sighed. Burke squatted and peered at me. "What's wrong with you, Cooper?"

Hank came to see me the next day. His visits were much less frequent now. I regarded him wearily as he squatted by my bed. "Cooper," he boomed, "what, you're not happy to see your Uncle Hank?" He scratched my ears and I leaned into it a little.

"We think Cooper's sick," Burke advised. "I'm going to get him to a vet."

"You sick, Cooper?" Hank asked me. "You don't look sick to me. He glanced over to Burke. "Maybe he's depressed."

"How can a dog be depressed? He gets to be a *dog.*"

"Yeah, but I've got you literally standing on your own two feet now. Dogs are like people—they need a job to feel like they've got a purpose in life. Cooper here is a working dog and you've forced him into early retirement."

I sighed as Hank and my boy played with the machine in the corner, the loud plates banging together as Burke grunted.

"I caught your dad playing guitar down at Cutter's Bar Saturday night," Hank said. "Give me four more of those, Burke. Man, he was *wailing* on that thing. I love their name, the Not Very Good Band. They sure do live up to *that*." Hank chuckled. "That's two, keep going. Your dad, though, closes his eyes and makes the music jump right out of that axe of his. I was so caught up in it I almost threw my underwear onstage."

With a bang the plates dropped. Burke was laughing. "He never plays for us. Says it will destroy our hearing."

"You Trevinos sure are interesting, I'll give you that. Never met a family that kept so much of themselves from one another. Like three islands in the same ocean, each one just over the horizon. Ho, did I just say that? I don't write down some of this wisdom, I'm never going to be rich. That was *poetry*. You ready for another set? What's with the face?"

"I was just thinking about school. I'm missing fall semester, and I still can't walk."

I glanced at my boy, remembering the children on the stone steps. Were we going to do School again?

"I'm gonna have you running the halls soon," Hank replied.

"You don't think I should just go in my chair? That's what my dad says."

"Hell, no! You go in on both feet! Listen to your buddy Hank, here. I don't care if you miss a whole 'nother year. You'll be the kid in your grade with a driver's license. Girls will be lining *up*. I'm gonna have to go as your bodyguard so's you don't get trampled by the cheerleading squad."

I wagged because my boy was laughing. Hank came over to pet me as he was leaving. "Remember, give this dog something to *do*."

TWENTY-TWO

Later, I watched dismally as Burke lowered himself into his chair without a good dog doing Steady. "Okay, let me try something," he whispered to me. He wheeled into his room. I closed my eyes.

"Cooper! Get the sock!" he called.

I opened my eyes, then shook myself off and padded into his room to see what he was doing. He had pulled out some objects I recognized—a soft, deflated ball, some clothing, a plastic cup, even Grant's nylon bone. "Get It! Get the sock!"

I sniffed around, finally settling on the deflated ball. I picked it up and looked at him. "Leave It! Get the sock!"

I hoped I would also do Leave It on the nylon bone. I jumped on the next most attractive item. "Leave It! Get the sock!" I tried again. "Yes! Bring It!"

I went over and spat the cloth thing in his lap. "Good dog, Cooper! Now get the glove! Get it!"

I was happy to play Get It but was overjoyed when Burke climbed out of his chair and then reached up for my harness. "Assist!"

That was not the last time I did Assist, but gradually the nature of the work changed. Now Burke would stand on his legs, leaning heavily on my back, and shuffle first one foot and then the other forward, and together we would transit the living room.

"Assist, Cooper!"

Hank very much appreciated how good I was being. "Look at you! You're ready for the fifty-yard dash!" Hank still came, just not as often, and he always told me I was a good dog, but then he and Burke would ignore me and play on the machine. Those days I would go check on what everyone was doing out in the fields, but they were never having any sort of fun, so I usually trotted back and lay in the kitchen in case Grandma decided to make bacon.

Normally ZZ and Chase Dad were off to one side and Grant and some afternoons Wenling to the other, but one day ZZ and Wenling were not around and Grant and Chase Dad were sitting with their backs to the slow truck, drinking out of cold, sweaty bottles.

"Can't believe what a difference it makes to have ZZ here," Chase Dad said.

Grant nodded. "Dad?"

"Yeah?"

"Did you mean it when you said I was a better worker than you were at my age?"

"Not just better. *Smarter*. My parents inherited this place and put me to work and I just didn't take to it at first. Was a long time before I found my rhythm. But you picked up the knife and went at the crops like you were born to it. You're still faster than I am. Pretty soon I'm going to just sit and watch you and ZZ do all the work."

"And Wenling."

"Her too."

"Wenling thinks we could grow grapes on the hill to sell to make ice wine."

"The hell is that?"

"You let the grapes freeze and harvest them. Brings out the sugar. Ice wine is served cold and is really sweet."

"Sounds wretched."

Grant laughed. "It's just an idea. We're not doing much with the slope right now."

"Because it's too hard to climb up and down the thing. My dad used to grow tomatoes on that hill, remember? Now his ashes are up there, overlooking the whole farm. I think he would've liked that."

Grant took a long drink. "So I was thinking."

"And?"

"So maybe I won't go to college next fall after all. Hang here and help out instead."

"I thought you said a college education was your ticket out of this hellhole."

"I'm still going; I just want to spend a little more time here."

I yawned, circled around, and flopped down in the dirt, my head by Chase Dad's outstretched leg. He stroked my head. "So what, until Wenling graduates, maybe?"

Grant didn't say anything.

Chase Dad stood and slapped his pants and dust puffed off them. I turned my nose away from the dry cloud. "Well, you know I'd appreciate the help, son. But it's got to be your decision."

Wenling came over that same day and she was sad. She and Grant went to sit under the apple trees and talk.

"How serious is it, Wenling?" Grant pressed anxiously. He sounded fearful. I stared at him in concern.

She shook her head, wiping a thin paper under her eyes. "No, that's not it. The doctor says a lot of people have heart murmurs. They're harmless. But . . . but it means I'm disqualified from applying to the Air Force Academy."

"No. *No*. Oh Wenling, I am so sorry. I know how important that is to you."

They hugged and I put my head in her lap. We sat like that for a long, long time. "So," she said with a quiet laugh, "I guess I'll try for Michigan. In-state tuition."

"Then I'll apply there, too," Grant responded instantly.

Wenling smiled at him with moist eyes. "I can still get my pilot's license. I just don't qualify to have people shooting missiles at me. I was so looking forward to that."

Grant laughed and I lifted my head and wagged, glad I was able to cheer them up.

One morning, when the leaves were falling to the ground in a relentless pour, we went to Grant's building, but Burke forgot his chair. His gait was uneven and sometimes he fell, and I did Steady while people stood in a circle to watch what a good dog I could be. "No, don't worry, Cooper's got this," Burke told them as he grasped my harness.

Not long after that, Burke could take his own car rides! We drove many places with warm foods and good friends but not with Wenling and not with Grant. I almost never saw her, but I could nearly always smell her on Grant. I always sniffed him carefully when Wenling's scent was pasted on his clothing, looking for Lacey, but never once found any signs of my dog.

"Hard to believe Grant's graduating this summer," Chase Dad

observed as he and Burke moved the odd equipment out of the living room and brought the couch back in. I wondered guiltily if anyone could smell how strongly I had painted my scent on that couch while it was in the barn.

We took a lot of walks, Burke and I, ranging farther and farther from home. We even walked in the snow! Sometimes he tripped and went sprawling, but he seemed stronger and more confident as the days grew warmer. I did less Assist and Steady, but I still had work to do. "Get the ball!" he would tell me. "Get the glove! Get the cone! Get It!"

I had a purpose.

"Wet start to the summer," Chase Dad observed. He eyed Burke. "Looking forward to having you helping out, son."

Burke started playing with plants with Grant and Chase Dad. The three of them seemed accustomed to not speaking to one another, though Grant and Burke often talked to me. I noticed that the next time Burke went to Grant's building, Grant forgot to go. Snow came and left; this was life on the farm and I was a good dog.

Warm days were just returning when my boy and I followed a small brook upstream to a pond lying behind a tall pile of sticks. The area reeked with the scent of some animals, though I couldn't spot them. Another mystery animal! "It's a beaver dam, see? There's a whole series of them on this stream. Let's go check it out."

We followed the creek as it threaded through the woods. Then it broke out into an open field and stopped twisting and turning and instead tracked in a straight line, which was much easier to follow. "The robo-farmers took out all the beaver dams and put in this cement trough, Cooper," Burke said. I looked at him expectantly. Get It?

"What's going to happen downstream if we get more than a

couple of inches of rain? Do these people not understand any-thing?"

That summer, we drove to a dog park to play with other dogs and to a lake to play with dogs on the beach and to a trail through the woods to play with dogs on the path. I loved the farm, but it was wonderful to be able to sniff and lift my leg on so many marks. Chase Dad and ZZ and Burke were mostly together on one side of the farm, and Wenling and Grant on the other, so I could always run back and forth, though usually I decided just to nap. I kept my eye on Burke, though—it was still strange to see him walking, and I wanted to be able to respond if he ever decided to go back to his chair.

One such day I drowsily opened my eyes when Chase Dad and Burke stood drinking water. I could not detect Grant and Wen-ling anywhere nearby, though ZZ was approaching from across the fields. "You know what I'd do?" Chase Dad asked Burke. "At Christmas break, when you graduate? I'd take some time off. Not race off to college."

Burke regarded Chase Dad sourly. "Maybe work the farm, like Grant's been doing? Now that he and Wenling are leaving in the fall?"

"Same arrangement," Chase Dad agreed cheerfully.

Burke was silent. I licked his hand because of the mixture of sad feelings coming off his skin.

I was a good dog that fine day, trotting out of the fields with ZZ, Chase Dad, and Burke. I could smell liver treats in Burke's pocket. As we drew near the house, I picked up the scent of Wen-ling and Grant in the direction of the barn.

Chase Dad held out a tool. "You want to put this away, ZZ?"

"Yes." ZZ took the thing and went toward the barn.

Burke and Chase Dad sat on the porch. Grandma appeared at the door. "Would you men like some lemonade?"

Burke wiped his forehead with his sleeve. "Sounds good to me!"

Grandma left to go to the kitchen. I weighed following her against the liver treats in my boy's pocket.

"Where did Grant and Wenling get to?" Chase Dad asked.

"I don't know and I don't care," Burke replied curtly.

"Hey!" Chase Dad said sharply. Burke and I both jumped. "When are you going to be done with this? I'm pretty sick of you not talking to your brother and pretending like you can't even *see* Wenling. Grant is family, and she's a friend and an employee. I'm tired of you acting like a spoiled child."

I could feel Burke getting angry. "Some things are impossible to forgive."

"Not when it's family."

"Yeah? I don't see you exchanging Christmas cards with my *mother*." Burke stood and stomped into the house. Now that he didn't need the chair, he could do an angry walk just like Chase Dad. He passed Grandma coming out the door with two sour-smelling drinks.

"Burke?" she said.

Chase Dad reached for one of the drinks. "Let him go. He needs to grow up and he's fighting it."

There was suddenly a loud, angry shout from the barn. Chase Dad stood up, alarmed. "That was ZZ."

Just then Wenling came running out of the barn. She was crying. She dashed to ZZ's car and jumped in and just a short time later ZZ angry-walked over and the two of them drove off in a cloud of dust.

"What in the world?" Grandma wanted to know.

Chase Dad looked at her. "I have a bad feeling ZZ just walked in on my son and Wenling doing something in the barn that he wishes he didn't see."

"Oh." Grandma put her hand down to touch my head. "That's . . ."

"Yes, it could be pretty bad." Chase Dad sighed heavily. "Like we need this right now."

Grant came out of the barn and I trotted down to greet him, but it was one of those times when a human doesn't want a dog, even though he obviously needed cheering up. Grant wasn't wearing a shirt, and his sweat popped in the sun. He passed into the house without saying anything to anybody.

ZZ returned later with Wenling's mother, who had been to dinner often enough that I knew her name was Li Min. She had hair and skin and eyes the same color as Wenling's, but her hands were more fragrant with delectable meats. Burke and Grant both emerged from their rooms at the arrival of the new people, but Chase Dad said, "We'd like to have a minute here, boys," so they both closed their doors. I heard Grant, though: he padded down the stairs to the bottom step and stood there hiding as if we all couldn't smell him.

They sat at the table sipping from cups. ZZ spoke, then Li Min spoke. "Zhuyong is sorry for the dishonor our daughter has brought to this, his place of employment."

Chase Dad shook his head. "No we're good, ZZ. Sorry you . . . well, I'm a parent. I understand."

ZZ and Li Min spoke together, and I could feel both of them getting angry. Finally she sighed. "ZZ wants them to get married."

"Oh!" Grandma exclaimed.

Chase Dad sat back in his chair. "Well, no disrespect, ZZ, but that seems an overreaction to the situation."

ZZ stared pointedly at Li Min and she sighed again. "Wenling tells me they are already engaged."

"*What?*" Chase Dad sputtered.

"Or engaged to be engaged, I guess," Li Min corrected herself.

ZZ spoke to Wenling's mother at length. Finally she held up a hand. "Okay, honey, let me explain. So: ZZ feels dishonored by Wenling." ZZ was shaking his head, frowning. "No, that's *exactly* what you're feeling," Li Min told him sharply. "He says that if they're engaged anyway and she's already behaving like a married woman, then there needs to be a wedding now. I'm telling you what he says; it is not necessarily my opinion."

"What is your opinion?" Grandma asked gently.

"Oh, and this is nothing against Grant, but I think a big part of it is that ZZ sees this as a way to keep Wenling from going off to college in the fall. He doesn't want her living so far away from her family."

ZZ was staring at Li Min. He spoke harshly and she held up a hand. It was the signal to do Sit, so I sat.

"No," she snapped, "do not tell me that has nothing to do with it, ZZ. And it won't work anyway—they'll just move to married housing."

Chase Dad and Grandma glanced at each other a little uneasily.

I heard Grant creeping stealthily through the living room and wandered in to watch him ease out the front door. Moments later he drove away.

I decided those liver treats in Burke's pocket needed my attention. I scratched at his door and when my boy opened it, I jumped on his bed and sat, looking very much like a dog who deserved a little snack. He finally gave me one. Yes! So I did Lie Down to try to elicit another, but he didn't react.

I heard ZZ and Li Min leave and then, much later, I heard Grant return. I slept with my nose pointed toward the pants

Burke had hung in his closet because there were still treats in the pockets.

Grant was not home that morning when Burke poured food in my bowl. I ate, then went out and reinforced my mark where the scent had faded, napped a bit, and then decided to head back to bed. I stirred when I heard Grant return, but I was far too comfortable to follow until I heard Burke yelling. "What? That's *crazy!*"

Burke was standing in the living room, as was Grant. Chase Dad and Grandma were both sitting on the couch. Burke pointed at Grant. "You do know she's only seventeen years old, right?"

Grant crossed his arms. "She's eighteen in September."

Burke whirled on his father. "Dad, you can't let this happen."

"It's not Dad's decision. It's our decision, Wenling and me," Grant said coldly.

"Everyone needs to cool down," Chase Dad replied.

My boy rolled his eyes. I went to him, anxious at all the powerful emotions swirling in the room. He pointed to his father. "Haven't you always said that one reason you got divorced was that you and Mom were married too young?"

Chase Dad stiffened. "I don't like you calling her 'Mom.' She gave birth to you, but *I'm* the one who raised you."

Burke made an odd noise. "What? *That's* what's important right now?"

At that moment a dog came blundering through the dog door. Grandma gasped and everyone started. It was Lacey! I jumped up and ran to her, wagging. I wondered if she had come back to have more puppies in the under barn. We immediately began wrestling, overjoyed to be together.

"Hey!" Chase Dad yelled.

"Cooper!" Burke shouted.

Lacey and I both stared at them, shocked. They sounded

angry, but who could be angry when something as wonderful as *this* was happening?

"What dog is that?" Grant asked.

Burke knelt and grabbed Lacey's collar. She wagged. "Don't you recognize her? It's the dog that gave birth in the storm shelter, the one Wenling named Lulu." He straightened, looking at Grant. "Your *fiancée* named Lulu."

"That was about the craziest thing I've ever seen. The dog just waltzed right in like she owned the place," Chase Dad marveled.

Burke did a sort of backward Assist, dragging Lacey to the door. "I'll call the owner and take her home. Come on, Cooper."

Once outside, Lacey and I followed Burke to the car and gladly piled in to the backseat. Car ride! The space was small, so we utilized all of it as we played with each other. "Hi. This is Burke Trevino calling again in case my first message didn't go through. I found Lulu and she's in my car and we're about to head out. I'll bring her home except I don't have your address, so please call me when you get this message, thanks," he said.

He sat for a minute and then started the car. "Okay, then, dogs. Until Lulu's family calls back I guess there's nothing better to do."

Lacey and I stuck our heads out our windows and breathed in the glorious goat farm and all the other rich odors floating on the afternoon air. We turned in a driveway and I could smell ZZ and Li Min and Wenling when Burke knocked on the front door. We had been here before!

Wenling opened the door but didn't let us in even though we could smell that they had beef cooking in there. "Oh my God! Did it happen again?" she asked.

"Lulu crashed into the living room in the middle of a, uh, conversation. I called the number on her tag and left a message."

"That's a little crazy."

"Wenling. I guess you and I should talk."

TWENTY-THREE

My nose told me ZZ and Li Min were in the house, but I didn't see them as we turned down a hall and into a room with a fire burning in a hole in the wall. Lacey and I rolled and played and chewed on each other, but reacted whenever Burke said "Hey! Settle down!" We could hear anger in his voice, so we usually did Sit, being good dogs, until one of us bit the other in the face.

"This isn't something you get a vote in, Burke. Please understand that."

"I do understand that. I do. I get that. But you're only seventeen!"

"My dad's sister was seventeen when she got married."

"Okay, that's certainly relevant. Um, I have to ask," Burke held his hand out in front of his stomach. "Are you . . ."

Wenling frowned. "Really fat?"

"Come on."

Lacey sprawled on her back, her teeth showing, and I put my jaws around her neck.

"No, I'm not. Doesn't it occur to you that maybe I *want* to do this?"

"Really, though? So you're not going to college?"

Lacey twisted and jumped up and I bowed, ready for more.

"Of course I am. No one said anything about not going to college. But speaking of that, it really hurt when I sent you a message about being disqualified from the Air Force Academy and you said nothing. Why couldn't you have answered me?"

I glanced at Burke because he seemed to be staring at the floor. "You're right. I should have. I'm sorry. I wasn't in a good place."

"Okay," Wenling responded quietly.

"But you're going to MU, right? Unless you're married, I mean."

"I am going to MU, and so is Grant. We're in love. People in love get married."

Lacey and I lifted our noses in exactly the same motion. A heavy rain was pounding its way toward us.

"People in love don't get married when one of them just graduated from high school. I mean they do, but, I just can't see *you* doing that. Is it because of your parents? Your father?"

Wenling shrugged, sighing. "Maybe a little."

"This is so wrong! He's got some insane ideas that are a hundred years out of date and you're just caving to him?"

Wenling was sad. She wiped tears from her face and Lacey was right there, wagging, trying to lick her wet cheeks, hoping to make Wenling feel better. "My father says I have dishonored the family."

"God, that's just so . . ." Burke lifted his hands and dropped them in his lap.

"He was raised with very traditional values. Honor is very important to him. I think it was worse that it was in the barn, where he works, than anything else."

"Why didn't you just use my bedroom? It has a first-floor window."

Wenling laughed through her tears.

"I'm actually *serious*." Burke was quiet a moment, his frown deepening. "Your dad is traditional. Plus he wants the farm, right? If you marry Grant, it will be in the family. Like you're a prostitute."

Wenling's mouth dropped open. Lacey nuzzled her hand. "That is the most offensive thing you've ever said to me, Burke Trevino."

"I'm sorry, but you told me he was pressuring you to find a Chinese boy when you were my girlfriend, and now he's all about Grant? Maybe it was because I was in a wheelchair and he couldn't picture me as a farmer."

"God, are you going to see everything through that lens for your whole life? You're out of the chair! No one cares how you spent your childhood!"

Wenling's shouts made Lacey and me uneasy. I sat by Burke's side, watching him for a clue as to what was happening. He took a deep breath. "Okay, I take it all back. I'm sorry. You're right. That was insulting, I get that. I'm just angry at your father. He's acting like you're not even your own person!"

The rain was now tapping at the house, a slowly building roar. Wenling reached out and stroked Lacey, who was also being a good dog doing Sit.

"I know. I could do no wrong when I was little, but when I

started wearing makeup I could see the distaste in Dad's eyes, like he thinks I'm going to turn into a hooker. Maybe marrying the son of a landowner does seem to him like he's found a way to save me from being a fallen woman."

"How does your mom feel about it?"

"Oh, you know. One minute she's totally against it, the next she is talking about wedding dresses. But she'll back me on anything I want to do. She paid for my pilot's license when my hours got cut."

"Wenling. I love you."

She drew in a sharp breath.

Burke held out a hand. "Not in a I-want-to-marry-you way. I love you because we were together all through middle school. You said it, we're best friends. Which means I really, really *care* about this. If you want to marry Grant, I'll be your maid of honor. Just . . . why rush into it? If it's meant to be, then you can date all through college, get married when you graduate."

She smiled. "He got down on one knee. It was so romantic."

"That's Grant, Mr. Romance."

"Stop. No, it was just, my father was all, 'I assume you're getting married since you are already acting like a wife,' and I tried to explain about what it means to be promised, but he goes storming off to talk to *your* father, like they're going to work it out between them, and then Grant comes over and I thought for just a minute, I'm *engaged*." Wenling stood up and twirled in a circle. "Then you show up and spoil it."

"Sorry."

"I'm kidding. I knew it was all fantasy. You're right. All day I've been trying not to deal with any reality." She shook her head. "This is going to really hurt Grant's feelings. He was so, I don't know, his face was so hopeful, you know? Like for the first time since I've known him, he's settled on exactly what he wants to do."

I was still watching Burke, but the anger seemed to have left the room.

"I see how he looks at you, Wenling. I know it's real."

"You want to see the ring?"

"He got a ring already?"

"This morning. I took it off when I heard you pull in the drive-way." Wenling stood and went to a table and opened a small box. She handed something to Burke Lacey and I could tell it was nothing edible.

Burke handed it back to her. "Pretty. Well, put it on."

Wenling was looking at the thing in her hand, a sad smile on her face. "No, I don't think I should wear it until I'm ready for what that means."

The quiet roar was steadily building, getting louder and louder. Burke looked up at the ceiling. "It's really coming down out there."

"They said like four inches."

"So, do you want me to talk to my brother?"

"No. I mean yes, wouldn't that be easy? But no. I have to be the one who tells him."

I snapped my attention to my boy, who had given a sudden start.

Wenling frowned. "What's wrong?"

Burke was on his feet. "The beaver pond. I forgot all about it!"

"What are you talking about?"

"I have to go. There's a family of beavers I found. This much rain will flood them out. Maybe I can do something to save them. Come on, Cooper."

"I'll go with you!"

Burke grabbed some tools from the garage and threw them in the trunk, and then Wenling and Lacey climbed with me into the car.

Car ride in the rain!

Burke was driving. "So the robo-drones are most effective when all the crop rows are straight and I guess that goes for streams, too. They wiped out all the twists and turns in the creek and forced it to go in a straight line in a cement trough all the way to the edge of their property. So there's nothing to absorb the flood. The water's going to come out of there like it's being shot from a cannon."

"What can we do?"

Burke gave her a grim look. "I don't exactly know."

It was still raining when he stopped the car, the fat drops flaring in the headlights, which Burke left on, pointed out at a small pond I recognized. Lacey immediately jumped in the water, but I stayed by Burke. I could tell by his mood he was going to need me. He pointed. "Look! The beavers are piling more branches on their den. The water must already be rising."

"There's a baby!" Wenling exclaimed.

My attention was drawn to some squirrel-like animals in the water. They were dragging sticks, as if they were dogs. One of them was much smaller than the other two. Burke opened the trunk of the car and handed something to Wenling. "Here's a hatchet. I'll take the axe. Let's go!"

Lacey and I watched, dumbfounded, as Burke and Wenling began chopping at small trees and running to throw them on a big pile of brush at the edge of the pond. The water squirrels immediately vanished. Lacey picked up a stick and ran around with it, thinking she understood what was going on, but my focus was on Burke. This was like Get It. It was Get It the stick. And then Get It another.

I plunged deeper into the woods, found a branch, and dragged it to Burke. "Good dog, Cooper!" He grabbed it and threw it on the pile. Lacey romped by with her stick and I gave chase briefly and then turned to get my own. I took it to Burke. "Good dog!"

A water squirrel came out and seemed to watch for a moment before swimming to the far side of the pond and paddling back with its own stick in its mouth. It scaled up the pile and deposited the branch and went back, followed by the two other water squirrels carrying their own twigs. We were all doing Get It!

Lacey wanted to chase the water squirrels, I could tell by the way she was watching. I went to her and did Steady, blocking her. She sniffed me. Didn't she know about Get It?

"The baby can barely drag the branches," Wenling said, "but she's doing it."

I noticed that the smallest water squirrel was hardly keeping its nose out of the water as it glided across the pond with its branches. "They know if they don't succeed, they'll all perish," Burke replied.

Lacey eventually sprawled on her belly and started chewing her stick to bits, while I went back to helping Burke and Wenling. Wenling cheered when the rain tapered off.

Burke broke off a tree branch. "We have to keep going; the water will rise for a while yet."

There are far more fun ways to play with sticks, but we played Get It for a long, long time. Burke looked around the pond and grinned. "Water's stopped rising! The dam is going to hold!"

Wenling hugged him and they jumped into the car. Lacey and I were soaked. We lay down together in the back, cold and too tired to do much more than nibble on each other's lips.

Wenling rubbed her hands together, shivering. "I'm freezing."

"Heat's on, it'll be warm in a minute." He held up his phone. "So Lulu's owners called and left a message while we were busy. Do you want to go with me to take her back?"

"Sure. Burke . . . that was fun and it felt . . . important. Thank you for including me."

"If we hadn't shown up, they wouldn't have made it."

"And I was thinking the whole time, here's this beaver mother and father and baby, and they know what to do because they're *beavers*. And they're side by side, making their life. That's how marriage is supposed to be."

"You do know beavers are rodents, right?"

"Stop. I am just trying to say, I don't know what I want to do with my life. I had this plan, join the air force, become a pilot. Then I decided I want to study agricultural sciences, horticulture, but maybe when I get to school I'll change my mind again. The beavers know for a certainty what to do, and until I do, too, I can't get *engaged*."

"Right, I think you said that back at your house."

"Would you please stop being so irritating? I'm saying this was a profound experience."

For some reason we dropped Lacey off at the same house where I had found her once before, a stranger's house, though Lacey ran right up to the door, which opened for her. Burke left me in the car with Wenling and followed Lacey, but he didn't grab her and bring her back to the car as I hoped. He briefly spoke to a woman on the threshold. Then we drove to Wenling's house and she hugged Burke and got out, and then we returned to the farm without her.

Almost none of the day made any sense to me at all.

I saw Wenling the next day, though. She drove over. Burke and Grandma and Chase Dad were all off somewhere. I was happy to see her! She and Grant sat under a tree and talked and at one point he yelled at her. I saw her hand him something and he angry-walked into the house and then she drove away.

I was nearly successfully catching squirrels when I heard Grandma's car in the driveway. I raced home. Everyone was carrying sacks filled with great food smells when I pushed through the dog door. Then Grant stomped downstairs in the angriest walk I had ever witnessed. He strode over to Burke and Burke set his bag down and faced him. Grant reached out with two hands and shoved, hard, and Burke stumbled and fell and I went to him to do Steady, but he jumped up on his own.

Chase Dad and Grandma darted swiftly out of the kitchen. "Hey! Settle down!" Chase Dad commanded in a loud voice.

Grant whirled. "Wenling broke off the engagement."

Chase Dad and Grandma looked at each other. "Grant," Grandma started to say.

"Because *he* said her father only wants her to marry me so that the farm will be his someday."

"That's crazy," Chase Dad declared after a moment. "ZZ would never . . ."

"It's what Burke told her!" Grant turned back and shoved Burke again, but this time Burke remained on his feet.

"You can hit me if you want, Grant. I won't fight back," Burke said quietly.

"There's not going to be a *fight*. Did you really say that, Burke?" Chase Dad demanded.

"I suggested it was a possibility, is all."

Chase Dad shook his head. "Well, that's just foolish. You owe your brother an apology. The farm is going to both of you boys equally. For you to share it, work it together."

Burke raised his hands and then let them fall to his side. "Dad . . . I want to be an engineer. I want to design and build dams, things like that. Grant's the farmer."

Grant snorted contemptuously. "Me? I'm not spending my life completely broke."

The fury came pouring off Chase Dad. He slammed his fist down on a table. "This farm has been in the family for generations and I am busting my butt every damn day to keep it going and you're just walking away?" he shouted. "This place means nothing to you? My whole life means *nothing*?"

"What about *my* life?" Grant screamed. "You work me like a dog, like a goddam slave! And then when I want to do something for me, everyone's against it. The best thing that's ever happened to me, and Burke ruins it!"

"She's only *seventeen*," Burke shot back. "Why can't you wait a few years? What difference does it make? Why don't you think of what's best for Wenling? You're no different than her father."

Grant's fists were knotted. "You're just jealous she picked me over you!"

My head whipped around. Grandma had fallen into a chair and was slumped sideways. I padded over to her, conscious of a foreign odor rising from her skin.

"You're not a slave, Grant," Chase Dad seethed. "That's ridiculous. This farm belongs to the family. We work it together. It's our source of income, of everything!"

I barked. They all turned and looked at me. I barked again.

"Mom?" Chase Dad ran to her chair. "Oh God, Mom! Grant, call 911." He pulled Grandma right onto the floor, faceup. He started pushing his fist into her chest. "*Mom!*"

TWENTY-FOUR

Grandma was taken away on a rolling bed and so much anguish followed her out the door that I whimpered. When Chase Dad and Burke and Grant jumped into a car and drove down the driveway I cried and followed, pursuing them on the road, until they stopped and Burke opened a door for me. After a short ride we arrived at a big building, but I didn't see Grandma again.

Not long after that the house was filled with sad, quiet people. A lot of them hugged Chase Dad. There were plates and plates of food, which I thought would make everyone happy—it certainly made me happy—but some people were so heartbroken they were weeping. I did not know how to help any of them and felt a little like a bad dog because of my failure.

Wenling went to sit with Grant and he got up and walked away so she sat with Burke. They talked in muted tones. ZZ and Li Min were there, and they murmured as well. I didn't know why someone didn't just throw a ball.

Grandma was not there. This was, I knew, why everyone spoke with such whispered sorrow. Life ends, for humans the same as goats, and when it does, people mourn and a dog must be there for hugs and silence.

Gradually the company left until it was just Chase Dad and Burke and Grant. They carried plates into the kitchen and started bagging things up. "Enough to feed an army," Chase Dad noted in wooden tones.

"When do you want to bury her ashes?" Burke asked.

Chase Dad wiped a cloth across his eyes. "Oh, tomorrow, I guess. Don't have the heart for it right now. Seems like just a short time ago that we were up there on the hill with Dad's ashes. I can't believe they are both gone." Chase Dad put his head in his hands.

There was a long, long silence. Finally Grant cleared his throat. "I'll stay for that, then."

Burke and Chase Dad both looked at him.

He nodded. "And then I'm leaving."

Chase Dad stood and held out his arms. "Come here, son. We're all hurting."

Grant took a step back, shaking his head. "My friend Scott says I can crash at his place until I figure things out. Down in Kalamazoo. Maybe I'll work construction or go to Western. Obviously *not* going to school at MU with Wenling. But I can't stay here anymore. I need to get *out*."

"Please, Grant," Chase Dad begged.

Grant walked to the stairs and started up. "You'll have to figure out how to run this place without me, because I'm never coming back. This is like a prison for me."

Chase Dad sat down. "I have never felt so old in my life," he whispered. I went to him and put my head in his lap.

The next day we climbed up the big hill that overlooked the farm, and everyone spoke quietly, and then Chase Dad dug a hole and put something heavy in it. I sniffed the dirt but I did not understand.

Grant and Burke eventually descended back down to the house, but Chase Dad sat on a rock and was so sad that I knew that to be the best dog possible I should remain with him. I put my head in his lap again and he stroked my ears and cried with deep, pain-filled sobs. I let the tears fall on my fur without shaking them off.

We were there for a long time, and then when we returned to the house, Grant was gone.

And, like Grandma, he didn't come back.

For a long time after that, I found myself going to Grant's room to inhale the scents in his closet, and to Grandma's room to smell her clothes.

I was doing just that when I sensed my boy behind me in the doorway. After all this time, it was still a shock to see him standing without my help. "Hey, Cooper, you miss Grandma? Let's go to town."

I assumed we were going to find Wenling and hoped Lacey would be with her, but instead we went to the dog park.

I *loved* the dog park. I *loved* leaving my marks everywhere. I was running and running with dogs when a huge, stocky male rushed aggressively toward me. I turned and faced him, tail stiff, ready for whatever he intended, but he slowed, politely sniffing between my rear legs. I returned the gesture, and immediately I recognized him: it was Heavy Boy Buddha, my brother!

We ignored all the other dogs and pursued each other around the park. I was quickly exhausted—Heavy Boy Buddha was much harder to tackle than Lacey, and could knock me right off my feet. He was panting, too, though, and after we chased off a couple brown dogs from the water bowl, we lapped up our fill and then collapsed together in the shade.

I didn't get up when a man shouted "Buddha!" and clapped his hands, though Heavy Boy Buddha clambered to his feet. I watched as my brother approached the man and followed him out the gates. Heavy Boy Buddha stopped on the other side of the fence, searching for and finding me with his eyes, and wagged his tail. I wagged back.

We were brothers.

This was what happened to dogs: we went to live with people. We were puppies with siblings and a mother dog and then humans intervened, and it was best, because when Mother was raising us in the den, she was afraid, and we were not fully nourished and had no purpose. Having a person to live with was the gift given to good dogs.

The rest of the summer passed pretty much the way the previous one did, only Grant wasn't there. Close to the time when Chase Dad started driving around with buckets of apples, Wenling came to see me and her car was packed so full of things I couldn't do car ride even if I wanted. I sniffed suspiciously—there was cloth and plastic, mostly.

Burke opened the other door. "Wow, you must have nearly a tenth of your closet in here."

"Stop. It's everything I own. Um, so did you and your dad talk it through?"

Burke shook his head. "Not really. He told me I should call Grant and apologize. Never mind that my brother deliberately left his phone and no one knows where Grant even *is*. Somehow it's my fault my brother took off."

Wenling turned and looked out into the fields. "Didn't you get the sense Grant was always going to leave?" she asked softly. "If there was anything he didn't want, it was to stay here and work the farm."

"That's true. He was just waiting for an excuse."

"And so I'm the excuse," Wenling observed.

"Right, you are basically the reason for everything bad that ever happens."

Wenling laughed quietly. I wagged at the familiar sound.

"So you haven't heard from him, either?" my boy asked.

"No. I broke his heart, Burke. I said we would always be together, but I didn't want to get married right then. But he said now or never. It was like watching him break himself apart, somehow. Like he was proving some point about me, about your family, everything."

Burke closed the door on his side. "Grant's always been angry about things he can't articulate. I'm not sure he even knows, deep down, what has him so furious." Burke walked around the car to be with Wenling and me. "So with me at Michigan State at semester and you at MU, I guess we're huge rivals and are not allowed to talk to each other anymore."

"That's a familiar state of affairs."

"Ouch. Yeah. About that. Wenling. I am so, so sorry for how I've been behaving. I was trying to punish you and Grant and wound up . . . well, I didn't accomplish anything, did I? I think back to how it was when we were together, the three of us, hanging out, and realize that even though I was in the chair, I was never happier. Then I ruined it."

"Oh Burke."

"No, I'm serious. I think of every time you smiled at me at school and I just looked away. How I'd see you and Grant together and immediately head off in another direction. I wish I could have it all back. I would do it so differently."

"It's okay, Burke. None of it matters."

They stood and looked at each other, smiling. "Go Green," he said.

"Go Blue."

"Good luck, Wenling."

They hugged for a long time. I did not understand what was happening, but I knew it was making them sad, especially when Wenling drove off and Burke just stood there, watching the car go until the sound of it had faded long away.

I was on the front porch later, digesting a very fine dinner of dog food, when I picked up the most wonderful scent possible: Lacey was near! I dashed down the driveway as she came scampering up. I was overjoyed to see her. I looked toward the house, wanting to share this amazing event with people, but no one was outside and I couldn't take the time to go get them, not with Lacey here! We ran and ran together in the fields, jumping on each other the whole way. We passed through the fields, scrambled up the hill, and raced past the rock where Chase Dad had been so sad. This was the farm where I had spent my whole life, and now, with Lacey here, I knew everything would be perfect.

My stomach felt heavy from dinner, and then, as we played, it felt heavier and heavier, as if I were still eating. A tight cramp gripped me. I felt the need to vomit but was unable to. I stopped playing. Lacey approached me, concerned, her ears down.

Panting, I turned toward home. I needed my boy. Burke would make it better. With every step, though, I felt my stomach expanding against my ribs, a painful pressure. Whining, I stopped and gazed helplessly at Lacey. I couldn't lie down, yet I could barely stand. I imagined Burke's hand in my fur, comforting me, finding the pain and making it go away.

Lacey barked, the sort of frantic sound a dog makes when it

needs a person. She turned toward the house and barked and barked, but it was a long way from us and no one came.

She touched her nose to mine and then ran away in the direction of home. I sank to the dirt, my breathing labored, yipping in agony when I fell on my bloated side. I heard Lacey barking in the distance and imagined her on the porch.

The barking abruptly ceased. "Cooper!" Burke called, his voice thin on the breeze.

I rose to my feet, drooling and staggering, and took a few steps before I had to halt.

I heard Lacey barking again. She was coming closer. I raised my head and saw Lacey running ahead of Burke, who was following her. He put his hands to his mouth. "Cooper!"

I could not be a good dog and do Come.

Then Lacey was there. She licked my face, crying. I heard Burke's footsteps. "Cooper! What's wrong?"

He knelt beside me and put his hands on my face. Then his arms came around me and he hefted me up, grunting. Though I felt a sharp pain, nothing has ever felt more comforting than being held against his chest as he carried me to the car. Lacey jumped in the backseat with me and carefully curled up against my body, guarding me.

After a car ride I could tell from the sounds and smells wafting out into the parking lot that we had arrived at the vet's, but when Burke tried to lift me out I cried and he left me there with Lacey. Lacey put her nose to mine. I wagged as best as I could.

I realized something then: this wasn't just about the agony in my stomach. Something much more important was happening. As vivid as any memory, I knew what was occurring now. I knew I would not be swimming in the pond ever again, or sleeping with my boy, or running with Lacey, or being a good dog doing Assist and Steady. If Burke sat in his chair and needed me to do Pull, I wouldn't be there to help him.

Burke gave me a purpose in life. It made me sad to think that my purpose was over.

When Burke returned the vet was with him. I felt gentle fingers probing my side. "Bloat and volvulus," the vet said. "His stomach is twisted."

"Can he be saved?"

"Help me get him to surgery."

Arms reached for me and though I knew they were trying to be gentle, the tearing pain made me cry out. Both men backed away. "Oh God," Burke said.

"Let me get Ketamine." The vet hurried off.

"Cooper. You're a good dog, the best dog. Cooper, hang in there, buddy. I love you, you know I love you. Such a good dog," Burke whispered. He kissed my face and I wagged. I felt the terror in my boy so I roused myself and licked his cheek and some of the fear became sadness, instead.

I lay there with Burke and Lacey. Burke was my boy, and Lacey was my dog. I was surrounded by those I loved.

The vet returned and, with a sharp bite at my fur, a warmth spread through me. The sensation in my stomach became a tolerable ache.

"We're losing him, Burke."

Burke pressed his face into my fur. I smelled his tears. "Oh Cooper, Cooper. You're such a good dog. Please, if you can, would you hang on, for me?"

I sensed that Lacey's snout was pressing against my lips, but I could no longer feel her there. I concentrated on them, Burke and Lacey, clinging to their scents as long as I could.

"I'm sorry, Burke. He's gone."

Burke's voice came from far away. "Cooper, that's okay. It's okay. I love you. You are a good dog, such a good dog. I'm going to miss you so much. I will never forget you, Cooper."

There with my boy and my mate, I felt at complete peace, and the pain receded and my vision went dark and I heard Burke calling my name over and over, but I could no longer see him. I could feel his love, though, as strongly as I had felt his arms when he hugged me to his chest.

I was glad Lacey was there to comfort him. Burke would need a good dog, now.

It seemed, then, that I was floating in warm water. My vision returned, but there was nothing to see except a diffuse golden light. I had the sense I was somewhere else, no longer in the parking lot with Burke and Lacey. I knew I had been here before, even if I didn't exactly know where I was.

"Bailey, you are a good dog," I heard a man say. His voice sounded familiar, as if I had heard it long ago and just couldn't remember who he was.

"I know this doesn't make sense to you now, Buddy, but your work isn't done yet. I need you to go back for me. Okay, Bailey? You are being a good dog, but there is still something very important for you to accomplish."

I wondered who the man was, and what he was trying to tell me.

TWENTY-FIVE

I was a puppy again.

I was able to accept this fact because there really wasn't any other choice. I had a mother, but she was a different dog than my first mother, and her fur and the fur on my puppy brothers and sisters were splashed with mottled whites and blacks and browns and they all had light eyes and pointed ears. My own body was small and light, my limbs uncoordinated, my senses dull.

I expected the floor and walls of the den to be metal, but when I was able to explore I realized that though we lived in a home similar to my first (because of the tight, low ceiling) it was otherwise a complete change—dirt floors and stone walls. Sunlight streamed indirectly at us from square holes cut into all four sides of this strange place.

Lacey had come back to me as a new dog, and obviously I was doing the same thing. Is this what every dog experienced?

I nursed, and played with my siblings, and when we crawled out the square hole into the light I saw that we were living in a space under a house. There was snow on the ground and my siblings rolled in it and bit at it as if they had never seen snow before.

I could not smell Burke, or any humans at all, really. No sounds or scents came from the house, which squatted by a small lake that was frozen over. I could pick up no trace of the goat ranch, or anything familiar.

Then a thought occurred to me: one of the puppies might be Lacey! I carefully sniffed each sibling, enduring their inevitable lunges and play, but eventually concluded she was not here. I would know Lacey if I encountered her.

It was a sunny day, almost painfully bright, and we were all out in the snow, taking advantage of some warmer weather. Mother was lying peacefully, then suddenly raised her head sharply, alarmed. She sensed danger, though I could smell nothing. Mother turned immediately to one of my sisters, seized her by the back of the neck, and carried her back to the den.

We might not have perceived the threat, but we knew enough to follow our mother. We scampered after her toward the square hole entrance. When I heard human voices, though, I stopped and turned to look behind me.

Several men were advancing toward us with long, gliding motions. They carried sticks in their hands and were wearing boards on their feet. I could tell they had spotted me.

"It's a puppy!" one of them exclaimed.

I wagged. What would happen now is that I would go to them and they would take me to Burke. I began bounding through the shallow snow, struggling with it, and then I felt my mother's teeth on my nape. I was yanked away.

"Wow, you see that?" I heard one of the men say. "I didn't know they did that in real life."

Mother dropped me inside the den. After a moment, shadows interrupted the stream of light from one of the square windows. Mother Dog's growl was fierce and I cowered with the rest of the puppies. A man chuckled. "I wouldn't stick my head down in there if I were you."

"Not going to. Just trying to see what's happening under there."

"Hey. I've got some turkey jerky in my pack. Hang on."

Mother Dog growled again, a low, lingering warning. When something came sailing in through the sunlight and landed nearby, she flinched, but remained pressed up against us.

Eventually, I could sense that the men had left. Mother Dog suspiciously approached the tossed object and ate it noisily.

I could feel how relieved were my littermates by how joyously they recommenced playing, but as I raised my nose to the fading presence of the men, I felt disappointed.

A few days later we were back out wrestling under a gray sky when I heard an odd squeaking noise emanating from above us. I glanced up and spotted several fat birds batting at the air with thick wings, making all sorts of racket as they circled the pond. I observed Mother watching them intently as they landed on the ice, skittering and crashing, sliding inelegantly on their bellies. They looked like ducks, except they were much larger, and while ducks make an irritating squawk, these made an irritating honk.

Mother, her head low between her shoulders, creeped down to the lake's edge, easing out onto the ice. She was going to catch one of the big ducks! I had never managed to ensnare a duck myself and I watched eagerly, hoping to find out how it was done.

The fat honking birds all warily regarded Mother as she tracked closer and closer to them. Suddenly she rose up out of her slither and began frantically clawing her way toward them, and then they were beating the air loudly with their wings and were in the air just before she reached them. Frustrated, she barked.

And then she fell through the ice.

She had turned to dash back to us and then her hindquarters collapsed as the surface beneath her feet gave way and she was nearly submerged, only her head visible. The distress and fear crackled through us all, and I whimpered. Then her two front paws came up to grip the ice in front of her, but that was all she managed. She just lay there, panting.

We milled around, not knowing what to do. I realized that we should be with her, and ran down the slope toward the pond. My siblings all flowed down the beach after me. We sprawled when our paws hit the smooth surface of the frozen lake, our little feet sliding out from underneath us.

Mother barked a high, sharp warning. I drew up short and my littermates did the same: we had never heard her make a sound like that before, but it carried a meaning we all somehow instantly recognized. She was telling us to stay back. Our heads bobbing in confusion, we crept forward, unsure, halting when she barked again.

I could feel everyone's rapid heartbeats as we pressed together in a flustered, frightened mass. This was our mother, our life source, and she was in such danger she wouldn't let us follow our most basic instinct to seek safety with her.

Another sound came to us then, something very familiar to my ears: a vehicle was approaching. I turned to see a boxy van make a sliding halt next to the house. A woman stepped out, shaking her long blond hair. She waded through the snow up to the house and opened the outer door. I saw her feel above the doorframe, then lift a small rug, and then pick up a wooden box. She returned to the door, opened it, and walked inside. She was not in there long, though, before she came out, her head down as she peered around at the snow. She traced our footprints, raising her head and starting in surprise when she caught sight of us. "Oh no! No, come back! Puppies!"

I broke from my siblings and joyously galloped toward the woman, who ran down to meet me. When she stepped on the ice, her foot broke through and black water pooled over her boot. "Oh!" She backed up to the shore, then fell to her knees and spread her arms wide, and when I reached her I jumped into them because I knew this woman, knew her by sight and smell and sound. It was Ava!

She had grown to be a very big girl.

The rest of my dog family might not have known her, or maybe they did, but they followed my lead and within short order we were all soon leaping and squirming at her feet. "Okay, okay, you're safe. Wow. We need to save your mother." She had her phone out and pressed to her cheek. "Yes! My name is Ava Marks with Hope's Animal Rescue. I'm out at Silver Lake Cottages and there's a dog who fell through the ice. It's the fourth cabin from the road. She can't get out without help. Wait. What? *What?* A couple of *hours?* No, please, I don't . . . you can't send anybody? She could be *dead* by then. *Please.* Okay, yes, yes, please do call me back."

She slipped her phone into her pocket. Some of my siblings were gazing out at Mother Dog and some of them were peering up at Ava. The puppies turning away from Ava were clearly more afraid than the ones focused on her. When dogs hand their fates over to a human, they feel much more secure than if they believe they must solve a problem themselves.

Out on the ice, Mother Dog hadn't moved. She was watching us, her ears back, her tongue out.

"Okay, puppies. I'm going to put you in the rescue-mobile,

okay?" She bent down and picked up one of my sisters, carrying her tenderly to her van—the same, or at least similar, van, I realized, that I had ridden in long ago. I knew inside there were cages and blankets and toys. Ava returned and reached for a brother.

I understood what she was doing because this had occurred before. Ava was going to take us to a place so that Mother Dog could find us. But how would that work? Mother Dog was still out on the ice, and I didn't think she could get out. Didn't Ava understand that we needed to help our mother?

Behind Ava, well down the snow-packed road, I spied a man coming. He was gliding on long boards, rhythmically punching the snow with sticks gripped in his hands. Ava bent down to pick up another sister, then straightened when she glimpsed the man. She waved. "Hey! Help!"

She went to the van and deposited my sibling and then put her hands to her mouth. "Hurry!"

The man was panting so loudly I could hear him. I looked back at my mother, who hadn't moved, and then to the last remaining puppy, a little male smaller than me. He was obviously afraid, and I decided a good dog would go to him. I pressed up against him, doing Steady.

The man stopped, still a little bit down the road, leaning on his sticks. He held up a hand, still panting.

Ava crunched a few steps toward him, her boots sinking. "There's a dog out there, she's fallen through the ice!"

The man nodded, looking out at Mother Dog and then at Ava. "Okay," he gasped. "Let me see if there is some rope in the cabin."

"I unlocked it."

"I know, you set off the alarm. Whew, I thought I was in better shape than this."

"I'm with Hope's Animal Rescue. We got a call there were puppies out at this cabin. I thought they meant *in* the cabin."

"I'll check for the rope." The man pushed off with his sticks and slid past us. As he did so, his scent came cleanly to my nose, and I was so surprised I nearly yipped aloud. This wasn't just any man, this was Burke!

Of *course* Ava would find me, and of *course* she would give me to Burke!

Burke was kicking off the boards on his feet. He looked the same, smelled the same—I knew he would be happy to see me. I made to run to him, but Ava scooped me up and then grabbed my fearful brother, who cried quietly.

"It's going to be okay, little guys. We'll save your mother," Ava whispered, nuzzling us. Since I was up this close to her, I licked her cold face, and she giggled.

"Got some rope!" Burke stepped back out.

I squirmed to squeeze out of Ava's arms and into Burke's, but she held me tightly. "Do you own this place?"

"Oh no. My buddy is the caretaker for the property managers and I am just helping him out so he can visit his parents. Okay, here's what I am going to do. I'm going to crawl flat on the ice, spread out my weight, and have a ski in each hand for further displacement. You hang on to the rope and I'll play it out. When I get there I'll tie it around the dog and you pull."

"Please be careful."

"Oh, you know it."

Burke carried his shoe boards down to the lake, and Ava followed, still clutching my brother and me against her chest. He lay down with the boards and gingerly wriggled forward, a rope railing out behind him. I squirmed again because he obviously needed Assist.

Ava held the end of the rope. "I called 911, but there are two house fires going today and they don't have anyone to spare."

"It's okay, this is working. The ice isn't even cracking. I think I'm inventing a new sport, here."

"Ice crawling?"

"Wait until you see my triple axel."

I watched as he slithered up to Mother Dog. The lake air was so undisturbed, I could hear him croon "good dog" to her. She panted but did not resist as he looped the rope around her neck. "Okay, now, pull!"

Pull? How could I do Pull?

Ava set us both down and grunted as the rope went rigid. I saw Burke grappling with Mother Dog, straining to lift her out of the water. "You've got it!"

When Mother Dog had all four feet on the ice she tried to run to us but her rear legs kept splaying. Ava hauled on the rope. "It's working!"

"I'm coming back!" Burke shouted.

And then he fell through the ice.

Ava screamed.

Burke's head had vanished and though I was only a puppy I ran to do Steady, to help him out of that hole. He needed me and this was what I had been trained to do.

"No, puppy!" Ava cried behind me. I ignored her and ran straight toward the black water into which Burke had vanished.

The only sound was the tap of my tiny feet and my mother's panting as Ava rapidly reeled her in. Mother Dog stared at me as I dashed right past her, bent on where I had last seen Burke.

His head popped up out of the hole. He stood, the water level with his hips. "Oh my God, is this water cold!"

I splashed through the last few steps as fast as my little puppy legs would let me and threw myself into his arms. Laughing, he hugged me. I was his Cooper dog. "I have to confess," he whispered into my ear, "I thought that was the end for me there, little guy."

He threw his long boards toward the shore and began wading, grasping me with one arm and breaking the ice in front of him with the other.

Ava was holding my little brother. "I had no idea the water was that shallow. Are you okay?"

"I guess compared to how I'd be if the lake was seventy feet deep, yes, I'm *wonderful*. But otherwise I'm leaking ice water from my underpants. How's the mother?"

Ava glanced over to where Mother Dog was anxiously nosing around the outside of the van. "She seems completely oblivious to being in the lake. You'd hardly know anything happened."

Burke stepped up on the narrow beach. "Well, she's tougher than I am, then. I hope to hell the cabin's water heater is working."

He carried me up the steps and into the cabin. I wriggled with pleasure at being held by my boy. He tried to set me down and I tried to stop him, frantically jumping up in his arms to lick his face. "Hey!" he sputtered. "I have to get out of these things!" He was laughing, obviously happy to be reunited with me.

I was sniffing Burke's sodden clothes, pooled up in a heap, when Ava walked in. The bathroom door was open and Burke stood being drenched by hot water, steam curling out. I wagged and ran to her, and when she dropped to one knee I leaped up, licking and licking, until she laughed and lifted me high. Ava! Burke! This was wonderful! "Oh my, you are so affectionate! What a cutie pie. Hey," she called, "are you going to be okay?"

"This is the best shower I've ever taken. Could you throw my clothes in the dryer for me?"

"Uh, sure. I'll maybe put them through a spin cycle first, otherwise they'll take forever."

"That's okay, I'm going to be in *here* forever."

Ava put me down and scooped up Burke's clothing, which dripped water as she carried them to a small closet and, banging around, put them in a familiar-smelling machine that made a loud noise. She returned to the bathroom door. "I can't believe you showed up. It was like you were sent by God or something."

"Or the alarm company, anyway."

I sniffed along the walls, finding the scents of other people.

"I'm trying to say thank-you for coming out here and saving the dog's life."

"I should thank *you*. My head was splitting with boredom. There's nothing to do but ski around and around the lake, checking to see if there's been a bear invasion or a new volcano."

Ava laughed.

"Well, I know one thing. If I ever bought this place, I'd put in a *much* bigger hot water tank," Burke announced. "We're losing heat already."

Ava turned back to the machines. "Okay, wait," she called over her shoulder. She brought out some towels as the water stopped and went back to the bathroom. "I put the towels in the dryer to heat them up for you. . . . Oh!" She pulled her head abruptly back into the living room. I glanced at her curiously.

"Hey, sorry," Burke said. "I guess I should have mentioned my strange habit of being naked when I shower. Could I have the towels?"

Ava threw the towels in the bathroom. Then she scooped me up off the floor. I licked her face. I wondered if we were all going to live here in this house. It was smaller than the farm.

We stood there for a moment. Ava was watching the open door. "So I put your clothes in the dryer."

"Thanks."

"I'll put my card on the table, if you ever have another box of puppies you need picked up."

"What about a bear?"

Ava laughed. "I'm sure we'd find him a good home." I was feeling so affectionate I gave her chin a nibble. She sharply pulled her head back from me. "I've got the van running with the heat on."

"How do you know the mother won't just drive off in it?" Burke padded out into the living room, his feet making wet marks on the wood floor. I wagged, wanting to get down and run to him. I ached to feel his hands on my fur. He had a towel around his waist and another one draped over his shoulders. "Nice of you to heat the towels for me." He stepped over to the machines and crouched and opened a door, sticking his head in. "I'm Burke, by the way," he announced, his voice muffled.

"Nice to meet you, Burt. I'm Ava."

Burke stood, pulling his head out of the machine. "Probably take another hour. Sorry, I know you said something, but I couldn't hear it."

"I said my name is Ava."

Grinning, Burke came across the room. Ava moved me to her other arm. "Nice to meet you." They held hands and then changed their minds and let go. They smiled at each other for a long moment. She shifted me back to the original arm. "So you're not the permanent caretaker, then?"

"No. I'm a grad student at Michigan State. Engineering. And you do rescue?"

"It's my dad's rescue, actually. His mother was named Hope. I go to Northwestern. Pre-law. We're on Christmas break. But yeah, rescue is sort of my life's passion. I was visiting my dad and his girlfriend when we got a call that some cross-country skiers saw a mother and puppies out here."

Burke shrugged. "My family doesn't really do holidays. I took this temporary job in part as an excuse to avoid going home to my dad's place. My brother hasn't been heard from in a couple of years, long story, and when he left it sort of broke up what remained of the family. My parents are divorced."

Ava nodded. "Mine, too."

Burke opened the refrigerator. "If we get snowed in we've got plenty of beer."

"I actually need to get going."

"Oh, I wasn't implying you should stay with me in this cabin and drink pale ale all afternoon. Though if you did it would be the second most exciting thing to happen to me today."

"When you fell through the ice, I really thought you were going to die."

"*You* thought. My whole life was flashing before my eyes when my feet hit bottom—it happened so fast I only made it to second grade."

Burke and Ava grabbed hands again. "Goodbye," Ava said. She carried me out to the van. She opened the sliding door, and my siblings, who were sleepily piled in a cage, leaped to their feet, instantly electrified. She kissed me on the nose. "You are such a special one, I'm going to name you Bailey," she told me. She opened the cage door and fended off my brothers and sisters, depositing me in the middle of the jumble. She shut the door and they were instantly on me, sniffing and then chewing me as if I'd been gone forever.

Wait, where was Burke? I shook off my littermates and put my paws on the side of the kennel, peering up at the small window, desperately trying to glimpse my boy.

Mother Dog was lying down, barely awake, in her own cage. Ava slid in the truck and sat for a moment, gazing at the cabin. "Burt," she said quietly.

I did not understand why, but she drove away and left Burke behind. I cried and cried. Why? I belonged with my boy.

Eventually I stopped sobbing and pondered all that was happening, stepping out of the endless scrum of jostling puppies to have some space for myself. Why was it that, as was true once before, when Mother Dog was pretty much done nursing me, Ava came along to take me to the world of people? And last time that world centered around Burke and I had a very important job, but my boy no longer sat in his chair—was that why we were leaving him after he went swimming? If I wasn't here for Burke, what was I supposed to do now? And what was a Bailey? I'd heard that before somewhere.

It turned out my *name* was Bailey. Ava named all of us, but I wasn't sure my siblings understood when she pulled us up to her face and said, "You're Carly. Carly, Carly, Carly." She called me "Bailey, Bailey, Bailey" and I got it, and when she was doling out treats, saying, "Sophie. Nina. Willy." I waited patiently for "Bailey" and didn't just surge forward and step on heads like my littermates.

We were in the same sort of building I remembered from my first life as a puppy. The air was heavy with the scent of the mystery animals that lived in barns. There were nice people all around who fed and cuddled us, one of them Sam Dad. "Hi, Bailey!" he would say to me.

But then it changed. After a long ride in the van, I was sent to live with a man who called me Riley, instead. His name was Ward and he was Chase Dad's age. He spent so much time sitting in his chair I thought perhaps he was going to ask me to Pull or Assist, but he could walk when he felt like it. When the sun turned warm he would spend time lying down in his backyard, drinking a sweet-smelling liquid out of a can and belching and then farting. When Ward threw a can out into the long grass I smelled it but he didn't say to Get It so I assumed it belonged lying in the yard.

I had no other people to watch over, and no job to do at all. Often other men would come over and either sit and yell at the TV or sit in the backyard and belch and fart with Ward.

My domain was that yard. I would sniff around the fence, hoping I might come across something new, but the only scents were the scraggly plants and the marks I had made lifting my leg. On the wind, though, I sometimes caught the faintest whiff of the goat ranch's unmistakable presence infusing the air. I would lift my nose, thinking if I could smell that, I could smell Lacey, but her scent eluded me. Mostly all I could smell was Ward.

A visit to the vet left me feeling sleepy and itchy. "Had to get old Riley fixed," Ward informed his friends.

"Fixed? You mean broken!" one of his friends hooted. "He was fixed when you got him!"

The men laughed so hard several of them farted. I retreated to the far side of the yard.

I wanted to go home.

Those same friends were drinking from cans and filling the air with pungent smoke from their mouths when I had an idea. They were laughing more than usual, and started painting over my marks with their own, weaving unsteadily to the fence and planting a palm to support themselves. I padded to the back gate and sat, waiting patiently. Eventually one of the friends pushed open the back gate and staggered through it, letting it swing carelessly behind him. I followed him out.

The man stumbled into the front yard and retched—it smelled even worse than Ward's belches.

I watched him for a moment. He was on his hands and knees and looked like he could really use a dog doing Assist, but then he stood and weaved his way back through the gate, closing it behind him.

With a general sense of the direction of the goat ranch, I confidently set out to find the farm, trotting along the road.

Before long, the smell of a completely new creature reached me. The moon was bright and I spotted something the size of a small dog scuttling across the pavement, its back hunched. I immediately set off in joyous pursuit.

The animal turned to face me. I romped up to it and play-bowed and it bared its teeth and charged me, front paws coming off the ground. I backpedaled furiously and it kept coming and I turned and ran. Whatever it was, it did not want to play! And, though it was much smaller than I was, I did not like the look of its fangs. It seemed some animals did not want to have fun in life, preferring to be hostile and unpleasant.

I began running when I was close to the farm. I'd pretty much expected to pick up Lacey's smell as I scampered up the farm driveway, but there was no sign of her on the breeze. The house was dark and quiet. I pushed through the dog door and stood for a moment, wagging, wondering what I should do. I could tell that Chase Dad was in his room, sleeping, his door shut. Neither Burke nor Grant were home, and neither of them had been there in some time. ZZ's scent was much stronger, and Grandma's was elusive in the air, a mere hint, now.

It felt so wonderful to leap up on my boy's bed and curl up for the night. There was enough of him left that I could imagine he was sleeping next to me, though because he wasn't, I took advantage of the situation and sprawled out on his pillow.

With morning there was sunlight and I heard Chase Dad in the kitchen. I jumped down and went to him, wagging, thinking this would be a good day for some bacon. His back was to me, but as I approached he whirled and dropped his coffee. "Yahhh!"

Startled, I hesitated a moment, but I couldn't contain myself. I ran to him and put my paws up, trying to climb up to his face.

"Hey! Down! Sit!"

I obediently did Sit. Chase Dad put a hand on his chest. "Who are you? How did you get in here?"

I didn't understand, but I wagged.

"Are you a good dog? Friendly doggy?" He held out a hand and I licked it. It tasted like eggs. "I guess you are. What are you doing here? Is this a prank? ZZ? Are you here?" He cocked his head, listening. "Burke?" He waited a moment. "*Grant?*"

I expected someone to appear, and it seemed Chase Dad did as well. He sighed, reaching for my collar and twisting it a little. "Riley. So your name is Riley."

He was calling me Riley, but here on the farm I was Cooper.

After a time, Ward came to get me. I was disappointed, but now I knew the route. It wasn't long before he was unloading groceries and I was able to slip out through the door to the garage and from there out to the driveway.

ZZ and Chase Dad were out in the fields and I was so excited to see both of them that I ran around with a stick, but they were busy with their inedible plants and didn't pay much attention. I recognized the sound of Ward's truck after most of the day had passed and was very disappointed—why was he coming to get me? I belonged *here*.

The best opportunities always presented themselves when Ward's friends came over to belch and fart. Inevitably I could wait alertly and squeeze through the gap when they opened the gate. Ward was always angry at me, but I kept returning to the farm. I couldn't figure out, though, how he always knew to find me there.

One afternoon a storm broke a tree in Ward's backyard. Some men arrived to chop it up with loud tools and I idled, seemingly paying no attention until one of the workers swung open the back gate, and then I was free.

Chase Dad was sitting on the front porch when I scampered joyously up. In his lap he clutched a box with metal strings holding it together, and his fingers on those strings sent familiar vibrations into the air that halted when he saw me. He started shaking his head. "Riley, why do you always come here? What do you want?"

I searched carefully. No sign of Burke. The boys had been gone a long, long time.

Chase Dad petted me and gave me water and was still sitting there with me when a car turned up the driveway. The driver got out and stood there, looking at the house.

It wasn't Ward, though.

It was Grant.

Chase Dad ran off the porch and up to Grant the same way I had run to him the morning he threw his coffee on the floor. He seized Grant in a tight hug. "My God, Grant, my God," he murmured. His cheeks were wet. I couldn't manage to wedge my head between them, so I stood on my rear legs and put my feet on Grant from behind.

Chase Dad finally released Grant from the embrace, holding him at arm's length. "Welcome home, son."

"I figured I'd help with the harvest." Grant finally bent over to let me kiss him. "You get a dog?"

"That's Riley. He doesn't belong to me; he lives with Ward Pembrake, the guy with the sandwich truck who sold to the field hands? Only there aren't any field hands anymore so he's pretty much retired. Crazy dog comes to visit all the time. I call Ward and he comes out, smelling like a brewery, and Riley heads off with him until the next time."

Grant stroked my ears. "Hey, Riley. You seem like such a good dog. For sure you've got Australian shepherd in you."

Chase Dad nodded. "I'm betting maybe Newfoundland, too."

Having Grant call me Riley and tell me I was a good dog made me realize that even when I was back home on the farm, my name was Riley now. They couldn't tell I was really Cooper, the way I could always separate Lacey from all others, even if she came as a different dog.

It was startling to realize that a dog could understand something a human couldn't.

"You really want to help with the harvest, Grant?"

Grant stopped petting me and stood. "I just thought maybe it was time to reconnect, is all."

"I'll take it. It was a dry start to the summer, but we've had some rain since."

We were sitting on the porch when ZZ arrived. "Look who it is!" Chase Dad called.

ZZ's boots made the porch boards creak. "Hi, Grant. Very nice," ZZ greeted. He held out his hand and Grant grabbed it and twisted it and then let it go.

"Your English has gotten a lot better, ZZ," Grant observed.

The men sat down, so I lay down at their feet. "He still doesn't say much, though, do you, ZZ?" Chase Dad remarked with a laugh. I could feel happiness coming off him, strong as one of Ward's belches. "And he gets his tenses and pronouns pretty mixed up."

"How long you stay? Stay-ing," ZZ asked Grant.

Grant shrugged. "Summer. Don't know. I was working for a paving company, sort of lost interest."

"You were what, standing in the road with a sign that said 'slow'?" Chase Dad laughed.

"Pretty much. I was in sales. Just got tired of it."

"Your brother's got a job for some firm that instead of building things, tears them down."

"They decommission dams, Dad."

"Wait. You talk to your brother?"

Grant nodded. "Yeah, well, just the one time. I decided if I were going to reconnect, I should start with him. I called him the other day, told him about coming up here. Figured before I burned the gas I should check to make sure you hadn't sold the place to the robo-farmers."

"That the first time you two've spoken since you left?"

"Yeah."

Chase Dad leaned forward. "How did it go?"

"Oh, about as you'd expect. Maybe worse. You could feel both of us wishing the conversation would hurry up and end."

"Tell you the truth, I don't talk to him much, either. My birthday. Father's Day. It's always awkward between us." Chase Dad sighed. "Miss my mom. She would have known how to put Humpty Dumpty back together."

There was a noise in the house, a trilling tone. Chase Dad stood up. "Hang on, I'll get that." He left us, and a moment later the noise stopped.

Grant clapped a hand on ZZ's arm. "You look good, ZZ."

"You well also."

"How is Li Min? And Wenling?"

"Both were fine, thank you."

"And, uh . . . is Wenling married? I mean, what is she doing now?"

"He in school to be agricultural engineer."

"Oh wow. That's great."

"She was not married. He lives with her boyfriend. His family will be from Qinghai province a long time."

"Ah. I think I get it."

Chase Dad pushed the door open and stepped out. I wagged. "You're not going to believe this. Ward's not coming to get his dog this time. He says if Riley likes it out here so much, he can just stay. Never even asked how I felt about it. Sounded drunk as a lord and it's not even noon." He sat down and frowned at me. "Now what?"

Grant scratched my chest with a finger. "You know what? I'll take him. He seems pretty smart. What do you say, Riley? Want to live here with me for a while?"

"Oh, we know he likes the farm," Chase Dad observed.

I yawned, wondering when my boy would get here.

I slept on Grant's bed that night.

Burke did come, but it wasn't until the apples were filling the air with their scent. I sprinted across the yard, sobbing, and tackled him the moment he stepped out of his car. "So you're Riley!" he greeted with a laugh, kneeling so I could climb on him and kiss him. He fell back and I climbed on top of him, rolling on him and loving him with frantic cries. "Okay, good, that's enough. Whoa! Okay!" He stood, slapping his pants. "So where is everybody?"

We walked out to the fields together, me dashing in circles around him, my joy uncontainable. When Burke saw Grant he began to run and then Grant was running, too, and they crashed into each other, laughing and slapping each other's backs. I jumped around excitedly, exultant that we were all finally back together. Dad came dashing across the fields, grinning, and joined his sons, holding them both.

Li Min made delicious beef in the kitchen and I followed her every move, ready to pounce if she dropped something. Everyone sat at the table and ate, and a tiny piece of meat fell from Grant's hand. I could always count on Grant!

"So tell us more about this Stephanie," Burke asked.

Li Min made a small noise and I glanced at her, hoping she was planning to feed the dog beef as well.

Chase Dad's leg, which always twitched a little, went still. "Not much to tell. She's a companion."

Burke laughed. "That's what people your age call it?"

"She's a hard person to get to know," Li Min observed.

"She's a groupie for the Not Very Good Old White Guys' Band," Grant said slyly.

"She is not a *groupie*," Chase Dad corrected testily. "You come up for Thanksgiving, you'll meet her then."

There was a silence, finally broken by Grant. "*What?* We're actually going to get to meet one of your girlfriends?"

I turned back to Grant and waited patiently for more beef.

Later, in the living room, Grant, ZZ, and Chase Dad sat while my boy and Li Min poured water on plates at the sink. The men were eating peanuts, so I picked the living room over the kitchen.

Chase Dad threw a peanut in the air and caught it with his mouth, just like a dog. "I wish you wouldn't leave, Grant."

"I've already stayed longer than I intended, Dad."

"ZZ and I could really use the help. And look, Grant, you were born to this work."

"Dad."

"I mean it."

ZZ stood up. "I see if I help him."

He passed into the kitchen and I was about to follow but just as I stretched and shook myself, Grant leaned forward and snagged some peanuts, so I did Sit, being extra good.

Grant sighed. "I appreciate it, but I need to make some real money."

"We're profitable here."

"Barely."

"With your help . . ."

Grant held up a hand, the peanut odor wafting off it so powerfully I involuntarily gave the air a lick. "Can we not talk about this, Dad?"

They were quiet for a time. Chase Dad shrugged. "What about Riley, then?"

I jerked my head up at my name. Peanuts?

Grant leaned over to look at me. "Could he maybe stay here with you? I'm not sure where I'll be living."

"Sure. We're getting used to him."

Later I was disappointed when Grant dug into the box of dog toys and pulled out his nylon bone. "Hey, Riley, want a bone? Huh?"

I did Leave It on the nylon bone, pulling out a rope toy and shaking it. Now *that* was fun!

Life was different now that I was Riley. Grant and Burke did not do School. They both left the farm for long amounts of time, but then they would come back and sleep in their old bedrooms with me. They were never at the farm the same time, though.

Sometimes a woman named Stephanie came to visit, and I liked her because she always threw the squeaky toy for me. The first time she helped Li Min in the kitchen I thought Stephanie was very clumsy because the pots and plates all rang with loud impacts on the counter. Then when Chase Dad cooked and Stephanie helped and there was no excessive noise, I realized that it wasn't her, it was Li Min making all the clatter. It happened every time Stephanie came to see Li Min and ZZ and me and have dinner. It seemed like Li Min's version of an angry walk.

Stephanie and Chase Dad liked to sit at the table and play "cards," a word I came to associate with no food being tossed down for me to catch. "You know Li Min doesn't like me very much," Stephanie complained.

I heard a light slapping sound: one of the "cards."

"That's ridiculous, Stephanie."

"She's never smiled at me. She barely speaks to me."

"She's a quiet person."

I turned and chewed at a particularly vicious itch on my foot.

"This is outright hostility, Chase."

"Well. Maybe she thinks you're out to steal ZZ away from her."

Another slap, but Stephanie's legs had gone very still. "Why would you make a joke like that?" she asked quietly.

"What? I didn't mean anything by it, Steph."

"It was really inappropriate."

"I'm sorry. I apologize."

"If anything, I feel like I'm stealing *you* from ZZ. The two of you are so close. Hard to believe what you said, that at first you two didn't like each other very much."

"It wasn't him, it was me. All I needed to do was hear that he was employed by TMH and I built up a whole myth about him that was completely false. I've apologized to him for it a bunch of times. Like you said, we're on pretty good terms. I couldn't make this place work without him; he does most of the heavy lifting."

Another slap of a card. Why weren't these people hungry?

"And I know ZZ will take over when you retire."

"Retire?" Chase Dad laughed. "Farmers don't retire, they just wind up under the dirt one day instead of working on top of it."

"Well, but you said you'd like to travel, see places."

"Right, and I'd like to wake up in the morning without sore knees. Not going to happen."

"I don't understand."

I flopped onto my side and closed my eyes.

"Even if I had that kind of money, take off to Tahiti, I couldn't do it, Steph. The farm won't let me go. There's always something that needs to be fixed, even in the winter."

"Well, then you could sell the farm."

"It's for the boys, you know that."

"The boys? Then where are they? If they want to inherit it so badly, why aren't they here?"

"That's between me and them, Steph. A father and his sons, working through some things."

"Only you aren't working through things. You said they still don't speak to one another, and they never call *you*, either."

Chase Dad didn't reply.

"The first time I met you, you were this carefree guitar player."

"Care*less*, you mean." Chase Dad laughed. "The only reason I sound good is because everyone else in the band is worse."

I wagged sleepily at the laughter.

Stephanie sniffed. "I'm trying to say you seemed so fun. So unburdened. Here on the farm, you are this whole other person. So serious all the time."

"Farming is a serious business."

A long silence was broken only by the sound of the cards and my long sigh.

"What are we doing, Chase?"

"Sorry?"

"We've been going out for more than a year. I've got shoes in your closet and a drawer in your dresser. And that seems to be it, as far as you're concerned."

"Honey . . ."

"I do not want to waste any time, Chase. I'm too old for that."

"You think we're wasting time?"

"You think you'll ever get married again, Chase? No, I don't mean to me, just in general. In life. No, you don't, do you? No matter what."

"I don't understand how we got on this topic."

Stephanie stood and I looked at her hopefully, getting to my feet as well. "I'm going to need some time, Chase, to think about all this."

"Think about *what*?"

Stephanie stopped coming over after that. I guess she didn't like cards after all.

I didn't know Chase Dad realized there was a dog park nearby until the day he drove me to town and then steered over to the same place Burke used to take me! I was so excited to mark everywhere and sniff so many dogs under their tails and run around. I expected to encounter Heavy Boy Buddha, but there was no sign of him. Instead I received a shock when a frisky dog galloped up and play-bowed. I knew this dog—she was Lacey's puppy! *My* puppy, all grown!

She didn't recognize me at all—that was obvious by the way she carefully examined my mark, getting to know me.

It had never occurred to me that a puppy I had known when I was Cooper would not recognize me when I was Riley. I knew Lacey, but this dog, named Echo, didn't know *me*.

I didn't understand any of it. Were Lacey and I somehow unique among dogs?

We played and played, Echo and me, with that easy freedom dogs feel when they like each other. Somehow it didn't matter that she didn't know who I was.

That winter, when the snow was deep, Grant drove up the driveway and there was another car right behind him, being driven by a horse I soon learned was named Lucky.

Lucky the horse seemed to me to be one of the most worthless animals I had ever encountered. She never came in the house—she obviously couldn't figure out the dog door, though I went in and out of it several times to demonstrate. She never chased a ball or a stick. And she never ate food, just chewed on dry grass without throwing up.

Chase Dad patted Lucky's nose. "Never heard of renting a horse before," he told Grant. He stood back, regarding Lucky's car. "Nice trailer, too."

"Want to take a little ride?"

When Lucky the horse did Steady it went all wrong and Chase Dad wound up stuck on her back for a time while she trotted around.

"Haven't done this in a while," Chase Dad called, grinning.

That night, Lucky was in the barn, but when I went to check on her she just stared at me, not even lowering her nose when I lifted my leg on some straw in a friendly fashion. I gave up on trying to be nice to a horse. Inside the house, Chase Dad and Grant played cards. I groaned and lay at their feet. If anyone would give me a treat during cards it would be Grant, but he was as distracted as everyone else.

Slap. That was the sound of cards. I decided I didn't like it.

"Time you leaving in the morning?" Chase Dad asked.

Slap.

"Not too early. You want to come?"

"Nah. I never was much of a camper. Especially in winter."

"It's not really camping. The route takes me to cabins and a lodge."

"Guess if I want nature I'll just hike up to my apple orchard."

Slap.

"I mean, it would be nice to spend the time with each other doing something besides working," Grant suggested softly. I picked up something like sadness and sat up to lick his pant leg.

"You'll have more fun without having to drag me along," Chase Dad replied.

The next morning Grant took me for a long car ride with Lucky the horse following right behind us—I smelled her the whole way. I did not understand how Lucky took a car ride by herself.

We parked and Lucky stopped her car at the same time. I had no idea what we were doing.

I was surprised when Lucky did Steady and Grant got stuck on top of her and we took a walk on a trail in the snow. There had been a lot of horses before us, as evidenced by their leavings, which had frozen solid and were even less interesting as ice than when they were fresh. We stopped along the way at some three-walled buildings that had nothing interesting in them, just piles of stale grass that Lucky chewed out of ignorance. We slept in a small wooden house by a frozen stream among other, similar houses, and Grant spoke to a few people. The air was thick with the tang of smoke. Lucky spent the night with some other horses, but they didn't play, they just stood around trying to think of something to do.

We went farther into the woods the next day. When we stopped that afternoon, Grant brushed Lucky and put her in a place with other horses while I played and wrestled with a big black dog and a smaller brown dog. A few horses watched jealously.

"Let's go to the lodge now, Riley," Grant called when he came out of the horse house. I followed him into a big, warm building with many smells and hallways with many doorways. A popping, spitting fire in a stone wall sent acrid odors and heat into the large main room, which rose up to a very high ceiling. Grant stood and talked to some people at a tall table.

Then I was jolted by an unmistakable scent, coming to me faintly, separating itself from the smoke and the people and the warm food smells.

Ava.

TWENTY-EIGHT

I put my nose to the air and, now that I had detected Ava's presence, there were signs of her everywhere. I tracked back and forth, searching. She had been in this big house, with its creaky wooden floors and couches and people laughing and drinking coffee. Been here not long ago—her scent was fresh, recent. I knew instinctively that I could find her, as if Find were a command, like Steady and Assist.

But I would have to venture outside. Grant was still standing at a table, talking to two women and not watching me, while I followed Ava's track right up to the front door. She was somewhere on the other side of it.

I did the trick that worked with Ward's farty friends at the back gate—I sat close to the threshold and waited impatiently for someone to go out or in. Finally the cold air rushed in and I rushed out. "Oh!" a man exclaimed as I streaked past his legs.

"Riley!" I heard Grant call sternly. But I was able to separate Ava from the other people who had trod the snow, and I was off on the hard-packed surface, following a path well traveled by people and horses and dogs.

When Grant yelled my name again, far behind me, I could tell that he had stepped outside the big house, but I felt driven to continue, lured forward, as if it was my purpose to find Ava the way it seemed to always be her purpose to find me.

The trail branched off several times, but her scent was gradually getting stronger, and I confidently picked the correct direction each time. Daylight was failing quickly now, the woods growing dark in the thickets, the snow glowing under my feet. I was panting but not tired—I felt full of energy, absolutely compelled to continue the course I had started.

Fewer people had taken the next turn, making the snow less compacted and therefore more difficult for me. I had to proceed more slowly, but I also, for the first time, smelled Ava on the air. She was much closer, now. I ran on as best I could, my legs sinking with each step.

The trail took me to the lip of some high rocks. I followed, realizing that only a few people had come this way and that she was one of them. Ava was just ahead. In the direction of Pull Right was a steep fall to flat, unmarked ground.

I arrived at a rope strung across my way. Here, all other tracks halted except one. I crawled under the rope. Now the snow was punctuated by a single set of footsteps that weaved in and out of sparse trees. Ava had come alone at this point, making her own pathway.

And then the scent trail ended and the footsteps stopped. I halted, confused. I could still smell her—it seemed as if she were right *there*, very close, but where? I squinted in the dim light.

Then I heard a small sound; a hopeless, diminished cry. I crept forward slowly, mindful of the sharp drop. When I peered over the edge, I could see a woman lying facedown in the snow, her long, light-colored hair splayed out in front of her.

It was Ava.

I did not know what to do. She was not looking at me. She was breathing harshly in shuddering breaths that communicated pain and fear.

Distressed, I whined and saw her go completely still at the noise. "Hello?"

I waited for her to tell me what to do. When she slumped back into the snow, I barked.

"Oh my God! Dog?" she rolled onto her back and cried out as she did so, a sharp, agony-filled exclamation, but then she was looking up at me. "Dog! Come! Please come help me!"

I wagged in confusion. She was much too far away to do Come. I could not jump down to her. She would have to climb up to me.

"Please! Come! Come here! Come! Come!"

I felt desperate. I tracked back the way I had come but did not see a way down. I returned to where she had spotted me.

"Okay. Where's your person? Hello!" she shouted loudly. "Over here! I'm hurt! Help me!"

When she inhaled, turning her head, I froze, thinking she was hearing something. She visibly slumped. "Okay. It needs to be you. Can you come? Here, dog! Come!"

I whined in frustration. Obliged to do *something*, I turned and galloped back through the snow, retracing my steps along the ridge. As more footsteps joined my route, the going was easier, and this felt like progress even though I was running *away* from Ava.

Soon I was at a split in the trail—that way lay the big house and Grant, but straight ahead the path was on a descending slope, which made for easier going. Without thinking, I pursued this direction, and when the declivity steepened I began taking exhilarating leaps, bounding ahead. I snaked through some big boulders and fallen trees and then I was at the base of the looming rocks. The path split again but I had no doubts—I turned toward Ava. Right up against the stone wall the snow was very thin and I was able to quicken my gait. Her scent filled my nose and I could hear her, hear her soft cries, and then I saw her lying in the snow, her arms over her eyes. She turned her head sharply as I drew near.

"Yes! Good dog! Such a good dog!"

I loved being a good dog for Ava. I jumped into the deeper snow and forged through it and got to her, licking her wet, salty face. I tried to climb on her and she screamed.

"Down! Stop! My leg!" she cried.

I knew Down, of course, so even though it was such heavy snow I sprawled out in it, crawling forward to kiss her some more. She seized my head in both her hands. "Oh, you are such a good, good dog. Okay, okay, let me think. I need you to get my pack, okay? I've got food in there, and things to make a fire, and maybe my phone is in the outer pocket. Think you can do that?" She played with my collar. "Riley? Think you can get it? It's right over there!"

I tensed, understanding she was telling me to do something.

"Get the pack! Riley, get the pack! Get it!"

Get It! I went to the base of the rocks and jumped on a stick. She didn't say Leave It, so I proudly took it back to her.

"Okay, good dog, but not a branch. I need my pack, okay, Riley? If I don't have my pack I won't stay alive long enough for anyone to find me. Okay? Get the pack!"

Get It! I saw another stick, this one redolent with her smell, and grabbed it. She groaned, but accepted it. "Not the ski pole. Thanks, good dog. But I need the pack, okay? Can you get the pack?"

I heard the word "get" but it didn't seem like a command. I tensed. "Get the pack, Riley, the pack!"

I bounded joyously through the snow, loving showing Ava I knew how to Get It. I smelled many things to bring her; this game could go for a long time.

I unearthed something made of metal and plastic and proudly trotted back to her.

"That's a snowshoe. Oh God." She put her hands to her face and I felt the fear and desperation and I creeped forward, not understanding. I whined and she petted me with a hand wet with her tears. "I don't want to die, I'm so scared to die," she whispered.

We played Get It with more sticks and what I recognized as a glove, but none of these made her happy. I felt like a bad dog, disappointing her when she so desperately wanted something from me.

Sunk down in the snow a little bit was another object with her scent painted on it. I picked it up—it was heavy, a heavy bag, and I was about to abandon it when Ava became excited. "Yes! Good dog! Bring It! Yes, that's it, Riley!"

It was easier to drag than to carry it, but I did Get It with the bag and Ava hugged me. "Oh Riley. You are so smart." She let out a loud gasp as she struggled to sit up, and then she was unzipping the bag. She pulled out a bottle and drank from it, and then a pouch of bread and meat she bit off. "Want some sandwich?" She offered me a morsel and I took it, nearly swooning with the glorious flavor. When I was done I ate some snow.

"No phone. I had it in my mitten, didn't I? I wanted to take a picture, which is why I snowshoed so close to the edge and fell.

So of course it's not in the pack." She looked around, shaking her head. Then she gazed at me. "This isn't going to work, Riley. I can't build a fire out in the open on top of the snow. Even if I could, we're supposed to get four to six inches tonight. I need to make it to the protection of the base of the cliff. Oh Riley, I have something else for you to do, can you help me? I need to make it over there somehow."

I could tell she wanted to play Get It some more and I tensed, ready. Instead she threw her pack, grunting, and it hit the rock wall and fell with a thud. Was I supposed to bring it back? Then she reached out with her hands, seizing my collar. "All right. This is going to be the hardest thing I've ever done, but I have to. Ready?" She kicked at the snow with one leg, pushing me a little, gasping with pain. "Help me, Riley!"

Though she didn't say it, this felt like Steady, so I held still. Grunting and wheezing, she pushed again, turning my head the way Burke did with Assist. Is that what we were doing? I cautiously took a step forward. Ava screamed and I stopped, turning back to her in alarm.

"No, it's okay. We have to do this. Sorry, it was just worse than I expected. Keep going. Please? Riley! Keep going!"

She grappled with my head, turning me back. It *was* Assist. We moved together, slowly and carefully, heading toward where her bag lay against the big rocks. She was sobbing, sucking in air with almost every step, but she didn't want to stop. When we reached the bag she collapsed, panting, and lay still for so long that I nosed her in worry.

"Okay." She winced as she put herself in a sitting position.

After that we played Get It with sticks. It did not take me long to understand that this was all she was interested in, which was fine by me—if I were a person I would want nothing but sticks and maybe balls and a squeaky toy. I was reminded of being in the rain with Wenling and Burke and the water squirrels.

Ava was pleased. "You're amazing, Riley! How do you know how to do this?" At one point she seized my head and stared at me as she had often done when I was a puppy. "Are you my guardian angel dog? Did heaven send you?"

When she was tired of the game she built a fire. "Okay. So I won't freeze." She looked around "No one knows I'm here, Riley. Is my leg bleeding internally? What happens when it snows?" She hugged herself. I did Sit attentively, ready to do whatever she asked of me next.

After a long time, the cold air brought me the salty tang of her tears. "I'm not ready," she choked. Her head drooped, her light hair swinging forward. "I've never had a man in love with me, never been to Europe, never . . ."

I licked her face and she wiped her nose and gave me a wry smile. "Riley. Okay, Riley. You're right." She cocked her head at me. "Newfie–Australian shepherd mix. I rescued some puppies just like you, back in the lower peninsula, a few years ago. Such a sweet face." She sighed. "Maybe someone will come looking for *you*, Riley. Someone loves you and gave you this fancy collar."

I was tired. I sprawled in the snow. I didn't resist when she took my head and pulled it gently into her lap. "Can you feel the storm coming? It's going to be a bad one. I don't know if I'm going to make it through the night, Riley." She was crying again. "Would you stay with me? If I'm going to die I want a dog with me. Then you can go back home." She stroked my fur and I closed my eyes. "Oh Riley," she breathed, "I was so stupid." She wiped her face with her sleeve. "This will be so hard for my dad."

Were we just going to sit here? I understood that Ava was frightened and in pain and cold, but I did not understand why, if that was the case, we didn't just return to the house with the many rooms.

A light snow began to fall. Ava gently, sadly plied my fur. I drifted in and out of sleep, conscious only of her breathing, the heat of the fire, and the steady motion of her fingers lovingly stroking my head.

TWENTY-NINE

Ava and I were both asleep, but my head snapped up instantly when I heard Grant's shout on the night wind. "Riley!"

He was calling me, but before I could move, Ava's hand shot out and grabbed my collar. "Stay with me, Riley!" I tensed—I wanted to bark, but her grip made me think I shouldn't. Ava pulled in a deep breath. "Over here! Help! Here!"

She waited, listening. "Hello?" Grant yelled back.

"Here! I've hurt my leg! Help!"

The air held a heavy, long silence. I smelled Lucky, and then, moments later, Grant. Out of the gloom I could see him picking his way forward at the base of the rock wall, pulling Lucky by her leash. I did not understand why Lucky had to be here.

"Here!" Ava called.

Grant waved. "I see you!" He stopped and looped the horse's

rope over a tree limb, and then made his way to us, his boots crunching the rocks. I wagged.

Ava released my collar. "Thank God," she breathed.

I bounded forward to greet Grant but not Lucky. He let me lead him back to Ava. He stooped, holding his hands to the fire. "Hi. What happened?"

"Oh, I was so stupid. I was snowshoeing and wanted to see the cliffs. It was so pretty and I was taking pictures and got so focused on what I was doing I fell right off the edge. My leg's broken. Is Riley your dog?"

"Yes. I'm Grant Trevino." He leaned forward and they briefly held hands.

"Ava Marks. I'm so glad you followed your dog."

"Oh no, he ran off from the lodge before dark. I thought he'd come back but he didn't, so after dinner I saddled up Lucky to come fetch him."

I looked up sharply. Dinner?

"How did you find us?"

"GPS on his collar." Grant grinned. "Riley here likes to run off on people, though this is the first time he's done it with me. Good thing he stumbled on you."

"He barked when he was up above me on the cliff."

"Want me to look at your leg?"

"It's not . . . I can feel where it is broken. Right under the skin."

Grant lifted his eyebrows. "Ouch! I'm so sorry. Well, there goes the idea of me carrying you on the back of my horse. I'll make a call, get the rescue squad out here."

"Thank you. My phone was in my hand when I fell and I have no idea where it went."

Grant turned to face Lucky and spoke into his phone. I nuzzled with Ava. She was much happier now that Grant was here, and so was I.

"Okay, they're coming." Grant knelt by the fire again. "You're lucky it's just your leg. That's got to be a thirty-foot fall."

"What's lucky is that Riley came along."

I wagged at hearing my name but did not know why they would be talking about Lucky, who was just standing there.

"I really thought . . ." Ava pulled in a shaky breath. When she continued, her voice was strained. "I really thought I was going to die of hypothermia. And then this angel dog appeared, and I asked him to fetch my backpack, and he did, and then I asked him to get me sticks for a fire, and to drag me over here out of the wind. He did it all as if we'd been practicing it his whole life. I'd be dead if it weren't for him."

Grant rubbed my chest. It felt wonderful. "Huh. I sure didn't train him to do anything like that, but he's a really smart dog. Figures everything out in an instant. First time I told him to lie down, he got it. So, are you staying at the lodge?"

"Well, I *was*. I imagine tonight I'll be in the ER."

Grant winced. "Of course. Sorry. Are there friends I should contact for you? Your boyfriend?"

Ava shook her head. "I'm here by myself *because* of my boyfriend. *Ex*-boyfriend. He dumped me after I'd paid for the trip, so I thought, why waste it?"

"Well, he must be an idiot."

Ava smiled. "Thanks. But if I could use your phone to call my dad?"

After some time, people arrived on loud machines. They strapped Ava onto a bed and carried her away. It was so similar to what happened the last day I saw Grandma that I shivered, pressing up against Grant.

We spent a few more days wandering around pointlessly with Lucky but not Ava. When we arrived back at the farm (Lucky closely followed us the whole way in her car, so she was back, too) the sun had gone down. I trotted through the dog door while Grant stayed with Lucky.

I knew the moment I entered the living room that something was wrong. Chase Dad lay on the couch with a wet cloth over his eyes and he did not say anything to me at all. Li Min and ZZ were both there, sitting rather oddly in chairs pulled up to the couch as if they planned to eat off it, and they didn't react, either; it was as if they did not seem to understand the significance of my return—there was a dog in the house now! Everyone should be happy!

Chase Dad's hand was dangling toward the floor. When I nosed it, he stirred with a groan. "Hi, Riley," he whispered. He drew his knees up to his chest.

He smelled ill and sweaty, and when his fingers touched me I could feel that he was in pain. I sat, anxiously watching him, understanding nothing at all.

Grant took a long time, but eventually he pulled open the door, stamping his boots on the porch and bringing the scent of Lucky into the house with him. He stopped when he saw us. "What's wrong?"

Li Min sprang to her feet. "Your father is sick and he won't go to the hospital."

Grant stared at her, then went over and looked at his father. "What's wrong?"

"Bellyache."

Grant glanced at Li Min and ZZ, then shook his head. "No, it's got to be more than that."

"He was not able to get up," ZZ said.

"He's in terrible pain!" Li Min exclaimed.

"I can stand up, for God's sake," Chase Dad snapped. "I just don't want to."

Li Min fluttered her hands. "It started at breakfast. He couldn't eat his eggs, and you know how rare that is. Then he threw up. He went out to do some chores and came back and lay down on the couch and has been lying there all day."

"I'm right here, Li Min," Chase Dad grunted. "You don't have to talk about me like I'm in the next room."

Apparently we were all going to stay in the living room for the moment, so I sat down, feeling the worry wafting off everyone.

"You didn't do your chores?" Grant shook his head. "It's got to be serious, Dad. Remember when I asked you if I could skip chores if I was the victim of a bear attack, and you said, 'Depends on how many bears'?"

Chase Dad barked out a single laugh that immediately turned into a cry of shock. "*Jesus!* That felt like getting stabbed."

"Scale of one to ten, with one being a stone in your shoe, and ten being a shark bite, how would you rate your pain?" Grant asked.

Chase Dad didn't say anything for a bit. "Eight," he finally murmured.

Grant's mouth dropped open. "*Eight?* My God, Dad, we've got to get you to the hospital."

Chase Dad shook his head. "No need."

"*Please!*" Li Min said frantically. "Please go, Chase!"

"Dad. You don't let us take you, I'm calling an ambulance."

Chase Dad glared at Grant. Li Min put a hand on Chase Dad's shoulder and squeezed. "You have to go."

ZZ and Grant carried Chase Dad out the door and drove off. I stayed close to Li Min because she fed me dinner and because she really needed a dog. She paced around the house, she kept looking at her phone, she stood at the window and stared out into the night. She cried three times. I dutifully followed her and did Steady whenever she needed a hug, glad to have a purpose in the midst of these perplexing circumstances.

When Grant drove up the driveway I slid through the dog door to greet him. He was barely out of his car before Li Min came running out. "Grant! What's happening with your father?"

Grant hugged her. "It's going to be fine. The appendix didn't burst. He's out of surgery and resting."

Li Min put a hand to her mouth and nodded. She was weeping.

"ZZ's going to stay the night up there with him. And the doctor says he won't be able to do any work for at least two weeks. *That's* what will kill him." Grant cocked his head, regarding her strangely. "You okay?"

She nodded, wiping her eyes. "I was just really worried. When you texted me I looked up appendicitis, and it can be very bad. You can die from it. And then I didn't hear anything else."

"ZZ didn't call you? I thought he called you."

She shook her head wildly. "It's been agony, waiting, no word all night."

"I am so sorry, Li Min. I thought for sure he was updating you."

She took a breath, shaking herself like a dog shedding water. "Would you like anything? Coffee?"

"I didn't actually get dinner."

I looked at him hopefully. Dinner was a great idea!

"Oh! Let me put some things out." Li Min was soon in the kitchen clattering pans, but not in an angry-walk way.

"What do you suppose *that* was all about, Riley?" Grant whispered to me. I heard my name and felt sure a repeat dinner was a real possibility.

It wasn't, but Grant did feed me a little under the table.

Chase Dad returned home after a day or so, but was tired and went to lie in Burke's room. Grant stood and watched him. "Get you anything?"

"Just need to rest."

I wondered if I should jump up on the bed, where I had spent many nights in my life. It was my boy's bed, but Chase Dad had never let me sleep with him—did that make a difference?

"I need to take off pretty soon, Dad."

"That's okay. I've got ZZ."

"And Li Min," Grant added.

"Right."

"She's here every day now?"

I still wasn't sure where to lie down. I yawned.

"Right. So's ZZ."

"That's nice. To have her here, I mean."

"What are you getting at, son?"

"Nothing. So I need to get back. I have to return the horse."

"You want to do me a favor?"

"Sure."

"Take Riley with you? He's really your dog as much as mine. I'm not supposed to be doing anything but sleeping and eating. Like being a teenage boy. I don't feel like I can do justice as a dog father under the circumstances."

Car ride with Grant! A long one, spoiled only by the fact that Lucky followed us all the way until we went to a horse-smelling place where many, many horses chewed at grass, looking for something to eat. Then we drove off and Lucky was so busy gazing at the other horses she forgot to get back in her car.

We ended the trip at a place with slick floors, where Grant's room was down a long hall with many doors. Grant, I concluded, liked big buildings full of people. I loved his home, because the bed was in the same room as the kitchen, but did not understand why we had left the farm. We were far away; I couldn't pick up any trace of it on the wind.

Grant brought home a squeaky toy! I loved it—when I attacked it, the sound reminded me of Lacey. He also pulled out a new nylon bone. That, I did not love so much.

After a few days, we took another car ride, this time to a house saturated with an instantly recognizable scent. Ava! Grant knuckled the door while I wagged excitedly. "Is that you, Grant?" I heard her call.

"It's me!"

"Come on in; it's unlocked."

I bounded inside as soon as Grant pushed open the door. Ava was in the living room and I was delighted to see she was sitting in a wheeled chair just like Burke's! Her leg, though, was sticking straight out. She petted me but didn't have any treats. The extended leg was wearing heavy, hard pants.

There was a nice, soft rug on the floor and I sank down on it while Ava and Grant talked, letting the sun warm me. Eventually the rays tracked off the rug and on to the wood floor, so I had to decide what to do: get up for the sun's warmth, or stay on the soft rug? I picked the rug.

"How's it been with the wheelchair?" Grant asked.

"Fine. Boring. And I sprained my left wrist in the fall, which I didn't even notice until I got to the hospital. So it's tough to get around in a wheelchair."

"My brother was in a wheelchair when he was younger."

"Oh, I didn't know you had a brother. You didn't mention him."

Grant shrugged. "We're not close. Long story. Anyway, he had a dog who would pull him around, help him in and out of the chair, stuff like that. We should see if we can train Riley."

I regarded him lazily.

"That's not easy to do," Ava observed.

Grant stood. "Got a rope?"

"There's a box of dog leashes in the front closet."

Grant opened a door. "You've got a *lot* of leashes."

"I'm in rescue, remember?"

When Grant put the leash on my collar I wagged, excited to be going for a walk. He handed the other end to Ava. "Okay, when you tell him to pull, I'll call for him to come to me."

I knew that word. Pull. It made sense; she was in the chair. I did Sit, ready to work.

"He's going to yank me right out of the chair."

"Just hang on tight."

"I don't know how to water-ski."

"This is how my brother and my dad trained Cooper."

I was so glad to hear the name Cooper. Grant went across the room. I ignored him. I knew what I was doing. "Tell him to pull!"

Even though it should be Ava commanding me, it was obvious what they wanted. I did as I had been taught, walking slowly forward, leaning into my leash and feeling the chair roll behind me. "Oh my God!" Ava exclaimed.

Grant was grinning. I did Pull all the way across the room. No one said Halt but I had run out of anywhere to go. "Riley, you are amazing," he told me.

"So wait, he didn't just figure out to do that on his own. Did you train him as a service dog?"

"No. Maybe it's got to do with your weight in the chair. He feels the resistance and it's like 'heel,' which he does know means move slowly by our side."

"So you're saying I'm fat."

I smelled the sweat pop on Grant's skin. "*No.* Oh no, no, huh-uh."

Ava laughed. "I'm kidding, Grant. You should see your face. Well, he for sure has Newfoundland in him and Newfies are often used to pull carts—I guess it could be instinctive. Is he a rescue? I see Australian shepherd in his coloring, that's obvious."

"I think he is? Remember I told you at the cliffs that he likes to run away? He belonged to a guy named Ward, but Riley kept taking off, and a lot of the time he would show up at my dad's farm."

"Ward *Pembrake*?"

"Yeah, that's it. You know him?"

"No, but I know this dog! I rescued him before he was weaned. His mother is mostly Australian shepherd, and of the whole litter, this one was my favorite." Ava held my head in her hands and gazed into my eyes. "It's Bailey! Remember me, Bailey?" She stroked my head. "Mr. Pembrake's brother is a friend of my father, so we let him have Bailey and I guess he renamed him Riley. What an amazing coincidence!"

I did not at all mind being called Bailey by Ava. It reminded me of being a puppy.

"Bailey's a good name," Grant observed. "I'm told we've had a Bailey or two in our family."

We did Pull several more times. I was ready to do Assist and Steady, but Ava apparently wasn't interested.

"So Ava," Grant asked, "do you want to maybe have Riley stay with you for a few days?"

She looked up in surprise. "What do you mean?"

Grant shrugged. "I just started a new job, so he'd just be alone in my apartment in Lansing all day anyway. He could help you get around. I'll bring over his bowl and food and his toys."

"Won't he be confused when you leave him here?"

"He's pretty easygoing. And he tracked you in the woods, remember? I think he remembers you from before. And I'd come visit." Grant's voice was hesitant. I regarded him curiously.

"Oh. Yes, I'd like that, Grant," she said softly.

Grant smiled at her. "Maybe it's not a coincidence that I wound up with Riley and he found you in the woods. Maybe it was meant to be."

They sat and stared at each other. I yawned.

Later a man knocked on the door and handed them some food in a flat box. I sat next to Grant due to his habitual generosity at dinnertime, but he was mainly interested in talking and not giving anything to a deserving dog.

"My mom moved to Kansas City after she and Dad divorced," Ava said. "She's the CEO of Trident Mechanical Harvesting."

"*Seriously?*"

"Why do you say it like that?"

"It's just that my dad pretty much believes her company is ruining America. Forcing farmers off their land. He's pretty intense on the topic; I'll warn him not to mention it around you."

"They don't force anybody. It's a pretty good deal. They buy the farm, cash it out, but the owner can lease it for a dollar a year if they want and continue to work it and keep the crops to sell. Usually after just a few years they decide they'd rather take their money and live in Florida or something, but they can stay there until they die if they want."

"I had no idea. A dollar a year, and they can keep their farm?"

"That's the agreement. My mother is very sensitive to exactly what you're saying, that people think her company is destroying the family farm."

Grant drummed his fingers. "Wow. I never heard that. So," he said slowly, "do you think your mom could get that deal for my dad?"

{THIRTY}

Now I lived with Ava. She did not ask me to do anything but Pull. I was frustrated, watching her struggle with her heavy pant leg as she moved from her chair to her bed and to the couch—I was right here, ready to do Assist, which she knew I could do from the night in the snow, but she never asked for my help.

Often Sam Dad and a woman named Marla came to see me and possibly also Ava. Marla smelled primarily of flowers and the chemicals in her dark hair. Sam Dad hugged her an awful lot.

"Do you want me to stay with you, Ava? I can get time off at the bank," Marla offered.

"No, that's okay," Ava replied. "I've got Riley."

Sometimes I would lie with my nose to the crack under the door, sniffing the dancing swirl of trees and animals and dogs and people. I could not smell Lacey. I convinced myself I could detect the farm, and the goat ranch, but it was such a minimal trace I might have been sensing something not really there. This was, I reflected, one of the oddest aspects to being a dog—humans deciding we lived where and with whom they wanted. I felt in my heart I belonged on the farm and wondered if we were ever going to return. Was Lacey *there*?

I had to accept my fate, of course, accept it the way I accepted having the vet ease my pain with a single prick and then realizing I had a new mother and was among a new litter of pups.

I also understood that my feelings had shifted. I still loved Burke, but now felt very strongly attached to Ava and Grant. This was something else about being a dog, I decided: the capacity to love many people.

Grant returned to see me often, and no matter how deeply I buried it in my box of toys, he always found the nylon bone.

One time he came over with flowering plants clutched in his fist, instantly flooding the house with their redolence. I was reminded of Marla. He thrust the plants at Ava in an almost violent motion. "I brought flowers."

"I can see that," she laughed. "They're lovely, thank you so much. If you're trying to sweep me off my feet, though, it won't work until I get my cast removed."

Grant nodded.

"It's a joke, Grant. Would you mind taking them into the kitchen? I'll show you where I keep a vase."

"I knew it was a joke. I was trying to think of a witty reply. My brother's the funny one in my family. I'm just good old reliable Grant." He kissed her and carried the flowers to the sink. He ran water and stuffed them into a tall glass, his back to us.

"I just know that when I first saw you, you were coming out of the mist with your horse, to save my life. Like a knight in shining armor," Ava told him softly. "If that makes you reliable, I'll take it."

Grant made dinner and tossed me small pieces of spicy meat while doing so. I was so happy he was home!

"It's a little scary to go off on my own, but I'm just not cut out for corporate law," Ava said later, at the table.

"So now what?"

"I already have my first client—Hope's Rescue, my Dad's non-profit. I thought that might be what I concentrate on, working with shelters, maybe veterinarian offices. But, like I said, a little scary."

A piece of meat hit the floor and I pounced.

"You'll make it work. You're smart."

"You bring me flowers, you tell me I'm smart. Your mother raised you well." There was a silence. "Wait, what is it? What did I say?"

"It was Dad who raised us. My mom divorced him, moved overseas, and started a new family with some guy. I don't remember her much. We haven't heard from her in a long time."

"I am so sorry, I had no idea."

Grant sighed. "I used to wonder what was wrong with me, that she never tried to visit or anything, but my grandma said her new husband is ultra-controlling and wouldn't let her. That's the story, anyway." He went quiet.

I nudged Grant's leg with my nose because there was still plenty of meat smell up there on the table.

"I can tell it still makes you sad," Ava murmured.

"Oh. I was just remembering when she left. My brother Burke was born paralyzed below the waist and she couldn't deal with it, so she took off."

Ava's mouth dropped open. "Did she actually *say* that? That it was because he was disabled?"

"She didn't have to. We all knew it. We all sat down in the living room and my parents asked us if we wanted to stay with Dad or go with her. And I was going to pick her, but I didn't want Burke to go, too. I wanted her for myself, and anyway she was leaving *because* of Burke. So I said Dad, because I knew that my brother would follow my lead and I could change my mind later. But then Burke says, 'I'll stay with Grant.' Not Dad, with *Grant*. So what could I say then? I was stuck."

"Wow, Grant."

"I know, why did he say it like that?"

I put a paw on Grant's leg and he gave me a small smile.

Ava nodded. "Sounds like he really loved you."

Grant looked away. "That's not how I saw it at the time. I thought it was some sort of ploy. Trapping me on the farm."

"I guess I can see how that bothered you," Ava agreed.

"I resented him for it practically my whole life," Grant replied.

"I don't have a brother or a sister," Ava observed quietly. "I guess I always imagined that if I did, she would be my best friend."

"Sure. It's not like Burke and I haven't tried. As adults, I mean. We've talked now and again. It feels like we're both faking our way through the conversation. There's just too much history between us."

"We have something in common. My mother left the child-rearing up to my dad while she fought her way up the corporate ladder. It was all right when I was young, I mean their arrangement, but she never felt my dad's work was important. You know, nonprofit. When they got divorced I stayed with my father. She switches out boyfriends about once a decade, while Dad's been dating Marla forever."

"I always thought my father saw me as a source of cheap labor," Grant replied. "With my brother in a wheelchair, it was up to me to do everything. I really resented it, but now I'm kind of grateful for how I was raised. Whenever I get a job, everyone always says I work harder than anybody. I get companies calling me sometimes, asking me if I would be willing to come back."

I went over to the window to check for squirrels, dogs, and other intruders. Nothing was out there.

"How's that going? The new job, I mean."

"Okay, I guess. My company helps rip out outmoded green energy equipment. Corporations can realize real gains if they upgrade. My territory is North America, so I'll be traveling a lot. Also, the company is headquartered in Germany, so I'll have to go to Europe from time to time. But, so, I can be based out of anywhere. Here, if I want. Meaning, if *you* want."

"Grand Rapids?"

"We'd see each other more often. I mean . . ."

"I'd like that, Grant. I'd like it a lot."

Later they went to Ava's room to lie down. She did not need me to do Steady because Grant helped her. They were wrestling but when I jumped up to join them, they both yelled "Off!" so I curled up on a pillow on the floor. Finally they calmed down. "Good old reliable Grant," Ava said, and they both laughed.

The next morning Grant made breakfast and tossed me some ham. "When does your dad need Riley back?" Ava asked him. "I'll be sorry to see him go."

"I just talked to him yesterday. He's finally up and around, but still can't work. And I told him about you, and how Riley is like the ghost of Cooper past."

I looked up at the odd sound of both of my names spoken so close together.

"He pointed out that Riley is as much my dog as anybody's. So he can stay as long as you want."

"Good dog, Riley," Ava praised. She also pitched me a piece of ham. She was catching on to how things should work!

"You can change his name back to Bailey, if you want," Grant offered.

I stared at him. Now *that* name. What were we doing?

"Oh no," Ava replied. "Riley fits him just fine."

Grant filled a closet and a dresser in a back bedroom with his clothing, but when he was home he slept in Ava's room. I usually slept with Ava when Grant was gone, but while he was there I preferred my dog pillow. Their bed was too active.

Just like Burke, Ava eventually put her chair away and began walking again. And, just like Burke, she had some trouble with it at first. I knew from experience that she needed me to do Assist but wouldn't want me to. When people put their rolling chairs in a closet, it's as if they put a dog's Pull in there, too.

Now that she was walking, Ava spent most days in a place I had been before, a house that contained dogs in cages, and Sam Dad and other nice people.

And cats.

I could not believe that *this* was the mystery creature I had wanted to meet my whole life, the always-fleeing barn animal with the smell that clung to so many people! Everyone called them "cats" and they were so much less interesting than I had imagined. The dogs were in large pens and liked to bark. The cats were in smaller pens and just *stared*, communicating nothing except maybe an undisguised contempt.

They were nearly the size of water squirrels, these cats, but they did not flee when I went to their pens to inspect them—in fact, the one time I pressed my nose to the wires, the feline within raked me with her tiny, slashing claws.

I spent so much time trying to make the acquaintance of one of these surly creatures, the one who lived in the barn and fled from the sight of me, only to find out they were so jealous not to be dogs they couldn't be friendly.

Nearly every day, people would come to visit the dogs and play with them, and sometimes the dogs would leave with the people and the dogs were always happy. And people also came and talked to the cats and carried them out and the cats did not look happy.

I remembered being a puppy in this place, and always bounded enthusiastically into the yard to play with other dogs, hoping Lacey would be among them. She was not. I sniffed everywhere for her, but never caught her scent. I wondered if Lacey was living with Wenling now.

When I slept, I sometimes dreamed I was on the farm, running with Lacey. Often she was my first Lacey, with the white chest and short hair, and other times she was the light-colored, scraggly furred dog I knew now. And sometimes I dreamed I could hear a man talking to me. *"Good dog, Bailey,"* he would say. I did not recognize the voice, though it sounded very familiar, as if I should.

I was happy to live with Ava and, occasionally, Ava and Grant. I knew I would be happier, though, if we were all on the farm with Burke and Chase Dad.

"We're headed back up north to your old stomping grounds tomorrow," Ava told Grant at dinner. "That dog-fighting operation I told you about? Death Dealin' Dawgs? The state police are going to shut it down and we're one of the rescues who are going to take care of the animals."

"Wow, that sounds a little . . . aren't you worried they'll be vicious?"

"Some of them might be, but with reconditioning, with love and kindness, nearly every dog can be resocialized."

I watched them both, alerted by the word "dog."

"I'll go with you, if you'd like," Grant offered.

"Really? We could use the help."

"Of course."

"Good old reliable Grant."

"Oh sure."

"No, it's sweet. I love that about you." There was a long silence. "I said I love it *about* you, Grant. I didn't say I love you. Don't look so scared."

Grant cleared his throat. "We taking Riley?"

I looked at him, hearing the question. What was I being asked? "Of course!"

It was still dark outside that morning when Ava and Grant loaded me in the van full of dog kennels and we went for a ride. Grant sat next to Ava. The empty cages rattled with every bump. I was in my own bed and I curled up and slept most of the trip, though I jolted awake when some familiar odors began filtering through the van interior. I smelled water, trees, and unmistakably the goat ranch. I excitedly got to my feet. We were headed to the farm!

No, we weren't. We first drove to a parking lot and there were a lot of cars there, all lined up.

Men and women wore thick clothing with heavy objects on their belts that clanked a little as they moved. They seemed anxious, so I nervously lifted my leg on several car wheels, not sure why everyone was so tense. "All right," a woman said loudly. "Let's move."

I smelled road dust as the van swayed and bounced. "I'm feeling apprehensive," Ava confessed.

"It will be fine," Grant replied. "Didn't they say we won't go in until we get the all clear from the SWAT team?"

"You're right."

Grant blew out a breath. The sound was so familiar—he was pretty much the only person I'd ever met who did that. "I've never been bitten by a dog before."

"Don't even think that."

I picked up on their anxiety. Whatever was happening, it was scaring them.

We turned up a very narrow driveway. I breathed in the scent of many dogs, and when we stopped, I could hear barking. Ava slid between the front seats and let me out of my cage and allowed me to stick my face out her open window, but we all stayed inside.

I saw our new friends running around in a stiff manner, like a fast angry walk. People dashed to the front door and when it opened, they pulled a barefoot man out and wrestled with him and pushed him to the ground. Another man bolted from the side of the house, and he was tackled and there was more wrestling. I wondered why they didn't let me out, because it's always more fun to play with a dog present.

Eventually a man wearing a hard-looking hat walked up to us. He put his hand up to my window for me to lick. "We're good, come on back. There are more of them than we were told."

We jumped out. The scent of dog was very strong now, and the barking was deafening. When we passed through an open gate, I hesitated. Dogs, in cages stacked on top of each other, were barking shrilly. I could feel their fear, their loneliness, and even some rage, could hear it in their voices. Feces and urine coated the hard-packed earth, strong enough to make me drool.

Ava was crying. A woman wearing a plastic hat came forward and spoke sternly: "Okay, one at a time. Remember. Assess. Stabilize. Control. Remove."

Ava turned to Grant. "Can you hang on to Riley's leash?"

Grant nodded. "Sit!"

I did Sit, feeling disappointed. The odors were almost a scream to me, urging me to leave my mark on top of so many others soaking the dirt in the yard.

Ava put on heavy gloves. She watched the barking dogs for a

moment, then stooped in front of a cage on the ground. The dog inside wagged and put its face to the wires. Ava opened the door. "This one is fine," she told the woman in the plastic hat. The woman exited through the gate, leading that dog away on an oddly stiff leash. The dog looked at me, ears back, but did not try to come over to introduce himself.

This was a bad place. I did not understand what we were doing here.

Ava knelt in front of another dog. This one watched her with cold eyes. Ava began speaking softly, and I saw his fear begin to subside in the way his muscles unclenched along his body.

There was a female in a nearby cage that drew my attention. She was not barking. She was staring at me, her tail stiff and wagging. Feeling compelled, I darted forward to the end of my leash, ignoring the dogs who were barking at me. "No, Riley! Sit! Stay!" Grant commanded sternly.

But I did not want to do Stay. My rope taut on my collar, I was nose-to-nose with the female through her bars, both of us wagging furiously. She was a stocky brown-and-white dog with a blocky head and ears that stuck up and flopped over. Her face and body had small, pitted scars flecked here and there. She looked and smelled nothing like any other dog I had ever met, but that didn't matter.

I had found Lacey.

THIRTY-ONE

Dogs were being led out on stiff leashes and put in one of several vans. When Ava released Lacey I was ecstatic, but Ava spoke sternly to me. "Down, Riley!" Lacey twisted, trying to get to me, but Ava put herself between us and commanded me to Sit and Stay, which I did until I saw Lacey being loaded into Ava's van, and then I strained against my leash, dragging Grant over so I could climb up and into Lacey's cage just as Ava was shutting the door. We immediately began wrestling.

Ava glared at Grant. "What are you doing?"

Grant was laughing. "Riley really wants to be with that dog!"

"That's beside the point, Grant. This dog might not be safe. She's been abused—you can see the scar tissue."

"You're right, Ava. Sorry."

Ava opened Lacey's cage door and called me and we both obediently jumped out. Ava grabbed my leash and said "go on" to Lacey, who leapt back in while I strained. Ava shut the door. "Did you make a girlfriend, Riley?"

I stayed in the van when Ava left. She returned with a male dog who was missing an eye. He didn't greet me; he curled up in the back corner of his cage and panted. He was frightened.

When all the cages contained dogs, Ava called me out of the van and I reluctantly obeyed. She shut the side door and slid into the front seat. "See you in a bit, Grant!" she called.

I was shocked when the van drove off. How could it be that I finally found Lacey and now she was going away? Without thinking I ran after her in fast pursuit.

"Ri-ley!" Grant called from behind me.

No. Lacey was in there! I couldn't let her go!

"Riley! Come!"

My dedication wavered. I slowed, panting.

"Riley!"

I dejectedly turned around and went back to Grant, my head down.

We spent some time there without Ava. Other vehicles led other dogs away until I was the only one left. Would I be taken somewhere, too?

I yipped with relief when Ava's van returned, but when the door was flung open, Lacey was no longer there. I wagged when Ava held me and kissed my nose, but I felt lonely and lost.

We were in the van doing a car ride somewhere else, Grant driving, when Ava put her phone to her face and talked. She put the phone down and turned urgently to Grant. "We have to turn around and go back!"

"Why? What happened?"

"The vet's office where we took the dogs for evaluation screwed up and somehow a couple of dogs escaped. The newsfeed is making it sound like there's a pack of killer animals on the loose and they're having a meeting and people brought *rifles*. They're going to shoot those poor dogs!"

I sat up, yawning anxiously. Ava was upset. What was going on?

"We'll find them. Nobody is better at tracking strays than you are, Ava. Everything will be fine."

We drove for a while as the sun dropped in the sky. When we stopped I was astounded: this was do School! I had done Assist on those stone steps for Burke so many times!

A man smelling like peanut butter approached Ava's side of the truck and she lowered her window. I wondered why he wasn't sitting on the steps with his friends. "They just left. It's insane, Ava. They came driving up with guns in their racks so the sheriff made them park off school property, and they wanted to argue about *that*. Eventually they sat in the gym and said the dogs are going to kill their chickens and their kids. The sheriff said if they saw a stray pit bull they should call it in and let the law handle it, and they *laughed* at him. They've got their bloodlust up."

"That's horrifying."

We did a very slow car ride, turning up and down streets, the scents changing only gradually. "Look at that, they are carrying their rifles like they're in the army!" Ava stormed as a truck blew by on a roar of machinery and a trail of men's laughter.

"That's not at all legal. Call the sheriff," Grant advised.

"Those dogs deserve a chance at a better life," Ava seethed, her phone in her hand.

The fear and anger and tension were so powerful I was panting with them.

Ava spoke and then put her phone in her pocket. "Good news. They've got most of them."

We pulled into a brightly lit parking lot. I wagged as Grant opened his door and let me out, snagging my leash in one hand.

"Get you something?" Ava asked.

"Black coffee would be great, Ava. Thanks." He turned to watch a large truck swing into the parking lot. "I know those guys. High school."

"They're armed to the teeth."

Grant began walking toward the truck.

"Grant," Ava called.

He waved his hand at the men inside the truck. "Hey, Lewis. Jed."

"Trevino?" one of the men asked. He stood up out of his truck. He was holding a thick, heavy stick with an acrid, familiar odor I could faintly pick up. "Thought you were in Florida or something." He transferred his stick to his other hand so he could pull on Grant's.

"I was there for a time. What are you guys up to?"

I turned to see that Ava was coming up to join us.

"You didn't hear?" The man looked at me. "Bunch of fighting dogs escaped. We're out huntin' them."

"You're hunting down *dogs*?" Grant snorted incredulously. "That's not even legal."

"It is when they're vicious," he asserted.

Ava stepped forward. "No it's not. Michigan chapter nine, 750.50b. You can get up to four years in prison. I am the attorney for Hope's Rescue. The animals are technically ours: we were asked by the county sheriff's department to take care of them. If you harm them in any way you will be sued, and I will file a criminal complaint against each and every one of you."

The man talking to Grant went rigid. Grant cocked his head. "Don't you have a wife and a kid now, Lewis?"

He blinked, turning his focus on Grant. "Yeah. Baby girl."

"Well, if you're so worried about packs of wild dogs, why aren't you home protecting your kid instead of driving around drinking beer with your buddies like it's the first day of deer season?" Grant leaned over and looked at the other two men in the truck. "You know how pissed the sheriff's going to be if you actually manage to kill a dog?"

Our new friends drove off. I nosed Grant's hand. We were close to the farm—more than smell it, I could *feel* it. I whined.

"What's wrong, Riley?" Ava asked softly.

"Maybe everything that's going on is making him stressed out. You know what? We should swing by and drop him off with my dad, long as we're so close," Grant suggested.

"It's a good idea. Riley, would you like to go be a farm dog for a while?"

I wagged.

When the goat ranch passed by my window I knew where we were going!

Chase Dad and ZZ were at the table. They leapt up when Grant opened the door, and everyone was hugging. I waited patiently for my own hugs, which I assumed would be coming. Chase Dad was grinning. "So this is Ava."

"Hello," ZZ said.

They were, of course, hugging me now, and I was kissing them back. "Hello there, Riley," Chase Dad said, turning his face away so I could lick his ear.

"We just dropped by for a moment, see if you'll watch Riley for a bit," Grant informed them. "We're out searching for a couple lost dogs."

"What do you mean?" Chase Dad asked.

While they talked, I slid out the dog door and stood with my nose raised. I could smell the ducks and, far away, some horses. I liked living in the small house with Ava and Grant, but I loved being here on the farm.

After a time, everyone stepped out on the porch to be with

me. Chase Dad put his hand on my head. "How you been, Riley? I've really missed you."

I stood on my back legs so I could reach his face with my tongue. I loved Chase Dad.

"We need to get going, Grant," Ava said.

"Are they actually dangerous?" Chase Dad wanted to know.

"Probably not, but maybe. They certainly will be disoriented and frightened."

I caught a bare hint of something on the air and snapped my head up. Was that what I thought it was?

Grant put a leash on my collar. "Okay, you're going to hang here for a bit, Riley."

I barked. Everyone jumped. Ava crouched down and put her head next to mine, peering into the darkness. "What is it? What do you see, Riley?"

Chase Dad pointed. "Look!"

Lacey stepped into the pool of light under the pole by the driveway. Ava took in a sharp breath. "It's one of the pits we rescued today."

Lacey! I was wagging furiously, straining to get to her. Lacey was wagging, too, but as she came closer she slowed, dropping her head.

Grant pulled on my leash. "No, Riley."

No? What could that word possibly mean in this context?

"That's the one Riley has a crush on," Ava said.

Chase Dad cocked his head at her. "What?"

"At the dog yard, Riley ignored everyone else but that one. Grant, I know it sounds strange, but let Riley go."

With a click my restraint was gone and I bounded across the yard to my Lacey. We greeted each other as if we'd been separated forever. I chased her and she chased me and we rolled and played and played. Of course she was here!

I didn't notice that Ava and Grant were at the van until Grant called me. I dutifully trotted to him and so did Lacey. Ava was holding a long stick with a loop at the end of it. "Good dogs!" she said. "Can you sit, Riley?"

I did Sit and glanced proudly at Lacey when she did the same. We were good dogs together! Ava took a step forward and lowered her stick and the loop went around Lacey's neck. "Good dog, sweetie, you are such a good dog." She exhaled a sigh of relief. "Just a couple more and this nightmare is over."

Grant clicked the leash back in my collar. "I'll wait here while you take the pit bull back," he suggested.

Lacey was put in the van, but not me. I was astounded and hurt when Grant held my leash and Ava drove Lacey away. Not again!

I tracked Lacey by scent until Grant took me into the house.

"I think Ava's right, Riley's in love," Grant told Chase Dad. "I had to hold him to keep him from running after them."

ZZ left. Chase Dad and Grant were in the living room and I sprawled at their feet, my leash trailing out from my collar. I sighed. I did not understand where Ava was taking Lacey and hoped they would soon be back.

"Did you read the paperwork I sent?" Grant asked.

Chase Dad settled back in his chair. "Glanced at it."

"It's a good deal, Dad. You can work the farm as long as you want. Sell your crops to whomever you want. The company doesn't get it until after you pass on."

"What about you boys?"

Grant blew out some air. "Burke's not interested, Dad. And you know my position. If I worked here I would literally be dirt poor."

"I am not selling the farm to the robo-farmers, Grant. I don't know how you could even think such a thing. Maybe you don't see the value in it now, but you could change your mind. Haven't you had what, thirty careers already? Seems like changing your mind is something of a specialty for you."

"Dad . . ."

"Want to talk about something else? Because this subject is closed."

I jumped up when I heard the familiar sound of Ava's cage van in the driveway. Grant met Ava at the door. I could smell the new Lacey on her pants and hands, but Ava was alone. "What happened?" Grant asked.

She ran a hand through her hair. "One of the dogs was killed."

Grant sucked in a breath. "That's horrible. How?"

"Boys with guns, Grant. Boys with guns. We caught the rest of them, though. They're safe." She sighed, stepping forward to put her head on his shoulder. "I'm exhausted."

"Let's stay here tonight, then. The weekend, even."

Grant and Ava slept in his room and there really wasn't enough bed for me, so I trotted into Burke's bedroom and circled a few times before curling up on his pillow. I was comforted by his scent, and wondered when he was coming back to the farm.

There was so much I did not understand.

Lacey ran with me in my dreams that night. She was the first Lacey, the one who left after we found the snake. When I awoke, I was startled she wasn't lying on Burke's bed with me.

The next day I followed ZZ and Chase Dad out into the fields and watched them play with plants, moving side by side. "Grant seems to think he's got something better to do this morning," Chase Dad drawled with a smile.

ZZ nodded.

Chase Dad stood up, pushing his fist into the small of his back. He watched ZZ keep working for a moment. "ZZ."

The other man looked up.

"Grant wants me to sell the farm to Trident Mechanical Harvesting. I saw their offer. It's a lot of money, ZZ. I don't know if it is because Ava's mother runs the company, or if it is because I'm more valuable being right in the middle of their whole deal. Every time they want to get from here to there they have to steer clear around my property. So . . . I could lease the place back for a dollar a year until I die, and then they'd get it. Continue to live here, to work it. Only I wouldn't have to worry about the bills anymore."

ZZ was watching Chase Dad very carefully. Chase Dad slowly turned his head, eventually twisting his body so that he went in a circle, as if taking in everything he could smell.

ZZ stood, a worried frown on his face. "I would still work here?"

Chase Dad nodded.

ZZ shrugged. "Okay," he said.

THIRTY-TWO

Here is Grant," ZZ observed.

At Grant's name I turned and could smell and see him striding out to us.

Chase Dad grunted. "Good. I'll tell him what I am going to tell you right now. I'm not selling. Understand me, ZZ? If my kids don't want it, then fine." Chase Dad stepped forward and put his hand on ZZ's shoulder. ZZ looked surprised. Chase Dad was staring at him fiercely. "When I die, I'm leaving this farm to you and Li Min, ZZ. You're a real farmer."

The two men stood looking at each other, and then ZZ stepped forward and hugged Chase Dad. ZZ was crying, but he did not seem sad. He did not speak, but he wiped his eyes and nodded.

Grant walked up, looking puzzled. "Did I just see you two hugging each other?"

Chase Dad laughed. "Our secret's out; that's really what we do all day out here."

Grant grinned. "I won't tell anybody. So, Ava had to leave. There's some big national organization that filed a lawsuit. They want all the Death Dealin' Dawgs put down. They claim the dogs can't be rehabilitated. They say the dogs are "slaves" who are "better off dead." The rescues that are housing the dogs have teamed up and hired Ava to represent them."

"Dog fights." Chase Dad was shaking his head. "Hard to believe such a thing could happen around here. I never heard a word about any of it."

Grant looked around. "I thought I might as well spend the weekend here, show you two old guys how to harvest cucumbers."

The three men spent the day not playing with a dog. It was evening when they finally decided to head back to the house. ZZ drove the slow truck and Grant and Chase Dad walked together while I ran ahead—and a good thing I did, too! I saw a creature I had encountered once before, with a hunched back and a scuttling walk. It was at the base of the big tree next to the barn, but when it saw me tearing across the fields it wisely dashed up the trunk. It jumped into a yawning hole high over my head, but I wasn't fooled, I could smell it in there.

I barked to let it know that it was out of options. Grant and Chase Dad shouted for me but I stayed on mission—whatever the thing was, I would not let it come back down.

"What is it, Riley?" Grant called as he approached. "What's up there?"

I saw the creature peer out of the hole—nose pointed and painted with light-colored fur, black circles around each dark eye.

"What's he got?" Chase Dad asked.

"He's treed a raccoon up there. See it?"

Chase Dad stood with his hands on his hips. "Yeah, I do.

When did that hollow get so big? I'm surprised the tree's still standing."

"Raccoon," ZZ repeated slowly. "Raccoon."

Grant petted me. "You don't want to mess with a coon, Riley. They can be vicious if they have to. Come on."

I was disappointed when Grant made me follow the men inside and shocked when he blocked off the dog door—I had expected to spend the rest of the evening periodically bursting out and giving that animal the fear of its life.

It was gone the next morning, though its pungent odor still clung to the tree. Denied the opportunity to punish it for its trespass, I sniffed carefully, and then did the only thing appropriate, which was to lift my leg to overwrite its scent with my own.

Grant and I eventually left to go find Ava. It turned out she had returned to her house. Grant packed a bag and departed like he always did and I went back to the busy place with Sam Dad and Ava's friends and dogs and the haughty cats. Most of the time Ava was there, but sometimes she would leave and Sam Dad would take me to his home at the end of the day and, when Ava arrived, she sometimes needed a dog because she was very tense. "I would love a glass of wine," she told Sam Dad as she collapsed in a chair. He handed her something pungent to drink and I curled up at her feet.

"So? How'd it go?" Sam Dad wanted to know.

"Today was heartbreaking. We heard testimony about their living conditions. Some were chained to buried car axles. We also viewed a video of one of the dogs attacking a person. They claim it's Lady Dog. You can see some guy going in with what they called a break stick to separate these two dogs, because the boxer mix is being killed by the pit mix. The idiot must have been drunk because he falls down and the pit is on him instantly. It's pretty brutal."

"Which one is Lady Dog?"

"She's got the mostly white muzzle. The one that Riley likes so much. She's the most gentle dog, Dad."

"You sure it's her?"

"That's the thing, the picture is so shaky you can't really tell. Same litter, maybe. Classic pit mix, strong body, grinning face. Somebody leaked the video and it has a few million views, so everyone is calling for Lady to be put down."

"Any dog in the middle of a fight can turn on a person."

"Sure, Dad, you know that, I know that, but it was pretty savage."

"This makes no sense. Those kind of people would never let a fighting animal live if it went after one of its handlers."

"I agree."

They both sighed. Sam Dad poured some more of the liquid. I could feel some of the tense sadness leaving them and was glad I was there to help.

"We're getting death threats against Lady Dog now," Ava continued. "One guy claimed he was headed over to my place with a rifle. I gave it to the sheriff."

"I'd feel better if Grant were there with you, Ava."

"He had to go straight to Tucson. Another week."

There was a long silence. I turned to attack an itch at the base of my tail. Sam Dad stirred. "He sure travels a lot."

"He's a good man, Dad."

"I am not saying he's not. But I can tell you're not happy."

"*He's* not happy, is the problem. He switched jobs again. Nothing satisfies him. But I guess we're happy. Don't look at me like that, Dad. It's the first real long-term relationship I've ever had. Usually they've cheated on me by now."

"Oh honey."

Ava waved her glass. "That's maybe the wine talking. But

there's some truth to it. I feel like I'm always loyal, and the men I pick . . ." She shrugged.

Sam Dad's jaw tightened. "None of them were good enough for you."

She gave him a soft smile. "I know. Maybe I'm just holding out for someone as decent as my father."

Marla walked in smelling like cats and flowers and, even though I was comfortable, I climbed to my feet to greet her. That's just one of the jobs of a dog, to make people feel welcome when they first come through the door. She pointed to a bottle. "Please tell me you have more of *that*."

Sam Dad sprang up and poured her some of the same strong-smelling liquid. "Tough day, hon?"

Marla shrugged and smiled. "Probably nothing like what Ava goes through." She accepted her glass. "If my department gets a loan package wrong, no animals get hurt."

Ava took me home and ate dinner and fed me noodles, which were just okay. I loved Ava even though she didn't eat much meat.

The next time I saw Grant, Ava had been touching her phone constantly. He dropped his bag with a heavy thud. "Well?"

Ava gave him a hug, but her tension didn't leave her. "The judge is deliberating and will render tomorrow. Basically I'm just texting with my dad and all the other rescues, second-guessing myself."

"I am sure you did great."

"All I know is that if she rules against us, the dogs will all die."

I sniffed Grant's pants, but there were no treats.

"Couldn't you appeal?"

"An appeal would cost a lot of money and take a lot of time. Meanwhile the dogs would be stuck in their cages, not being rehabilitated, while the system grinds on. I don't know if any of us have the stomach for that." She pressed her lips together. "It would have meant a lot to me if you had been there, Grant."

There was a long silence. "I had to work, Ava. Come on."

The next day Grant ate bacon and Ava didn't but she was at the same table, so I sat and watched them both alertly. When I heard a familiar noise, both of them went stiff.

"This is it," Ava whispered. "Either the dogs live, or they don't." She picked up her phone, took a breath, and spoke to me. "Hello?"

I went to Grant because he was so tense his leg was hopping under the table.

"Yes. Yes, thank you. Bye."

Grant jumped up.

"We won!" Ava shouted.

They ran together and hugged. They were so happy they gave me bacon. They left together, but when they came back they brought Lacey!

Grant unsnapped her leash. "It's the killer dog of Michigan, Riley! Be careful!"

I was so happy to see my Lacey. Normally I was not supposed to run around in the house, but I figured these circumstances called for such behavior. I jumped up on the couch and then leaped on her back. We crashed into a lamp.

"Lady! Riley! Sit!" Ava commanded sternly.

My butt hit the floor. I felt like a bad dog. Lacey did Sit next to me.

"She's well-behaved, anyway," Grant observed.

"Which is good because she's our dog now."

"What do you mean?"

"I'm not even going to try to adopt out a dog that was all over social media as the most vicious creature in the universe. I'm not sure Lady would even be safe with someone else. She has a lot of anti–pit bull fanatics who want her dead since she's the poster girl for Death Dealin' Dawgs."

"Our dog," Grant repeated.

Lacey and I were still doing Sit. We looked at each other, unsure how much longer this was going to last.

"My dog, then, Grant. Lady's my dog and Riley's your dog, okay? Happy?"

Ava put us out in the backyard and Lacey and I played until it was dark. When we were let back in the house, we collapsed on a rug on the floor. I was so happy and exhausted I could barely raise my head.

Grant and Ava were eating, but even the tantalizing smell of hamburger couldn't make me move off that rug. Grant poured something into Ava's glass. "Hey, Ava. I'm sorry. You're right; I should have been there for you, and I wasn't."

"I do like a man with an apology."

"So I was thinking we should take a trip together. Go to Hawaii."

"Wow. You must *really* feel bad."

"I've got airline miles, hotel points—we'll go first class all the way."

"What about the dogs?"

"We'll take them to the farm and my dad will watch them for us. I actually think it might be good to get Lady out of here for a while, in case one of those nut jobs actually does show up to hurt her."

It was not long before we all returned to the farm! Lacey bounded out of the car and ran straight to ZZ, who seemed surprised at her enthusiastic greeting, for some reason. Lacey was also thrilled to see Li Min and then ran through the house, sniffing. I knew who she was looking for: Wenling, of course. I had no way to tell her that Wenling and Burke were not here, but dogs very quickly figure out that sort of thing.

Lacey was now "Lady," just as I had once been Cooper and was now Riley. That's the sort of thing dogs will never understand. To me, she didn't need a different name just because she looked like a different dog. She was still my Lacey.

Grant and Ava left us the next day. Lacey and I scarcely noticed; we were running and wrestling and playing all over the farm. When we dashed down to the pond, I took care to remain close to Lacey in case she went after another snake, doing Steady to block her from wading into the marshy area, but she was more focused on harassing the ducks.

After a time, we trotted out to the fields to check to see if ZZ and Chase Dad were interested in giving us treats. They weren't, but we stuck with them anyway. Most of the time, a dog feels better if there are humans within sight and smell.

Every day was the same for us: playing, playing, playing, then out to the fields to nap near Chase Dad and ZZ.

"Well, ZZ, I think that'll do it today," Chase Dad would say, which was a signal to get up because the men would walk with us home for dinner.

"ZZ?"

On this day, Chase Dad was frowning, and I felt Lacey tense. She went straight to ZZ, who was standing oddly, a bit bent over, not moving. "You okay, ZZ?"

ZZ fell to his knees. Lacey barked in distress. "ZZ!" Chase Dad yelled.

ZZ toppled face-first into the dirt.

THIRTY-THREE

Chase Dad pulled out his phone and spoke harshly and then threw it from him. He flipped ZZ on his back and started pushing on ZZ's chest. Lacey was circling the men in agitation, whining, so distraught she snapped at me when I went to try to comfort her.

I felt sure I knew what was happening, and I felt sad for Lacey, and sad for Chase Dad, whose tears were falling down in dark splats on ZZ's shirt. "Come on, ZZ! You can do it!" he shouted, his fear scraping his voice raw. "ZZ! Please, please no, ZZ!"

Lacey and I looked up when a long, thin wail pierced the summer air, growing louder before it snapped into silence and a heavy rumble accompanied a big truck up the driveway and out into the fields. It drove directly to us and two men and a woman leapt out, carrying boxes and kneeling next to ZZ and putting something over his face. One of them pushed on ZZ's chest and Chase Dad sank back, his hand covering his eyes.

I padded over to him. He was breathing in great, shuddering gasps, still weeping. He touched me when I nosed his hand, but I could tell he was not even really aware I was there.

"ZZ!"

I looked up. Li Min was running toward us, her mouth open, face contorted in terror. Lacey scampered to intercept, but Li Min dashed right past her. Chase Dad stood, visibly gathering himself, and spread his arms for her. "*Li Min,*" he grated hoarsely.

They fell into each other's hug, sobbing. Lacey and I were close by, distressed we couldn't help. The new people put ZZ on a bed and lifted it into the back of their truck, and Li Min and Chase Dad got in with them and they all drove away. Lacey pursued for a little bit, but at the end of the driveway she stopped, forlornly tasting the dust of the truck as the loud wail again split the day.

Eventually Lacey returned to me, ears down, tail tucked, uncertain and scared. I gave her nose a kiss and led her back home, through the dog door and onto Burke's bed. I knew from Grandma that this was the sort of thing that sometimes happened, and when it did, a person was taken away. That person would not come back, but everyone else would. Good dogs would wait, because when the people returned from wherever they had been, they would need their best friends.

And people did come. First Chase Dad staggered in the front door by himself, slumping into a chair to sit and stare and finally put his head in his hands and grieve with loud, frightening howls. I whined because he was in such pain. He eventually stood and took faltering steps into his room and closed his door.

Then, within just a day, Burke was there! I was so happy to see him I ran around the yard in mad circles, Lacey pursuing in bewilderment. When he reached down I jumped up to lick his face. "Wow, you are just about the friendliest dog in the world, Riley."

My boy seemed subdued. I realized that he didn't understand that I was Cooper, and obviously he had forgotten about the day we went swimming in the frozen lake.

Burke glanced up as Chase Dad opened the front door. "Hey, Dad." I understood, then, that he was feeling the same as Chase Dad about ZZ.

The two men hugged each other. "It's been too long, son."

"I know, Dad. I am so sorry about ZZ."

"Yeah."

"I'm sorry it took something like this to bring me back. . . ."

"You're here now, son. That's all that matters."

"How's Li Min?"

"Wenling is with her now. Not doing so well, I guess. Grant and his girlfriend are cutting their Hawaii trip short to come back for the funeral."

"That's really nice of them."

"ZZ was family." Chase Dad turned and looked at his farm, then shook his head. "Come on inside."

I slept on my boy's bed for a bit that night, but Lacey was agitated and confused, so eventually I jumped down and lay next to her on a rug. Dogs need dogs as much as people do.

At breakfast the next morning, I sprawled hopefully under Burke's feet, thinking he'd toss me a treat for old times' sake. Lacey lay under Chase Dad's feet because she didn't know how rare it was for him, of all people, to feed us under the table.

"How's business?" Chase Dad asked as he sat down.

I heard Burke pouring something and the heavy smell of coffee filled the air. "Best dam business ever."

"Anyone ever laugh at that one?"

"Just me." Burke chuckled. "It's still the most rewarding job you can imagine. Every time we decommission a dam, nature immediately sets out to make amends for our sins. Marshes return, whole ecosystems rebuild, fish appear as if from spontaneous generation."

"Did you go up the hill to see the dam TMH put up there? Supposed to help with all the flooding."

"They have flooding because they turned all the streams into cement-lined ditches and then paved three acres to build their fruit processing plant," Burke replied.

Chase Dad grunted. "They needed to put in the plant so they could run me out of the orchard business. Past two years, I'm selling my apples and pears at a loss. Remember Gary McCallister? He gave up on his cherries completely."

I looked up at the clink of silverware on plate, which caused Lacey to look up as well. Her reaction caused me to sit up and so she sat up. The two of us stared eagerly, being very good dogs.

"Have you met Grant's new girlfriend?" Chase Dad asked.

"No. I don't . . . I really don't see Grant, Dad. We're just better off if we don't run into each other."

"What did I do wrong that my two sons don't want to have anything to do with me or each other?" Chase Dad lamented.

"God, no, you didn't do anything, Dad. It's just . . . I just . . . I don't know. It's just so damn awkward between us. We say we don't have issues, but it sure doesn't feel that way. And you . . . I just always felt your, I don't know, disapproval. That I haven't managed to be a better brother to Grant. That I decided to be an engineer instead of working with you on the farm."

Chase Dad was staring in disbelief. *"Disapproval?* My God, Burke, I am so proud of you my heart's bursting. Please, whatever I did to make you feel that way, forgive me. I love you, son. You mean everything to me."

They hugged each other violently, slapping and clutching at each other. I wagged uncertainly. Eventually they sat back down. Chase Dad cleared his throat. "So, Burke, I was thinking. From what I can tell, your job has you on the road pretty much every day. You could move back to Michigan. Hell, you could live *here*. Pellston has commercial flights."

"Dad."

Chase Dad drummed his fingers on the table. Finally he leaned back, sighing. "Just miss everybody."

There was another long silence. Lacey glanced at me in disbelief. Were they really going to completely ignore us?

"So let me ask you, Burke, what's it going to be like for you when you see Wenling?"

"I honestly have no idea. The real question is what's it going to be like for *Grant*."

"You in touch with her much?"

"I wouldn't say 'much.' Messages. She was in Kansas once for a conference, so I drove over from Kansas City where I was consulting. We talk on the phone, sometimes."

"But no . . ."

"Romance? I don't think either one of us would have much interest."

"But there's a chance?"

"So now you're a dating service?"

"I'm just at the age where a man would like to have some grandkids to spoil."

"Well, if there's going to be the pitter-patter of little farmer feet running around, it's going to be from Grant. I haven't met anyone."

When Wenling and her mother arrived, Lacey greeted them

the way I'd first greeted Burke, racing around the yard, yipping and crying, kissing Wenling's hands. Wenling, I saw, didn't recognize Lacey any more than Burke recognized me.

"What a crazy dog!" Wenling looked up and saw Chase Dad and Burke coming down the steps. She pushed her hair out of her eyes. "Burke."

"So sorry about your father, Wenling."

They hugged. Chase Dad went straight to Li Min and they held each other and both of them wept a little.

"That's Lady," Burke informed Wenling. "Ava's dog. Ava is Grant's girlfriend."

Wenling nodded. "Mom said. I think she's the one I met, the rescue girl? Her name was Ava, I think, is it the same one?"

"Oh." Burke shrugged. "I actually don't know anything about her at all."

We were attentive dogs and followed everyone into the house. Lacey wanted to wrestle, to work out her joy with frenetic play, but I did Steady, and she was puzzled enough to stop leaping around and nosed me, perplexed. I understood that when people were sad, they wanted to sit and speak softly and not have dogs try to cheer them up. Some things happen that even a dog can't fix, and ZZ going away in the back of that big truck, never to return, was one of them.

That's why, when Ava and Grant arrived, I did not jump on them like Lacey. I sat, wagging, as they stood up out of their car. "Hey there, Riley, good dog," Grant greeted. "Down, Lady Dog. Down!"

"Look at how calm he's being. It's almost as if Riley gets it's a sad occasion." Ava took my head in her hands. "You're a good dog, Riley. An angel dog."

"Well, let's get this over with. Come on in and meet my brother," Grant sighed.

Ava patted his arm. "It will be okay."

Lacey barged in through the dog door ahead of them, but I waited and followed Ava through the people door. Everyone else was at the table drinking coffee, but they stood with smiles.

"Hey there, Burke," Grant said softly.

"Long time, Grant."

Wenling stepped forward. "Grant." They hugged.

"So sorry about your father, Wenling. This is Ava. Ava, that's Wenling; her mom, Li Min; you've met my dad, Chase; and the dumb-looking one is my brother, Burke. Everyone, this is Ava."

"Oh my God!" Ava blurted.

"It's *you*!" Burke was grinning in delight.

All the people looked at one another blankly. Lacey gave me the same look. "You two know each other?" Grant asked.

Burke and Ava hugged, a little awkwardly, so Lacey stuck her nose in between them to add affection. "I never put it together," Burke said.

"I didn't either. I mean, I thought you said your name was 'Burt.' But honestly, it was so long ago, I forgot."

Chase Dad cleared his throat. "I don't know about everyone else, but I'd sure like to be filled in on what we're talking about, here."

I heard a car coming up the driveway and ran out the dog door to greet it, Lacey in hot pursuit. It was two women bearing warm dishes of food that caused me to salivate. They weren't the last people to show up bearing meals, either. When a house is full of sadness, people bring food, but the only ones happy about it are the dogs.

That night I lay on the bed dodging my boy's restless feet. Back when I did Steady and Assist for him, he never kicked out in his sleep, but now I groaned and moved out of the way with every twitch. Still, I was content. I had what I had always wanted:

everyone together on the farm. Lacey paced restlessly in the living room, waiting for Wenling to return, before finally climbing upstairs to sleep with Grant and Ava. I hoped Wenling and Li Min would come back soon so that Lacey would stop worrying.

And they did, but only after a long day, which started with everyone getting dressed in noisy shoes in the morning and then leaving their dogs alone all day. Lacey was impatient with my attempts to play with her—reuniting with Wenling and then watching her drive off made Lacey frustrated in a way I completely understood.

Everyone was sad on the day of noisy shoes. Until the sun fell, people stood around and murmured mournfully and ate food, but neither Lacey nor I tried to elicit treats—this did not seem the right time for that.

A few people gave us treats anyway. A good dog is hard to resist.

When the house emptied, Lacey lay at Wenling's feet. There were long silences, then someone would speak quietly, and there would be a long silence. Li Min made some of the vile stuff I had learned was called "tea." Wenling put paper to her face and wiped her eyes or honked her nose.

Chase Dad slapped his knee, a sudden sound that made everyone jump. "I've made a decision." He glanced around the room. "I'm going to sell the farm."

Lacey and I looked up because of how everyone in the room suddenly went rigid. There was a long, apprehensive silence.

"Why would you even say that, Dad?" Burke asked.

"Because without ZZ I don't see how I can make it. Hell, we've lost money four years running. Grant was right, Grant has always *been* right. I'm swimming against the current here."

No one spoke for a moment.

"So, sell to Trident Mechanical Harvesting?" Grant asked. "Then work it for a dollar-a-year lease?"

"No, hell, just give it up and be done with it," Chase Dad told him bitterly.

Lacey sat up and yawned in agitation at the rising disquiet.

"I'll help," Li Min said quietly. Everyone looked at her. She shrugged. "ZZ was . . . he wouldn't hear of me working the crops. To him, an American wife can't be in the fields, it reflects poorly on him. But my hours at the shop have been cut down to almost nothing, so I could go out in the fields and work with you, Chase. Every day if needed. I'm not ZZ, but I can learn."

"I'll move home, too," Wenling declared. Now everyone's eyes were on her. Lacey put her head in Wenling's lap. "In honor of my father. To help my mother. I'm working in a lab because that's just what you do with a degree in horticulture, but I think I'd rather be outside, see if anything I learned can be applied to a family farm and not just a"—she looked at Burke and grinned—"a robo-farm."

Later Grant was up in his room when Burke knocked lightly on the doorframe. It was still odd to see Burke upstairs without me doing Assist to get him there. I wondered if Burke would ever decide to go back to using his chair.

"Talk to you a minute, brother?" Burke asked.

"Yeah, sure."

I had to scoot fast to keep from being left out when Burke shut the door behind him. He leaned up against it. "I was thinking maybe you should hang around here for a bit."

Grant tilted his head. "Hang here," he repeated.

"As in, move back to the farm for a while."

Grant snorted. "Dad tell you to come up here and say that?"

"No, Dad has nothing to do with it."

"Sure he doesn't."

"Grant. Yes, he could use your help. But that's not why. I think you should move here for yourself."

Grant barked out a laugh. "Sure."

"For yourself, and maybe for someone else."

THIRTY-FOUR

As I sat there looking at the two brothers, I heard Lacey on the other side of the closed door. I hoped someone would open it, but Grant was staring at Burke, doing an angry walk with just his eyes. He pointed his finger. "I think maybe you should just keep a lid on whatever it is you came here to say."

Burke shook his head. "Wow, you so sound like Dad. But you don't see that you've spent your whole adult life running from the only two commitments that ever mattered to you?"

"Commitments."

"The farm. And Wenling."

Grant's grunt was full of disgust. "I don't want to be a farmer. I've spent my life leaving the farm."

"You don't want to be anything *but* a farmer, and maybe you've been leaving the only place you belong."

Grant sat down heavily on his bed, and Burke settled into a chair. Grant folded his arms. "Wenling and I broke up."

"Yeah, a million years ago. And you two didn't 'break up,' you just took off on her. She didn't want to be a child bride, but that didn't mean it was over. Come on, Grant. I've been in the same room with you all day. I've seen who you look at whenever you think no one is watching. And it sure as heck isn't Ava."

"Yeah?" Grant challenged. "I see *you* looking at Ava."

"That's true, she's really pretty," Burke admitted. "I hate to tell you this, brother, but with Ava you've peaked."

Both men laughed quietly. On the other side of the door, Lacey drew in a deep huff of air through her nose, surveying the room—she knew we were in here and that she was out there.

"Did . . . did Wenling say something to you?" Grant asked tentatively.

Burke grinned. "Ho ho, so, there is some interest, then."

"Just answer the question."

"No, Grant. She doesn't have to."

Grant stared at him. Burke stood and opened the door, and Lacey bounded in and I fell on the floor so she could straddle me and bite my face.

After breakfast the next morning, Ava and Grant strolled down to the dock at the pond, so Lacey and I followed. I was surprised when Lacey didn't leap in the water after the ducks, but at least she barked at them. We both did, going into a frenzy until Grant yelled "Cut it out!" at us. I didn't know what he was saying, but his meaning was pretty clear.

I lay at Grant's feet and Lacey dropped down next to me, putting her head on my back.

"Those two really love each other," Grant observed.

"What did you want to talk to me about?" Ava asked.

"How do you know I want to talk to you about something?"

"Seriously? You've been acting weird all morning. I know something is going on."

"Well." Grant blew out a breath. "Without ZZ, I'm really worried about my dad. How he is going to make it through the fall harvest, I mean. So I thought I would spend a few months up here, help him out."

"Just like that? What about your job?"

"I texted them and said I needed to take a few months off for a family emergency."

"You *already* texted them? Without talking to me?"

"It's not like that, Ava. I wanted to see if they would give me the time off."

"And they did?"

"Sure. Well." Grant cleared his throat. "What they said was I could reapply for the position when I got back."

"I see." Ava stretched her foot out and ran it along Lacey's back. Lacey groaned and rolled onto her side so Ava would have better access to her tummy.

"Dad says I'm probably better at farming than he is," Grant added.

"And he needs the help."

"Yes, it's a tough job."

"What about Wenling?"

"Sure, she's okay. I mean, she can help, but I don't know if she can replace ZZ. Or how long she's going to want to stay; she's a scientist, not a farmer."

"No, I am asking, what about Wenling? Does she have anything to do with this decision?"

"She did just lose her father."

"So the rambling man suddenly wants to live on the farm. With Wenling. His former fiancée." Ava sounded bitterly angry, and both Lacey and I raised our heads to look at her.

"Come on, Ava, that's not what I am saying."

The next day Grant and Ava took us on the long car ride back to Ava's house. We wanted to put our heads out the windows, but with them rolled up we elected to wrestle in the backseat until Grant turned and hissed "Stop!" at us. Again, the word was unknown, but we had no problem interpreting the tone.

"I think you should hire a security service. Ava? I'm serious. I know these death threats seem pretty looney, but you never know when one of those anti–pit bull nuts might make good on his bluff. Lady's the poster dog for their cause, a fighting pit bull that lives like a pet."

"You haven't been worried about it until now."

"Right, well, with me around, it . . ."

"Except you haven't been around," she interrupted him. "You travel all the time, Grant. If someone is going to try to shoot Lady, they're going to try, whether you're in Denver or Toronto or up at the farm with Wenling."

Grant made an odd, dissatisfied sound. It was mostly a quiet car ride after that.

Lacey and I burst into Ava's house ahead of them, excitedly sniffing around, then curled up on a rug and fell asleep. We padded out to the kitchen when Grant prepared dinner, though, because whatever he was doing had a delicious cheese-and-meat odor. He served plates for himself and Ava but not dogs.

"Grant."

"Mmmm?"

"I want you to sleep on the couch tonight."

"What? Ava . . ."

"Stop. I think you are a good man, Grant, I really do. And I think that you are doing your best to tell the truth, but something changed for you yesterday, and maybe you haven't admitted it to yourself yet, but saying you and Wenling aren't still stuck on each other is as ridiculous as saying Li Min isn't in love with your father."

"What? Li Min? That's ludicrous, Ava."

"And *that's* what you find ludicrous about what I just said? Li Min?" she challenged softly.

After dinner, with no treats given, Ava let us out into the backyard to scamper around and sniff. We were back by the fence when I smelled a man—Lacey smelled him, too. She emitted a low growl.

"Lady! Want a treat? Lady?" the man whispered. With the word "treat" the succulent odor of beef joined the man's scent on the air, and Lacey stopped growling. We pushed our noses up to the slats in the fence, drinking it in. He was hunched over and wore dark clothing. I instantly did not like him and did not wag. I felt myself readying for a growl of my own. The man raised his arm and made a throwing motion. "Here ya go, Lady!"

With a thud a small piece of red meat landed in the dirt, virtually at my feet. There was something wrong with it: clinging to its surface was an odor foreign to any treat I'd ever encountered. I lowered my nose, suspicious. My hackles rose at the strong sense of danger.

Lacey lunged to grab the meat, so I picked it up and ran, with her in fast pursuit. The smell instantly became a sharp, sour taste in my mouth. Something told me we should not eat this strangely delivered meal, something similar to a memory except not based on anything that had ever happened. It was bad. We should let Ava and Grant decide what to do with it. We needed humans to help us; this was outside of a dog's capabilities.

But Lacey wouldn't leave it alone. When I dropped the hunk of beef to examine it more thoroughly, she dove at it and I was forced to snatch it up again. Finally, exasperated, I snarled at her, clicking my teeth. She bared her own fangs in response. Why didn't she understand? She pressed forward and I was shocked at how fierce she appeared. She did not sense the same threat I did. She was ready to fight for this, even though it might hurt her.

So I ate it, turning away from her and bolting it down on the run. I could not let Lacey have it. I had to protect her from this menace, because it came from a sinister man, crouching on the other side of the fence with evil intent.

When I finished the meat, an unpleasant tang remained in my mouth. Lacey sniffed the grass where it had lain, and then my jaws. I wagged, but she did not play-bow. She went back to the fence, probably hoping for a repeat performance, but the man's smell had faded away.

That night Grant stretched out on the couch in the living room, and Lacey sprawled on Ava's bed. I was confused. I tried to climb up with Grant, but there was no room. Yet sleeping with Lacey and Ava seemed wrong, somehow. I worried about Grant being comfortable without a dog draped across his legs.

"Lie down, Riley," Grant told me.

I did as I was told, closing my eyes, then snapping them open. The floor suddenly didn't feel right; I had the sense it was tilting. I remember my first mother and the first den, with the metal walls. Those strange forces of torsion that threw around my siblings and me were, I had learned, the sensations of a car ride. I'd become accustomed to such things, but not when I was splayed out on the floor.

I lifted my head, panting, looking at Grant. I remembered lying in a field after playing with Lacey, my stomach feeling as if it was biting me from within. Something very similar was happening to me now, and I was fairly certain how it would end.

I staggered to my toy box and pushed my nose to the bottom for the nylon bone. Drooling, I carried it carefully and set it on the couch next to where Grant lay sleeping. When he woke up he would see it and know that I loved him. I stumbled back to my bed and fell heavily into it.

That long-ago day in the field, my last as the good dog Cooper, Lacey had been there, loving me, concerned and caring. Now, as if she sensed I was thinking of her, she eased off Ava's bed, nosed open the door, and padded out to see me. I licked my lips. The sour taste from the forbidden meat was very strong on my tongue, and Lacey put her nose to it.

Lacey was, I realized at that moment, an old dog in a younger dog's body. She had had a difficult life, and it aged her. The thought made me sad.

I urgently maneuvered to my feet, feeling suddenly sick in my belly. I went to the door and scratched at it, but by the time Grant was there to let me out, I was heaving up dinner. "Oh! Riley, what's going on? No, Lady! Get back!"

Grant turned on the lights and began cleaning up the mess. I felt like a bad dog. Lacey knew I was in distress and nuzzled me helplessly.

Ava walked in, tying a robe. "What happened?"

"Riley threw up. I'm getting it."

"Riley?"

I glanced at her but was having trouble seeing her. "He's really sick, Grant, look at him."

My legs collapsed and I fell to the floor. I was panting, unable to draw in air.

"Riley!" Grant shouted.

Lacey's nose was right there. I felt her love and concern, even as my vision blurred.

Ava was sobbing. "I think he's been poisoned, Grant."

They both knelt by my side. Lacey dropped to her belly and crawled forward until our snouts were touching. I felt the caressing hands on my fur, the distress of everyone in the room, the sensation of rushing water.

The pain in my stomach unclenched. I was with Lacey and Grant and Ava. I loved them all, just as I loved Burke. I was a good dog, but something was happening to me now, something I had been through before. "We'll get him to the vet," Grant said.

"Hurry!"

Lacey licked me tenderly as Grant put his arms under me. She would be with Ava and Grant, now. I was glad for that. People need a good dog, especially when another one dies. Grant lifted me up into the enfolding darkness, and I felt myself keep rising, up and up and up, until I was far, far away, floating in inky waters.

"Bailey," a familiar voice soothed. "You are such a good dog, Bailey."

I could see a golden light, now. I had been here before. I liked being called a good dog by this voice. I felt his love for me in every word, even if I couldn't understand what he was saying.

"Your work is almost done, Bailey. Just a few more things for you to fix. One more time, Bailey, just need you to go back one more time."

I thought of Ava, and Grant, and Wenling and Burke, and Chase Dad and Li Min. I pictured them all at the farm, running with Lacey.

The thought made me very happy.

THIRTY-FIVE

Awareness came gradually, but it was all familiar: the warm, nourishing milk of my mother, the squeaking, squirming presence of my siblings. When my nose began reporting on my surroundings, I even knew where I was: a building with dogs in cages and cats who stared with hostility.

And the first person I smelled was, of course, Ava. When I was old enough to see her I would rush over any time she was near the den and my brown-, white-, and black-colored siblings would irritate me by doing the same thing, as if they all belonged with her. She was *my* Ava. Some of my littermates chewed on her fingers, but when she picked me up I always just tried to kiss her nose.

Sam Dad played with us, too, taking us out into the yard where I first met Lacey. Lacey wasn't there, though. The grass was dead and the snow was piled in some places, but I could tell the days were getting warmer.

Ava loved to pick me up and stare into my eyes. "This is my absolute favorite," she told Sam Dad.

"So, let me guess. You're naming him Bailey."

I glanced at him. What did it mean that he was saying that name?

Ava laughed ruefully. "No, I think I've gotten all the Baileys out of my system. Every single dog I ever named Bailey was re-named by the new owners. No, this one is Oscar. He's only a puppy, but see how he looks at you? He has the eyes of a wise, old dog."

"An old soul," suggested Marla. She swept her dark bangs off her forehead, and when she petted me the oils and fragrances from her hair were painted on her fingers.

Ava nodded. "Exactly."

"What kind of dog are you, Oscar?" Marla asked.

I heard the question in her voice but didn't recognize a word.

Sam Dad chuckled. "Retired woman who brought in the pups said her expensive, purebred German shorthaired pointer hunt-ing dog 'somehow got pregnant.' So we don't know exactly."

"I'm saying cocker, maybe," Ava added.

Marla kissed me on my nose. I liked Marla.

We were in the yard when Ava opened the gate and an aging dog trotted in, white nose to the ground. She was piebald with brown patches all over. I didn't need to smell her, I recognized her by sight.

Lacey.

Her arrival set off a stampede, my brothers and sisters trip-ping over themselves to get to her. I wanted to greet her without their interference, but when they reached her they mobbed her, leaping up, gnawing at her, squeaking. Lacey was gently tolerant of all of it, wagging her tail, sniffing the puppies, allowing them to try to gnaw her lips.

"Good, gentle Lady Dog," Ava murmured.

Finally I stepped on one of my sisters and was nose to nose with my Lacey. She immediately play-bowed and began leaping and twisting, as excited to see me as I was to see her. Of *course* she knew me!

"Lady is sure jazzed to meet these pups!" Ava observed to Sam Dad.

"I love it when an older dog is energized by younger ones," Sam Dad agreed.

I wanted to chase Lacey around the yard, to wrestle with her and roll with her, and I could see she wanted the same, but we were stymied by my tiny size.

When I was bigger, we'd be back to harassing ducks on the farm.

The gate opened and I was delighted, though not surprised, to see Burke standing there. I ran over to see him and of course my idiot littermates did the same. He grinned. "Hi!"

"Burke? Wow!" Ava, beaming, ran to him and he kissed her on the cheek, taking care not to step on any of the puppies pooling at his feet. "It's been what, three years?"

"Yes, but I promise I thought about you for an hour every day."

Ava laughed. "What brings you here?" she asked.

"I've been thinking of adopting a dog," Burke replied. "And I was driving past and I saw your sign on the highway, the one with the puppy video? And I thought, this is where I should go."

"Dad, this is Grant's brother, Burke."

"Nice to meet you," Sam Dad said, sticking out his hand so Burke could pull on it briefly. "I'm going to go clean out the cat cages."

"The glamour never ends." Ava laughed.

I put my paws on my boy's pants, straining to reach him. He rewarded me by stooping over and yanking me high into the air, so that we were staring into each other's eyes.

"That's Oscar," Ava said. "He's the sweetest one of the litter. Absolutely loves people. Especially you, it looks like."

"Hello, Lady Dog, long time no see," Burke greeted as Lacey came over to be petted. He glanced at Ava. "I thought you weren't supposed to allow dogs and puppies to mingle until they've had their shots."

"There are two schools of thought on that one. Personally, I think it is better to take the risk and let the puppies socialize with other dogs as much as possible. More dogs are put to death for not being socialized than die from viruses—inoculated dogs have herd immunity just like humans. So wait, you're getting a dog? I thought you Trevino boys were all about not letting your feet get stuck in one place."

I gazed up at my boy's face in adoration. He nuzzled me and I licked his cheek. "Funny thing is that I just took a job doing a mechanical survey of all the dams in the state. I'm going to be a Michigander for the foreseeable future. I picture driving around with a dog next to me. Keeping me company while I tromp around looking at rusted pipes and crumbling cement. Can I have Oscar?"

"Seriously?"

"Look at him. Who could resist those brown eyes?"

"Well, he's not quite old enough to adopt just yet. And you do know you have to get him fixed, right? We pay for it, but it's a requirement."

Burke put me down. I ignored the other puppies and tried to climb back up his body. "I imagine if you drew up the contract it's pretty ironclad."

"You have no idea."

I was disappointed when Burke left a short time later. Once again, people were behaving in ways a dog couldn't begin to fathom.

Not long after Burke's visit, my siblings began to depart one by one, Ava reaching into our cage to gently take each wiggling, eager puppy away. I knew they were going to new homes, with new families, and that made me happy.

I was sleeping on top of Lacey, my little puppy head rising and falling as she breathed, when the gate opened and Burke was there again! This was his new trick, I decided.

Ava stood. "Hi!" She looked at her wrist.

Burke shrugged apologetically. "So sorry I'm late. I ran into a woman who mistakenly thought she owned a dam just because the pond backs up onto her land. When I told her my job is to assess whether it was safe and by every measure I can think of that one is not, she wanted to argue the point rather vehemently. What's wrong?"

"Sorry? Nothing."

"You're looking at me sort of strangely."

"Oh, I was just thinking you look . . . nice." Ava dropped her eyes.

"Thanks. I washed my hair, even though I already did it last month."

Ava laughed.

I was carried to a small room and Burke sat at a desk to rattle and scratch some papers. Ava sat across from him. Lacey stiffly eased onto a dog bed and I climbed in with her. I was settling down for another nap when something occurred to me and I sat straight back up, staring at the two people as they talked.

Burke didn't just always find me—he always found Ava, too! And they were the only people in the world I had ever done Pull for. I had even done Assist for Ava in the snow! So, even though it had never before seemed to me that Ava and Burke were connected, they actually were.

Burke bent over his papers. "I'm glad to see Lady. After Riley, I kept thinking they would keep trying to hurt her."

"They had to back off after all the bad press. The guy the cops caught was a volunteer for the, let's just call them the 'organization that shall not be named.' They tried to disavow him, but he was on their donor rolls."

"What kind of time did he get?"

"Time? He had a fine and community service. I filed an objection when he petitioned to have his volunteer work for that same horrible organization count toward his hours, as if attending meetings to discuss putting pit bulls to death is somehow for the *community*." Ava picked up the papers and stacked them. "So, have you spoken to your brother lately?"

Burke shook his head. "No. We were not on speaking terms for so long that it's hard to get back into the habit. I talk to Wenling sometimes though."

"Ah, Wenling, the black magic woman. So you're under her spell, too?"

I snuggled closer to Lacey, my mate, loving being with her, with Ava and my boy in the same room.

"You don't know? She was my girlfriend before she was Grant's."

Ava's mouth dropped open. "No, I did *not* know. When was this?"

"Long, long time ago. Funny how important it all seemed back then. Now it's just kid's stuff. She dumped me for Grant."

"Really? He never said a word about that. His own brother?"

"Okay, wait, I don't know why I said it like that. I dumped her, to be honest. Long story, but I had this image of myself being suddenly very popular with the girls, and I wanted to be free to pursue that. When that didn't work out, I became pretty jealous, which was stupid—she was going to date *somebody*, right? But I was in a bad place and said some things to my brother at the time, harsh things. Grant's got a lot of my dad in him—he has a tough time forgiving people."

"So when you talk to her . . ."

"Right, we're just friends."

"No, what I am meaning to ask is about Wenling and Grant."

"Ah." He gazed at her steadily. "They're a couple, yes."

Ava laughed dryly. "Sometimes I need someone to explain to me why every single man I've ever dated has left me for somebody else."

"You probably just picked the wrong guys."

"That's what my dad says. Whatever Wenling's got, I need to get some."

"From what I see, you've got more than enough."

Ava laughed delightedly. "I've never heard *that* one before."

Burke just stared at her, a small smile on his face, and eventually Ava glanced away. "You want to have dinner with me tonight?" he asked.

"Oh," Ava replied. Lacey and I looked over at her, sensing a rising tension in the room.

"Oh yes or oh no?"

"It's just that it is short notice."

"I'm trying to be spontaneous. Everyone thinks engineers are controlled and predictable. Last night I tore off my clothes and howled at the moon."

Ava chuckled. "You planning to do that again?"

"Let me buy you dinner and we'll see."

That summer, Burke and I took long car rides to wonderful places. I swam in lakes and streams, I tracked animal scents through thick woods, I slept with him in a small cloth room that he folded up and put in his truck each morning. We would smell *wonderful*, our odors blending together. And every few days we would drive over to see Ava and Lacey.

Lacey was always there at the door to greet us when Ava opened it, until suddenly she wasn't. "Hey there," Ava said. Burke kissed her while I pushed past both of them and anxiously went to Lacey, who was lying in her dog bed. She lifted her head and wagged but didn't get up when I nosed her.

"I am here to visit your shower," Burke announced.

"Our relationship began with a shower."

"That's right. But that time I hadn't been sleeping in a tent with a dog for four straight nights. Hi, Lady, how are you doing, old girl?"

Lacey wagged, but I could feel a draining, depleting sickness within her. She was, I realized, coming to the end of this life of hers, a good life where we had been together for much of it and where she was loved by people like Ava.

"Did I tell you about that first time? That first shower?" Ava asked.

Burke pulled his shirt over his head. "What I remember is that after submerging in a frozen lake, that hot water was the best thing that's ever happened to me. Highly recommended. We should open a spa. Shove people into a hole in the ice and then let them shower while their clothes are in the dryer."

"I could see you in the mirror. Not well, the glass was fogged up, but I stood and watched you."

"Why didn't you join me?"

Ava laughed.

Burke started running water. "Why don't you join me *now*?"

I went to Lacey. We sniffed each other carefully, noting changes. I was no longer a puppy, I was a truck dog whose job it was to ride around with my boy and visit fun places and chase squirrels. And Lacey was hurting inside. Soon enough, the pain inside would emerge to her outside, so that people would notice.

"I have to be up north next week," Burke remarked at dinner. "I thought maybe you'd like to come with me. You and Lady Dog."

Ava regarded him with a puzzled expression. "What do you mean?"

"Stop by the farm. Visit my dad. Wenling told me Grant is going to be gone."

"Does your brother know about us?" Ava asked after a moment.

"I haven't mentioned it to Wenling, so no. I figured that we'd start with her and Dad and let them tell Grant."

"You mean you wouldn't delight in his reaction when you tell him I'm your—" Ava abruptly ended her sentence.

"I do still owe him for shoving me off a cliff when I was in a wheelchair."

"No exaggeration in that story, Burke."

"It was a one-hundred-foot drop into a lava pit. No, I think I'm long past wanting to torment my brother, not that he would believe it." He was silent for a moment. "I know what you almost said there."

"Excuse me?"

"You were going to say 'girlfriend.'"

Ava looked away. "Sorry."

"So are you? My girlfriend?"

Ava stared at him. Burke shrugged. "I tell everyone you are. That we're exclusive. I guess I should have cleared it with you, first."

She was quiet for a moment. "We're clear," she finally said softly.

They kissed so much after that, I got bored and fell asleep. I woke up, though, when Lacey stirred and moaned. I licked her lips and her tail wiggled feebly. I thought about all the wonderful times we had shared, running and playing and wrestling. Lacey and I belonged together—I understood that above all else.

The next morning was Lacey's last. It began, as usual, with Ava setting out bowls of food for us. Lacey didn't stir from her bed. "Lady? What's wrong, honey?" Ava asked, stroking Lacey's face. Lacey briefly lifted her head. "Oh no. Lady," she whispered.

Sam Dad and Marla came over a little while later. Lacey had begun panting, but still hadn't moved from her bed. I stayed right by her, providing what comfort I could. Sam Dad felt her up and down, looked in her eyes, shaking his head. "She's in real distress. Could she have eaten something?"

"She's been lying there since I got home last night," Burke said.

Sam Dad stood up. "It's your decision, honey, but if it were up to me, I would end her pain right now. I don't know what is going on, but it's really hurting her. Who knows what damage was done to her insides at Death Dealin' Dawgs. Surgery probably isn't an option even if we could get a diagnosis, but she's had a long life."

Ava dropped to her knees and wrapped her arms around Lacey. "Oh Lady, you are such a good girl, I am sorry I didn't see how much pain you've been in."

"She hid it from you," Sam Dad advised. "She didn't want you to be worried."

Marla stroked Lacey's head. "You've given her such a wonderful ending to her life after such cruel beginnings, Ava. You gave her love and a good home."

I hung back respectfully, letting the humans love their dog. Lacey's gaze met mine and I saw what comfort she was taking from all the attention, how it was alleviating whatever was hurting her inside.

When everyone else stood, Ava hugged Lacey for a long, long time, her silent tears falling down on Lacey's fur. Lacey raised up and gave Ava a kiss, then exhaustedly let her head drop back down.

It was Lacey's last kiss. Sam Dad readied something for Lacey and I went to her side. I was glad to be there for her, a dog who loved her and could help her move on to whatever was next.

We both knew what was happening now, and we were both grateful for it. Of all the wonderful things that humans do for dogs, this was one of the best—helping us when we are in the sort of pain that can only be eased with death.

Lacey was leaving this life, but I knew I would see her again.

THIRTY-SIX

The smell of Lacey was still strong in Ava's house the morning we all piled into Burke's truck. It was not difficult to help them cheer up, because not only was I excited for a car ride, I was thrilled because I imagined how much fun Ava was going to have staying in the little cloth room with Burke and me.

"Oscar! Calm down!" Burke commanded, laughing.

Getting people to laugh after something sad has happened is one of the most important jobs for a dog.

I became ecstatic when I picked up the telltale odors that told me where we were headed. The farm! Even better!

Chase Dad was sitting on the porch, but stood when he saw us pull in. I ran to him, wagging. "Hello, Oscar, good to finally meet you," he greeted. I licked his hands. He was looking at Burke and Ava, though, a funny expression on his face. "Burke, hey."

"Hi, Dad."

"And . . . Ava."

"Hello, Mr. Trevino."

"No, please, call me Chase." He hugged her. "I have to admit, I am not sure I know what is going on."

Burke smiled. "It's exactly what it looks like."

"What it looks like is that you and your brother confound conventional norms."

Ava shrugged. "I just knew I was going to settle for one of them or the other."

Everyone chuckled, but I could feel some uneasiness in all of them. "Li Min is in the barn working on the tractor." Chase Dad put his hands to his face. "Hey, Li Min! Come see!"

Burke looked puzzled. "Working on the tractor?"

"Yeah. I told her we could afford a new one, but I think she likes the challenge of keeping the old one going," Chase Dad replied.

"No, I mean, I guess I didn't know she could do that," Burke explained.

"Oh," Chase Dad said with a nod. "Li Min can do *anything*."

When Li Min came out of the barn I ran to her, jumping up in greeting and smelling her oily fingers. She hugged Burke with her hands draped oddly at his back, not touching him. "Nice to see you, Ava," she said. "I'd offer to shake, but my hands are a little greasy."

"You look like you've spent the morning being fingerprinted by the FBI," Burke observed.

"I'm going to go clean up," Li Min said. She climbed the stairs and went inside the house.

Chase Dad turned to Burke. "Grant and Wenling are in town, but I'm expecting them back momentarily."

Ava and Burke glanced at each other in alarm. "So Grant's here?" Burke finally asked.

Chase Dad nodded. "His trip got postponed." His eyes widened. "*Oh.*"

"Huh," Burke commented with a shrug. "Okay, then. We'll deal with it."

Since Lacey was not at the farm, I went down and barked at the ducks in her honor, lifting my leg on one of the dock posts for good measure. Running back up to the house, I veered sharply when I picked up a smell both new and familiar. A goat! A baby goat! I stuck my head through the fence and she came skipping right over to meet me, lowering her head to rub against mine. Then she tore around her pen, leaping high, while I watched, a little perplexed. What was she doing?

Standing there watching the goat's antics, I remembered Grandma talking to Judy, long ago on a day just like this. Though their smells had been washed away by time and snow and wind, for a moment it was as if I had their scent in my nose, fresh and present, and could hear Grandma's gentle voice. I had met many wonderful people in my wonderful lives, but I would never forget Grandma.

When a car glided up the driveway I abandoned the goat and gave chase, jumping on Wenling and Grant as they emerged from it. I was so thrilled at this development I lay on the ground, wriggling in joy, as Wenling petted me. "Who are you?" she asked.

"That's Oscar," Burke called from the front porch. He tromped down the steps and gave Wenling a hug, then turned and faced Grant. After a moment, the brothers embraced each other a little stiffly.

"To what do we owe this honor?" Grant asked.

"I came to see how badly you're messing up Dad's operation. Hey, I have to tell you something. Both of you, actually."

They stopped, regarding him warily. I did Sit, being a good dog.

"Ava's here."

Both Grant and Wenling started in surprise. "Ava Marks?" Grant asked sharply. "That Ava?"

"That Ava, right."

Grant looked to Wenling. "I don't know what she's doing here, Wenling. I swear." He turned to Burke. "What does she want?"

"From you? Nothing. She came up with me. Ava and I are together now."

There was a long silence. "That's great," Wenling offered.

Grant was angry. "What the *hell* are you doing, Burke?"

Burke spread his hands. "I ran into her when I went to adopt Oscar. I took her to dinner, and we just . . ."

I looked up at my name, though I was prepared to be called Cooper or even Riley here on the farm.

"You 'ran into' her? Like we're supposed to believe that?" Grant seethed.

Wenling turned to him. "Why is this such a problem for you, Grant? What's it got to do with you?"

He stared at her in disbelief. "You don't get it? It's got everything to do with me. Why else would he do something like this?"

"You're being ridiculous," Burke snapped.

"Are you saying you're still interested in Ava?" Wenling demanded.

I wagged uncertainly at her distress.

"What?" Grant shook his head. "*No.*"

"Then what's the problem?" Wenling asked tightly.

"The problem is his motivation. The problem is that this is some sort of *revenge.*"

"You know what I'm sick of?" Burke responded angrily. "I'm sick of you turning every wound and injury into some sort of lifelong trauma that we're all supposed to make excuses for. After Grandma died, you *vanished*. For years! And now you're saying what, you have some sort of lifetime hold on Ava Marks, because you dated each other for a while? When are you going to grow up?"

Grant's fists were clenched.

"Now *you're* being unfair, Burke," Wenling responded tersely. "None of us can undo what's done. Grant tells me all the time that his biggest regret was how he turned his back on you."

Burke seemed to soften, his shoulders losing their tension. "You say that?"

Grant looked away, then nodded.

"I say the same thing, Grant," Burke said quietly. "How I wish my brother and I would figure out a way to talk to each other."

Wenling was looking back and forth between them. "I think I'll go in and chat with my boyfriend's ex-girlfriend."

"Or, you could go in and talk to your ex-boyfriend's current girlfriend," Burke told her.

With a small laugh, Wenling turned toward the house. Burke and Grant headed down to the pond, which was good because I was ready to give the ducks another working over.

"So you and Ava? Is it serious?" Grant asked.

Burke nodded. "Seems to be."

"You maybe could have said something before this instead of springing it on me," Grant observed.

We reached the dock and I ran to the end, glaring at the ducks. They stared back. Ducks sometimes shake their tails, but it is far from being a true wag.

Burke kicked a stick off the dock and into the water and I tensed, wondering if I should go get it and bring it back to him. "I didn't want to tell you at all. I knew you'd overreact."

"How am I overreacting? You show up unannounced with my

ex-girlfriend. Hell, yes, you should have told me. Or texted Wenling, like you do practically every damn day, my brother and my girlfriend talking to each other. Because you have to have the last word on everything."

"Well, that was a compound—complex complaint if there ever was one. I don't text Wenling every day, not even every month. And I didn't phone you because you and I don't *talk*, and anyway so what? You dumped Ava for Wenling, remember? Did you expect Ava to join the nuns? And don't we have a fine tradition of stealing each other's girlfriends?"

"God, is everything a joke to you?"

"Is *nothing* a joke to you?"

The stick was still floating on the water. I stared, mesmerized. I was stuck between getting it and not getting it. Why throw a stick into the water if you don't want a dog to retrieve it? But no one was encouraging me to jump in. People usually become really excited when they throw a stick, but not Burke, not this time.

They were quiet for so long I became bored and flopped down on the dock, mournfully watching the stick bob away.

Burke laughed softly. "Remember when you duct-taped me to the chair and left me in the barn? I got Cooper to pull me over to the tools and managed to stick a pruning knife under the tape. Took me all day, but I freed myself and was back in the house like nothing happened when you went to the barn to check on me."

"Cooper was a good dog."

I glanced up.

"Kind of a metaphor for our lives, isn't it? We're always messing with each other. But not this time, Grant. I swear, just like you and Wenling had nothing to do with me, Ava and I have nothing to do with you."

I heard the sound of the front screen slamming and sat up.

Ava and Wenling were stepping down the front stairs together, talking animatedly.

Grant blew out a breath. "Well, *this* could be bad."

"Yeah, they might compare notes. If either one of them talks the other into higher standards, we're sunk."

Wenling raised her hands to her mouth. "We're taking a walk. I'm going to show Ava the orchard!" she called.

Walk! I was grateful to have the decision about the stick made for me. I ran up the hill and joined the two women as they headed out into the fields. Soon we were in the place where the pear trees grew in thick rows.

Wenling reached up and pulled on a low bough. A bottle hanging off the branch made a tinkling sound. "See? The pear grows inside the bottle. When it's mature, we sell the finished product to a distiller who manufactures pear brandy. We're doing apples and apricots, too. Instead of making less than a penny a pound selling to the baby food company, we're making around ten bucks. *Profit*. Chase says it is the first time in his memory that the people in the bank are glad to see him walk in the door."

I sniffed the tree limb and saw nothing remarkable about it.

"Growing fruit in a bottle," Ava marveled. "I had no idea such a thing was possible."

"It fails about half the time, but we're getting better with practice." Wenling released the branch. "When did you and Burke start going out?"

"So, you remember the story of how Burke showed up when the dog fell through the ice?"

"That's right. You told us at Dad's funeral. I guess I had forgotten. You already knew each other from that."

"Exactly. Even though we barely talked that day, I never forgot how this stranger so casually risked his life to save a poor dog.

And then one day out of the blue, Burke shows up at my dad's rescue to adopt Oscar and wound up asking me to dinner. It was all pretty spontaneous. And also not, not spontaneous—more like fate. Do you believe in that?"

Hearing my name and the word "dinner" uttered aloud certainly got my attention. I did Down, being on my absolute best behavior.

"Fate? I guess I do. Something like that," Wenling replied without mentioning me.

"Although," Ava added, "knowing him now, I realize he was planning something. He showed up the second time dressed in nice pants. Burke never wears nice pants."

Wenling laughed. "I know what you mean."

Ava and Wenling faced each other. "This is pretty weird. We've both dated both brothers," Ava said. "I mean, it's weird for *me*, anyway."

Wenling nodded. "Burke and I were sweethearts when we were just kids. Grant, though, he was my first love."

"Is he talking about leaving? Taking a new job? Going back to Europe? Africa?" Ava asked.

"Grant? No, not at all."

"When Grant and I were together, all he wanted to do was be somewhere else. After a while, I knew he also wanted to be with some*one* else. When I saw you two together, I figured out who that person was."

They began walking slowly and aimlessly, like people do. Normally I would run ahead of them to scout for creatures to chase, but having heard the word "dinner" I decided my best move was to stick close to them.

"Ava," Wenling said after a moment. "I'm sorry how it happened. I swear, I didn't plan it."

"I don't think Grant planned it, either, Wenling. He said he was staying to help his father, and I think that was true. Mostly true. Partially true."

Wenling smiled.

"Besides, if I had still been with Grant, Burke would never have asked me out. No matter what Grant thinks, Burke doesn't hate him."

"So you and Burke are happy?"

"God, I hope *he's* happy. He's pretty much the best thing that's ever happened to me. He's kind. He calls me when he's on the road. He asked *me* if we were exclusive, which made me realize I've always been the one to do that. Until I met him, I never failed to make bad choices. Not Grant, of course. But every other man I've ever met has wound up dumping me eventually. I guess that's why I'm in animal rescue—a dog will stay, will give you all the love you want, and never run off with someone else."

The words "dog" and "stay" confused me, because we were still walking.

"That's not Burke, though," Wenling agreed. "He's, what's the word? Steadfast. Even when I started going out with his own brother, he continued to hold my best interests in his heart."

"He's never told me he loves me, though," Ava confided.

"Oh. The Trevino men aren't very good with expressing themselves like that."

"I've noticed." The two women stopped, smiling at each other, and then hugged. I decided they must have forgotten all about dinner and I wandered off to see if I could locate a rabbit.

When Burke went back to traveling and spending nights in the soft folding room, it was still just the two of us. I was sad for Ava that she had to stay home and couldn't come with us to sleep on the ground and roll in dead fish, though after I did that Burke decided to give me a bath, for some reason. "My God you still stink," he told me that night as I sprawled across him. I didn't know what he was saying but I licked his face to let him know I was happy.

We were back to see Ava shortly after that bath. They hugged each other in the hallway and hugged all the way down the hall and into the bedroom, so I stretched out on the couch and waited for dinner.

"I won that case I told you about," Ava said later at the table. "The court gave us custody of those poor, abused dogs that drug dealer had chained in his yard. One of them has a crushed vertebra and can't move her back legs. Oh Burke, it's so sad. I saw her today. She is so sweet and loving, but the vet says we can't do anything for her. She'll be at the shelter tomorrow."

"Are you going to put her down?"

"I don't want to. She's full of life, but seeing her drag her hindquarters is heartbreaking. I don't know what sort of life she could have."

Burke was quiet.

The next morning he and I decided to visit Ava's dog-and-cat place. I wagged when I saw Sam Dad, who petted me. "Hi, Oscar," he said. "Hello, Burke."

Marla was there, too. "Did Ava tell you I'm volunteering full-time down here now that I'm retired? Also the one up north."

Burke laughed. "She said she and her dad double-teamed you."

Ava put her arm through Burke's. "Let's go back; you have to meet Janji, that dog with the paralysis I was telling you about. She's got the best disposition."

"Janji?"

"It's Malay. The drug dealer's wife was from Singapore, I guess."

There were only a few dogs in the cages in the back. Burke and I waited while Ava opened the cage for one, a black dog with pointy ears and bright yellow eyes. She didn't walk like a normal dog—her back legs scraped the floor behind her, and her tail was limp. Curious, I approached her, sniffing.

Ava reached out and stroked the female's head. "Janji, meet Oscar."

I yipped in shock because it was Lacey! I immediately climbed on her, joyously knocking her on her back, rolling on her, and then careening energetically around the room, coming back to barrel into her. She panted and dragged herself after me. "Oscar! Stop that!" Ava scolded.

"Oscar!" Burke said sternly.

We had apparently done something bad dog, so I did Down and tried to contain my desire to play and play with my Lacey. She was panting, excited to see me, too, but wasn't scampering around like I was.

Burke stooped and stroked Lacey's ears. "What a sweet dog." He looked up at Ava. "How much time does she have?"

"Oh. I don't know, honey, it's tough to look at that happy face and make that decision. It's not like she's in pain."

Burke straightened. "Can you give me a week?"

"Give you a week? What do you mean?"

THIRTY-SEVEN

A few days later we were back to visit Lacey at Ava's building of dogs and cats. Burke led me into an open-topped cage in a big, empty back room and then brought in Lacey, carrying her as if she were a puppy. I whined and Lacey stared at me with those bright eyes: we both wanted to be playing together, but instead Burke set Lacey in a chair like the one he'd had as a boy, with big wheels on either side. Ava helped hold Lacey while Burke fastened some dog collars around Lacey's waist.

Apparently my boy missed his chair so much he had decided to give one to Lacey but not to me.

Ava seized Lacey's collar and they walked around and around the perimeter of the room, as if a person could do Pull for a dog. Lacey kept glancing frantically at me the entire time. I sat, utterly perplexed and feeling ignored. Agitated, I ducked inside the doghouse at the end of the cage and then, finding nothing worthy of notice, backed out. "Good dog, Janji, that's it," Ava praised.

"She seems fine with it. Why don't you let go of her and I'll call her?" Burke suggested.

"Okay." Ava released Lacey.

"Come, Janji!" Burke called.

Lacey shook, realized she was free, and then bolted for me. The chair twisted and fell over and dragged her down with it, though within an instant she was back up and towing the fallen apparatus behind her.

"Janji!" Ava darted forward and grabbed Lacey's collar.

I wondered if "Janji" meant "Stay."

"Well, crap, she bent the harness; let me fix it," Burke muttered, playing with the chair.

"This isn't working," Ava said sadly.

"Just give her time."

"Burke, we can't let her injure herself with this thing."

"It will be all right. Okay, Janji, don't be so wild, okay? Steady, girl."

I started in recognition. *Steady.* Of course! Lacey was falling out of her chair. She needed a dog to do Steady.

Ava walked Lacey around in circles some more, but every time, when she released Lacey's collar, Lacey lunged and the chair careened onto its side.

"Janji!" Ava cried. She seized Lacey and stood gazing at Burke with a mournful expression. "She's just too young and wild."

Well, enough of *this*. Lacey had shown me how to escape from similar kennels: I climbed on the doghouse and then leapt nimbly over the sides of the cage. I went straight to Lacey and did Steady right there beside her.

"Oscar! What are you doing?" Burke demanded.

Lacey yanked herself out of Ava's grasp and made to climb on me and I nipped at her, showing teeth. She reared her head back in shock. Then she tried to race away for a game of Chase the Dog, but I was right there, blocking her.

"Are you seeing what I am seeing?" Ava asked, astonished.

I did Assist, pushing Lacey to the wall, pinning her, and then forced her to take slow, measured steps forward. She was panting with incomprehension, but she allowed me to guide her around the room. Several times she grew impatient, but I always blocked her from scampering off.

That's how we played that day, in that big empty room. Lacey wanted to wrestle but I understood that while she was in the chair we were working and she needed to focus on doing her part. Burke and Ava sat and watched. Whenever Lacey decided to break away I corrected her sternly. She was utterly baffled at first, but after a time seemed to understand that if she went in a straight line, her path was easy, but if she tried to dart sideways the chair would tilt and I would do a rigid Steady until she calmed down.

Later I went for a car ride with Ava and Burke, feeling like a good dog.

"It's like Oscar was trained to be a support animal . . . for a dog," Ava marveled.

"Do you believe dogs can come back? Like, reincarnation?" Burke asked.

"I don't know. I've met a lot of people who think so, they'll swear to me that their new dog is the old soul of a pet they had a long time ago. Why do you ask?"

"Because it is as if Oscar is channeling Cooper. Oscar? Are you Cooper?"

I barked at the name Cooper and they both laughed.

Over time, Lacey seemed to understand that her chair required her to be calm, to move in a straight line in the big empty room and not bound around erratically. "She's getting pretty good at that," Burke observed.

"It will be hard to adopt out a dog who needs a cart, though," Ava responded.

Burke slapped a hand to his chest. "Adopt out Janji? Our girl? Our child? How could you even think of such a thing? What kind of mother are you?"

Ava laughed and they kissed. I wagged—they were doing that a lot, lately.

When the snow fell, Lacey had difficulty moving when we took our walks, but Burke knew what to do. He tied a leash from Lacey's harness to mine. "Okay, we're going to try something. I'll walk ahead of you and you pull, okay, Oscar? Like being a sled dog," he told me.

I understood the moment the leash was tied to Lacey's harness and my own. Burke walked backward in front of me, patting his legs. I did Pull, slow and measured as I had been taught, and Lacey moved much more easily. I was happy to be doing my work again. "Wow," Burke breathed. "This is unbelievable. I just . . ." He stood staring at me in silence for a long time, and Lacey and I waited patiently. Finally he looked around as if verifying we were alone. "Oscar? Pull Right."

I immediately turned Pull Right. Burke gasped. "Pull Left!" I switched course. "Halt, Oscar!" I stopped dead in my tracks.

Burke was breathing raggedly, gulping in air. His fingers trembled as he undid the leash to Lacey's chair and tied her to a stair railing. Those stairs led up to a dark, cold building. I watched curiously as he lay down in the snow. He grabbed my harness and turned my head toward the building. "Oscar? Assist!"

At last! I triumphantly turned to do Assist for Burke up those steps, wishing there were children sitting on them to watch.

When we reached the top, Burke was weeping. He grasped my head in his hands. Below us, Lacey stirred restlessly. "Cooper?" his whisper was ragged. "Are you Cooper?"

I was his Cooper dog. I wagged happily. Whether my name was Cooper or Riley or Oscar, I loved being held by Burke. He wiped his eyes. "My God, Cooper, is it really you?" He crushed me to his chest. "I don't know what I believe, but if it's you, Cooper, if it's really you, I've never stopped loving you. Never forgotten you for a moment. You're my best friend. Okay, Cooper?"

I closed my eyes, loving my boy.

We drove to the farm when the snow was deep and there were lights in everyone's trees and shrubs. As often happens when the air is cold, the farm had a tree growing inside it, which I sniffed suspiciously. I had always felt pretty sure that if I lifted my leg on the indoor trees I would be breaking a rule.

The baby goat had grown to be a lot bigger. She slept in the house that used to belong to Judy. Her name was Ethel the goat.

Everyone seemed relaxed and happy, and I was pretty sure I knew why: We were all finally at the farm together. Well, except Lacey, who stayed back with Sam Dad and Marla, for some reason. I figured Lacey would show up eventually.

"So Dad has something to tell you, and then Wenling and I have something to tell you, too," Grant announced. He looked pleased with himself.

Chase Dad shifted uncomfortably. "Well."

Burke nodded. "Well?"

Chase Dad took a long sip of his drink. People were very thirsty that night. "Li Min sold her house."

Burke nodded. "Sure. Okay." He cocked his head. "And?"

Ava brightened. "Oh!"

Wenling smiled. "Exactly."

Burke frowned. "Exactly what, exactly?"

Chase Dad cleared his throat. "Li Min and Wenling both live here, now."

Burke was looking at everyone. Ava elbowed him. "That's wonderful," she pronounced pointedly.

Burke regarded her with a perplexed expression. "Wonderful?"

"Yes, Burke," Ava said patiently, "it is *wonderful* that Li Min *moved in with your father.*"

"Oh," Burke said. His eyes widened. "Oh!" His mouth dropped open.

Chase Dad gave him an embarrassed grin. "Yeah."

Burke turned to Li Min. "That's great, Li Min."

Li Min beamed. "It took him long enough to ask. And then he said only, 'Maybe you should put your house on the market.'"

Everyone laughed. "The Trevino men, so romantic." Wenling sighed to more laughter. I wagged at all the joy, thinking they might want me to bring out a ball or a squeaky toy, but not a nylon bone.

"So what do you want to tell us, Grant?" Ava asked.

Wenling and Li Min glanced at each other, smiling broadly. Grant stood up. "I am pleased to announce that this coming June, right here on this piece of profitable property, Wenling is going to marry me."

Ava jumped to her feet with a squeal. "Oh my God!" She ran to Wenling and they hugged and then everyone stood, so I barked.

"Wait, Wenling, are you enormously fat?" Burke asked, and she laughed along with him.

Li Min brought out the odd-shaped box with metal cables. She handed the thing to Chase Dad, who pulled it into his lap as if it were a puppy.

"Dad's going to play?" Burke demanded in disbelief.

Grant nodded. "Oh, Li Min's brought a *lot* of changes to this house. She sings with the band now."

Burke made a surprised noise, so I looked at him.

"We changed the name," Chase Dad said with a nod. "Now we're Four Bad Musicians Plus a Chick Who Can Sing."

Everyone laughed.

They all sat in a tight circle and Chase Dad ran his fingers along the strings, filling the air with a hum. "Here's one I wrote. I call it, 'Dry Start to the Summer.'"

Everyone laughed again. I nosed my way into the middle, carrying a squeaky toy, knowing this was what they would actually want.

For some reason, Lacey never showed up that visit, so we returned home to be with her. Burke and Ava talked the whole way while I slept in the backseat.

The next time we were on the farm, the days were long and the grass was fresh and soft. Lacey stayed home to be with Marla and Sam Dad *again*, which made no sense to me at all.

I bounded out of the car and Wenling and Grant were there to greet me. "There's the bride-to-be," Burke said. "How is everything going?"

"Chaotic, but fine," Wenling replied. "So you decided not to bring Lacey?"

I glanced up at her, hearing Lacey's name and a question. I wondered if she was asking where Lacey was, something I was questioning myself.

"Lacey?" Burke replied. "Wenling, you mean Janji?"

"I said Lacey?" Wenling laughed.

Ava was pulling a bag out of the trunk. "Janji's cart is great on pavement, but we didn't think she could maneuver on the terrain here. So Dad and Marla are watching her."

Grant grabbed a bag himself. "Hey, Burke, you want to help me string some lights in the trees a little later?"

"I think I'd rather hear more speculation about Wenling's dress. I just can't get enough of that subject," Burke replied.

It was a hot, hot afternoon, and I found myself frequently taking advantage of the water dish. Burke and Grant climbed the big tree next to the under-barn stairs, trailing ropes after them. I figured they were going to pull the doors off again. There was no lingering scent of the creature who had once taken refuge in the large hole—I had terrified it, obviously, and it never dared return. "Remember how I climbed higher than you and then dropped eggs on your face?" Burke laughed.

"It was one egg. So I jumped down and pulled the ladder away and you were stuck until at dinner Grandma asked where you were and Dad made me tell because my laughter gave it away."

"Climbing trees was easy for me; dropping to the ground without working legs, not so much. Hey, Grant."

"Yeah?"

"I'm really happy for you. You and Wenling."

"Thanks, Burke."

They smiled at each other, and it was at that moment that the wind hit like a slap. I turned my face to it, drinking in a blast of wet, cool air. The tinkling ropes Burke and Grant were hanging began swinging in the stiff breeze.

"Whoa," Grant said, "where did that come from? It feels twenty degrees cooler."

After a short time, I heard a deep, low rumble, so low I could feel it in my chest like a growl. I looked up into the tree, where Grant and my boy were still talking and playing with ropes.

Chase Dad came out, the door banging behind him. "Looks like we're going to get some weather." He peered up at his sons.

"You about done? I don't think it's a good idea to be in a tree in an electrical storm."

Grant smiled down at him. "If the lights aren't perfect, it will ruin the wedding."

"The dress might save it. Ava has seen pictures. I'm not allowed because I'm the best man, but I'm allowed to hear about it for seven straight hours," Burke noted. "It's probably the most beautiful dress and it will look perfect on Wenling's skin, but Ava is too pale and if it were her dress she would wear a slightly less blue white. More of a cream white or possibly an ecru white, but never a blush white because on her it would look tacky."

Chase Dad grinned. "Come on down now, you two."

There was a crack of thunder and everyone jumped. They turned their heads. "Man, look at the sky," Burke said. "You ever see it so dark? And yet right over there it is still sunny."

Grant dropped down off the ladder next to him. "Crazy."

The wind carried with it the smell of rain. I raised my nose to it.

"So Dad, Grant shared with me that you asked Li Min if she wanted to make it a double ceremony and she told you that if you mentioned anything to Wenling about the two of you getting married, *that* would ruin the wedding," Burke observed slyly.

Chase Dad put his hands on his hips. "Did Grant also tell you that I asked him not to tell anyone?"

"I'm just thinking this is a pretty fraught situation," Burke drawled.

Chase Dad shook his head. "I sure stepped in it. I thought it was a reasonable question, but Li Min acted like I suggest we commit murder together."

"So you're engaged to be engaged? Last time I heard of somebody in our family trying that, it didn't go so well," Burke replied.

"Lucky for Dad he doesn't have a *brother* sticking his nose where it doesn't belong," Grant said pointedly.

Far away, a roar was building. It was faint, but somehow felt *huge* to me. I looked up at my people, but they were laughing and talking. If they weren't worried, should I be?

"Hey, Dad," Burke said, "in all seriousness, how did the guy who turned down every eligible woman in the county wind up wanting to get married again?"

Chase Dad smiled. "Every woman in the county." He reached down and petted me in that way people do when they're not really aware what they're doing.

"Seriously," Burke persisted.

Chase Dad drew in a breath and blew it out, Grant-style. "I don't think I ever felt loved by a woman before. Least, a woman who didn't want me to leave the farm, or be someone I wasn't. When I'm with Li Min, I'm at peace. She was there in front of me the whole time, and when I finally saw her, I knew she was the one."

Grant nodded. "I know the feeling."

Chase Dad cleared his throat. "I want you boys to know there was never anything going on with Li Min while ZZ was alive."

"I would never think that, Dad," Burke replied. Grant nodded.

"ZZ was my best friend," Chase Dad continued.

"We know, Dad," Grant reassured him.

My hackles rose. I looked off into the distance, not seeing the threat, not understanding it, but sensing danger.

"What is it, Oscar?" Burke reached down and gave me a reassuring pat.

Then the wind died down completely, as if someone had shut a window. The men all frowned.

"The calm before the storm," Grant observed.

"Let's head in before we get wet," Chase Dad suggested.

I sat and watched, anxious, as they put the ladder in the barn and picked up some papers and then finally began walking toward the house. The roar was louder now, and then, rising sharply to the top of it, I heard a howl, forlorn and eerie. The men heard it, too: they all turned their heads at once, gazing toward town.

"Tornado siren," Chase Dad noted.

Ava stepped out onto the porch. "Is that what I think it is?" she called.

"We better get to the storm cellar," Chase Dad said tensely.

Ava turned back toward the house. "Wenling! Li Min! Come on, we need to go into the tornado shelter!"

Burke turned. "I'll get the goat!"

I could not only hear the angry roar, now. I could *feel* it.

Something was coming.

THIRTY-EIGHT

I chased after Burke as he darted to the goat pen and flung the gate aside. Ethel stared in shock as my boy ran to her and swept her up into his arms. Staggering a little, he turned and raced back to the steps to the under barn. The doors were lying open and Grant and Chase Dad stood at the top helping Li Min follow Ava and Wenling downstairs. I was last, after Burke and the goat. Chase Dad pulled the big metal doors shut with a bang and a light popped on.

I sniffed carefully but could find no sign of Lacey and the puppies. But everyone else was there, sitting on one of three benches hanging off the walls.

"Okay," Chase Dad said, rubbing his hands together. "Battery for the lights will last five days and I have two backups. Water, food, enough for thirty man-days. The toilet's there, hand pump—

tight quarters in there, but it'll do. Flip it up and you can take a shower. Woodstove for if it gets cold."

"Why don't we all just live in here? It's like a vacation resort," Burke observed.

Wenling laughed.

I eased over to the stone steps and looked up. The heavy doors sealed out much of the wind noise, but I could hear it and knew it was increasing. I growled softly.

Burke snapped his fingers. "Here, Oscar. It's okay. Come here."

I obeyed his summons, wagging. Ava was looking at her phone. "I just texted my dad and told him we're okay."

"For at least thirty man-days, anyway," Burke replied.

I examined Ethel the goat and she blinked at me. I knew that a version of doing Steady for her would be for me to pretend I knew what was going on. I hoped it comforted her.

A high, shrieking howl caused everyone to look up. "Man," Grant said uneasily. Then a loud rattling sound hit the metal doors.

"That's hail!" Chase Dad shouted over the barrage. Li Min scooted closer to him on the bench, and Chase Dad put his arm around her.

Ava stirred and I picked up her rising anxiety, so I crossed the small space and leaned into her, doing Steady, offering support. She stroked my fur.

The drumming on the metal doors just kept getting louder and louder. I smelled water—a small trickle was seeping in through the cracks between the doors and dripping on the steps. Chase Dad shook his head. "Should have weather-sealed the door seam."

"I'm really scared, Chase," Li Min said into his shoulder.

A howling roar was building outside. Burke and Grant glanced at each other.

Now *everyone* was afraid. I yawned, panting.

"It's coming right at us!" Grant yelled. He embraced Wenling with both arms. I whined and my boy reached and pulled me up next to Ava and wrapped us up in a tight clutch.

With a bleat, Ethel the goat hesitantly trotted over, too, her body rigid with alarm. Chase Dad picked her up the same way Burke had me. Apparently everyone would be carrying the goat now.

Impossibly, the roar increased force, punctuated now by booming blasts directly overhead. Thuds shook the walls, a screeching, tearing sound obliterating all else.

"We're losing the barn!" Burke shouted.

For a long, long moment, everyone held themselves perfectly still, as if we were all doing Steady. Then something enormous slammed the double doors with a crash so deafening, everyone jumped. I barked.

"It's okay, Oscar!" Burke told me. "Hang on!"

I could barely hear him.

"What the hell was that?" Grant demanded at the top of his voice. No one answered.

Just as the noise was reaching the level of physical pain there was an abrupt shift. The thrashing roar dulled to a rumble, and the shrieking quieted, and I heard everyone exhale. Within moments the only sound was the steady beat of rain hitting the metal doors—I could smell it, cold and wet.

"Wow," Grant said into silence. "That was really something."

Chase Dad nodded. "I'm almost afraid to go up there. It sounded like a bomb on the doors."

Grant put a hand on his shoulder. "I think we took a direct hit, Dad."

Dad gave Grant a grim, resigned look. "I know."

Wenling chuckled softly. "Remember, Burke, when you told me about the huge tornado that wiped out the town, and said we'd be safe down here? I thought you were crazy. We don't get *tornadoes.*"

Li Min reached for Wenling and they hugged. "That was the most frightening moment of my life," Li Min murmured.

Chase Dad stood. I jumped down, wagging, ready to do what was next. "Guess I'll check it out."

Grant stood as well. "Are you sure? It's really coming down out there."

Chase Dad stepped over to the stone stairs. "Just want to see what I have left. If anything." He trudged up, reached the metal doors, and slid the heavy bolt. Then he just stood there. "Boys, give me a hand? Door's stuck."

Burke and Grant joined him. I followed, not sure what was going on but ready to participate. They put their hands on the doors and grunted.

Grant blew out a breath. "Wow."

The men tromped back down the steps, climbing up to the benches. Burke sighed. "Now we know what that huge crash was. The tree with all the lights blowing over. Either uprooted or it snapped clean where the hollow was. It's right on top of these doors." He looked over at Wenling. "I'm afraid this ruins the wedding."

"I guess we're trapped down here for a while. Now what?" Grant asked.

"I don't have a signal," Ava announced.

Everyone dug out their phones.

"I don't either," Li Min agreed.

"Looks like the tornado took out some cell towers. I'm not up, either," said Burke. "Anyone?"

They all shook their heads. I returned to the area beneath my boy's bench, which had a cushion on it, wondering if I would be allowed back up even though the loud noise had passed.

"So what do we do?" Ava asked.

"Well," Burke replied, "after thirty man-days, we resort to cannibalism."

"We don't know what it looks like up there, and we don't know what the tornado did to the town. Not sure anyone will come looking for us anytime soon," Chase Dad stated evenly.

"I get the shower first," Wenling said.

Everyone laughed softly.

"I didn't really plan on this many people, but we're still okay. Three fold-down bunks. Three couples," Chase Dad announced reassuringly. "We really can last a long time here, if need be."

There was a long silence. "You have some cards down here?" Grant asked.

"Cards," Chase Dad repeated. "That would have been a good idea."

Ethel retreated to a corner and folded her legs as she lay down. I padded over to her and, after a moment, curled up with her as if she were a dog. She smelled wonderful. I slept for a time but woke up when I felt alarm spike through the people in the room. I raised my head. Burke and Grant were at the woodstove. Black water was seeping out of it. Burke stood and looked at the pipe that ran to the ceiling, encircling it with his hands. "Dad, you have a hammer down here?"

"A hammer?"

"We need to bust this duct and plug it. *Now*."

"Are we maybe overreacting? It's just a little rainwater," Grant objected.

"It's coming from the woodstove because the chimney vent was sheared off. Whatever's left of the barn is filling with water," Burke replied. "And that's happening because of Trident Mechanized Harvesting. Their water management system was never

designed for this much runoff. Their paved pad up there is dumping water into their cement canal and it's jumped the banks, so
all that water's coming down the hill and to the low points on our
property, like the pond. And into the barn's foundation, which,
because it is below the freeze line, is like a swimming pool. And
this," he said, knocking on the pipe, "is the drain in the bottom
of the swimming pool."

The water had gone from a trickle to a steady misting spray. I
watched in utter confusion as everyone went into motion. "The
bunk pads? The stuffing?" Wenling asked.

"Perfect," Burke replied.

Ava and Wenling tore apart a cushion, yanking out handfuls
of white stuffing. Ethel jumped up and seized a mouthful. "No,
Ethel!" Li Min scolded, throwing her arms around the goat. I
knew, though, that Ethel trying to eat the stuff was just her way
of trying to make sense of what was happening, like a dog running
to a toy when humans were being too confusing. She was not a
bad goat.

Chase Dad stood at the pipe with a hammer. Burke seized
the woodstove. I wagged, picking up their tension, not understanding.

Grant gathered the stuffing from Ava and Wenling. "Okay, I'm
ready," he said, crouching next to his father.

"What can I do?" Li Min asked.

Chase Dad pointed. "Check that green box; I might have some
duct tape in there."

Burke shoved, grunting, and the woodstove shifted. Chase
Dad swung his hammer and it rang against the pipe. "Seam's
splitting!" Grant shouted. Chase Dad whacked the pipe again and
water began shooting from the point of impact. I backed away,
lifting my paws gingerly out of the puddle forming on the floor.

"Hit it!" Burke bellowed.

Chase Dad clenched his jaw and smashed the hammer down again and again and then the pipe was broken. Water came hosing out of it. Grant rammed the stuffing up into it, blinking in the blast. "This isn't working!" he cried.

Burke grabbed a plastic bag and ripped it, dumping blankets onto a bunk. The puddle sloshed around my feet. Burke wadded up the plastic and crouched next to Grant, thrusting his hand up into the pipe. The water slowed to a trickle.

"That's not going to hold!" Burke declared, his arm plunged in up to his elbow. He turned his wet face away.

"No duct tape!" Li Min announced. "Chase, the broom handle!"

"She's right, Dad!" Burke urged.

Chase Dad pulled out a broom and put it against the wall and stomped down on it, snapping the wood. He waded over to the pipe, fell to his knees, and nodded at Burke. "On three!"

"One . . . two . . . three!"

Burke yanked out his hand and Chase Dad shoved the wooden stick up into the pipe. He grimaced, struggling to keep it there, his arms trembling. "No good!"

"Wenling! Tool box!" Li Min said urgently.

Wenling grabbed a plastic box and shoved it under the stick. When Chase Dad released the stick it thumped down onto the closed lid of the box.

For a moment, the only sound was Chase Dad's panting and the steady splash of water leaking out of the pipe.

"Think it will hold?" Grant asked.

Burke looked grim. "For now. Depends on how deep it gets up there."

No one said anything for several moments.

"Okay. Everyone get up out of the water. Put everything we need to be dry up on the bunks," Burke directed.

"What's going on, honey? Why are you concerned?" Ava asked.

Grant climbed back up on one of the benches. "You really think we're going to drown down here?"

Burke reached down and lifted me up. "I'm not worried about drowning, I'm worried about hypothermia. We've got to get dry and stay warm until somebody finds us."

Chase Dad picked up Ethel the goat and placed her on the bench next to Li Min. The goat and I stared at each other, completely baffled. Chase Dad opened a plastic crate and handed out towels, and everyone started drying their feet, throwing sodden socks into the rising pool below us. The men pulled off their shirts and put on clean ones.

Chase Dad stared at the stream pouring out of the pipe. "It's coming faster. What do we do when it rises above the bunks?"

Burke drew in a breath and everyone watched him, waiting, so I did, too. "I don't know."

We all sat together on the padded shelves. I gazed down at the swirling currents with interest, thinking about swimming in the pond.

The rain continued its pounding assault on the doors. Everyone went silent, staring at, as far as I could tell, nothing at all. I felt fear and sadness in each of them.

They stretched out on the small beds. They were lined up so close together I could leap from one to the other. I sat with whoever seemed most afraid, doing Steady because they needed a good dog. Ethel lay next to Li Min, who I supposed needed a good goat.

Morning came. I heard birds. Gray light poured through the cracks in the door, which continued to drip with the falling rain. I looked down: the water was almost up to the level of the bunks. I wondered how much longer we were going to stay here.

I was ready to leave.

THIRTY-NINE

Ava sat next to Burke, Wenling next to Grant. Chase Dad and Li Min were sleeping. The loud trickling noise continued, much more audible than the steady patter against the metal doors at the top of the stone steps.

"Someone will come soon," Grant murmured.

"Won't the water drain off?" Wenling whispered.

"No, it will have to be pumped out," Burke replied.

Grant looked down into the water. "Pumped out," he muttered.

"I'm scared," Ava said. Burke put his arm around her.

Chase Dad stirred and sat up, rubbing his face. When he took in how deep the water was, his eyes widened in shock. "My God," he breathed.

"Hey, I have a surprise for you." Grant dug in his pocket, then turned and handed something to Wenling.

She took it with two fingers. "The original ring! You said you lost it in a poker game."

I sniffed but couldn't smell anything of interest.

Grant was grinning. "Yeah, well, I lied."

Everyone was quiet.

"I love you, Ava," Burke blurted. "I'm sorry I never told you before."

"Oh my God, now I'm terrified," she replied. "You think we're going to die."

"No. I don't think so. I think what is going to happen is we're going to get out of here, and that Grant and Wenling are going to get married, and they'll be so happy that we'll want to get married, too."

Everyone was staring at him, and he continued. "Something's going on; the water level keeps rising and falling outside. Otherwise, we'd have all drowned by now. They've got motorized pumps up the hill; they're running them to bail out their flood. Each time they do, our water rises and we get more in here. But they're not running them consistently. Their overflow is a twenty-four-inch pipe down to the river, and it must be getting clogged with debris, so they have to clear it, and that's when they start pumping again. They have to; their multimillion-dollar plant will flood out if they don't. But they can see what their pumping is doing to our hill, our property, and probably the road—every time they turn on the motors, they're doing more damage. When they stop pumping, the water in the barn starts going down and the pressure in the pipe drops and the levels in here stop rising as quickly. I've been trying to figure out why we're still alive and that's the only explanation."

"So you're telling me you've been sitting there trying to figure out why we're *alive*?" Grant demanded.

"I can't help it, I'm an engineer. So the barn's foundation isn't perfect," Burke continued. "There are cracks, and the floor itself is dirt. When they aren't pumping, the barn is slowly draining. We're not going to die."

"I love you, too, Burke," Ava whispered. He squeezed her hand. I wagged at the affection between them.

"The water's gone way up the past couple hours," Chase Dad noted grimly. "And it's still raining. So unless they can keep the drainpipe clear up there, they're going to keep pumping and we'll keep getting more water."

Burke nodded. "Sort of a wet start to the summer."

Wenling was staring at the water. "Hypothermia is supposed to be an easy way to go. So is drowning."

Ava shuddered. "Oh God, Wenling."

"If it happens," Wenling continued, "I'm glad it is with you. With all of you."

Chase Dad's expression was sour. "I guess I never noticed that this bunk was a little lower than the others." He lifted the pad he was sitting on, ruefully examining the wet stain on the bottom of it. "Li Min, honey, I need you to wake up. The water's still rising."

Li Min sat up. Burke threw some blankets to his father, who folded them several times. Li Min and Chase Dad perched themselves on the folded blankets, their heels near the water. "What did I miss?" she whispered.

"Burke says we're not going to die," Wenling responded finally. Ethel reacted to the water touching her skin and stood, her posture stiff and afraid. Grant pulled her to him.

"That's not all. Didn't Burke just propose to Ava?" Grant demanded.

Li Min put a hand to her mouth. Everyone stared at Burke. "I guess I did," he observed with a shy smile.

"Well, son, if you don't mind me saying, that was one of the lamest marriage proposals I've ever witnessed," Chase Dad chided gently.

"I got down on one knee, myself," Grant volunteered. "Just saying."

Burke eyed the rising water. "One knee," he repeated dubiously.

Wenling reached into her pocket. "Here," she said, handing the same small, uninteresting object to Burke. "You can borrow this until you get one of your own."

Burke took it. He turned to Ava, getting to his knees on the shelf, his head almost at the ceiling. "Ava, you are the love of my life. Will you marry me?"

Ava wiped her eyes. "Of course, Burke."

I was startled when everyone clapped. I glanced at Ethel, but she didn't seem to know what was going on, either.

"The rise seems to have slowed," Chase Dad commented after a long silence.

"Maybe," Burke agreed. "Look at the doors. The sun's out. No more rain."

"I saw Mom," Grant blurted. "Patty."

Everyone stared at him in shock.

Grant sighed. "She hasn't lived in Paris in years. I tracked her down to Neuilly-sur-Seine. Lots of rich people."

"Why in God's name would you do something like that?" Chase Dad demanded angrily.

Li Min put a hand on his shoulder. "Let him tell it, darling," she urged softly.

Grant's mouth twisted. "We met in a café. She brought money. That was the first thing she did, was slide this envelope across the table to me, like I was there to blackmail her. I slid it back. Then she tells me how furious her husband would be if he found out she was meeting with me. One of her *sons*."

Everyone sat quietly, leaning forward to hear over the sound of the dripping.

"She has two daughters, but she wouldn't show me a picture of them. She also doesn't like dogs."

Everyone glanced at me, for some reason. I wagged, unsure.

"Oh, and when I told her you weren't in a wheelchair any longer, Burke, *she had no reaction at all*." Grant shrugged resignedly, blowing out a breath. "She didn't leave because of that. Because of the . . . challenges of you being paraplegic. I was wrong, Burke."

"Then we were both wrong," Burke murmured.

Chase Dad stirred, but Li Min put a restraining hand on him and he said nothing.

"So," Ava asked after a moment, "why did she leave? Did she tell you?"

"Yeah, after I asked her a couple of times it was like a pot boiling over. She told me she hated the farm. Hated the town. Hated Michigan, being broke. Her whole life here, the way she described it, was utter misery. She was taking French lessons for free at the library because she was planning to leave and go to Europe. And then the French teacher's brother showed up, and she saw him as her ticket out." Grant shrugged. "Sorry, Dad."

"Nothing here I didn't know," Chase Dad grunted. "Nothing here I didn't tell you."

"We were kids, Dad," Burke protested mildly. "We didn't understand."

"After a while I realized she still carries a grudge. Not just against Dad," Grant continued, "but all of it. The farm, you, me, Grandma. So listening to her, I guess I saw it in myself. Me, I carry a grudge. Against you, Burke. And you, Dad. I'm so sorry about how I've behaved."

There was a long pause punctuated only by the constant drip of water.

Wenling put her hand on top of Grant's. "Ava told me she thinks you were always searching for something and never finding it. Was it your mom? When you found her, did that make you okay with living here?"

Grant shook his head, gazing at her. "No, *you* make me okay with it."

The mist from all the drips coated my fur to the point where I had to shake them off. Everyone leaned away from me when I did, and Ethel blinked. Then we sat some more.

Burke cleared his throat. "I am sort of afraid to tell you this, but I think Oscar is Cooper. I mean, I'm *convinced*."

I wagged at my boy.

"Grandpa Ethan always said that his dog Bailey came back to him," Chase Dad replied. I wagged at Chase Dad.

"This is more than that. Oscar knows Assist."

"Assist?" Ava repeated.

I did not know why they were saying Assist and hoped they would not ask me to do something that involved jumping into the water.

"It's how Cooper helped me across the floor. And up the stairs," Burke explained.

"Which is not as easy as it looks," Grant interjected.

"So you were able to train Oscar?" Li Min asked.

Burke shook his head. "That's what I'm saying. He *already knew it*. And he knew Pull, and Pull Left, Pull Right. With no training, Li Min. Not in this lifetime."

"Riley knew Pull from the first time he heard it, remember, Ava?" Grant asked.

Ava smiled. "And Riley found me when I fell and broke my

leg. If he hadn't, I wouldn't be here today. I always said he was my angel dog." Ava leaned forward and looked at me. "Are you Riley, Oscar? Are you my angel dog?"

I wagged at her and licked her hand when she lifted it to me. Her tears were flowing freely.

"Can I just say, to hear this now, right now and right here, is giving me some comfort?" Wenling remarked in a soft voice. "If Burke believes it, then I believe it, too. Which means . . ." Wenling trailed off.

"Which means if no one finds us, there is something else after this," Ava said.

I saw that everyone was holding hands, and I wagged. Li Min had her eyes closed and was moving her lips as if she were talking.

I shifted my gaze: the spray from the pipe was suddenly more pronounced and louder.

"Pump's back on," Chase Dad stated flatly. Everyone shuffled and I got up, thinking we were leaving this strange, wet place, but after much rearranging of padding and blankets, everyone was sitting back down.

"Try to keep your feet dry, Li Min," Chase Dad urged. He turned to his sons. "If we're going to die today, I want you to know how sorry I am I could never figure out how to get my two sons to talk to each other. And how glad I am the two of you are talking now."

Grant nodded. "We get out of here, I'm never letting us be strangers again. And if we die . . ." His voice trailed off.

Burke cleared his throat. "If we die, we won't find out if the food would really have lasted for thirty man-days."

Ava shook her head. There were still tears in her eyes. "If we die then I'm dying on the happiest day of my life."

Burke and Ava kissed. Everyone was hugging, and when I pressed close, Burke hugged me, too.

"*Damn*, it's coming up fast," Chase Dad hissed. Everyone struggled to their feet on the shelves. I shook, feeling soaked even though only my lower legs were underwater.

"It's so cold," Li Min whispered.

They all held hands, their heads bent up by the ceiling, their feet gradually submerging in the rising water. Li Min was shivering.

"If we were standing on the floor now, our heads might be underwater," Chase Dad observed grimly.

I whipped my nose up. I heard something; a splashing sound. No one else was reacting, though, so I didn't make any noise myself until I smelled her. Lacey! She was right outside! I barked.

Burke blinked at me. "What is it, Oscar?"

I barked again and Lacey answered.

"There's a dog!" Wenling exclaimed.

Everyone stared at the doors at the top of the steps.

"Hello?" a faraway voice called from outside.

"Dad!" Ava screamed.

"In here!" Burke yelled.

"The storm cellar!" Grant shouted.

There was loud splashing and a shadow flitted across the cracks. "Ava?"

It was Sam Dad. I barked again.

"We're all down here, Dad!" Ava called.

"Okay, hang on, we need to throw a chain around this tree," Sam Dad replied.

"Hurry, Dad! The water keeps rising!"

We waited tensely. Everyone was shivering now. There were thuds and bangs and a loud rattle and then the metal doors fell open and the sunshine poured into the small under barn. Lacey and Sam Dad and Marla and some men I didn't know were staring down at us.

We went swimming! Grant held Ethel at the reach of his out-stretched arms and waded with his head underwater, but I plunged in and paddled toward the sunlight. I greeted Lacey joy-fully at the top of the steps, careful not to let her tip over her chair.

"My God, you could have drowned," Sam Dad said.

The goat darted past us and Lacey stared at me for an expla-nation, but then we both felt the shock in our people when they emerged from the under barn. "Oh . . . ," Chase Dad murmured. I went to him.

Everything was different! Large pools of muddy water were everywhere. I wanted to run through them and do Get It with all the sticks I saw, but the somber mood of the humans restrained my joy. The barn was missing, as was most of the house—I could see into the kitchen, and the sink was there and nothing else. I was utterly baffled. Did Sam Dad do this?

"It's all gone," Chase Dad whispered. Li Min put her arms around him.

Marla passed out blankets and they were gratefully accepted. I was happy just to have the sun on my fur and my Lacey at my side. "I'm so sorry, Dad. I know the farm meant everything to you," Burke said.

Chase Dad turned and looked at him with wet eyes. "Is that what you think? No, Burke, *you* mean everything to me. You, and your brother, and Li Min, and Wenling and Ava. The farm was never just a building, it was a way of life—life with my family."

Chase Dad and Burke hugged, and then Grant joined them, and Ava and Wenling, so I went to them and stood on my hind legs and pressed against them so they would have a dog.

"Well," Ava declared, "when it's time to rebuild, I promise my mother's company will pay for it."

"You sure? Isn't it an act of God or something?" Chase Dad objected. "You really think they'll pay?"

"They will when her daughter the attorney calls to explain things," Ava vowed.

"We were going to leave," Sam Dad marveled. "When we pulled up, we could see no one was here. We figured you must have made it to a shelter in town. There are hundreds of people missing in the county. But Janji was barking, and when we let her out she was running around, sniffing, and we thought maybe she had a scent of something. Some*one*."

"I guess we shouldn't have worried about her maneuvering the cart on the farm," Burke observed.

"Good dog, Janji," Ava praised.

I wagged because I was a good dog, too.

A few days after we all swam in the under barn, we gathered in a big building and Grant and Wenling and I stood in front of a crowd of people and I chewed at an itch at the base of my tail and people cheered. When the leaves began falling we all trooped back to the same building and this time Li Min and Chase Dad stood in front of people and I did not have an itch.

A winter and summer passed and my life with Lacey, who the humans insisted on calling Janji, and Ava and Burke, who kept the same names, was very happy. Ava and Burke were happy because they had two dogs.

I was thrilled at how much time we spent at the farm. There was a new house and a new barn but the same ducks. I did Assist with Lacey whenever she wanted to roam off the driveway and into the fields, and she understood I was there to guide her.

Burke took Lacey down to the pond and lifted her out of her

chair and held her in the water. She batted at the pond's surface with her front paws, but when Burke released her, she was swimming! I joyously paddled out to be with her and together we made a go at the ducks until they flapped away, and then we just swam in circles. I understood something, then: as much as Lacey liked the chair, this freedom to swim made her feel like the dog she used to be, a dog who could go anywhere she wanted.

Apparently everyone enjoyed building houses, because when they finished building one they put in another one down by the pond. Ava and Burke moved in, and then Lacey and I never left the farm! I thought of our place as the new new house and the bigger one as the new old house.

We had a big gathering at the farm so that everyone could sit in chairs and watch Lacey and me stand with Burke and Ava while they talked, and then people had a wonderful dinner of chicken, and Lacey and I were richly rewarded at the tables.

"We're married, now, so you and Janji are legitimate, Oscar," Burke told me. His hands smelled like chicken.

A few winters later, Burke painted the back bedroom and put a wooden cage in there. He and Ava spent a lot of time just standing around by the new cage, talking. Lacey and I were bored with it all.

"Now that we know it's a boy, I want to call him Chase. Chase Samuel Trevino," Ava said at dinner.

"That would be wonderful. Both dads will be thrilled," Burke replied.

That summer, Ava started walking strangely, not angry walking, just a side-to-side waddle. She spent a lot of time holding her stomach, which had swollen up into a round belly so that she looked a little like Ward the Belcher.

We were upstairs in the new old house one quiet afternoon. Burke and Lacey were in the new old barn, but I was with Ava. I had a sense that she wanted me there, or perhaps that she *would* want me. It was an odd feeling, but I didn't question it. Knowing when you're needed was just part of being a good dog.

Ava was playing with the clothes of the bed. "Oh," she said suddenly. "Oh no." She sank to her knees. "*Oh.*"

An odd pain radiated off her. I whined anxiously. "Where did I put my phone?" she whispered. "This is too sudden."

I barked. She was sitting on the floor and a new, strange odor wafted off her, mixed with the familiar scent of human fear. I barked again.

Down below, at the new old barn, Lacey answered. I went to the window. She had wheeled out of the barn and was standing there, looking up at me. I barked yet again and her reply reminded me of the time I felt sick in the field and she barked for Burke to come get me.

My boy stepped out of the barn, regarding Lacey curiously. I was barking and she was barking. He looked up at me and I barked some more.

Burke ran across the yard toward the house.

I was anxious when he drove off with Ava and didn't return right away, and initially so was everyone else in the house, the tension crackling off their skin, and then suddenly they all relaxed. People do that, change moods very quickly, and there's no sense trying to figure out why. They were all sitting after dinner in the living room and feeding Lacey and me cheese treats, which made them so happy they were laughing and talking excitedly. When Burke walked in they all jumped to their feet and hugged him.

"Welcome home, Dad!" Chase Dad boomed.

"Congratulations, Dad!" Grant said.

Dad? I was very confused by this, but Lacey seemed unperturbed.

A few days later, Ava finally came home, carrying a tiny baby human who smelled a little sour. I was not interested, though Lacey was right there in the middle of everyone. They passed the infant around while I went outside to see the goat.

Burke liked to put the little child in a shopping basket and carry him around. After a day went by, people became bored with the baby, except Ava, who held him constantly. Sometimes the baby squawked and sometimes he slept quietly. Everyone called the baby "Chase," which just seemed wrong. We had a Chase Dad, now we were going to have a Chase Baby? And Burke was Burke Dad?

When my boy put the baby shopping basket down on a low table, I decided the time had come for me to examine the thing. The child was awake and scowling at me as I approached, leading me to believe he didn't understand how important I was to the family.

Ava came over and knelt on my other side stroking me. "See the baby, Oscar?"

I put my nose right on the baby's stomach and inhaled his odd odors. "Good dog. Gentle dog," Burke said softly. "Good dog Oscar."

I suddenly had a strong memory of another voice saying "Good dog. Good dog, *Bailey*." A man's voice, coming to me as I moved in golden light.

I took another deep whiff of baby. No, not a man's voice, *Ethan's* voice. With a jolt I remembered Ethan now—and I recalled more than that. I now had memories of many lives, lives I had long forgotten. Not just running and playing with my boy Ethan, but helping to Save people. And I recalled my girl CJ, and other people I'd loved: Hannah and Maya, Trent, Jakob, Al. . . . I was, I realized, a dog who had been born and reborn over and over, living a vital purpose, fulfilling an important promise. I did not know why I had forgotten, or why I remembered it now, but I did remember—I remembered everything. I had been Toby and Molly and Ellie and Max and Buddy and Bailey.

And I knew who this was, this baby sitting in his basket in front of me, his eyes squeezed shut. As easily as I could recognize Lacey no matter if she was Janji or Lady or any other dog, I could recognize this tiny little person.

It was Ethan.

AFTERWORD

W. BRUCE CAMERON

Maybe this has happened to you: I worked my whole life toward accomplishing a single objective, only to have my goal change on me once I accomplished it.

The goal was to be a successful novelist—and by "successful," I meant "published." And man, did I fail at *that* for most of my life. I worked a variety of jobs to support my writing habit, raised a family, had dogs, and couldn't convince any agents or publishers that the nine novels I wrote during this time period were worth a look. Nine novels!

Then I stopped failing. Finally, my books were in bookstores.

So just when I thought I had arrived, someone moved the goal posts on me. Suddenly it wasn't just about being published, it was about making a difference. I decided to try to do some good in the world.

I wrote the first novel in the *A Dog's Purpose* series to convince my then girlfriend, Cathryn Michon, that despite the pain of losing her dog Ellie, we should adopt a puppy. (It worked: we brought little Tucker into our family, and Cathryn liked the story so much she married me!)

For some people, the lessons in *A Dog's Purpose* help them heal from the wound left when a canine best friend passes out of our lives. The book was a huge success. As a result, I've been able to support hundreds of animal rescue organizations by donating books, signed movie posters, and other items for silent auctions and other giveaways.

I've had readers tell me A *Dog's Purpose* moved them to rescue a new dog. Look, if my work persuades even one family to adopt a pet, I have accomplished something very important.

The second novel in the A *Dog's Purpose* series, A *Dog's Journey*, touches on some important issues affecting humans. First, the groundbreaking work by my friend Dina Zaphiris and others to train dogs to detect cancer at *stage zero* is a key theme in that book. It's my hope that both the novel and the movie A *Dog's Journey* will raise awareness of this fascinating and hugely promising technique. Also, I am a firm believer in the hospice movement and its potential to bring dignity and peace to the end of people's lives, which is explored in the novel (we didn't have enough movie running time to incorporate it into the screenplay).

As I was writing the A *Dog's Purpose* series, it occurred to me that the lives of Bailey (and Ellie, and Toby, and Max, and Molly, etc.) would each make excellent stand-alone younger reader novels. We call them the Puppy Tales. Some, like the award-winning *Ellie's Story*, are distinctly based on the A *Dog's Purpose* series, while others, like *Toby's Story*, bear almost no connection to the "grownup books." I mention these novels here because I have been told by parents and educators that the Puppy Tales, with their dog point of view, help children who don't normally like to read to fall in love with books. In other words, I never knew I would be writing children's books, never had it as a goal, but now the letters and emails I receive from classrooms everywhere have turned this aspect of my career into one of the most rewarding—I am proud to be doing good.

The only complaint I get is that I'm not writing the things fast enough!

It is also an honor to participate in generous giveaway programs that help bring literacy to children in schools across the nation and other places where children find books. I always enjoy meeting young readers and I am complimented to donate my work to such worthy causes. For their special efforts in these endeavors, I'd like to extend a special thank-you to my friends at Scholastic Book Fairs and Clubs.

As I write this afterword, my publisher is getting ready to start printing up *A Dog's Promise*—the third novel in the *A Dog's Purpose* series. Unless you're the sort of person who always reads the last pages of a story first, you've finished the novel. My goal was to have the message of hope, of the promise that love is a force that transcends lifetimes, resonate with you. Because that's what I feel when I look into a dog's eyes: hope. They seem to be promising that no matter what, we will always be with the ones we love.

A Dog's Purpose, A Dog's Journey, A Dog's Promise. I didn't know I would be writing a trio of "dog books," but I'm very glad to have done so. As a writer, I have discovered my purpose.

{ACKNOWLEDGMENTS}

I remember learning in economics class years and years ago that no single person can make a pencil.

There's a point to this, I promise.

See, the graphite has to be dug out of the ground by somebody, shipped by somebody else, and fabricated into the pencil lead by yet another entity—hundreds of people involved right there. Then someone has to design the pencil: why not put the eraser in the middle? What color should it be? Will little children refuse to stick it in the sharpener if there is a baby unicorn at the top? The eraser is mined from, oh I don't know, an eraser mine, by seven men singing "Heigh ho, heigh ho, it's off to work we go." There's a metal band around the top of the pencil, which is different from a *heavy* metal band in that no one loses their hearing, but still involves a lot of people. Then there's transportation, the box the pencil goes into, marketing, and on and on. So, as it turns out, everybody on the planet is required to participate in order to manufacture a pencil.

That's why I learned to type as early as I could—I couldn't possibly write with all those people hanging around.

So it is with the writing of a book. When I sit down in front of the blank page, I bring with me the culmination of all my life's experiences, and all of the people who helped contribute to those experiences. For that reason, I must first thank every human being and animal living, or who has ever lived, during my time on this earth. Oh heck, I should also thank all the plant life as well. And, well, oxygen, gravity, water . . .

With that out of the way, I will note that there are a number of individuals I should call out, er, individually.

First, I want to thank my editorial team: Kristin Sevick, Susan Chang, Linda Quinton, and Kathleen Doherty. There are others at Tom Doherty Associates/Forge as well, including, for example, Tom Doherty. Sarah, Lucille, Eileen, and everyone in sales and marketing—thank you for helping my books become so popular. And, of course, a special shout-out to Karen Lovell, who has been my publicist since the very beginning. Good luck to you in your future endeavors, Karen. Without each and every one of you I would have to be printing my books and carting them to the nearest bookstore for people to buy. Probably if I had tried that method I would still be working on manufacturing my first pencil.

The connective tissue between an author and the publishing world is the author's agent. In my case, Scott Miller has been that person for me. Yes, Scott, you are my ligaments. Without you, my bones would collapse, and I would find it very difficult to throw a baseball. (I was doing okay with the pencil thing but I feel like I have sort of lost it with this connective tissue metaphor.)

I also have agents helping me with the world of show business. Sylvie Rabineau and Paul Haas, at William Morris Endeavor, thank you for nurturing my Hollywood career. I would say you are my connective tissue but I already used that one.

Sheri Kelton used to manage professional boxers and now she manages me. She keeps promising to get me a fight—I am starting to worry that I will never have a shot at the title. Meanwhile, though, she has helped steer my career away from my preferred trajectory of sloth and indifference. (I would point out that no champion boxer has ever brought this much laziness to a fight—it will be so unexpected, I would be certain to win! Or, at least, come in second.)

Whenever anyone offers me a deal, Steve Younger is the attorney I call in to work out the legalities. Steve, my wife says if I cook tonight she will clean the kitchen. What do you think? What sort of penalties can we enforce if she balks at cleaning because all I did was heat up the food that she made yesterday? (May I treat her as a hostile witness?)

I also have a criminal attorney. Thank you, Hayes Michel, for keeping me out of jail for another year! They will never catch me alive, ha ha ha. I guess actually he's more of a "litigator," but that sounds a lot like "ligament" and people are already sick to death of that term.

Gavin Polone, to whom this novel is dedicated, was the first person to believe that this series should be made into movies. Well, to be entirely accurate, he was the second person—my wife, mentioned elsewhere in these acknowledgments, was actually the first person to say that. At any rate, without Gavin, there would be no Cameron movies other than those by that James Cameron guy—as if *he* will ever amount to anything. So thank you, Gavin, for all you have done for me and for the dogs.

My crack staff has learned from me the special skill of blaming others for our problems, but Emily Bowden, my Chief of Staff, has adopted the odd policy of accepting responsibility for everything that happens with all of the working dogs here at my office. Emily, thank you for managing this sprawling, chaotic situation so that I don't have to. Because, as we both know, I wouldn't actually do any of it. Andrew, nice of you to join us.

Mindy Hoffbauer and Jill Enders are just two of the many

people who have helped keep my fans in touch with me and each other. Thank you, everyone in the secret group, for helping spread the word that I write these dog books where the dog doesn't die in the end. I would reveal more about the group, except that it's a secret.

Thank you, Connection House Inc., the huge multinational corporation that designed my new websites and at various times has assisted with certain marketing projects. Your president is like a son to me.

Thank you to Carolina and Annie for allowing me to be the Godfather.

Thank you, Andy and Jody Sherwood, for your cameo appearances in my novels. I so appreciate everything you have done for my family, in particular my mother. Same goes to you, Diane and Tom Runstrom: you are rays of sunshine desperately needed in my mother's wintery life. Okay, that sounds pretty grim but you all live in northern Michigan and I live in Los Angeles. I was just up there and, yes, it was wintery.

Thank you to my flight instructor, TJ Jordi, for introducing me to Shelby and for all you have done for the animals. Thank you, Megan Buhler for coaxing Shelby to reach for the stars. The two of you have made a lot of difference in a lot of lives. Thank you, Debbie Pearl for your vision, and Teresa Miller for sharing the cold and the really bad sandwiches to help Shelby become an Oscar-worthy actor.

Thank you, director Gail Mancuso, for loving dogs and infusing the movie A Dog's Journey with that love. Thanks to Bonnie Judd and her team for coaxing and praising wonderful performances out of our canine actors.

Along the journey with this three-book series, I have made friends with and have been so supported by the good people at Amblin Entertainment and Universal Pictures. There are far too many to name here—moviemaking and marketing takes a village. And thank you, Wei Zhang, Jason Lin, and Shujin Lan of Alibaba, for helping to introduce my work to China—the message that dogs are thinking, feeling, caring beings has now gone global!

The people in the family I grew up with are, of course, all mentally crazy. That is a prerequisite to becoming a successful author. Aside from that, though, I have to thank them for all that they do to support my career. My sisters, Amy and Julie Cameron, force people to buy my books and drag hundreds of individuals to my movies. If they don't cry, my sisters yell at them. My mother, Monsie, is an independent bookseller, meaning, she's independent of any bookstore—she just sells my books to every single person that she meets. If the people do not want to buy the book, she gives it to them. It means the world to me that my family is so supportive.

My family has grown beyond that initial nucleus and so I now have people younger than I who are also solidly supporting me. Special thanks to Chelsea, James, Gordon, Sadie, Georgia, Ewan, Garrett, Eloise, Chase, Alyssa. I have never for a moment felt anything but sincere support from you except for when you were teenagers.

My family has also grown to encompass Evie Michon, who besides giving birth to some very important individuals, has also been there as sort of a top secret research department, providing me with things like magazines from the time period in which my novel *Emory's Gift* is set. Thanks, Evie, and thanks also to Ted Michon and Maria Hjelm, not just family but good friends. Because of Ted and Maria we have three people who are very important to me: Jakob, Maya, and Ethan. Anyone who has read *A Dog's Purpose* will recognize those names.

While I'm on that topic, I'd like to recommend that book to you—*A Dog's Purpose* is the first novel in this series, and explains who Ethan is, and how Bailey comes to realize he is being re-born for a purpose. *A Dog's Journey* is the second, continuing the lives of Bailey as he returns again and again to CJ, a girl and then a woman who needs a dog to help her along life's journey. (Don't we all?)

Finally, like the grand finale of any self-respecting fireworks show, I present to you my wife, Cathryn Michon. She is my co-screenwriter, my life partner, and the person to whom I hand every draft of my novel for her sharp editorial eye. She designed and has been running our marketing efforts for years. And she is that person I can turn to when I'm feeling lost, full of self-doubt, and blocked, or even when I'm effusively happy and creatively en-ergetic. She's also a female director in Hollywood, something most executives consider very inconvenient to their narrative, which claims people only want to go to movies directed by men. (As of this writing, *A Dog's Journey,* directed by Gail Mancuso, is not yet in theaters, so we don't know if audiences will want to watch the movie or if they will say, "Directed by a woman? No way I want to see that!")

Thank you, Cathryn. You are a gift to me from God.

W. BRUCE CAMERON
Frisco, Colorado
February 2019

Discover More Great Reads from
W. BRUCE CAMERON

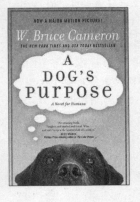

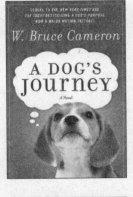

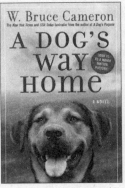

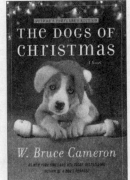

Tor-Forge.com **BruceCameronBooks.com**

W. BRUCE CAMERON BOOKS